NEPTUNE'S DAUGHTER

When Gwen MacIvor is widowed she surprises everyone by embarking on an entirely new life. She buys a derelict tower by the sea, sets about restoring it, takes a lover, and a job, studies astrology and learns to enjoy life – at last. Unfortunately, her daughter Eleanor, a successful executive of 30+, has other plans for her. For Eleanor is pregnant and intends to go back to work as soon as her baby is born, and naturally she assumes that her mother will bring the baby up. It is not an assumption Gwen shares...

NEPTUNE'S DAUGHTER

NEPTUNE'S DAUGHTER

by

Beryl Kingston

Magna Large Print Books
Long Preston, North Yorkshire,
BD23 4ND, England.

British Library Cataloguing in Publication Data.

Kingston, Beryl
    Neptune's daughter.

    A catalogue record of this book is
    available from the British Library

    ISBN   978-0-7505-2649-4

First published in Great Britain in 2005 by Transita

Copyright © 2005 Beryl Kingston

Cover illustration by arrangement with Transita

The right of Beryl Kingston to be identified as the author of this work
has been asserted by her in accordance with the Copyright, Designs
and Patents Act, 1988

Published in Large Print 2007 by arrangement with Transita

Magna Large Print is an imprint of Library Magna Books Ltd.

Printed and bound in Great Britain by
T.J. (International) Ltd., Cornwall, PL28 8RW

CHAPTER 1

The tower stood in an empty water meadow by the edge of the sea, its ancient brickwork silhouetted against a sky that shone like liquid gold under drifting clouds the colour of wisteria. It was a round tower and formidably well built, topped by a white beehive cap, and four storeys high, with long deep-set windows, a studded oak door, and right at the summit, a glass-fronted gallery overlooking the sea. To Gwen McIvor's dazzled eyes it looked wilful, like a huge, in-your-face act of defiance, uncompromising and untamed. She knew at once that it was exactly the sort of place she would like to live in. Then she saw the For Sale notice propped against the landward wall and knew, in the same unreasonable, instinctive way, that she was going buy it, even though the idea was totally out of character and battered her mind with surprise, for she wasn't the sort of woman who went around buying derelict properties she'd only just seen. She was Mrs Gwendoline MacIvor who lived in Fulham and had been quietly married for the past thirty-six years, and had two grown-up daughters, and was the sort of middle-aged woman nobody noticed, the sort who never put a foot out of line. Or at least she had been until that afternoon.

When she'd left her house a mere two and a

half hours ago, her emotions had been in such a tangle she hadn't even known where she was going. She'd just finished eating her usual quiet sandwich with her usual well-sweetened mug of tea and she was facing the fact that she would have to go back to work again on Monday now that the funeral was over. Not that there was any rush, because it was only a part-time job helping out in the local newsagents four afternoons a week, but over the years they'd come to depend on her and she didn't like to let them down. And at that moment she became aware of the clocks.

The noise they were making seemed to be getting louder and louder – ticketty-ticketty-ticketty from the tin contraption in the kitchen, clunk-clunk-clunk from the wall clock in the hall, a rising chorus of mutterings and scratchings and whirrings and clickings from every room in the house. Her irritation grew with the noise. There were so many of the damned things and none of them were any good. Never had been. Couldn't even tell the real time, which was hardly a surprise given the way he would keep tinkering with them. Now they just sat on the shelves and the walls, making stupid noises, sounding off the minutes of her life in their hateful, uncaring, mechanical, crushing way. And without any warning, her feelings suddenly boiled over in a rush of frustration and anger. She seized the kitchen clock and hurled it into the garden, where it lay on the lawn, trembling but still ticking, then she snatched up her bag, ran from the house, tumbled into her car and drove, heading south because any other direction would have taken her into the thick of the London traffic, but without knowing where she was actually going, sure of one thing and one thing only, that she had to get away – from the house and her life in it, from clocks, calendars, porridge-coloured walls, dull food, out-of-date clothes and boring television, from endless chores and the clutter of all her husband's useless 'collections', milk bottles, Toby jugs, cigarette cards, clocks, clocks, clocks, from the deadening, stultifying sameness of the life she'd lived for the past thirty-six years and couldn't bear to live another ticking second.

After a few miles, when she'd carved up yet another driver in her haste and been given the finger and a mouthful of abuse, her first sharp outburst of revulsion began to calm a little and she realised that she was driving to the danger of other road users and must think what she was doing, but by then she knew she couldn't stop until she'd got there – wherever there was. It was a glorious summer day, just what she'd expect for mid-July, blue skies heaped with cotton-wool clouds, windscreens sparkling, girls in pretty dresses, tin-hatted builders stripped to the waist, babies in sunhats and Rastas in berets, curled cats sunning themselves on window sills, every tree heavy with foliage in perfect summer green. Enjoy it, she told herself. Just be alive and enjoy it. You've got nothing else to do. There's no invalid to be looked after now, no funeral guests to feed, no housework that won't wait, no urgency. The day's your own. You can do whatever you like with it.

So she drove to the sea.

11

After an hour or so she realised that she was heading for Worthing and decided against it because it was a town and she wanted solitude; she took the next road west because it was a simple turn; admired Arundel as she passed below it but didn't stop there; noted that she was passing Chichester but didn't stop there either. Then an approaching road sign caught her eye and her attention. 'Seal Island' it said in its high, clear print. The words lifted her into remembered delight. Seals, she thought, and instantly saw them, lying on the rocks of her childhood sunning themselves, their dry fur mink-brown, scratching their heads languidly with their flippers, gazing about them with those great liquid eyes of theirs, lolloping over the rocks to slide into the sea, softly and easily, as though their bodies became water at the moment of contact. Seals. Naturally she followed the sign.

Within minutes she was in a wide flat landscape driving slowly south along winding roads towards the blaze of the sun and feeling quite extraordinarily happy, eased and pleased by everything she saw, here a flint house crouched under thatch and a long slate-roofed barn standing sideways to the road, there a herd of black and white cows browsing in their gentle untroubled way, there a row of greenhouses glinting like green water in the afternoon sun. Even the trees provoked her fellow feeling, for they'd all grown into distorted shapes, pushed sideways by the force of the prevailing south-west wind and that's just like me, she thought, pushed into his life-style all these years.

Presently the road narrowed to cross a short causeway with water on either side, a lagoon shimmering with waves and sunlight to her left, a shallow pool shining on her right, so she assumed she must have reached the island. Minutes later she was driving, very slowly, through the main street of a small village labelled Sutton, where holidaying families ambled from store to store with their kids trailing after them, licking ice creams. Then the village was left behind and the road was lined with Edwardian houses and she knew she was heading for the sea, for there were gulls wheeling overhead and she could smell the tang of salt.

There was a narrow promenade at the end of the road, and a gravelled space facing the beach where people parked their cars. She found a corner, eased into it, and got out to have a look round.

The sea was a joy to the eye, peacock green and summertime calm, sending ripples gently in to shore where half a dozen children splashed and squealed and tried to swim with their rubber rings haloed above seal-wet heads. There was a cheerful family directly below her, sitting on rugs eating sandwiches from Tupperware boxes and balancing thermos flasks among the pebbles, and a few yards further along the beach, three old ladies sprawled in deck chairs, either asleep or sunning their faces. Down at her feet the promenade was littered with tarred pebbles and shards of blackened weed and above her head the gulls soared and protested, their legs like scarlet threads against plump white breasts. It was all so exactly what she needed that she felt as though she'd come home. I'll take a stroll along the beach, she thought. Why not?

Which was how she found the tower. She'd walked until she had the beach to herself and had reached the point where the narrow promenade stopped and the pebbled beach sloped towards a marshy field, and suddenly there it was, looming up before her, so immediate and dominating that she simply had to go and take a closer look. She scrambled up the pebbles and strolled into the field, singing as she went.

As she drew closer, she could see that it was deserted and that it stood in a large walled garden, which had obviously been neglected too and for a very long time, for the weeds were waist high, the paths cushioned with moss and lichen, and there were two chipped trowels and a fork with a single prong rusting against the corner of some sort of outhouse. The garden wall was made of flint and almost low enough for her to climb over but, on the landward side next to the outhouse, there was a gap where a gate had been so she simply walked in, a little surprised at her daring but too full of curiosity not to go on.

The outhouse was made of brick and flint and thatched like the village houses, but it was little more than a ruin, all the windows broken, the thatch grey and sagging and growing grass, the one room inside full of rubbish – rusting tools, old shoes, broken flowerpots filled with spiders' webs as thick as old socks, and crates full of empty bottles, mostly cheap gin and whisky. The sight of it made her shudder. But the ground was good, even if it had been neglected. You could grow vegetables out here, she thought, picking up a clod of earth to crumble it in her fingers, and soft fruits. Clear those weeds, make a compost heap, double-dig. I'll bet it was a lovely garden once.

But it was the tower she'd really come to look at, that extraordinary defiant tower. She began to walk round it, peering in at the windows, and giving the door handle a pull in case it was open. Like the outhouse, it was very run down, the windows smeared with grime and the single room inside empty except for a scattering of old papers, a chipped butler sink and a broken chair lying on its side. But oddly its dereliction made it all the more attractive. It had such possibilities. Like the garden. She began to imagine how she could rescue it and turn it into a home – flowers on a table set to catch the sun, a new plaster and a colour wash on those chipped walls, a sofa with lots of cushions, part of the curved wall shelved for books, no clocks.

Then she took three more steps and saw the For Sale sign. The frisson of shock, delight and realisation closed her throat. I shall buy it, she thought, resting her hands on the cold stone of the sill. It's meant to be. I shall buy it and live here. With one half of her mind she knew she was being ridiculous, but a contrary tide was running in her too, carrying her into a new possibility, a new way of thinking, a new single life. I shall buy it.

The estate agent's was easy to find, being in the main street like everything else in the village.

There were three desks in the office, but only one agent, a fair-haired young man who was sprawled in his chair, drinking a cup of coffee.

But he set his cup aside at once, straightened his tie and stood up to greet her, rapidly assessing her potential as a client – classy diamond on her finger (good), hair severe and old-fashioned in a sort of bun (dubious), dress from Marks and Spencer's (middling), expensive handbag and sandals (good), car middle of the range and five years old (not promising). 'Good afternoon,' he said. 'How may I help you?'

Her answer was a surprise.

Being local, with a reputation for fair trading to maintain, he told her that the asking price was £100,000 and added, 'But you'll probably need twice as much again to make it habitable. It does have its drawbacks.'

He was impressed to see that the figure didn't throw her and waited while she thought about it. In fact to a woman used to London prices, £100,000 sounded reasonable and possible. The Fulham house had to be worth three or four times that, at least. 'I'd like to see it,' she said.

'No problem,' he said and introduced himself as he reached for his car keys. 'My name's Tom, by the way.'

'Gwen MacIvor.'

'Right then Mrs MacIvor. Shall we go?' And he led her out to his nice classy Volvo and was pleased to see that that didn't impress her either. So she's either used to money or an eccentric.

'It was a corn mill to start with,' he explained as he drove her to the site, 'but I expect you saw

16

that. There used to be dozens of mills round here in the old days, tide mills most of them. The last miller in this one went bust and they turned it into a watchtower. Napoleonic War and smugglers and things like that. For the last few years it's belonged to an old feller, which is why it's run down. This is an executor's sale. He was a bit of an eccentric, to be truthful. Kept himself to himself.'

'I've seen the outhouse,' she told him.

'Right,' he said, thinking, she doesn't miss much, and adding, 'There's no main drainage. I'd better tell you that. He had a septic tank. Might need some attention. They don't last for ever. There's electricity of course and he had the gas laid on some years back, I believe. But drainage could be a problem. I don't want to put you off or anything because it's a super position and a good price – all things considered – but you'd better know the worst.'

Difficulties could be overcome. She hadn't expected it would be easy. 'It's not that far from the village,' she said. It might be possible to get connected.

'Not as the crow flies, no,' he agreed encouragingly. 'It's an easy walk along the footpath. Anyway, here we are. Let me show you round.'

There were four floors, as she expected, getting progressively smaller as they rose, and the wooden staircase was rickety and would need repair. But the view from the top was so stunning, even through dirty glass, that it lifted her into breathless delight.

It was like being a bird, flying high and wild and

free in a huge expanse of clear blue air and wondrously multicoloured cloud, lilac, apricot, smoke blue, layer on layer of it. Below her, the Isle of Wight stretched like some mystic creature risen from the sea, still for the moment but poised to swim away, the sunshine glossy on the slopes of its green hills, its beaches ochre above the peacock green of the sea. To her left, the distant tower blocks of Southsea rose white on the western horizon and there were more ships than she could count, for as she now realised, she was looking down on the shipping lanes of the Solent, and they were full of tankers and cargo ships and white ferries, all following their appointed routes until they were mere black silhouettes against a far-distant apricot sky. As she watched, a ferry passed immediately below her. She could see right down onto the deck where the passengers were walking about and leaning over the rail, could watch the long lacy pattern of the wash foaming out behind it, white and straight in waters striped by sand and sunshine. If there had been any doubt in her mind it was melted away by the sheer joy of this view.

'It was a look-out post,' Tom explained.

'It still is,' she said. Imagine getting up in the morning to enjoy a panorama like that. My own look-out.

But the words brought an uncomfortable echo into her mind, for that was what her daughters said to one another when they were arguing – 'All right then. Go ahead. It's your own lookout,' – and until that moment she hadn't thought about them. They won't approve of this, she thought, and quailed a little. They'll think I've lost my senses. And I suppose I have in a way. Or come to them. But the thought was fleeting. Her decision had been made, there and then, at first sight, like falling in love, and now she was being driven by it.

The estate agent was waiting, being patient.

'I shall buy it,' she told him.

'Yes madam.'

'I shall have to arrange for a structural survey to be done. Do you know a reputable firm?'

He most certainly did.

'My capital's all tied up in my London property at the moment,' she said, pleased to think that her property-buying neighbours had inadvertently taught her the language to use. 'I assume you'll need a 10% deposit to secure this?'

He'd never made such a simple sale. By the time she left his office for her drive back to Fulham, the survey had been arranged, she'd promised to send him a cheque for £10,000 'as soon as it can be made available' and the matter was as good as settled.

As she crossed the little causeway, her common sense returned to sober her and she knew it was going to be difficult to explain what she'd done to Eleanor and Lucy. Perhaps it would be better not to tell them just yet. After all, it might not come off and there was no point in worrying them about something that might never happen. She knew it was a cowardly decision, but comforted herself that there was good reason for it. She didn't want them to be upset. She'd never wanted them to be upset. Never. She loved them both too much. Although of course they often had been. And this would upset them. She knew it would. It was bound to, a change as sudden as this. No, she decided, I'll wait until it's all signed and settled. I can tell them then and it'll give me a bit of time to think out exactly what to say. There's no rush. I've got to sell the house first and that could take months. The property market's very unpredictable. And I'll have to wait for the survey to be done. That could put the mockers on it.

But it wouldn't. She knew it wouldn't. The place was as good as hers. I'll get a few local builders to give me an estimate for the stairs and the plastering, she thought, and then I'll make enquiries about the drainage. I must be practical. But she wasn't being practical. She was being rash, for the first time in her life, and she was high with the shock and delight of it. No amount of cold-water conscience could bring her down. Inside her head she was singing with the joy of deliverance. Now, and at last, she could begin to live her own life in her own way. She could hardly believe her behaviour or her luck.

CHAPTER 2

Lucy MacIvor was in Heathrow Airport waiting with fidgety impatience in front of the designated gate, among a crowd so closely packed that she could barely see anything except the heads and shoulders of the people in front of her. Her sister's flight from New York had been announced nearly half an hour ago, but it was over two hours late then and she was beginning to feel buffeted by the combination of lengthening delay and enclosing crowds. If she doesn't hurry up, she thought, it'll be too late to get to Mum's this afternoon and I must know what this is about. She shifted her weight from one foot to the other, sighed and glanced at her watch again. And when she looked up, there was Eleanor sashaying towards her, tall, slim and elegant, and smiling her greeting smile, with a porter labouring behind her pushing a trolley stacked with travelling cases.

'What a flight!' she said, as she and Lucy touched cheeks and made kissing sounds into the air. 'I thought I'd never get here. I'm so glad you could meet me. It's such a bind not having a car. They'd better have it ready for me in the morning. God, I feel an absolute wreck.' She was exquisitely well-groomed, as always, her carefully blonde hair curved about her cheeks in two neat swathes, scarlet lipstick newly applied, eyelashes thickened with mascara, eye-catchingly stylish in a long cream jacket and high-heeled cream boots that Lucy hadn't seen before – I'll bet she bought them in New York – her skirt fashionably black, straight and long and without a single crease despite the long flight. How does she do it?

They headed off to find Lucy's car, making conversation as they walked. 'How was New York?' Lucy asked.

'Horrendous,' Eleanor said. 'Everything had to be done yesterday. You know how they are. Some great parties though. How's the overtime?'

'Horrendous. So what's new?'

Eleanor teased. 'And I always thought account-ants were the lords of the earth.'

'Not this accountant.'

'You should find another firm.'

'I did, if you remember. They're all the same. Determined to work us to death.'

'Yours and mine both. How's Henry?'

Lucy shrugged. 'OK as far as I know. I haven't seen him for ages. Not since Dad died.'

'Ah! Then it's…'

'Off,' Lucy said, closing the subject by her tone and her expression. 'How's Pete?'

'In Birmingham with Scatters doing a com-mercial. Indigestion tablets or something. That's why I asked you to meet me. Are we going straight there?'

'Yes.'

They reached the car park where the luggage was loaded and the porter took his tip and departed, but then there was an awkward pause as they drove away. Now that they were sitting side by side, Lucy was a little too aware of her sister's stunning good looks. They made her feel ordinary to the point of dowdiness and acutely conscious of the contrast between them, that her own hair was straggly for need of a cut, and mouse-brown – she always felt mouse-brown when she was sitting next to Eleanor – that she hadn't polished her boots in ages, that her jeans were faded and her jersey out of shape, that she drove an old Ford Fiesta instead of a new Renault Espace, that she was five foot four instead of Eleanor's willowy five foot nine, that her eyes were ordinary hazel instead of Eleanor's resplendent blue. When she'd dripped out of the shower that morning she'd simply put on her usual working-at-home clothes in her usual careless way. Now she wished she'd made more of an effort.

'So,' Eleanor said at last as they headed for the M4. 'Why have we been summoned?'

Lucy kept her eyes on the traffic. 'I don't know,' she admitted. 'She just said she wanted to see us. Before tomorrow.'

'Why tomorrow?'

'I don't know.'

'Didn't you ask?'

'Yes,' Lucy said, watching the traffic and tense with attention because she was on the motorway slip road. 'I did, as it happens, but she wouldn't say. She was sort of odd.'

'In what way?'

'I don't know. I can't put my finger on it. It was the words she used I think. I mean she usually says "Are you coming over? I'd love to see you." Like a sort of hint. And this time it was "I need to see you." and "Will you tell Eleanor?" She'd tried your number apparently and couldn't get through. It wasn't like her.'

'Delayed grief,' Eleanor said decisively. 'I thought as much when you rang me. We shall have to handle her very gently. It can do odd things to people. I've got a book about it.'

'A what?' Lucy said. Now that she was safely on the motorway she could relax a little.

'A book,' her sister repeated patiently. 'One of those self-help things. It's in my bag. There you are. See. I thought it would come in useful.'

It was a thin, brightly covered paperback, called *Step by Step with Mourning* and as Eleanor flicked through the pages, Lucy could see that it contained page-sized snippets of crass advice –'Let it all hang out', 'Dream away', 'Dealing with bottle-necks', 'Life after the funeral', 'Sweets and sweeties'.

'Oh Eleanor,' she said. 'For God's sake! She's our mother. Don't you think we might be able to handle her without a guidebook?' And when Eleanor raised her neat eyebrows in a disparaging grimace, 'All right, I know it was a shock, him getting ill like that and dying so quickly, but she took it wonderfully. Think how she was at the funeral. Quiet and dignified. Just right. Now wasn't she? We both said so. I think she's managing very well.'

'Yes,' Eleanor agreed. 'People do. And then they collapse afterwards.'

'Not two months afterwards. We're into September now.'

'Six months sometimes,' Eleanor insisted.

'Even a year, so the book says. You never know. We have to remember how quickly it all happened. Six months ago he was alive and well and everything was normal.'

'Well she didn't sound as though she was grieving,' Lucy said. 'Honestly. She sounded... Well if it hadn't been Mum, I'd have said businesslike.'

'She could be in denial,' Eleanor said. 'People do odd things when they're grieving. There's a whole section on Inappropriate Behaviour in that book'

'I can't imagine Mum's behaviour ever being inappropriate,' Lucy said. 'She's totally predictable. It's the best thing about her.'

'Well we shall see,' Eleanor said and stifled a yawn. 'God, I'm knackered! I think I'll just have a quick nap. You don't mind do you?' And was asleep before Lucy could answer.

Typical! Lucy thought. She's tired so she goes to sleep. I drive the car. It doesn't occur to her that I might like some conversation. Her sister's untroubled selfishness had always been an irritation. But what could she do? Except drive and wake her up when they arrived – and wonder what their mother was going to tell them.

Gwen MacIvor was wondering that herself. The last eight weeks had passed so quickly and pleasurably that what with selling her old home and redecorating her new one, she hadn't had time to think about anything else. But now, everything was rushing upon her. The completion date had been brought forward by nearly two weeks because her buyers were eager to take

25

possession, the kitchen was still being fitted down at the tower and she had one afternoon to break the news to her daughters. It was really quite alarming. I should have talked to them earlier on and not been such a coward, she thought. Cowardice and change are bad companions. But it was always the same, putting things off because she didn't know how to handle them. When she'd leapt into the joy of buying her tower, she hadn't thought any further than the change she longed for and couldn't resist. Now she was having to face the fact that any change brings others after it, as inevitably as a train starting a shunt, and that not all of them are either easy or pleasant.

Still, at least it was pleasant out in the garden feeding her bonfire. It was a very large fire, made of cuttings and old papers and all the garden debris she'd cleared in the last few days, and it was stacked so high it was clouding the sky with smoke and spitting red sparks higher than the plum tree, crackling and roaring. I've cleared the house, she thought, feeling righteous, and cleaned it from top to bottom, and the garden's neat and tidy, it's only the last of his horrible old newspapers to burn and the job's done. She stooped to pick up the final cardboard boxful and hurled it into the middle of the flames so that they flattened and spat sparks towards the trunk of the plum tree. Now, she thought, I can give my entire attention to telling Eleanor and Lucy. Oh I wish I'd told them earlier – and I wish they'd hurry up and get here.

In fact, Lucy was cruising along Crescent Road at that very moment, looking for somewhere to park, and Eleanor had woken up.

'Home!' she said, gazing out at the long row of Edwardian semis. 'No matter where I go, this place will always be my home, I just love it. Right then Luce, girls to the rescue.'

They rang the bell three times but they didn't get an answer and eventually Lucy fished out her door-key and let them in, calling as she went. But there was no answering call and no sign of their mother in either of the downstairs rooms, which looked oddly empty.

'There are things missing,' Eleanor said, scowling at the furniture. 'You don't think she's been burgled do you?'

'It's the ornaments,' Lucy realised. 'Dad's Toby jugs have gone for a start. And the pictures. And the clocks. Maybe she's decorating.'

'Where is she?' Eleanor said, as they headed for the kitchen. 'That's what I want to know. All that fuss to get us here, you'd think she'd be waiting for us. Ah! The tea's ready. That's something.'

'I can smell burning,' Lucy said, sniffing.

Her sister sniffed too. 'Oh for heaven's sake!' she cried. 'It's a bonfire. They've started already and he's barely in his grave. Poor Dad. People are so heartless. They know what he thought of bonfires and now the minute he's dead, they start.' She strode to the window to spy out the culprit. 'Look at all that dreadful smoke. I think it's next door.'

Lucy joined her, pulling the neat checked curtains aside for a better view. 'It's not,' she said, blinking with disbelief. 'It's us. It's in our garden. Oh Ellie, somebody's lit a bonfire in our garden.'

'We'll soon put a stop to that,' Eleanor said. 'Find a watering can.' And she opened the kitchen door and strode off towards the billows.

A figure emerged from the smoke, a small female figure in gumboots and trousers and a tattered jersey, with a rake in her hand.

'Hello you two,' she called. 'I didn't hear you ring. Tea's all ready. Did you have a good flight, Ellie?'

In a moment of exquisite shock the two girls recognised that this wild-looking woman was their mother, their neat, quiet, well-dressed, gentle mother in gumboots and trousers. Eleanor's face was a study in disbelief, blue eyes rounded, reddened lips falling open. 'What on earth are you doing?' she said.

'Making a clearance,' Gwen told her.

'But you've got a bonfire.'

'It's the best thing for a clearance.'

'You've cut your hair!' Eleanor said. It was more an accusation than an observation.

'Yes,' her mother agreed. 'So much easier than all that fuss with a French pleat. One quick brush and I'm ready for the day. Do you like it?'

Eleanor didn't like it at all and was gathering breath to say so when Lucy intervened. 'You said you had something to tell us,' she reminded them all.

'That's right,' her mother agreed. 'Come on in and I'll tell you over tea. It's...' Oh God! How was she going to begin? 'About the will for a start. It's not a great deal but I thought you ought to know.'

28

And she told them as she made the tea.

It wasn't a great deal. Their father's will was short, fair and to the point. He had left the house and all its contents 'to my wife, Gwendoline Mary MacIvor' and had directed that 'such monies as are left in my savings account after my funeral expenses have been paid are to be divided between my two daughters, Eleanor Frances and Lucy Anne'.

'It comes to £3,225 each,' Gwen told them. 'You'll be getting a cheque from the solicitor. In the next few days, he says.'

'So everything's settled,' Eleanor said, relieved now that she knew what this was about.

Gwen put down her teacup and smiled at them. But it was an odd smile, as Lucy was quick to notice, half defiant, half guilty, like a naughty child caught out in some minor misdemeanour but hopeful that she could charm her way out of it. 'Well not quite everything,' she said. Her heart was throbbing most uncomfortably. She put her left hand against her ribcage as though she could hold it still or calm it by pressure. If only she'd done this step by step and earlier.

'There's more?' Eleanor said.

Gwen looked from one to the other, bracing herself for what she was about to say. 'I'm moving,' she said at last. 'I've sold this house and bought – another one. We exchanged contracts on Thursday, just before I phoned you Lucy.'

Eleanor couldn't believe her ears. 'What do you mean, moving?'

'I'm going to live by the sea,' Gwen explained, speaking softly in an effort to placate her, 'in a place called Seal Island.'

Eleanor was so shocked she couldn't disguise her fury. First the bonfire and then the hair and now this. 'I knew something like this would happen,' she said to Lucy. 'Didn't I warn you?' She rounded on her mother. 'You can't sell this house. It's out of the question.'

Gwen took a breath to steady herself against her daughter's anger. 'I can, Ellie,' she said. 'I've done it. I'm moving tomorrow. That's why I asked you here today.

'How could you possibly do such a thing?' Eleanor said. 'You should have talked it over with us.'

True! True! And very painful. 'It would only have upset you.'

'No it wouldn't. We'd have advised you not to, wouldn't we Lucy? Oh come on Mother, see sense. You can't sell this house. It's your home. Our home. Our family home.' Her face was so distraught that Gwen couldn't bear to look at her any longer.

Lucy had absorbed the information rather more quickly and, although she was as surprised as Eleanor, she tried to be practical. 'Do you need a hand with the move?' she asked. 'I could take a day off and come with you, if you like.'

'No,' Gwen said, smiling at her gratefully. 'Thanks for the offer but I can manage. I'm not taking much. Just my books and clothes and a few bits and bobs. It's all packed up in the garage. I've never liked this furniture, to tell the truth. I shall be glad to see the back of it. I've sold it to the local second-hand store. They're coming

30

for it this evening.' Telling them about the furniture was easier and made her feel marginally better, especially as Lucy's expression was encouraging and loving. 'Now I've got the chance to start again from scratch,' she said, and the words gave her a sense of release. 'A clean slate. It's going to be fun.'

'Fun!' Eleanor exploded. 'Fun! You sell the family home and you call it fun.'

Wrong again! Gwen thought. Was it any wonder she'd put this off? When she'd known all along how difficult it was going to be. But it was a mistake and a bad one. 'It hasn't been much fun clearing it out,' she said, trying to deflect the impact of her unfortunate choice of word. 'You never saw such a load of old junk. The milkman took the milk bottles – bit by bit – and I sold the Toby jugs to the man from the Antiques Emporium. Got quite a good price for them actually. Apparently they really are collectable. But the clocks were a nightmare. He had an entire cupboard full of bits and pieces. I had to put them in the dustbin, and most of the clocks too. And then there were the old football magazines and he'd got more copies of the *Radio Times* than you'd ever believe and piles of theatre programmes and files full of letters, all gone brown and brittle and no use to anyone. I've been burning them for days.'

'But they were Dad's treasures!' Eleanor protested, glaring at her. 'He kept them.'

By now Gwen was so distressed she took refuge in a joke. 'Didn't he just!'

Her flippancy was beyond Eleanor's understanding. She turned to Lucy in exasperation. 'Speak to her!' she commanded. 'I can't handle this.'

Lucy didn't think anything she said would make any difference to their mother now, but she made an effort. 'Are you sure you're doing the right thing?' she asked. 'I mean, it's a major upheaval, moving house, the third most stressful life event after death and divorce. We wouldn't want you to move and then be miserable, or wish you hadn't and not have enough money to get back.'

'Quite right,' Eleanor approved, trying to damp down her anger by a show of good sense. 'It's a risk. You must see that.'

Gwen refilled their teacups to give herself time to think. 'I wasn't going to tell you all this,' she said at last. 'Not until later. But I suppose now's as good a time as any. For a start I've got plenty of money, so you don't need to worry on that account. I made a marvellous price on this house. And I shan't be miserable.'

Eleanor was aggressive. 'How can you tell? You might...'

Her mother's face opened into a smile of such transparent happiness that it stopped the words in Eleanor's throat. 'Because this is something I've wanted to do for years,' she said, 'something I never thought I'd be able to do. I wouldn't have either if he hadn't died. I'd have gone on cooking the same old meals in the same old kitchen, shopping in the same old supermarket, watching the same old programmes on the telly, living the same old half-life, day in, day out.'

32

'But you were happy,' Eleanor protested weakly. 'You and Dad. You were a happy couple.'

Oh dear, Gwen thought. This is going to hurt her but I can't help it. I've started now and I'll have to go on. If I don't they'll never understand. I can't keep pretending. Not now. 'No Ellie,' she corrected. 'Your father was happy. I endured. I spent thirty-six years living the way he wanted to, putting up with his collections, living his life style, and now I'm free of it. I've only myself to please. I'm fifty-six but I've got my life back and I can do what I choose with the rest of it. And that's the truth.'

Eleanor's face had fallen with distress and shock. How can she be saying such things? It's grief. It must be.

Lucy was more perplexed than shocked. 'Don't you miss him?' she asked. 'Just a little bit?'

Gwen smiled at her ruefully but she went on telling the truth. 'I missed him a lot when he first died,' she said, 'not having to get up in the night to attend to him, not having to give him his medicine and turn him, that sort of thing. But after a while it was different, as if the clouds had cleared. I suppose all prisoners miss their jailers at first, but once you've got used to freedom, you're glad not to think of them. Oh God! That sounds awful. But it is the truth and you'd better know it, if you're to understand what I'm doing.'

'You didn't love him.' Lucy understood.

'I went one better than love,' Gwen told her. 'I obeyed him. You've no idea what effort that cost. Propped him up, never criticised, allowed him to be himself, shielded him. You can't give any man more than that.'

Lucy winced. To be privy to such secrets was exquisitely painful. It made a nonsense of everything they'd all believed. She must have loved him a little, at least at first, even if he wasn't the most loveable man come the finish. 'But you did it freely,' she hoped.

Her mother's answer was uncompromising, although it was given half-laughing. 'I did it chained hand and foot.'

'You had a choice,' Lucy insisted.

'Sorry to disappoint you, chick,' her mother said, 'but no, that's exactly what my generation didn't have. There was never the slightest degree of choice. We went where our husbands took us. Lived where he wanted to live. Ran our houses to suit him. Underpinned him. That was our function. Husbands earned their living, paid the mortgage, supported the children. We stayed at home and made life comfortable for them. No matter what it cost us.'

Lucy turned away from the bitterness on her mother's face. 'This is awful,' she said.

'Not a bit of it,' Gwen told her, being too brisk because she was aching with distress at the damage she'd done. Poor Ellie was too upset to speak. 'This is freedom. Now I can live my life in my own way. It's going to be wonderful. Truly. It's a good thing.'

Eleanor's mouth began to tremble. She took her mirror and lipstick from her handbag and began to make repairs, painting herself into control, watching the effect as she worked. 'We must go,' she said lightly. 'Jet lag, you know.

Pete's expecting me. Are you ready Luce?'

Lucy was torn between the urgency of Eleanor's desire to escape and her own craving to make sense of what her mother was saying. Eleanor's needs won. She stood up slowly, smiling at her mother to show that she approved of what she was doing even if she didn't entirely understand it. 'You'll let us know if you want any help,' she said. 'You've only to ask. You know that, don't you?'

'Yes,' Gwen smiled back, but bleakly. Dear Lucy. At least she's taking it sensibly. 'Don't fuss. I shall be fine.'

So they left.

To her credit Eleanor maintained her control and waved to her mother until they were out of sight of the house, as if the visit had been normal. Then she collapsed into bewildered weeping. 'How could she do such a thing!' she cried. 'To sell our home. I can't believe it. Our home. Where we were all so happy. She's cut the ground from under our feet. All our memories gone. Everything. Why didn't she tell us? We could have talked her out of it. Now... Our family home! I can't bear it. All our memories gone.'

'Memories don't go,' Lucy said. She was determined to be sensible. 'They stay in your mind as long as you let them. You can't get rid of the bloody things sometimes. As I know.'

But that reduced Eleanor to shrieking. 'Don't be reasonable!' she yelled. 'I can't bear it. She's sold our home.'

'Your home is your flat in Chelsea,' Lucy pointed out tartly. There was no need for this sort of display. It was excessive. 'Where you live with Pete, when he isn't in Pimlico.' Your great big, expensive, minimalist flat. 'Mine is my house in Battersea, where I live with Helen and Tina. We've all moved on a bit since we lived round here.'

'Oh that's right!' Eleanor cried. 'Take her side. I should! Pretend it doesn't matter.'

'I'm not saying that,' Lucy said, watching the road as she took a right turn. 'It does matter, of course it does, but we've got to accept it. It's her house.' And when Eleanor went on weeping, she added, 'It's no good crying. We've just got to make the best of it, that's all.'

'But she'll be miles away.'

'We've both got cars. We can drive. It can't be that far.'

'You don't understand,' Eleanor wailed. 'It's got nothing to do with cars and driving. I need her here. I'm pregnant.'

The day changed character like a bud opening into bloom. 'Oh Ellie!' Lucy said, turning to look at her, briefly because the traffic was thick. 'That's wonderful! A baby! You lucky thing. Why didn't you tell Mum?'

Eleanor dabbed her eyes. 'How could I? She wasn't listening.'

'She'd have listened to that. When's it due? Does Pete know?'

'Not yet. I'm only six weeks. I mean, I'm not sure myself yet. I was only just sort of wondering about it when I went Stateside. Well I suppose I am sure, in a way. I mean, I haven't seen anything since I came off the pill.'

36

'When was that?'

'May, June.' Eleanor said vaguely. 'When Dad got ill. I'd been thinking about it for a long time, off and on. The old biological clock and that sort of thing. I mean it wasn't sudden. I'd been sort of brooding up to it, if you know what I mean. And then when he got ill and we knew it was cancer and inoperable and everything, I thought *this is the time*. I thought being a grandfather would give him something to live for. And then it was all over so quickly there wasn't time to tell him anything. Sod's law!'

Lucy was touched. 'Oh Ellie! What a lovely thing to do.'

'It wasn't just for him,' Eleanor said, wiping tears from her cheeks. 'I mean, I'd have done it anyway, sooner or later. It was always on the cards. He was – well, the precipitating factor I suppose. Poor old Dad. And now look at the mess I'm in. She'll be miles away just when I need her. How could she do such a stupid, stupid thing? She must have known I'd want a baby and how can she look after it if she's sixty miles away? I mean I can hardly drive it up and down to the coast every day. I'd never get to work in time.'

'You're going back to work then?'

'Oh yes. Of course. I mean you can't not, can you? Not these days. I thought I'd got everything sorted. I mean she's so good with babies. And now...' Her mouth squared ready to weep again.

Lucy forestalled her by being practical. 'So when's it due?'

'I don't know. April probably. Depends when it started. I mean I haven't had a period since Dad died but that was probably the grief and everything. You have to expect that don't you? Some people wait months according to the book and they say you can't count the first month anyway. It takes time for your hormones to settle down.'

'You and your books!' Lucy laughed. 'Some people click first time. Susie did. Get a kit and make sure. And then ring and tell me. Oh, Ellie, you don't know how lucky you are. I'm really envious.' Which was true – true as steel and cut as keenly, even though she'd taken care to speak as though she were joking. To be carrying Pete's child. It made her yearn to think of it. 'Look, we're nearly here. Would you like me to stop for a minute and you can make some running repairs? You look as though you've been down a coal mine.'

'Oh shit! Do I?' Eleanor said, and reached for her mirror to check 'Look, don't say anything to Mum just yet. I haven't told anyone except you – in case it's a false alarm, you know.'

'Don't worry,' Lucy reassured her. 'I'm stumm. Get that kit, that's all.'

CHAPTER 3

Peter Halliday was so effortlessly handsome that he'd begun to boast – in a half-joking way – that now he'd reached the grand old age of thirty-five he was too lazy to think about his appearance. Five years ago when he was pushing a rather disgruntled thirty, he'd achieved his fifteen minutes worth of fame by appearing as the sultry hero in a series of coffee commercials for TV, and had cashed in on his temporary popularity by taking an executive position with a small but prestigious company called Sheldons which made advertising shorts for film and TV. Now he was growing restless again and beginning to wonder whether it was time to move on. Sheldons wasn't big enough to contain his ambition for very much longer, even though it paid well and allowed him to continue his acting and modelling career part time.

At six foot three and well-built, with athletic shoulders, slim hips, long legs and an easy rangy walk, he was still the ideal model he'd been in his twenties, especially as he still possessed a mop of thick, corn-coloured hair – although slightly more artful than it had been – high cheek bones, an easily tanned skin, wide-spaced grey-blue eyes and a lazy smile, long since honed to perfection. He was the sort of young man who was welcome at any party and caused a stir when he entered any room, particularly if he was escorting Eleanor MacIvor, for they made a glamorous couple and she was as skilled at working a crowd as he was. His agent, a stout rugged man called Sandy Scatters, compared him to the young Robert Redford and stressed how unassuming he was and how easy to work with, which was usually true. Although, as they both knew privately, he could be morose and irritable after a tricky shoot.

He came back from Birmingham that evening with the remains of a hangover and stabbing indigestion, aching for space, order and sympathy – and a properly cooked meal. So naturally, instead of returning to the bachelor chill of his own penthouse suite, he drove straight to Eleanor's nice, white, well-ordered flat for a bit of tender loving care.

He was in for a disappointment. Eleanor pounced on him before he'd had a chance to sit down on her white four-seater. 'Mother's gone mad,' she said. 'Do you know what she's done?'

He slumped into the sofa and closed his eyes to show how unwelcome this was. 'Spare me,' he begged.

But she didn't spare him a single angry detail.

'So,' he said, when she'd ranted for five minutes and he'd poured himself a G and T to sustain him through the onslaught, 'it's her house. At least you know where she is. She's not disappearing to the ends of the earth like some I could mention. You should count your blessings. She could have gone to India or Afghanistan or Nicaragua or somewhere. Then you would have something to complain about.'

She recognised that he was making a bid for her sympathy but she'd moved too far into her distress to respond to it. 'But what about the baby?' she wailed.

He was surprised but not alarmed. She was given to dramatic statements. It was part of her charm. 'What baby, for fuck's sake?'

Her blue eyes looked quite wild. 'Mine.' Now she would tell him. It wasn't the best moment because she was so cross, but it was a chance. She took a deep breath. 'Actually...'

He choked her words before she could give tongue to them, speaking quickly and sternly in his clear TV voice, irritated that she should be talking nonsense when he was in need of attention. 'Allow me to point out to you,' he said, 'you haven't got one.'

To be deflected so quickly threw her a little but she persevered. 'But I might have,' she insisted. 'I mean what if I wanted one?'

He leant against the low back of the sofa and closed his eyes to indicate that the conversation was ridiculous. He wasn't in a fit state for hypotheses and he had no intention of allowing this to go any further. 'You don't,' he said firmly. 'So there's no problem.'

'You don't know I don't,' she cried, truthfully if inelegantly. She'd been anguishing ever since she'd let herself into the apartment, and now she was hot with distress, pacing the polished floorboards, flexing her fingers. 'I've got a biological clock the same as everyone else. I'm thirty-five in case you hadn't noticed and not

41

getting any younger. This is the future we're talking about. Our child. The future of our child. I can't help thinking about something like that. I mean it's there, in the back of your mind, all the time.'

'Not in mine,' he said with feeling. 'As you well know.'

Her eyes were wilder than ever. 'You're not a woman.'

'Wowee!' he said, grabbing her as she passed and pulling her down onto his lap. 'You've noticed. What are we having for dinner?'

I should have told him I'd come off the pill, she thought. Then he'd have been prepared and this would have been easier. But if she had told him, he might have turned against her and then none of this would have happened. 'That's all you ever think of,' she complained. 'Your bloody stomach.'

'I've had three days eating take-aways in various shades of inedible plastic,' he told her. 'Earning our crust, so to speak. Now I think I'm entitled to something just a teensie bit more palatable. So can we just leave this and do some cooking?'

But she was stuck in her distress and roaring with incomprehension. 'How could she do such a thing? That's what I can't understand. I simply can't.'

He released her, giving her his weary expression. 'There's no point trying to understand your parents,' he said, as she returned to her prowling. 'They're a law unto themselves. Look at mine. "Good morning Peter. We're off to India. See you around!" And then they're away for nineteen years and you barely get a peep out of them. Christmas card now and then but apart from that they're totally fucking useless. Don't talk to me about parents.'

She wasn't listening to him, having heard it all before. 'She must have known I'd want a baby sooner or later,' she said. 'I mean, most women want babies at some time in their lives.'

He made a superhuman effort to be reasonable. 'But you're not most women,' he pointed out. 'You're a senior executive in a multinational company, for fuck's sake. A career girl. And lovely with it! Take a look at yourself, if you don't believe me.' And he stood up and steered her towards the mirror, holding her by the shoulders. 'You're gorgeous. What are you? Look at that belly. Those tits. Superb and you know it. Totally fucking superb. Now tell me you want to spoil all this for some horrible puking baby.'

Eleanor was examining her image with a rather more clinical interest. I'm bursting out of my bra, she thought, admiring her burgeoning curves. There was no denying how attractive they were. They were turning Pete on good and hard. 'Um,' she said, leaning back against him and lifting her throat. 'I might though.'

'No you won't,' he told her, kissing her neck. 'Babies are the biggest single cause of poverty in this country, right? They stink, they howl and they're totally selfish. They make endless demands, day and night. They break up marriages. They wreck careers. They're total fucking bad news. You spend your entire life pouring milk in at one end and cleaning shit off the other. They are not for us. We agreed.'

They had. It was true. 'But...'

'No buts,' he said, turning her in his arms to kiss her properly. 'We've got better things to do than talk about stupid babies. Have you missed me?'

She pretended to think about it before she answered, playing their familiar teasing game. 'Might have done. A bit.'

'A lot,' he said happily, fondling her breasts. 'Look at the state of you.'

'And you're calmness personified,' she teased, and put down a hand to feel his erection. 'Oh God yes.' The baby was forgotten, and so was her mother's stupidity. There was nothing but pleasure now and driving need.

Much later that night, when they'd satisfied all their appetites and were lying sated and easy in her king-sized bed, she returned to the subject, this time lazily and without distress. 'She'll never stick it,' she said.

He smiled at her equally lazily. 'Who cares?'

'Stuck out there in the wilds. Think how cold it'll be. She'll hate it.'

He was murmuring, halfway to sleep. 'Then let her. The sooner she hates it, the sooner she'll come home.'

Yes, Eleanor thought, she will. She's bound to. All right then, I'll convert the games room into a nursery and a granny flat and have it all ready for her. I've got months yet. I can have it all done in plenty of time and when it's ready I'll drive her up to see it. I'll wait till she's really fed up and miserable and wanting to come home and then I'll surprise her. Poor Mum. I can't bear to think of her miles away and miserable. And with her mind full of such happy and almost altruistic thoughts, she drifted into sleep.

She was woken – much too early – by the stupid trilling of Pete's mobile phone. Why must he bring that dammed thing into the bedroom? she thought tetchily. Well answer it then. Don't let it ring. I can't sleep with all that noise. And was relieved when she heard his voice.

'Hi! Yah! Back yesterday evening... Horrendous... Well that's Stagger's all over...' Then his voice changed. 'Is that right?' he said seriously. 'Who d'you hear it from?... Right. Right. Who's in the running?... No, no, not to worry. No problem... Yah! Absolutely. No problem. Breakfast'll be fine. I'll be there in –let's say forty minutes. See yah!'

She didn't even bother to open her eyes. It had to be business. The tone of his voice was unmistakeable and he was already on his way to the bathroom. 'That was Jaz!' he said. 'Sheldons is up for grabs.'

'Can't be,' she said lazily and teased, 'Who'd want a little two-bit organisation like that?' The insignificance of the firm he worked for had always been something to taunt him with.

'Two multinationals, according to Jaz,' he said. 'After a toehold in the UK. Could be good news for the shareholders.' He and Jaz were both major shareholders. 'Anyway I'm off for a quick breakfast to talk it over.'

'I've got something to tell you,' she said. But he

was in the shower and whistling and didn't hear her, so she turned over and settled back to sleep. It was much too early to get up. She'd tell him tonight when she'd taken the test and knew for certain.

Her mother had been up since first light that morning, to strip her bed and pack away the bedding, scrub the quarry tiles in the kitchen for the last objectionable time and give the toilet its last thorough clean, for it was a point of honour to leave the house immaculate and she wanted everything to be done before the removal men arrived. When Lucy called to her through the letterbox she'd just put the kettle on for breakfast.

'Oh Lucy!' she said, touched to think that she'd given up a day's work to come and help her. 'You really are the dearest girl.'

'I couldn't have you moving house all on your own,' Lucy said, kissing her. 'Now what needs doing?'

'Just the breakfast things when we've had breakfast,' Gwen told her. 'The men'll do everything else.'

Which they did, remarkably quickly and efficiently. Within an hour and a half, after she'd locked up and given the keys to the estate agents, they were on their way to the coast in a cheerful procession, with Lucy's dusty Fiesta following her nice clean Fiat and the furniture van trundling along in the rear. From time to time she wondered what her daughter would think of the tower and anxiety made her scowl but, once

46

they were over the causeway, the joy of being so near possession was so overwhelming that she forgot about everything else.

And then there she was, with the smell of the sea in her nostrils and gulls wheeling and calling overhead and waves crashing on the shingle a mere hundred tousled yards away and the tower rising before her like a fortress. Home. The field before her was ribboned with sky-blue puddles, squashy with mud and full of vehicles – builders' vans, mud-spattered cars, a skip full of planks – and inside the walls of the garden there was a white delivery van, labelled Makepeace Kitchens backed right up to the door of the tower, which was wide open and emitting a steady throb of very loud pop music accompanied by calls and whistles and the intermittent thwack of hammers. It was wonderful, life-affirming stuff and she was the cause of it. She was so happy that her cheeks ached with smiling.

'What d'you think?' she called to Lucy.

Lucy had been thinking all through the journey, wondering what this new house would be like and imagining a seaside bungalow, or a house on a neat estate, or even a thatched cottage, but no amount of speculation could have prepared her for this. She parked alongside her mother's Fiat and eased from the driving seat, to stand beside her looking round in amazement. 'Ye Gods!' she said. 'Is this it?'

Gwen was breathing in the view. 'Yes,' she said, rapturously. 'Isn't it stunning? Wait till you see inside. It's going to be wonderful. I've been planning it for weeks. I'll leave the picnic things for now. Let's go and see how they're all getting on.'

But before she could move, the removal van growled up alongside and the foreman sprang from his cabin and strode across to her, dark with complaint.

'We'll never get it through a gate that size,' he said.

His objection didn't worry her in the least. 'Yes you will,' she told him cheerfully, and she leant into her car to retrieve a folder from the passenger seat. 'You've got a foot clearance. I've measured it.' She opened the folder and held out a pencilled plan for him to see. 'Look.'

'Measuring's one thing,' he told her darkly, 'squeezing the bugger through's another. It's very tight, is that. We'll have a go but I doubt we'll do it. And another thing. That van'll have to shift. Even if we do get through, we can't back up with that in the way.'

'I'll tell them,' she said. 'Don't worry. I'll have it clear in a jiffy.' And she went striding off across the mud to attend to it, her hair bouncing with energy and determination.

Following her, Lucy was struck by how much she had changed. She wasn't a bit like the unobtrusive woman who'd kept house and cooked and washed and cleaned all those years in Fulham, the woman she'd always thought she knew. 'You're amazing,' she said as she caught up with her. 'You've got everything organised, haven't you?'

'Most things, yes,' Gwen said. 'It's like my Dad used to say. Plan to the last detail and then you can cope with anything, no matter what turns up. Very sound advice.'

'Did you plan to tell us about it?' Lucy ventured.

'That was the difficult bit,' Gwen admitted. 'I did. But later. When I'd thought out the best way. But then it sort of all caught up with me.'

Lucy made a grimace. 'Didn't it just!'

'Don't scold me,' Gwen begged. 'Not today. Come and see inside.'

I can't say anything now, Lucy thought, as she followed her mother into the tower. Not when she's so happy. But we'll have to talk about this sooner or later, for Ellie's sake.

The ground floor had been divided by a newly built wall into a large arc-shaped living room and a smaller arc-shaped kitchen with an arched doorway between them. Both rooms were full of workmen. One was plastering the living-room walls, two were in the kitchen surrounded by packing cases, hard at work assembling the foundations of her new kitchen units, and there was a plumber lying on the floor among the debris easing a piece of copper piping into position beside one of her new radiators. The first flight of her new staircase curved against the grey of the newly plastered wall, looking sturdy and richly coloured, there was a new picture window over the new sink and all three original windows in the living room had been double glazed and looked pristine after the grime of their predecessors.

'Coming on!' she approved. 'The sink arrived then.'

The senior fitter nodded to her. 'Friday morning first thing,' he said.

'Good. Is the water on? Splendid. We'll have a cup of tea presently. Soon as I've unpacked my teapot. Is Mr Makepeace anywhere about?'

The fitter thought that was a rare old joke. 'Mr Makepeace!' he laughed. 'Here? Oh that's rich. You won't find him where there's any work to be done. He's a salesman. Take world war three to winkle that one out the office. You got a problem?'

She explained what it was and a key was found and tossed to the apprentice with instructions to go and deal with it. Then as the removal van was eased through the gate – 'Steady as she goes! No. Come on. You've got room,' – she and Lucy set to work. First a space had to be cleared in the centre of the living room to make way for everything and three old sheets unpacked from the first tea chest to be brought in so that the furniture could be covered over and protected from paint and plaster. Then they boiled the kettle, unpacked teapot, milk, sugar and mugs and provided tea for both the removal men and everybody in the building. After that the work on the new staircase had to be inspected.

'It's all going to be lovely and bright,' Gwen said as they climbed to the first floor. 'I've had enough of porridge and safe colours to last me a lifetime. I'm having the living room scarlet. Think how grand these new treads will look against that. And this is my bedroom, which is going to be buttercup yellow, with a white and gold bathroom. I've found some gorgeous tiles.

And up here's the spare room which is going to be blue or wisteria. I haven't decided yet. There'll be a toilet and shower in this little bathroom, when it's done. And up there is my look-out post. Wait till you see that.'

'You really love it here,' Lucy said as they stood side by side looking out over the Solent. The play of light from the sea was casting a magical rippling pattern across the wall behind her mother's head, like a shimmer of little fishes.

'Yes,' Gwen said, turning to smile at her. 'I really do. I knew I would the minute I saw it. I simply had to buy it you know, Lucy. I suppose the thing is, all you ever hear about these days is the single life and how wonderful it is, so it's in your mind. The gossip columns are full of it, and there's all those books cashing in on the Bridget Jones thing, and *Friends* and *Ally McBeal*. They all say the same thing. Be single. Live for the moment. Don't have responsibilities. It's there all the time, day in, day out, like a sort of lifestyle wallpaper for the rest of us. Until your father died, I used to read about it and watch it and think *lucky for some* and wish I'd had the chance to live like that when I was young. And now suddenly I've got plenty of money and plenty of time and it's my turn. I can be a singleton too and live the way I like. It's not just a twenty-something thing. You can do it at fifty-six. The minute I saw this tower I knew I was going to do it. I've think I've earned it, after all these years, don't you?'

'Yes,' Lucy said. 'You have.' It would have been churlish to say anything else.

51

Eleanor had dressed with the greatest care for her office debut as an expectant mother. She chosen her smartest suit, the Dolce e Gabbana black, set off by diamond stud earrings, a Gucci shirt and her new cream boots, her new American eye-gloss and mascara, which certainly did make her eyes look excessively blue – the beautician had been right about that at least – matching nails and lips, gold watch highlit by the white cuffs of her shirt. Pete should be here to see me now she thought, as she gave her mirrored image one last thorough check before she left. It had taken over an hour, not counting the ten minutes she'd spent on toast and coffee, but it was well worth it.

Her car having been repaired to her satisfaction, she drove off in style, stopping on the way to buy her pregnancy kit, preening herself with contented anticipation. She rushed to the toilets to use the kit as soon as she arrived, and then, smiling enigmatically, returned to the office, kit in hand and put it down casually on Monica Furlong's desk 'Watch that for me, will you,' she said.

Monica screamed, as she'd known she would. 'Aargh! You're never preggers! You lucky thing!' And within seconds every girl in the office was gathered about the desk, squealing and shouting and pushing one another aside for the best view. 'Yes! It's coming! Look! See it! Yes! Yes!' as if they were all having some sort of multiple orgasm. It was very gratifying.

But then, just as she was accepting their congratulations and telling them how fit she was and explaining that being pregnant wasn't going to make the least bit of difference to her, 'well, I mean, it doesn't, does it, not in this day and age', Helen de Quincy, the great white chief herself, swanned into the room, looked down her long nose at the kit on Monica's desk and asked Eleanor if she could 'spare a minute'.

It was really aggravating to have such a very short triumph when she'd hoped for at least half an hour's worth, but the de Quincy word being law, there was nothing for it but to follow the lady into her private office and face whatever music she intended to play. Not that it was possible to guess what it would be, for Ms de Quincy's face was its usual well-controlled mask and her body cues never told you anything that you didn't know already – that she was stick-thin and superior, kept her distance, could hire or fire at whim, spent a fortune on designer clothes, all of them in classic black, and changed her make-up and hair colour every week, like the style icon she was. This week's hair was straight, short and so red as to be virtually scarlet. It flamed above the cool chrome and black leather furnishings of her office. Whatever else you might think about her she certainly had panache.

She flung herself behind her great desk and fitted a cigarette into her long black holder, used it as a baton to direct Eleanor to where she should sit, and lit up, elegantly.

'Good feed-back from New York,' she said, narrowing her eyes against the smoke. 'Feather in your cap, I think.'

Eleanor thanked her. You always thanked Ms de

Quincy, no matter what she said to you.

The lady blew smoke out of her nostrils in a long stream and Eleanor watched her, thinking that she looked like a redheaded dragon. 'I trust that kit didn't belong to you,' she said.

'Well actually,' Eleanor admitted. 'It did. But it's no problem.' Then she realised that she was blushing and ducked her head, hoping to hide her cheeks, feeling embarrassed and irritated.

'I'd have said it could be a major problem,' Ms de Quincy drawled. 'I hope you're not going to go all mumsie on me. There's too much work in the pipeline for the patter of tiny feet and you've got too much to lose.'

'I know that,' Eleanor said, lifting her head and her chin, because she had to look at the woman, and willing her cheeks to pale. 'I know exactly what it would cost. I've seen it happen.' She marked off the points on her fingers, the way she did when she was giving a presentation to a client. 'First, you lose all the money you would have earned while you're bringing the kid up, which is bad enough; second, you come back to a beginner's pay with all your colleagues streets ahead of you; third, you're out of the running for promotion because the world's moved on while you were away and you've got to catch up; and fourth, as if all that weren't bad enough, you get a diminished pension at the end of it all. Oh no, any woman who disappears into the domestic wilderness because of a baby is simply cutting her own throat.'

'Very well put,' Ms de Quincy approved. 'Couldn't have argued it better myself. So I

54

gather you've made arrangements.'

'Of course,' Eleanor said and began to improvise some. 'It's going to be born in the Easter holiday, the first day of the Easter holiday. I've got it all fixed up. If I do take maternity leave – and I shall take as little as possible – I can work at home. I've already got an office there, as you know, so that's no problem.' She gave what she hoped was an artless laugh. 'I shall be back at my desk before you know I've left it.'

'I trust you've arranged for suitable child care too.'

'The best,' Eleanor smiled. 'My mother.'

It was a clinching argument. 'Glad to hear it,' the lady said, blowing smoke again, this time more lizard than dragon. 'We lose far too much talent to maternity these days. It's such a waste and it can spread through an office like measles. Send Mr Cuthbert in will you?'

Eleanor walked out of the sanctum and strolled back to her desk, giving her colleagues a sly smile to show that she'd been congratulated and to forestall any idea that she might have been summoned for a wigging. Well that's it, she thought as she took her seat, Mum'll have to look after it now. I'm committed. I must ring Lucy.

She was annoyed to be told that Lucy was working at home and really cross when she rang the Battersea number and got the answering machine. She's gone to help Mum with the move, she thought. How stupid! But typically Lucy. She's too tenderhearted. That's her trouble. Now I've got to wait till tomorrow to tell her my news.

CHAPTER 4

The first thing Gwen saw when she opened her eyes the next morning was an enormous herring gull gliding past her window. It was so close that she could see every detail of it, white breast feathers ruffling in the wind, round eye sharp as a jewel, even the blood-red tip of its yellow beak. The room was full of bright light and the familiar scents of beach and brine, and above the shriek of the gulls she could hear the sea shushing the shingle and the steady creak and plash of oars. She'd crawled into bed at midnight too tired to keep her eyes open but now she was instantly and joyously awake. 'Here I am,' she thought. 'Where I want to be.' She was tingling with energy, greedy for the day.

She threw the duvet aside, scrambled into slippers and dressing gown and sped upstairs to her look-out post, eager to survey her territory. And oh what a reward it was, the sea so calm there was barely a ripple on its surface, pale, pale blue and burnished with sunshine, the dinghy brown as a nut, its rower wearing a fishing cap and navy blue jersey and pulling easily on red-bladed oars, and further out to sea two tankers, long and flat and stained with rust, and a cruise liner sparkling with white paint, its decks pale as paper in the early morning sunshine and every porthole black as ink. 'And all this is mine,' she thought. 'Every day for as long as I like.'

That afternoon, after a lunch of fresh bread from the local bakery and cooked meats from the local butchers and one of the best green salads she'd ever made or tasted, she drove off to explore the island, under a summer blue sky between hedges yellowing towards autumn.

She soon discovered that there was only one other village on the island and that it was a very small one, no more than a cluster of thatched cottages, a large manor house which, it didn't surprise her to discover, was now an old people's home, and a very small church which stood, looking more like a relic than a place of worship, all by itself in the middle of a vast graveyard. It reminded her of the church on the island where she'd grown up, so having found a little gravelled car park nearby, she crunched into it, left the car and went to explore.

There was nobody about and the air was full of unfamiliar birdcalls. The sounds seemed to be coming from beyond the flint wall that bordered the graveyard, so she strolled through the headstones to see what was there and discovered she was looking out over the mud flats of a large natural harbour. It took no time and little effort to clamber over the wall and then she was alone in a wild, wind-licked world of pan-caked mud, whispering sedges, tussocks of harsh rough grass, long sand spits, sky blue water – and wild birds. A grey heron stood statue-still on one long black leg at the water's edge; mallards bobbed like corks on the shallow water or rose in a sudden, straggling formation to fly to a safer place, five yards away, honking like horns; a redshank ran neat and quick on its stick-thin legs, and scores of pale brown plovers were feeding on the saltings, all heads pointing in the same direction, their black beaks busy and accurate. There was even a cormorant, tall and black, long-necked and inelegant, perched on a rotting tree stump, hanging out his wings to dry.

She stood at the water's edge, breathing in the smell of the sea and surrounded by birds, completely in her element. It was sheer bliss. Her jeans and trainers were spattered with mud, her jacket had a green stain down one arm, there were twigs in her hair and salt on her lips, but what did it matter. I can have a bird table in my garden, she thought, the way I've always wanted. There's no one to forbid it now.

Lucy was hard at work that morning with an intractable set of figures, trying to pinpoint the error that had sent them into absurdity, so when the phone rang she answered in the vague voice she used to deter her colleagues at moments of concentration. 'Ye ... e ... s.'

Eleanor wasn't deterred in the least. 'I gather you went down to this Seal Island place with Mum yesterday,' she said. 'So how did it go?'

'OK,' Lucy said, still studying the figures. 'It's not a house though. It's a tower.'

Eleanor was horrified. 'A what?'

'A tower. And before you ask, it's very run down and she's restoring it.'

'She's off her trolley,' Eleanor said, her voice sharp at the other end of the line. 'I mean, a tower, for Christ's sake. I never heard anything like it. Grief you see. I told you so. Well it won't last. She'll be back by Christmas.'

'I don't think so,' Lucy tried to warn.

'She will,' Eleanor insisted. 'Trust me. I'm going to get her back. Ask me how I got on with the test.'

'You've done it then. Well?'

'That's why I'm ringing,' Eleanor said. 'I thought you'd like to know.' And she plunged into a highly coloured account of the entire incident, from Ms de Quincy's initial reaction, right down to her own skilful improvisation.

It disappointed her that Lucy wasn't as impressed as she'd expected. 'You're not really though are you?' she said, her eyes still on the screen.

'Not really what?' Eleanor asked.

'Going to have it induced.'

Until that moment Eleanor hadn't really thought about it. It had been a ploy, that was all, to satisfy the great white chief. But being opposed stiffened her resolution. 'Well why not?' she asked.

'Because it's unnatural,' Lucy said, looking away from the screen. This was too important to be given half her attention. 'Why can't it stay where it is until it's ready, poor little thing?' She found she was yearning for the child, her belly aching with something that felt like anguish. Was anguish. This is Pete's baby we're talking about, she thought. You can't drag it into the world before it's ready.

Eleanor drew in her breath with annoyance.

'That's the way things are these days. Life's tough for all of us. The sooner it gets used to that the better.'

'Well I think it's horrible. You're treating it like a commodity.'

'Now look,' Eleanor said, crossly. 'This is my baby in case you haven't noticed and if I say it'll be induced, it'll be induced. I've got to do what's best for me. I've got a career to consider here. More to the point we've got to get Mum organised to look after it afterwards.'

'Who's *we?*'

Eleanor was so aggrieved she missed the chill in her sister's voice. 'You and me,' she said. 'She's our Mum. I thought you might say something to her the next time you go down. Sort of prepare her.'

'Oh no!' Lucy said with feeling. 'Like you just said, it's your baby. You tell her.'

'You'll see her first,' Eleanor began, still arguing her case. But Lucy had hung up. Well, how rude!

In fact it wasn't impoliteness that had cut them off, it was misery. Ever since she'd heard about this baby Lucy had been holding back an impossible grief. She knew there wasn't anything she could do about it, that she had to be sensible – and she had been sensible, eminently sensible, congratulating Ellie and keeping her secret from Mum, putting on a bright face and not letting anyone know how she really felt about it – but that didn't stop the pain. Now tears were roughening her throat and if she wasn't careful they would spill into her eyes. She found a tissue and blew her nose quickly before the others

60

could see she was in a state. Open plan offices are the worst possible places to be when you're upset because there's nowhere to hide.

Sure enough Yvette got up and strolled over to ask if she was all right.

'I think I've got a cold coming,' Lucy told her. 'I've been sniffing all morning.' And sniffed to prove it.

Yvette was sympathetic. 'D'you need some paracetamol?'

'No, no. Thanks,' Lucy managed to smile. 'I've got some. Never travel without a packet. 'Specially when I'm fighting the Leicester account.'

'Oh is that what it is?' Yvette said, stooping to look at it. 'That's a real pig! They gave it to me last year. Drove me to drink. It won't stop us clubbing will it, this cold of yours?'

'No. Course not,' Lucy told her. 'It's only a cold. I'll shake it off. You know me.'

'Only I've seen this gorgeous top in Selfridges,' Yvette said. 'Sequined. Really slimming.'

The day carried her along. She and Yvette strolled down into Oxford Street in their lunch hour and bought the top. The Leicester account took all afternoon and wasn't sorted until six o'clock. Then it was home to Battersea and a quick tea, her two flatmates to fight for the bathroom and the serious business of dress, hair and make-up to attend to, and then the three of them were on the road and off to the club with Helen driving, as it was her turn. And once there the noise was so intense there wasn't space or peace in which to think or feel anything, which was just as well, given the mood she was really in.

She was greeted by her clubbing friends, many of them already cheerfully drunk but happy to accept another at her expense, she danced until her feet were sore and the sweat was running down her spine, she laughed at every stupid joke and agreed with every stupid opinion and finally when she was more than a little drunk herself and the pairing up had begun she made up her mind to pull the best-looking male in the place, just to prove she could do it. That was how Eleanor coped with distress and if it was good enough for Eleanor it was good enough for her.

In the musk and darkness of the clubroom, with the pulse of the laser beam to confuse her sight and the throb of the loudspeakers to assault her breathing, it took her some time to make her choice, but eventually she settled on a blond hunk with a strong jaw line and broad shoulders – six foot tall, gold medallion, gold watch, no beer belly, quite a good dancer – at least what has to pass for good among city types. He'd been eyeing her all the evening, so he was open to invitation. Having marked him down, she danced through the heaving mass on the floor, pushed various shouting or snogging bodies aside, and contrived to bump into him. 'Oops! Sorry!'

He turned out to be a bloke she'd met at an office party the Christmas before last, name of Toby, ran a Porsche and had a relation who was a Sir Something-or-other, rather full of himself, as she remembered, and he wasn't nearly as hunky close to as he'd seemed from the other side of the room. But he put his arms more or less round her waist and shouted that it was great to see her, so as he was the best that offered and seemed to know the form she decided to play along. Then Helen signalled that she and her partner were leaving so that was her lift home gone too and after that the end of the evening was rather inevitable.

He took her home in his Porsche, which was this year's model and even flashier than the one she remembered. He asked her how things were at 'what was it? Gloria Cosmetics?' which showed he remembered something. She told him life there was horrendous and remembering his job in the nick of time, asked how futures were holding up. He then spent the rest of the journey explaining the state of the market and his part in it, in full and exquisitely boring detail.

But once they were in her flat – still empty, or quiet at any rate – he moved instantly into seduction mode and did all the right things in the right order as if they were being filmed in close-up on TV, kissing her as though he was eating her mouth, pushing her towards the bedroom with his body – how does he know this is the door? – stripping her as though he was frantic for it, 'God you're beautiful!' tearing off his own clothes with a harsh ripping sound – does he use Velcro? – pushing her into the bedroom and down onto the bed in what felt like one movement, and humping into action 'God you're beautiful! Beautiful!' with such speed and determination that he'd come before she'd even made up her mind whether she was interested or not.

She lay beside him while he got his breath back, wondering whether she could ease out and go for a pee without annoying him. But she didn't have to wonder for long because he sat up and began to put on his clothes.

'Was I good?' he asked as he pulled his shirt over his head.

She was thinking what a spotty back he had. 'What?'

He repeated the question. 'Was I good? Did you come?'

'Oh that,' she said. 'Yes. You were terrific.'

'That's all right then,' he said, retrieving a shoe from where he'd kicked it. 'Must go or the wife'll be wondering where I am.'

'Wife?' Was he really married?

'Joke,' he said and laughed to prove it. 'Ha-ha! I'm not that sort of fool.'

She didn't care whether he was or not. 'Right.'

'See you at Dirty Harry's on Friday?'

'You might.'

He stood up, fully dressed again. 'Right.'

'You won't forget to shut the front door, will you.'

'Cheers!' he said. And went.

She listened until she heard the Porsche roaring expensively away. Then she turned her head into the pillow and gave herself up to tears. Life's so unfair, she thought, as her sobs made rhythmical patterns in the quiet room and her tears spread a dramatic dampness on the pillow. Eleanor is Daddy's pet; I help Mum with the washing up. Eleanor wins a place at Cambridge; I'm sent to

64

Sussex. Eleanor gets the fast track job; I toil over figures all day. Eleanor gets Pete and she doesn't even try and probably doesn't even want him much; I get that nerd Henry and Toby Whoever-he-was. She gets pregnant. Oh God! She gets Pete's baby. Pete's baby and she's going to have it induced. It's not fair. All I want is a little love. That's all. Just a little love. But now that she had the time to think, she realised that since her mother's extraordinary outburst she hadn't actually been at all sure what love meant. She'd always assumed it began with a blaze of glory, the way it had done when she first saw Pete Halliday, and then settled down into the sort of content-ment she'd seen at home. Or imagined she was seeing. Now she knew that her parents' love had been a pretence, and that it hadn't been love after all, she felt there was no certainty to anything. What had Mum said about it? 'I endured.' Was that what love was? Putting up with somebody. Enduring. Were there no 'transports of delight'? No 'right true end of love'? What had just happened in this bed certainly hadn't been love or passion. It hadn't even been good sex. And all I want is someone to love me truly. Is that too much to ask?

By this time her tears were spent and she was beginning to feel ashamed to be wallowing in so much self-pity, so she got up, went for that deferred pee, had a wash and put on a tee shirt and her towelling wrap. Then, since crying hadn't comforted her at all, she took down her two precious photo albums, turned on the bedside light and opened the pages into the well-remembered images of the past. Pete aged fourteen sitting on the wall between their two houses, the way she'd first seen him, long legs spread out before him, thick hair golden in the sunlight. Pete sprawled in a deck chair, reading – not such a good shot really because Ellie was in the background in that bikini. Pete aged seventeen, on his motorbike. Eighteen on his first 'vacation' pretending to stagger under the weight of the books he was carrying. Twenty, just back from the Mediterranean with a straw hat and a dazzling tan. Oh Pete! I've loved you for so long and it just gets worse and worse.

There was the sound of a key scraping in the lock, two pairs of feet scuffling, someone giggling and bumping about, then Tina's voice whispering, 'Leave off you idiot! You'll have us both over.'

And that's not love either, Lucy thought. And switched off the light.

CHAPTER 5

Perhaps it was just as well Gwen MacIvor was unaware her younger daughter was in distress. Had she known, she would have driven straight to Battersea feeling she had to do something about it and that would have cut short her first idyllic week beside the sea. As it was, she drove into Chichester that afternoon in happy ignorance and treated herself to a winter cape, a splendidly dramatic garment made of black wool with a dashing purple lining. Then, having dared so far, and because the black needed something to set it off, she added a squashy hat in mauve and purple velvet. She had never looked nor felt so grand.

Every day brought richer colours to her life. Domestic maples glowed wine-red against the flintstone walls. Pyracanthas spotted the village gardens with clusters of blood-red berries. Hedges grew grey-webbed with a lacy profusion of Old Man's Beard. Soon the fields were ploughed brown, grasses began the day dew-spangled, and the trees thinned their summer foliage and dappled into a magnificence of scarlet, gold and tawny. The two great oaks at the northern edge of the village yellowed hour by hour and the avenue of beeches carpeted her daily walk with a bronze fall. The richness of this new life of hers would have been delight enough without any other pleasures. But other pleasures there were.

The tower was gradually becoming the home she'd planned. Her look-out post was now a high-rise conservatory with sea-green walls, cane chairs and a profusion of busy-lizzies; the blue and white bathroom on the third floor was tiled, her fitted furniture was being made, the phone was promised for Friday, and although the kitchen was taking a long time, at least the hob and the sink and the fridge were in use, so it was nearly done, even if the walls and floor were bare and she didn't have the oven yet or any of her fitted cupboards. Another week, she wrote to Lucy and Eleanor on Thursday evening, and I shall be settled and holding my housewarming.

The next morning she woke to find the sea was grey and choppy and a strong breeze was blowing. It was so sharp it tossed the gulls about like scraps of paper, and so full of moisture she could smell the sea even inside the tower. When she opened the door to take in the milk, it blew her hair into her eyes and bellied her dressing gown like a sail. It made her feel so wonderfully alive that she stood where she was for a minute just to enjoy the power of it.

'Blow wind,' she called to it, quoting King Lear, 'and crack your cheeks.'

She was answered by a renewed gust – followed by a thin pathetic mewing. Whatever's that? Not a cat, surely, not out here. But there it was, staggering out of the outhouse, not much more than a kitten, small, black, yellow-eyed, long-legged, miserably thin and crying. Poor little thing.

'What are you doing there?' she called to it. And at that, it ran to her on its stick-thin legs, calling piteously, and she picked it up and held it against her dressing gown, running the palm of her hand along its back to comfort it. Its fur was so wet it was stuck together in ugly clumps and she could feel every bone in its spine. 'Why you're just skin and grief,' she said, full of pity for it. 'You'd better come in and have something to eat.'

She warmed up some milk, which it lapped frantically. Then she found an old towel and gave it a good rub down. And was touched when it started to purr. She was still drying it when the postman stuck his head in at the open window.

'What you got there?' he asked.

'This is my cat,' she said, because it was. There was no one to tell her she couldn't have a cat. Not now. She could keep it if she wanted to. And she did want to. 'It's called Jet.'

'It looks like one of them imps,' the postman said, looking at it dubiously. 'The ones in the videos. Jump out at yer, they do, all claws an' yowlin'. An' then you fall down and all the blood comes spurtin' out yer eyes, an' you die or get a plague or go mad. I can't remember which it was in that one. Terrible things them imps.'

She leapt to the cat's defence. 'It's a witch's cat,' she said, drying its front paws. 'Black all over. There isn't a bit of white on it anywhere. And that's rare.'

'Oo-er,' the postman said and went, quickly, leaving her letters on the sill.

'Imp indeed!' she said to the cat, and settled it

69

on her new sofa while she went to collect her mail. One from Lucy hoping everything was going on all right, one from the furniture maker to ask her what sort of handles she wanted, 'brochure enclosed', and a third from the water board about her application to be connected to main drainage. That one wasn't encouraging.

'Your application will be considered in due course,' it told her. 'However, it is only right to inform you that it will have low priority. Ordinarily we do not connect to a single dwelling occupied by a single person.'

'In other words,' she said to her cat, 'they'll only take it seriously if it's from a company or a group of buildings. Rotten buggers. Well I'll just have to see if I can get any of my neighbours involved.' There was a, farm not far away. She'd seen it on one of her walks. 'I'll stroll over there this after-noon and see what they say. What do you think?'

The cat narrowed its yellow eyes at her as if it approved.

'That's settled then,' she said, enjoying the fancy that they were having a conversation. 'Now I must get washed and dressed or I shall have the workmen here before I'm ready for them.'

It was really extremely pleasant to have a cat for company. It scrabbled up the stairs after her and sat outside the little bathroom while she showered, followed her down to the kitchen while she made her pot of tea and then curled up on one of the cane chairs in the look-out post, and was perfectly at home while she ate her breakfast and admired the view. Now that it was dry it didn't look quite so odd, and she noticed that it cleaned itself very thoroughly, young though it was.

It was still sitting in the chair when the telephone engineer arrived but after that the day was so crowded that she had no more time for it and was relieved that it seemed to be keeping out of the way. While the engineer was at work the builders arrived to paint her scarlet walls, the bedroom carpets were laid and the rest of the bathroom fittings man-handled up the stairs. In fact, there was so much going on that it wasn't until mid-afternoon, when she came back from a brisk walk down to the bakers, that she realised the kitchen fitters hadn't turned up. She was rather put out but, as she now had a phone, she rang the showroom and reported it to Mr Makepeace.

He was unctuously charming. Couldn't understand where they'd got to. Should have been with her at 8.30. Not to worry. No problem. He'd look into it and get back

He didn't, although she stayed in and waited for his call all afternoon. Finally, when all the other workmen had finished for the day, she sat in her newly scarlet room and phoned again. This time she got an answering machine which told her that the showroom was closed until nine o'clock the following morning. This time she was annoyed.

'It's a real nuisance,' she said crossly, as the cat came lolloping down the stairs to rejoin her. 'I was going to see about the drains today,' she told it, 'and now they've held me up. Still never mind. We'll have tea, shall we, and you shall have some

71

more milk, because you've been a very good cat, and then I'll go and find that farm. What do you think about that for an idea?'

It was easy to find, for there was a wooden signpost pointing the way, so all she had to do was follow the track. The morning gale had blown itself out and now it was a mild afternoon, breezy and autumnal but pleasantly warm. She could hear cows lowing on the other side of the hedges, a tractor rumbling somewhere to her left, a man's voice calling. Soothed and happy again, she walked into the farmyard.

It was a sizeable place, with a range of farm sheds on three sides, full of tractors and trailers, and a brick and flint barn on the fourth, roofed with terracotta tiles that were obviously very old, for they'd faded to a dusty pink and were edged with green lichen. The farmhouse stood somewhat apart, beyond the barn, and was a sturdy Georgian building, made of brick and knapped flints like the barn and beautifully balanced and proportioned. It had a green front door – left on the jar, she noticed – and was surrounded by a walled garden. The sight of it encouraged her.

There was a farmhand crossing the yard, stooping sideways against the weight of the bucket he was carrying, so she stopped him to ask where she could find the farmer.

'Mr Langley?' he said, frowning at her as though he wasn't sure who they were talking about. 'Well now, he'd be in the milking shed if he's anywhere. Follow the path to the gate and turn left.' And waved a hand to show her which one he meant.

It was a very long earth path but as she set off she could see the dairy at the end of it, a group of low buildings with slatted roofs and walls the colour of bleached linen, and rising beside them a silo of some kind, smooth and silver and glinting in the sun. Cows were lowing again although she couldn't see where they were and as she walked a cock pheasant jumped out of the hedge and strutted before her, stiff-legged and haughty, trailing its tail over the stones of the path.

This is lovely country, she thought, following it, and she wondered vaguely what the farmer would be like. He seemed to have a lot of cows. There were several lying in the field to her left, big black and white beasts, slumped on the grass, lazily chewing the cud, and as she reached the end of the path and found her way barred by the predicted gate, another smaller herd came ambling out of the dairy buildings towards her, bellowing as they swayed along the path. They were so big and so loud she was quite alarmed by them, especially as their leader had an ugly ring through her nose. It was made of yellow plastic like a child's toy, but it was hideously spiked and made her look unexpectedly aggressive when she raised her head. Do cows charge you? Gwen wondered, staying on the safe side of the gate. And how dirty they are, their flanks caked with mud and their hooves spattered with trodden cowpat. They don't milk them in that state, surely.

For a second she wondered whether she ought to go back to the tower and try again another time. But having come so far, she waited until the cows had all passed, shook off her timidity, edged through the gate – taking care to close it after her – and walked towards the shed.

It was a very dirty walk. After a few yards her shoes were as spattered as the cows' hooves had been, even though she was walking very carefully and watching her feet all the time. But the cow-shed was even dirtier, for here she was walking on an earth floor that was green with ancient excrement and sploshed with new pats at every step and she couldn't avoid walking in them, dodge though she might. On one side was a huge barn, divided into sections like a cattle market, and heaped with bales of straw, on the other a long narrow area packed with waiting cows, pushed in so close to one another that they were standing flank to smeared flank. Now she saw that every cow had a white number painted on its rump and realised that they were standing in that cramped space waiting to be milked. The dairy itself must be the covered area immediately in front of them. She walked on to find the entrance.

It wasn't what she expected at all. Until that moment she'd had a vague idea that a dairy would be white-tiled, well-lit and spacious, but this was a small narrow area with two lines of cows standing diagonally to each other, like lines of parked cars, each tightly wedged into a very narrow stall with a small manger in front of her and her hind legs at the edge of a trench in which the dairyman stood, his hands at the level of her udders. The enclosed air was sweet with the scent of their breath, and full of subdued sounds, the faint swoosh and knock of the milking machines, the occasional shuffle of hooves.

The farmer was down at the far end, squatting on his heels and talking to the dairyman. She couldn't hear what they were saying, but the tenor of their voices was low and serious, so she waited for a while until the farmer stood up and straightened his back

Then she called out, in as clear a voice as she could manage. 'Mr Langley.'

His answer sounded bad-tempered. 'Who's that?'

He's cross, Gwen thought, and instantly felt anxious, as she always did in the face of someone else's irritability. 'I'm your neighbour,' she explained. 'Gwen MacIvor. I've bought the West Tower. Just moved in.'

He wasn't the least bit interested in who she was. 'Who the hell let you in?' he asked.

She tried not to be discouraged. 'I've come to see you with a business proposition,' she said. 'If it's the wrong time–'

'Wrong time!' he said. 'Ye Gods! We've only just recovered from the worst foot and mouth crisis we've ever known. Don't you read the papers? You could be putting my herd at risk.'

'I'm sorry,' she said, continuing although the fury in his voice was making her heart throb with alarm. 'I thought it was all over. I mean there weren't any notices to say I'd got to keep out.'

He jumped into the trench, strode through it and leapt out again, menacing towards her until they were standing face to face. There was no doubt about his anger now. He was threatening her with it, making her feel extremely un-

75

comfortable, and yet at the same time and to her horror, attracting her strongly. I shouldn't have come here, she thought. It was a mistake. And I shouldn't be feeling like this, especially for a man I've only just met. It's not right or proper. I must stop it at once. But it couldn't be done. If anything it was getting worse. She wished he wasn't such a very large man. But he was. Over six foot tall and bull-bulky with very wide shoulders, a rock-hard chest and large strong hands. The sort of man who could pick you up and throw you out bodily if he wanted to.

'You've got no business here, notices or no notices,' he said fiercely. 'It's against the bloody regulations and it's too bloody dangerous. Just bugger off.'

It upset her to be attacked but she tried to defend herself. 'There's no need to be so–'

'Yes,' he said, 'there is. I've just built up a new herd and I want to keep it.'

She outfaced him, met his gaze and held it, thinking what bold blue eyes he had and what a tough face, all hard angles and defiance, with a broken nose and a chin as strong as his hands. It was a small triumph when he looked away first, dropping his eyes with a sweep of such thick dark lashes that she was turned on all over again.

'I'm sorry I've troubled you,' she said stiffly and turning on her heel, walked out, straight-spined with anger at his rudeness, annoyed by her unbidden – and unexpected – reaction to him. All right, maybe she shouldn't have walked in, not after all that foot and mouth business. But there weren't any notices and there was no need to treat her so rudely. He could at least have been civil.

He was back among his cows before she'd walked out of the shed, talking to the dairyman, his voice businesslike. 'I'll get Ed to come in and have a look at her.'

As she followed her footsteps back across the meadow Gwen realised she was still shaking from the violence of their exchange. Things change so quickly here, she thought, and it occurred to her that there was a dark edge to this newfound freedom of hers. She could live where she wanted, eat what she fancied, dress how she chose, keep a cat, but she was open to mistakes too, adrift in a world she didn't entirely understand, where there were arguments and difficulties waiting for her, and where she could upset people even when she didn't mean to. Still, she thought, he may have sent me packing but he hasn't changed my mind. There'll be other neighbours somewhere round about and I'll bet some of them would like to be on main drainage as much as me. I'll find out where they are and go and see them. And as the wind blew her towards her front door, flicking her cape before her, she was pleased to think that she was still determined and still optimistic.

The cat was asleep on the sofa but it woke and yawned as she stepped into the room and then stood up for a wakening stretch, arching its bony spine and straightening its little thin legs until they trembled with the effort it was making and gave way suddenly so that it toppled sideways into the cushions, looking angrily surprised.

'Daft thing!' she laughed at it, and went on to

77

tell it the news as she stroked its head. 'He was a very unpleasant man, little Jet, you'll be sorry to hear. Not at all nice. I'm not going to let him get me down, though. I shall find a way round him. Now I think we'll have fish and chips for supper. How would that be? I should say we've earned it, wouldn't you? I hope they fix the kitchen on Monday.'

Monday came and went without any sign of the fitters. Both bathrooms were tiled, the last wall painted, the fitted furniture delivered and eased into position, but there was still no sign of them. By ten o'clock on Tuesday morning, the circular carpet for the living room had arrived and lay under the stairs waiting to be unrolled, but the kitchen was still as it had been left on Wednesday afternoon.

'It's nearly a week now,' she said to Mr Makepeace when she phoned him, 'and they still haven't put in an appearance.'

He couldn't understand it. But not to worry. He'd look into it. No problem.

'That's what you said last Friday,' she reminded him. 'And nothing's happened and it is a problem. I've been living on takeaways since I moved in and there are packing cases all over the place It's not good enough. I want something done about it.'

'I told you,' he said. 'I'll look into it.'

She felt she was being given the push-off. 'No,' she said, 'I don't think you understand what I'm asking you to do. I don't want you to look into it. I want you to send the fitters back to finish what they started. And I want you to do it now.'

His tone sharpened. 'Can't be done,' he said.

'Why not?'

'They're in the middle of another job.' His voice was flat and final and brooked no argument.

She might have known it. 'And how long's that going to take?'

'All week. It's a big fitting. I can't expect them to leave it in the middle, now can I?'

'I don't see why not. They left my job in the middle. Sauce for the goose, sauce for the gander.'

'Now what I suggest, Mrs MacIvor, is you leave it to me and stop worrying. I'll see what I can do.'

How bloody condescending! 'And what I suggest to you Mr Makepeace,' she said, allowing her anger to grow, 'is that you fulfil your contract. I pay the money, you do the work, and you do it to my satisfaction. Which you're not doing at the moment. So let me make it clear to you. If this kitchen isn't finished by the end of tomorrow afternoon, I shall withhold payment.' And she put the phone down, feeling pleased with herself for taking such a strong stand.

His Volvo was in her garden within ten minutes and he was on the attack as soon as she let him into the tower.

'Read that!' he shouted, pushing a paper into her hand. 'That's the contract you signed. See your signature on the bottom. That is your signature on the bottom, I suppose? You do recognise it? You're not going to try and deny it? All right then, read the small print and you'll find I've fulfilled my part of the contract. To the letter.

79

You read it. All I was bound to do was provide the units. Well, I've provided the units. You can't deny it. So now, you've got to pay for 'em. That's the legality of it. It's not up to me to see 'em fitted. That's another company altogether. Sub-contracted. You read the small print. If they renege on you that's nothing to do with me.'

She moved away from him, reading the contract, willing her hands not to shake, too frightened to think or speak. Was she really going to be caught out by the small print? Surely he wasn't going to walk away with the money and leave her here with the kitchen half fitted. But how could she fight him?

He raged as she read. 'Don't you think you fool me for a minute. This is all about money. That's what this is. Money. And if you think you're going to cheat me out of what's mine by rights you've got another think coming, I can tell you. I'll take you to court.'

Through the fog of her fear, she realised that there was another voice speaking, somebody outside the door, which, she now noticed, Mr Makepeace had left ajar. 'Hello?' it called.

She moved away from her adversary at once, glad of a diversion, but when she saw who'd arrived she felt as if she was being nipped in a vice, for her visitor was Mr Langley and he looked even more massive than she remembered him.

'I'm sorry,' she faltered. 'It's not very con-venient at the moment.'

'So I hear,' he said cheerfully and walked into the tower as it he'd been invited. 'Oh it's you,

Tony. Thought I recognised the voice. What's all the hollering? I hope you're not bullying my old friend.'

His intervention stopped Mr Makepeace in mid roar. 'What old friend?'

The farmer grinned. 'Gwen MacIvor. The lady you're trying to bully.'

'I'm not trying to bully anybody,' Mr Makepeace said, his voice instantly reasonable and conciliatory. 'We got a problem here, that's all.'

'Which you're making worse.'

'Which I'm trying to explain.'

The farmer grinned at him again. 'You could have fooled me.' Then he turned to Gwen. 'So what is this problem then? Never knew a problem yet that couldn't be solved with a bit of common sense.'

He was so reassuring and seemed so totally in command of the situation that she told him, as briefly as she could. 'The kitchen's not finished and his men have taken off to do another job and now he says I've got to pay him whether it's finished or not because it's not his responsibility. It was supposed to be done by Friday.'

'I told you, Mrs MacIvor,' Mr Makepeace began, 'you can't expect to have everything your own way.'

'I don't see why not,' the farmer said amiably. 'If you'd undertaken to finish by Friday, then that's what you should have done, or you'll get a bad reputation all round the village – and you wouldn't want that.'

'I'll see what I can do,' Mr Makepeace said, taking refuge in a return to vagueness. 'I can't say

81

fairer than that, now can I?'

'Oh I think you can,' the farmer said. 'How about "I'll see they're here this afternoon." Try that.'

'That's not possible.'

'Oh I don't know,' the farmer said smoothly. 'Anything's possible when a reputation's at stake.'

The answer was grudging but given. 'I'll do what I can.'

'Then they'll be here this afternoon?'

And apparently they would. It was agreed. He was actually smiling about it. Then he was gone, as suddenly as he'd come, and she was left on her own with Mr Langley, feeling relieved and surprised and totally exhausted.

'I'm sorry,' she said, 'I shall have to sit down.' And did, sinking into the nearest sofa because her legs were too wobbly to support her.

'Name of Jeff,' he said, taking a seat on the other sofa, 'as we're supposed to be old friends. Jeff Langley. You don't want to take any notice of Tony Makepeace. He's all mouth.'

She gave him a rueful smile. 'He was all threats before you arrived.'

'He's a salesmen. That's his trouble. He can't think of anything except the money he's going to earn. They're all the same, double-glazing, kitchens, cut-throats the lot of 'em. Still he's done me a good turn this morning.'

She was beginning to recover. 'Has he?'

'I came here to make amends,' he said, and explained, 'You caught me on the wrong foot on Friday, I'm afraid. The outbreak was an absolute nightmare, but that's no excuse for the way I spoke to you.'

Oddly, she felt she had to reassure him, which wasn't at all what she expected to be doing. 'I shouldn't have come barging in,' she said.

'So,' he said, and smiled at her. He really was extremely attractive when he smiled. 'How would you like to come out to dinner with me?'

That was such a surprise she could feel her jaw falling. What an extraordinary man he is, she thought, one minute he's telling me to bugger off and the next he's inviting me to dinner. But it would be nice to have a cooked meal. 'I've been living on takeaways for days,' she told him, 'so yes, I think I would.'

'Tonight?'

She laughed at that, thinking what a quick worker he was. 'Well I don't know.'

'Eight o'clock?'

'I haven't said yes yet.'

'Then say it.'

She dithered, caught between the temptation of the meal and the fear of appearing too eager. Luckily there was a scrabble of feet on the stairs and Jet lolloped down to join them.

'It's a stray,' she said, as the little cat approached them gingerly. 'I think it's been living in my outhouse. It seems to have adopted me.'

He turned his attention to the animal. Temporarily. 'Have you had it checked over?'

'No. Should I?'

'I'll do it for you if you like.'

She would like. It would give her a pause in which to think.

He stooped, picked the cat up in his big hands and examined it quickly, stroking its fur the wrong way, looking in its ears, opening its mouth, turning it over onto its back. 'Well for a start she's a female,' he said, 'so you'll have to get her spayed pretty soon or you'll have every tom on the island caterwauling outside your window. And she's got fleas, which you'd expect, so she'll probably have worms too, and canker in her ears.'

'I suppose I'll have to find a vet then.'

'Take her to Ed Ferris,' he advised. 'He's first rate. And not far away. Just up Mill Lane. I use him all the time.'

She remembered his voice in the milking shed saying 'I'll get Ed to come in.'

'Well that's that then,' he said, and put the cat on the floor, setting it down neatly on all four paws. 'Let me know if your fitters don't turn up. See you at eight, right?'

And as he looked so cheerfully confident she had to agree.

After he'd gone she realised she hadn't asked him where they would be going. But what did it matter? It would be a proper cooked meal. And company. 'I've got a date, Miss Jet,' she said to the cat. 'What do you think of that?'

He called for her at eight o'clock on the dot, according to the dial on her new cooker, twenty minutes after the kitchen was finished and the fitters had left, so she invited him in to inspect the work.

'Excellent,' he said. 'Shows what the dreaded Tony can do when he tries. Ready for the off?'

84

His car was a Land Rover, which was predictable, and he drove it well, which she also expected, taking her slowly through the village, past a row of small thatched cottages and out into the countryside.

'This is such a pretty place,' she said, as they passed the last cottage. There were roses tumbling above the front door, creamy white in the darkening evening, and the living room was rich with yellow light. The curtains weren't drawn and there seemed to be a card game of some sort going on inside, eight grey heads clustered round two card tables. 'It looks really romantic.'

'You wouldn't say that if you knew what you were looking at,' he told her, laughing.

'What am I looking at?'

'The dark abode of Mrs Agatha Smith-Fernley, village gossip.'

She laughed too. 'Heavens! Is she as bad as she sounds?'

'Worse!'

'Then I must take care not to give her any reason to gossip about me.'

'We're going to the Lobster Pot,' he told her. 'I thought you'd like some local food. It's a good place. Off the beaten track. Nice and quiet.'

And very pretty, crouched beside the curve of a riverbank and built of wattle and daub, with a thatched roof that sloped down so low at the sides of the building that it seemed to be resting on the water butts. In fact the entire building was so far below the level of the road that there were three steps leading down into the restaurant. But once inside they were enclosed in warmth and mellow light, for there was a log fire burning on the ancient hearth and every table was candle-lit.

'Now,' he said as they settled for a table by the fire, 'what shall we drink to celebrate the defeat of the avaricious Tony?'

'That was your victory, not mine,' she said. 'If you hadn't come by when you did he'd have beaten me hands down.'

'No, he wouldn't,' he told her. 'He's all mouth is our Mr Makepeace. All you had to do was stand up to him.'

'You make it sound easy.'

'It is.'

'Not to me.'

'The best line of defence is to attack,' he said. 'You just have to feel powerful. Or pretend you are. Come on strong. Growl first.'

'Yes,' she said. 'I suppose so.' But she was thinking, I couldn't do that. It's not my style.

'I don't like being defeated,' he said. 'So I rarely am.'

Looking at the power of those shoulders and that stubborn jaw, she could well believe it.

'Except by bureaucracy,' he went on, 'and that's a bugger to fight.' A waitress had arrived and was hovering beside his chair. 'Evening Bet. Now then, what do you fancy?'

They made a very good meal, choosing lobster thermidor washed down with a bottle of very good Chardonnay and they talked of food and wine and places he'd visited and enjoyed, which made her feel quite envious, and the longer she spent in his company the more she liked him.

By the time they reached the coffee and chocolates stage, they were talking as easily as if they really were old friends.

'How was that?' he asked as she set down her cup.

'Very good,' she said warmly.

'Not what you expected,' he guessed.

That confused her a little because it felt as though he was probing her initial judgement of him. 'Well no,' she said, and decided to tease. 'But then you're full of surprises.' And much nicer than the angry man in the cowshed.

'Man of many talents,' he agreed.

'As I see,' she said, and teased again, amazed at her daring. Was this really quiet Gwen MacIvor teasing a strange man she'd only just met? It must be the wine. 'But not modest.'

He took her seriously. 'Modesty's a fool's game,' he said, in his outspoken way. 'If you know your worth you should own it.'

'And if you don't?'

He answered her with an alarming directness. 'Don't you?'

'I'm not sure,' she told him honestly. 'It's not something I've had much cause to think about. Not while I was married. I think I'm finding out.'

'Was married?'

'I'm a widow. He died in July.'

'That makes two of us. I lost my old darling two years ago.'

His face was shadowed by such sadness that she yearned to comfort him. 'I'm sorry,' she said and wondered if that was what had made him so bad-tempered.

87

'Yes, well,' he shrugged. 'You get over it. So they tell me. She was so ill in the end I was glad to let her go.'

'You miss her,' she understood.

'Yes,' he admitted. 'I do. She was a good woman.'

She poured herself a second cup of coffee, wondering what she could say that wouldn't sound crass, but he spoke again before she could think of anything.

'You've got good hands,' he said, watching her.

The compliment surprised her. She wasn't used to being praised and certainly not for the state of her hands.

'Hard working,' he said.

That was true. 'Always have been,' she told him, looking down at them. 'My father was a fisherman. I used to help him with the nets when I was quite a little thing. He said it was good for me. Toughened me up.'

He smiled at her. 'Quite right,' he said. 'I can't stand poncy hands. Long nails and varnish and that sort of thing. They're sure signs of idleness. And the boys are as bad as the girls these days. Do you know there are young men who actually have manicures right there in our village.' He pretended to shudder.

She enjoyed 'our village' but thought of Lucy and Eleanor and felt she ought to defend them. 'Nail varnish is part of the uniform in London,' she said. 'My daughters couldn't go to work without it. They'd be drummed out the office.'

He leant across the table, picked up her left hand and held it. 'Good strong honest hands,' he

88

said. 'They say a lot about you.'

His touch was extremely pleasurable. 'This is like something out of Mills and Boon,' she said laughing to cover her embarrassment.

'Is that what you read?'

She grimaced. 'Oh please! Do me a favour!'

'It takes all sorts,' he said. 'My old darling used to gobble 'em up like sweeties. Loved 'em. She knew they were a load of old trash but she couldn't get enough of 'em. She said they cheered her up when the weather was bad.'

She tried to withdraw her hand, feeling he'd held it quite long enough, and laughed to show that she wasn't taking him seriously. But he held on to it, daring her to pull away, so she decided to tease instead. 'This is getting personal, Mr Langley.'

He smiled at her, still holding her hand. 'Yes, Mrs MacIvor. Isn't it fun?'

'And more Mills and Boon by the minute.'

'Not quite,' he said, letting go. 'If it was, you'd be a farm hand of some kind. A milkmaid probably. And I can't see you milking cows. Not after the way you barged into my dairy.'

Now she could be openly embarrassed. 'I'm sorry about that. Like I said...'

He brushed her apology aside. 'Water under the bridge,' he told her. 'Just as a matter of interest, what do you read?'

'Very highbrow stuff,' she said. 'Booker prize-winners and that sort of thing. I took a degree in English and Sociology when I left school. I thought I was going to teach. But then I got married and brought up a family instead. Bit of a waste really.'

'Nothing in nature ever goes to waste,' he told her. 'It just gets ploughed back.'

It was a comfortable philosophy but, before she could digest it, the waitress approached with the bill. 'I hope you're going to let me pay my share,' she said.

'I am not. This is my treat. Your turn next time. How's that?'

'That I can agree to.'

'Glad to hear it,' he said and put a credit card on the saucer.

It was late by the time they drove back into the village. The pubs were shut, Mrs Smith-Fernley's cottage was a brooding shadow, the High Street deserted and unfamiliar. They turned into the unlit darkness of Mill Lane and he parked the Land Rover and got out.

'I'll walk you to your door,' he said. 'It's black as pitch down here of an evening. Don't want you tumbling into ditches.'

So they walked along the narrow lane together and he took her hand again and tucked it into the crook of his arm. There was something so old-worldly and protective about the gesture that she allowed it without comment and even curved her fingers about the rough cloth of his jacket. And it was dark, for the moon was new and what little light it gave was obscured by drifting cloud.

'The stars are so bright down here,' she said, looking up at them. 'You can hardly see them in London. And hark at the sea.' The waves were crashing onto the shingle and hissing back in a long shushing sigh. 'I think that's what I like most about this place, the sound of the sea. I really missed it when I left home. Living in a town was quite a culture shock. I felt as if I was out of my element, if that's not a silly thing to say.'

'Maybe water is your element,' he said. 'My old darling could have told you. She was into all that sort of thing.'

'Horoscopes you mean?'

'Astrology,' he said. 'She was studying it. Had all the books and a computer all set up for it. Tell her the day and hour you were born and she could tell you all the stars that were influencing you and what to learn from them. Personally I thought it was pretty daft, but it meant a lot to her.'

So you went along with it, Gwen thought, surprised again. That's how much you loved her. And she felt envious of this woman to have been given such affection.

'If she were here now,' he said, 'she'd probably say you were born under the influence of Neptune. That's the one for affinity with the sea. Water and mist and tears, mystery, fairy tales, castles in the air. I learnt that much, you see.'

'It sounds fascinating,' she said and meant it.

'I'll show you some of her books if you like.'

Yes. She would like it very much.

They had reached the end of the lane and there was her tower solidly dark against the skyline with a faint mist rising from the sea towards it.

'Sea and mist and castles in the air,' he said. 'And here you are, Neptune's daughter. Safe and sound, back at the water's edge.'

CHAPTER 6

Mrs Agatha Smith-Fernley was, in her own estimation, the conscience of the village. She was a big woman, in every sense of the word, physically, morally and politically, a woman of unflinching purpose and unquenchable determination, tall, weighty and flat-footed, with a bosom like a well-stuffed bolster, tightly permed, brass-coloured hair and a voice that could carry from one end of the High Street to the other. She had acquired her reputation and her double-barrelled name by dint of marrying and subduing two timid husbands and outliving them both. Now she lived on her own in the romantic rectitude of Dove Cottage and made it her business to keep her suspicious black eyes on all the goings-on in the village.

She led an extremely well ordered life. Her weekly bridge party was invariably followed by a coffee morning at Ye Daynty Tea Shoppe so that the scandals aired in her living room the previous evening could be mulled over and embellished by a larger circle of acquaintance. Naturally she had an acolyte to escort her to the tearooms and agree with everything she said, and a special seat reserved for her in the centre of the bay window, where she was served coffee filtered to her exact specification and a selection of her favourite chocolate biscuits. There were people who said –

but privately, of course, and only in front of their dearest and most trustworthy friends – that they sometimes thought she could be a trifle overbearing, but it was generally accepted that if you wanted to know what was happening in the village the place to find out was the Ye Daynty Tea Shoppe when Mrs Agatha Smith-Fernley was holding court.

On that particular Wednesday morning, her acolyte arrived pink-cheeked and breathless with a very choice item of news. 'You'll never guess what I saw last night,' she panted.

'I never play guessing games, Teresa, as well you know,' the great lady said. 'So you'd better tell us.'

Teresa O'Malley was born to be a shadow. Unmarried, small and pale, with a peaky face, a subservient manner and the Irish trick of giving assent by an echoing statement, her greatest excitement was to live at the edge of Agatha's thunder. 'I will,' she said, eagerly.

'Well go ahead then.'

So Teresa went ahead. 'I was just getting ready for me bed last night so I was. I'd not been long home from the cards, not above half an hour at all events, and I'd had me little cup of cocoa and seen to me hair and I just went over to the window for a minute to ease it open, the way I do. I like a touch of air of a night time. It keeps the pipes clear. Well then, I ease it open, and who d'you think I see walking up Mill Lane in the dark clinging on to Mr Langley's arm?' She paused, round eyed with the delight of scandal.

'Well go on, woman. Who?'

'Her-in-the-tower,' Teresa said, rosy with the

power of denunciation. 'Clinging on to Mr Langley's arm so she was. Bold as brass.'

'What did I tell you?' Mrs Agatha Smith-Fernley said, looking round at her audience. 'She's a bad lot. I told you that the first time I saw her. Strolling about the village with mud all over her trousers – and I do not approve of women in trousers, as well you know.'

Now that she'd given them their lead, the coffee group dedicated themselves to criticism. Her-in-the-tower was roundly castigated and all her sins remembered. How she told Mrs Gurney's boy she was a witch. 'Admitted it to his face. Mrs Gurney told me herself. Frightened the life out of him, poor kid.' How she kept a black cat 'which proves it'. How she looked the part in any case, striding about the village in that ridiculous cloak of hers. 'Have you ever seen a woman in a black cloak in this village before? No. Well then that says something.' How she never ate anything but take-aways. 'The extravagance of it. Rich you see. More money than sense.'

'And now she's got her claws into our poor Mr Langley,' Agatha Smith-Fernley said. 'You'd think he'd have had enough after losing all those cows.'

There were loud murmurs of sympathy for the farmer. 'Poor man.'

And at that point Connie ran in hotfoot from the Post Office where she'd heard a splendid piece of gossip about Mr Makepeace. The meeting shushed itself quiet to hear her.

'Well,' she said, 'you know he's been fitting a kitchen for Her-in-the-tower.'

They did. They'd been following it closely.

94

'Well she's refused to pay him. Refused point blank. Shouted and raved and called him all sorts of names. Terrible it was. His secretary's just been telling me. And then refused to pay. Point blank. What d'you think of that?'

'It doesn't surprise me in the least,' Mrs Agatha Smith-Fernley said, stout in her seat of judgement. 'We shall have to keep an eye on her.'

'We will,' Teresa O'Malley agreed. 'We will so.'

As Gwen eased out of Jeff Langley's Land Rover in the car park of the Lobster Pot, the air around her was prickly with the smell of burning. She was instantly and cheerfully alerted, but there was no sign of a fire, no flames or smoke as far she could see, only the leaning shapes of several wind-distorted trees, black against the indigo blue of the sky, the bosky outline of the restaurant, and a peppering of bright white stars above her head.

'Someone's got a bonfire,' she said, sniffing the air. 'I do like the smell of a bonfire.'

'Fire's my element apparently,' he told her as he walked to their nook in the chimney corner.

'Now that's no surprise,' she laughed. 'I suppose that's why you live dangerously.'

'No I don't.'

Over the past two weeks she'd learnt how pleasant it was to tease him by contradiction. 'Yes you do,' she said, as she took her seat. 'This is the fifth time we've come here in a fortnight, I hope you realise. We shall get a reputation if we go on like this.'

'Fifteen days, if we're counting,' he said. 'Tuesday to Tuesday. Anyway we had to be here tonight. They've got red mullet. Special treat.'

He's so kind, she thought, looking at his craggy face, and so easy to talk to. 'You spoil me.'

He laughed. 'It's a tough job but someone's got to do it.'

'That funny old biddy of yours was watching us when we drove past. Did you realise?'

He was unconcerned. 'Let her.'

'Aren't you afraid of gossip?' she asked, shaking out her napkin. 'I know I am. What if they start talking about us?'

'They're probably talking about us already,' he said dismissively. 'They're easily shocked. It gives 'em something to do. Let 'em get on with it.'

It rather pleased her to think she was doing something shocking. 'And here's me never done a single scandalous thing in my life. You're a bad influence.'

He took the menu from the waitress. 'Glad to hear it. You're the sort of woman who benefits from a bad influence.'

She smiled at him. This easy, kidding style of theirs was such fun. It made her feel young and adventurous. 'That's a back-handed sort of compliment, if ever I heard one.'

'They're the best sort. Red mullet twice and scampi for starters.' He looked a question at Gwen and she nodded. 'With garlic bread.' And as the waitress left them. 'So. What's new?'

'Nothing much,' she admitted.

'Don't tell me you've run out of something to say,' he teased.

They'd talked non-stop at every single meal they'd shared – and all the way home – and well into the night, once they'd established that they had their coffee in the tower.

'I've already told you more about myself in two weeks than I told Gordon in thirty-six years,' she said. Which was perfectly true, for there was something about this man that encouraged confidences. 'Your turn tonight. How was your day?'

'If I start on that you'll be bored to tears.'

'No I won't.'

'Yes, you will. It'll be about milk yields and butter prices. I've spent the whole afternoon doing the accounts.' He grinned at her again. 'Your turn. Tell me what you really want to talk about.'

'All right then,' she said and rushed into the topic that had been occupying her all afternoon. 'What I really want to talk about is the drainage. I can't stand that horrible septic tank. It stinks to high heaven.'

He gave a roar of delighted laughter. 'Which must be quite the most romantic thing any woman's ever said to me.'

She was afraid she'd overstepped the mark and began to flutter. 'Oh I'm sorry. I didn't mean to...'

'I'm sure you didn't. That's part of your charm.'

She still wasn't used to his compliments. They were offered so suddenly and usually when she wasn't expecting them, so they confused her and made her blush, as this one was doing now.

'Well you've started,' he said, enjoying her heightened colour, 'so you might as well go on. What's the problem?'

'I want to be connected to the main drainage but the water company's being iffy. That was what I came to your farm to talk about.'

This time he smiled with understanding. 'I gather you put in an application and they turned you down. Right?'

So she gave him the story, keeping it as brief as she could.

'Doesn't surprise me in the least,' he said when she'd finished. 'They said the same thing to me.'

So he's tried too, she thought, feeling encouraged. I'm not on my own. 'When was that?'

'Couple of years back. When Dot was ill. I should've fought them over it, but what with her being so bad and worrying over the foot and mouth, I let it slide. So what will you do next?'

'Visit some of our other neighbours?' she asked. 'What do you think?'

'I shall put my mind to it,' he said. 'If there's two of us, that's better than one, but what we need to clinch it is another applicant with a heavier demand. We might try Mr Rossi.'

'Who's he?'

The scampi was arriving, steaming succulently. 'Tell you later,' he said, picking up his knife and fork. 'When I've fixed it.'

And that was all she could get out of him, although she tried twice during the meal and once when they arrived back at the tower. 'Am I going to be told about the mysterious Mr Rossi now?' she said, as she put the key in the lock. 'We're all on our own. I think you could risk it.'

He was sniffing the air. 'I can smell rain,' he said.

'That's right!' she said, pretending to be annoyed. 'Be infuriating!'

'No, seriously. I can. You smell bonfires, right? I

98

smell rain. It'll be chucking it down in an hour or two.'

She turned the key and stepped into her nice scarlet room. 'I'll take your word for it.'

'That being so,' he said following her, 'I think I ought to stay the night. It's about time.'

For two long seconds she was too confused to answer, as thoughts spun in her head as if they were being tumble dried. Is he suggesting we sleep together? she thought. Does he know how I feel about him? My God, what if we did? No. This isn't happening. I'm reading too much into it. He's joking. Must be. So she decided to answer joke with joke. 'That would cause a stir.'

'Is that yes or no?' he asked.

She felt she was being challenged. 'How can I answer that? It depends what you mean.'

'Now I would never have put you down as dim-witted,' he said, as near to laughing as he could get without making a sound. 'I mean I want to sleep with you.'

She was panicked by such directness, felt cornered, turned away. It was too soon. She knew too little about him. He was good company, he'd rescued her from the odious Mr Makepeace, he could turn her on just looking at her, but there were other darker sides to his nature, the power of his temper, the heavy dominance she'd seen when they first met. She stumbled into an excuse, trying to speak lightly. 'I think we're a bit too old for – that sort of thing, don't you?'

'You do talk bollocks,' he said and he tucked his forefinger under her chin, lifted her head and kissed her long and sweetly, full on the lips.

Then there was no denying how she felt.

'Still too old?' he asked, his eyes teasing.

'Well no,' she admitted. 'Look, perhaps I should have said out of practice. It's been a long time...'

'Sounds like a wicked waste to me,' he said. 'We must put it right, mustn't we?' And he kissed her again, this time with more passion – and after every sentence. 'You're too beautiful not to be loved. You must know that. And too gentle. And too kind. And too daft.'

It'll happen sooner or later, she thought. And I do like him. And it's only sex.

'Don't worry,' he said, reading her expression. 'I shan't rush you.'

And he didn't.

She woke at daylight, remembered with a rush of pleasure and surprise and put out a hand to touch him just to reassure herself that she hadn't been dreaming. And was disappointed to find him gone.

He'd left her a note propped against the cafetiere, which was still standing where she'd left it the previous evening primed and ready and unused.

'*Six am,*' it said, in his large bold hand. '*Just off to the farm. I didn't wake you. You looked too peaceful. Will ring later. Didn't I tell you it would be fun?*'

And it had been fun, she thought. Not just sex but a revelation. Not just pleasure either but a wonderful sense that she was special and appreciated. And all that after years of being an obedient wife and letting Gordon do his boring worst whenever he got the urge, and then accepting a sort of dumb celibacy when he lost interest.

'I've got a lover, Miss Jet,' she said to the cat, which was purring at her ankles hoping to be fed. 'Don't you think that's amazing? This is a new life and no mistake. What would my girls say if they knew?'

Fortunately both her girls were preoccupied with their own affairs. Lucy had so much work to do that for the last five evenings she'd still been in the office and struggling with it at nine o'clock, Sundays and all. And Eleanor had bought herself a book called. *Why Suffer?* and purporting to be 'All you need to know about pain relief in childbirth' and was psyching herself up for her first appointment at the maternity unit of her local BUPA hospital.

Of course she was already a regular visitor to the hospital, which was where she and Pete had their six-monthly check-ups, but this visit was in a different category altogether. This was a cause for celebration, a reason to be admired and petted and given special attention, for now she had a special status as Ms Eleanor MacIvor, expectant mother. She sashayed in through the plate glass doors as though she was gracing a catwalk.

She'd always liked the hospital. It was so cool and modern with its white foyer and its discreet signs and fresh flowers everywhere to scent the heated air. It pleased her sense of style that the nurses and junior doctors were uniformly dressed in white, and that the consultants wore suits that were fashionable and beautifully cut. The one who interviewed her that morning was charm itself, smooth and reassuring and

101

beautifully dressed, which was just as well because she'd had to cope with a midwife and a very junior nurse before she was finally ushered in to see him and although the midwife was quite nice in a plump sort of way, the nurse was too young and needed glasses. All she had to do was weigh and measure her and she couldn't do that properly. She'd got her height right but she was way way out when it came to estimating her weight.

'61 kilos,' she said, when Eleanor took off her dressing gown as instructed and stood on her ridiculous scales.

'Impossible,' Eleanor told her, speaking sharply because she was so affronted. 'I've been 56 kilos for years. I never vary.'

'Scales differ,' the nurse said, speaking lightly as if it didn't matter. 'The main thing is for us to watch your weight and see you don't put on too much over your pregnancy.'

'That,' Eleanor said firmly, 'is most unlikely. I'm very very careful about my weight.'

The consultant soothed her complaints away. 'Nurse is right, of course,' he said. 'Scales do vary. A great deal more than our patients realise. But looking at you I should say you'd have no worries at all in that direction. No worries at all.' He glanced at the file that was open on the desk before him. 'I see you've had regular check-ups here and they've all been more than satisfactory. You've always maintained an admirable weight. Oh no, no worries at all.'

So having established that she was the same slim Eleanor she'd always been, she allowed the consultation to proceed. It was as encouraging as she'd expected. He agreed with her entirely that she should suffer 'no unnecessary pain' at the birth. He demurred slightly when she hinted that she would like to be induced 'if it goes on too long', joking that his babies all did as they were told and arrived on the expected date give or take a few days. 'But we will always decide on the course which is best for you.' In fact, mulling it over as she drove back to the office, she had to admit that they'd only had one difference of opinion and that was over what he called the EDA, the expected date of arrival. He would insist on calculating it from the date of her last period, which was ridiculous when she'd just come off the pill and particularly when it would mean that the baby would arrive at the end of February instead of the start of the Easter holiday. But she'd had the good sense not to argue with him. It wasn't wise to put your consultant's back up, everyone knew that, and in any case it wouldn't matter in the long run because the baby would come when she said it would and he would be proved wrong.

In Seal Island, Teresa O'Malley was dialling Mrs Smith-Fernley. She was shaking with excitement at the news she was about to pass on.

'Agatha!' she said, when the great lady had announced her number. 'He was there again last night, as ever was. I saw him with my own eyes so I did. Oh she's the bold one and no mistake. Bold as brass. I was just taking a bit of a stroll to get the air – I like a bit of air of an evening – and I thought I might as well walk the few extra yards to the bend in the road and there he was. Well not him exactly. His car. Parked right up against her front door at ten o'clock at night. Now what d'you think of that?'

'I think she's got her hooks into him, poor man.'

'And that's not the half of it. I was just upstairs putting a bit of silver polish on the candlesticks – they run to verdigris in the damp weather, green in seconds they are – and who do I see walking across the field? Arm in arm if you please. In the broad daylight.'

Mrs Smith-Fernley was suitably outraged. 'Scandalous!' she said. 'You'd think he'd have more sense. Where were they going?'

'Well that's the mystery of it. I watched them all the way, thinking just exactly the self-same thing. Where are they going? I thought. He'll hardly be taking her to the farm. Not in broad daylight and not in front of everybody. He's got more sense than that, surely to goodness. And no, sure enough, they took the footpath to Mr Rossi's caravan site. Now what do you think of that? Isn't that a curious thing altogether?'

'She's wasting her time if she's after a caravan,' Mrs Smith-Fernley said. 'I saw Mrs Rossi in the baker's this morning and she told me they're closing the site this afternoon. That's why they've come down. We shall have to keep an eye on her.'

'We will. We will.'

CHAPTER 7

Mr Rossi took up his position on the hard standing beside his expensive caravan and waved goodbye to the last of his clientele. 'Goodbye Madge! Goodbye Jon! See you next year!' It always saddened him, this boarding up and stowing away, these too jolly farewells, for now winter was on its way and there would be no more sea and sunshine for any of them until the first faint warmth of Easter and that was five cold months away.

He was an odd-looking man, short and stout with a fringe of black-hair around a totally bald scalp, thick black eyebrows, moist red lips, mottled cheeks and a belly so perfectly round that he looked like an amiable Russian doll, especially as he had a habit of rocking on his heels when he was concentrating and always wore a bow tie and an extremely bright waistcoat – even when he was supervising the emptying of the cesspits. But he was a businessman for all that, with a talent for arithmetic and a shrewd eye for a bargain.

'Another year gone,' he said mournfully to his wife, who was sitting just inside the door of the caravan, swathed in wool and busily knitting.

'Soon be spring,' she comforted. And then looked up as two figures walked onto the site. 'Hello? Is that Mr Langley? Well here's a surprise.'

'How nice to see you,' Mr Rossi said, rolling forward to meet his visitor and be introduced to Gwen. 'From the West Tower, eh? I've heard a lot about you. Come in, come in. What can I do for you?'

They climbed into the caravan and were instantly stifled by heat.

'We like it snug,' Mrs Rossi explained. 'Cold creatures the pair of us.' She was almost as plump as her husband and wore a thick cardigan over her shirt and trousers and an even thicker scarf round her neck. 'Would you like some tea?'

'Tea, Mother?' Mr Rossi said. 'We can do better than that.' And produced a bottle of cognac and four crystal glasses from one of the overhead cupboards. 'Just nice time for an aperitif, eh? Your good health Mr Langley, Mrs MacIvor.'

The cognac was overpowering in the fug of that overcrowded little room. 'So what can I do for you?' Mr Rossi repeated.

'Actually,' Jeff said, 'it's more what we can do for you. We've come with a business proposition.'

'Have you now?' Mr Rossi said, sipping his brandy. 'It wouldn't be the other half of this field would it, by any chance?'

'Could be. Depends on what we decide this morning.'

The shrewd eyes smiled. 'Go on.'

'Seems to me you'd get a lot more trade if you could offer a swimming pool and shower rooms and so on.'

'Very true, but the cesspits wouldn't take it. We'd be emptying out every fortnight.'

'Precisely. Now if we were to go on to mains

106

drainage it would be a different matter.'

'We?' Oh very shrewd now.

'You, me and Mrs MacIvor.'

'Expenses split three ways?'

'Three ways or thereabouts.'

'Let me do some maths,' Mr Rossi said, 'and I'll get back to you. How's the herd?'

'Is that it?' Gwen asked, breathing in the cool air as she and the farmer walked out of the site a few minutes later. She was surprised that so little had been said and couldn't help feeling that nothing would come of their visit, intriguing though it had been.

'That's it for the moment,' Jeff told her, striding along the footpath beside her. 'He's taken the bait. Now he'll work it all out and see if it's worth it on balance. He wants the rest of the field, you see. An ambitious man our Mr Rossi. He'd like to run a caravan village like the one along the coast. If he really got going here he'd be on his way and a swimming pool would be a draw.'

'Just as a matter of interest,' she said, 'what are you getting out of it?'

'Capital,' he told her. 'I lost my herd because of the foot and mouth and it's taken a long time to build it up again, especially with milk prices falling. I'm on the way but not into profit yet. Set-aside doesn't help much either.'

'What's that?'

'Set-aside? It's what the EEC pays you not to farm. See that field over there where the tractor is? Well that's going to be set-aside next year, all forty acres of it. Won't grow a thing from

February to September. They pay you not to touch it. Wicked waste if you ask me, but that's farming these days. We can't grow what we like any more. We have to do as we're told.'

His voice and expression were so bitter she looked at him with concern. 'But why waste good land?' she asked. 'That doesn't make sense.'

'It makes economic sense, I'm afraid,' he said. 'If we cut back production, we decrease the corn supplies and that keeps the prices up for the big dealers.'

'That's awful.'

'That's business,' he said. 'It's all rules and regulations these days, how much insecticide to use and when to use it. Cows not allowed into the food chain over a certain age.'

Gwen thought of all those gentle beasts waiting in the cowshed, numbered and patient. 'But you don't kill them off young, surely?'

'No,' he said. 'Most of them last seven years, with a calf a year to keep up the yield. Some have to go earlier but seven years is about average.'

'And what then?'

'Then we slaughter them and burn them. Don't make that face. It's not all loss. They pay us for each carcass.'

She'd grimaced at the thought of the poor things being slaughtered and burnt. It brought back all those awful TV images of cows being burnt in the fields. And it upset her to realise how callous he sounded. That was a side of him she hadn't seen before and she wasn't sure she liked it. 'It's all so brutal,' she said.

'Farming is,' he told her. 'Always was. We don't

keep animals for pets. We keep them for milk and meat. Or we used to when times were better. Can't even keep our land these days. In fact...'

She pulled her mind back to the conversation, prompting, 'In fact?'

'This is just an idea,' he said. 'I haven't told anyone about it yet, so keep it under your hat. If I can get the mains laid on, I can build a clubhouse over there by the holm oak. Kit Voller owns the next farm, you see – the one over there. See the chimneys behind those trees? He's toying with the idea of turning over three of his fields for a nine-hole golf course. If I were to offer him an extra field and a clubhouse, I reckon we could go into partnership. And that would solve quite a few problems. You're making a face again. I know it'll mean more good land not being farmed, but you have to diversify in the farming industry these days, the same as everywhere else.'

'And I thought you were doing all this for me,' she said.

'There's that too,' he told her seriously. 'You revived the idea and I'd like to get rid of that septic tank for you. But no businessman is ever altruistic. It's not in the nature of the beast. We do what we do for profit. Or mostly for profit. If you can help someone you like on the way, that's a bonus but it's never the main reason.'

'Well at least you're honest about it,' she said, equally seriously.

He pulled an invisible forelock. 'Well thank 'ee ma'am.'

The gesture brought a lurch of desire, which surprised her after the disquiet of some of the

109

things he'd been saying. She slipped her hand through the crook of his elbow, found she was glad of the contact, and walked on in companionable silence for a few minutes, while she digested what she'd heard. Love is so unreasonable, she thought. One minute I'm upset because he sounds callous and the next I'm turned on by him. It's not logical. But then maybe it's not love either. Maybe it is just sex.

They'd reached the first stile and she had to let go of his arm. 'Can I ask you a personal question?' she said.

'You can ask whatever you like,' he said as she stepped over the stile.

She looked down at him from the top step. 'Would you say we're having a love affair?'

He threw back his head with a roar of delighted laughter. 'Well I don't know what else you'd call it.'

'Neither do I,' she said. 'That's why I asked.' She paused, considering what to say next as he climbed the stile too. 'I suppose,' she said as they walked on between the hedges, 'it's because I don't really know what love means. The word, I mean. Or the word as it's applied to husbands and wives. I know what it means between mother and child. I love my girls to bits. Always have. If anyone hurt them I wanted to wade in and tear them to shreds. But I'm not sure I ever loved poor old Gordon. Not with that sort of passion anyway.'

He'd listened to her seriously. And ventured a personal question of his own. 'Why did you marry him then?'

'I thought it was the thing to do,' she said. 'And he wanted to marry me. He kept on and on and on about it. And I thought... Well actually I can hardly remember what I thought. Not what I'm thinking now, anyway.'

'And what are you thinking now?'

'I'm wondering whether this is love. What we've got.'

They had reached the parting of the ways where the signpost signalled three directions and another stile blocked the path to his farm. He put one foot on the stile and turned to face her. 'Would you like it to be?'

'Yes. I think so. Would you?'

He smiled at her, a warm, easy, gratified smile. 'If you ask me we're well on the way to it already,' he said. 'I'd say it was coming along nicely.'

'You make it sound like a crop.'

'It is in a way,' he said. 'If you want strong healthy growth you have to take time. Time and nurture. And good feeding. You can't rush it.'

'And that's how you see it,' she observed. 'As something that grows. What about love at first sight?'

'Romantic twaddle,' he said in his forthright way. 'Love's a different matter altogether. Love takes effort and argument and compromise and sharing things. It's a very complicated business.'

'Tell me about it,' she said wryly.

He lifted his head to listen to the sounds coming from his farmyard. 'Gotta go,' he said. 'See you tonight then, Neptune's daughter.'

'Naturally,' she said, and thought, with a rush of happiness, how natural it was. Unreasonable,

111

yes, unpredictable, surprising, yes, but natural.

He was already striding off along the footpath but turned to look back for a second, his craggy features silhouetted against the autumnal blue of the sky. He sensed that they'd passed a turning point in their affair and, even though he wasn't quite sure what it was or how they'd reached it, he felt he ought to mark it with a gift. 'I'll bring some of Dotty's books over for you to have a look at,' he said. 'If you like.'

In Barbados the sky was cobalt blue, the sand white, the sea turquoise and the heat enervating. Peter Halliday had spent the entire morning rising sun-tanned from the sea, doing his best to look young, handsome and carefree while holding in his stomach as tightly as he could. Now after more takes than he could count, he was feeling decidedly jaded and more than a little irritable.

'Time for a break?' Staggers asked, to forestall trouble.

'Sounds reasonable,' Pete agreed. 'Unless you want a shot of me melting away.' And he waded back into the sea, knowing exactly what he needed, short swim to cool down, shower, clean clothes, ice-cold beer.

He had to admit he didn't enjoy these tropical shoots any more. They'd been all right once upon a time, when he was in his twenties and being glamorous was easy. Now they were just a pain and the less he was required to wear, the more he suffered, stuck out here in the heat with indigestible food to eat, and never enough to drink, and scorpions in his shoes, and hordes of half-educated, so-called technicians to irritate him, the way this lot had been doing all morning. Haven't got the fucking cradle marks off their fucking bums, he thought, as he trod water and looked back at the shore, and they think they know it all. And they're on the pull all the time. Shag, shag, shag. Like fucking rabbits. And they all talk crap.

There were three of them wah-wah-wahing away as he showered. On the next balcony probably, which was a fucking nuisance because that meant he couldn't go outside or he'd be drawn into their stupid conversation. But in fact he was drawn into it whether he would or no because they were talking about the Sheldon take-over.

'I see Sheldon's shares were up again yesterday,' a voice said. 'That's the third time in a week.'

'So you reckon it's on then,' another voice said.

'It is according to my broker. I'm buying more shares.'

That provoked laughter. 'What with? I thought you were skint.'

'So is it J.R. Grossman's, d'you reckon?'

'Yep. That's what the smart money's saying.'

It was exactly what Pete wanted to hear. if it is Grossman's, he thought, the shareholders'll make a killing. I wonder if Catherine knows anything about it. She used to be pretty thick with the chairman of Grossman's a few years back. It might be worth giving her a call.

It took four calls and much grumbling impatience before he finally got through to the lady's apartment in New York and then some fool on the other end of the wire told him she wasn't 'available right now' and suggested he called back later that evening. But at last, when he was beginning to despair of phone lines altogether, her number actually rang and Catherine herself took the call.

'Well hi there,' she said. "What can I do for you, you old reprobate? I haven't seen you in ages.'

He'd forgotten what a sexy voice she had. 'I'm a disgrace,' he agreed, 'but I'm doing my darnedest to put it right, believe me. Fact, I shall be in your part of the world in a day or two. Could we meet?'

'Let me find my filofax,' her voice said coolly. 'Right. What day did you have in mind?'

It was a device to keep him at arm's length and they both knew it. 'Hey!' he protested, contriving a hint of laughter in his voice. 'Do you book in all your lovers these days?'

'Only reprobates and people who call me for a favour.'

He laughed out loud at that and then moved smoothly on, deciding to outface her with the truth. 'Actually,' he confessed, 'I've been hearing rumours about Grossman's and a take-over. You don't happen to know anything about that, do you?'

'You want an invitation, right?'

'Sorry?'

'I'm giving a reception for the chairman. Wednesday week. Tell me where you are and I'll send you an invitation.'

It was providential. 'You're a star,' he said.

Now all he had to do was to set his broker to work to buy a few more shares – well a very large number of shares actually – and book a ticket to Kennedy. Providential! Absolutely fucking providential! Good old Catherine. It occurred to him that he'd better phone Eleanor too and let her know what he was doing. He glanced at his watch to check the time. If he was quick, he could catch her before she left for work.

When the phone shrilled through the minimalist calm of Eleanor's flat that morning, she'd just picked up her mail and noticed, with an unexpected lurch of excitement, that the top letter was from the hospital. But as soon as she knew the call was from Pete, she put the bundle down on the bed beside her unopened, and settled down to tell him her news.

'Listen,' she said. 'I've got something to–' But his voice cut in before she could say another word.

'I haven't got you out of bed or anything, have I?'

'No, no. It's half past seven. The postman's just been. Listen, I've got something to tell you.'

'So have I,' he said. 'Just wait till you hear this. Will you be pleased or will you be pleased. Sheldon's are up for grabs. I told you so didn't I? And it is J.R. Grossman's. Good or what? I'm off to the States tomorrow to see what else I can find out. It's all booked. I thought I'd better let you know or you'll be giving me stick. No, just a joke. Hold on just a minute.' And he spoke into the room. 'It's open. Just push. Oh it's you Staggers.

115

Hold on just a minute.' Then he returned to talk to Eleanor again and this time in such a rush he barely gave her time to answer. 'Look. I'll have to go. Staggers has just arrived. I'll see you when I get back.'

'When?' she asked. 'Only I've got–'

'Coupla weeks,' he said. 'Month maybe. Depends how long it takes. I'm not going to rush it. This is important. See ya.' And hung up.

As Eleanor put the phone down she had to admit she felt defeated and irritable. His refusal to listen was hurtful, as if he were pushing her away. But then, that was Pete all over. It was nothing new. He was always rushing off somewhere or other, making money or a film or an impact, and paying no attention to anything else. She couldn't say she wasn't used to it. Just as well I've got a life of my own, she thought, opening her first letter.

As if to show her how right she was, it was an appointment for a scan. You see, she said to the phone. They're offering me a scan. They're taking it seriously even if he isn't. When is it? Next Tuesday. For heaven's sake. They don't give you much notice.

It occurred to her, as she put the letter down and opened the next one, that she ought to tell her mother about the baby. It was the middle of October now and more than three months since she'd started thinking she might be pregnant. If she didn't say something soon it would start getting obvious and then the poor old dear would think she'd been deliberately left out of it. She'd got a bit of a belly already but nothing that couldn't be disguised by clever clothes. When do you really start showing? Four months is it? Or five? I shall have to look it up. I'll write one of my notes, she decided. Let her know I'm thinking of her. That sort of thing. But I won't say anything about the baby yet. I'll have this scan first and get the nursery built and then it'll all be plain sailing. So it was a short note and said very little.

Dear Mum,

Keep thinking about you and wondering how you are and whether you've settled in now. Sorry I can't get down. Work is horrendous. I hardly have time to breathe. Pete is in Barbados, lapping up the sun. Lucky thing!

Will come and see you the first chance I get.

All love, Ellie.

After that she plunged back into her life again. There was another major presentation to prepare – it ran to thirty-seven pages already and she was only two thirds of the way through – there were lunches with clients and parties and dinners, and the plans for the nursery had to be completely thought out before the work could begin, because she didn't want to run into any snags there. Everything had to be perfect so that her mother could come back to civilisation as soon as possible. She was probably getting sick of it by now, down on the coast in all this nasty weather, poor old thing.

In fact the poor old thing was happier than she'd been in her life. The mist might be rolling up from the sea in long white swathes and there might be a winter chill out in the village, but inside the tower it was warm and colourful, she had Jet for company and, since Jeff had started to bring over Dotty's books on astrology, she had plenty of reading material to keep her entertained and intrigued when she was on her own.

Because she was now firmly nicknamed Neptune's daughter, it was the book about Neptune that she tried out first. She began it rather sceptically, thinking it would be about horoscopes and fortune telling but it wasn't, and the further she read the more fascinated she became. Soon it was part of her day to retire to her lookout post after lunch and sit in the sun and read for an hour or two with Jet on her lap.

'It's really rather academic,' she said to Jeff when they were at dinner one Thursday evening and he asked her how she was getting on with *her new study*, 'and it makes such sense. I didn't think it would, but it does.'

It pleased him to think he'd given her something to enjoy. 'Couldn't see it myself,' he told her, 'but that's what Dotty always said.'

'I recognise things,' she said and tried to explain, as much for her own benefit as for his. 'Even the titles of the books make sense to me. The one I'm reading at the moment is called *Neptune and the Quest for Redemption* and it covers all sorts of things I read at college. Creation myths and stories about redeemers, psychology, even courtly love and I'd forgotten all about that. In fact there's a whole section on love which is really fascinating.'

'I prefer the real thing to reading about it,' he said, smiling at her.

She smiled back 'I've noticed,' 'she said, and went on pursuing her thoughts. 'The really extraordinary thing is how familiar it all is. I can see myself in it.'

'Well you would, wouldn't you,' he teased, 'being Neptune's Daughter. What did I tell you?'

'Apparently we're prone to self-sacrifice,' she said. 'And that's me to a T. Or at least it was until I came down here. And that's in the charts too. The need for escape and withdrawal and a love of the sea. Then there's the need for poetry and music. I've had that all my life. Even the mist makes sense. Mistiness and blurred vision. I think I had that all the time I was with Gordon. I'm only just beginning to see straight now.'

'And fish,' he teased, deliberately keeping the conversation light. 'I'll bet you've found them in the book too. How's your Dover sole?'

'Superb,' she said. 'Which reminds me. I think it's about time I cooked you a meal. I've got the hang of my new oven now and it cooks wonderfully. How about Saturday?'

'Sounds great,' he said. 'It's going to blow a gale so the forecast says, so it'll be nice to be indoors. I might even stay the night.'

'Surprise, surprise,' she laughed.

CHAPTER 8

Saturday was an eldritch night, sloe-black and rain-sodden, whipped by a wind that howled in the chimneys, shrieked through the alleys and lashed the naked trees until they groaned: a night for witches, devils, poltergeists, hobgoblins, a night for loathsome deeds, a night when even the sturdy street lights of South London flickered and dimmed as though they were as vulnerable as candles.

'We're going to regret this,' Lucy said to her flatmates as they scurried to her car, bent double under their umbrellas. 'I can feel it in my bones.'

'No we're not,' Tina said, scrambling into the passenger seat. 'It's gonna be great. Rick's gonna be there.'

Lucy hurried to check that they were all in the car and that the doors were shut. Then she slipped into gear. 'Big deal!' she said.

Helen was teasing out her new hairstyle with her fingers, admiring the resulting fizz in her hand mirror. 'What's it matter?' she asked. 'We shall be indoors. Right? I've never seen it rain in the Candy Kitten.'

The little club was as crowded as ever and the noise level as loud but although it was rain-proof, the wet weather was noticeable because it had intensified the smell of the place, adding a strong odour of damp clothing to the usual mixture of sweat and musk, heavy scent and pungent after-shave. Once her eyes had adjusted to the darkness, Lucy could see that most of her usual crowd were there, either dancing or standing in groups shouting at one another, and that the teenagers were already out of their skulls and dancing with such arm-flicking abandon it was a wonder they didn't poke somebody's eye out. Still, having struggled here through the gale, she decided she might as well enjoy herself and pushed into the middle of the throng to dance with the rest.

No matter where she was, whom she was with, however bad her mood, dancing always gave her a lift. It was the most sexy occupation she knew and full of sensation, a recreation in every sense of the word, feeling the beat as it pulsed upwards from her feet to the top of her head, shaking her belly and making her scalp crawl with pleasure, moving her entire body to the rhythm, on and on, never wanting to stop, until there was nothing but darkness and music and the joy of un-restrained movement. It was sensual, blissful, orgiastic, orgasmic. It couldn't be beaten.

But it could be interrupted. She had barely been on the floor more than a quarter of an hour before she became aware of a body intruding itself upon her and opened her eyes to see who it was. Henry! Oh shit!

'Great to see you,' he bellowed at her. 'Long time no see. Where've you been?'

'Working,' she said, turning away from him and continuing to dance. What had she seen in him?

'We must get together,' he said, following her. 'D'you fancy a drink? An E? What about supper?'

121

'You're treading on my feet,' she shouted back and danced away from him as quickly as she could, slipping through the smallest gaps between the dancing bodies where he would be too bulky to follow. And then just as she'd lost him, she looked up to find herself staring into the flushed face of Toby Whoever-he-was.

'Hello!' he shouted, seizing her round the waist and pulling her towards him. 'Your place or mine?'

The evening crashed, suddenly and totally like a computer. She was filled with an unreasonable, driving urgency to run, although she had no idea where to. Somewhere new and different, where there was clean air to breathe, open countryside, vast seas, great wide skies, and people who didn't tread all over you and expect you to have sex with them the minute they suggested it. She struggled away from him, throwing off his arms as if they were chains, darted through the crowd as if she was in a panic – and found Tina, who was snogging some huge hulk with very black hair.

'I'm off!' she shouted at her. 'Tell Helen will you?'

Tina didn't open her eyes. 'Um,' she said. 'See you in the morning.'

No; Lucy thought, you won't because I'm going to Seal Island. She knew that now. It was the obvious place to go. But there wasn't time to explain. There wasn't anything except this surge of adrenaline pushing her on, out of the club, into her car, back to Battersea, into her room.

She changed into warm clothes, packed an overnight bag, and was off again, driving south, peering through the rain-streaked glass of the windscreen at the string of red tail-lights that blinked and bobbed before her, at the sudden scurrying shapes of a late night crowd bent against the rain, at a muddle of cars and buses at a junction, at a glimpse of greasy road and a pile of trodden garbage, cigarette packets, crushed beer cans, chip wrappers and used condoms, escaping.

Epsom was a confusion of traffic, the long stretch of road past Dorking was lit but virtually empty, and then she was out in the countryside and in such obliterating darkness she could hardly see the edge of the road even with her headlights full on. And that sobered her. This is dangerous, she realised. You could have an accident on a night like this. Damn you Henry and damn you Toby Whoever-you-are. Why couldn't you have stayed at home and then I wouldn't be risking my neck out here. But she wasn't going to turn back. Not now, not when she'd come so far, and needed to escape so much. If only the rain would stop. Or the moon come out or something.

But the moon remained hidden and the rain continued and the road was endlessly and hideously empty. And after a few more miles she began to feel decidedly afraid, aware that the bends in the road were full of threatening shadows, the overhanging trees black and sinister, the hedges ash-grey and flickering with menace. She drove faster and faster, eager to get the journey over and done with, glad to mark off the road signs as she passed – 'You are entering West Sussex', 'Billingshurst', 'Pulborough' – and most relieved of all to reach the sign for Seal Island. Now, she comforted herself, it would only be a matter of minutes and she would be in the tower and warm and welcomed.

There was a police car skewed across the road right in her way, blue light flashing, red stripe fluorescent, and so close to her that she had to stand on the brakes, tyres squealing, and even then she only just stopped short of it. Oh Christ! she thought, tense with alarm. Now what? A policeman loomed through the curtain of rain, in a yellow fluorescent waistcoat, his striped cap dripping water, to signal to her to let down the window.

'Would you mind backing up, madam?'

How the hell am I going to do that, on a little winding lane like this, and in this dark? 'Can't I just slip past?' she said. 'I'm only going to the tower.'

He was adamant. 'Afraid not Madam. There's been an accident. I've got an ambulance and a salvage truck coming through.'

Now she could see the grey outline of a truck of some kind, keeled over into the ditch with its bonnet embedded in the hedge. Its rear wheels were right in the centre of the road and plainly no one was going to get past – unless they were on foot.

'OK,' she said, and slipping the car into reverse, began to inch backwards. It was hideously difficult. For a start she'd stopped right on the bend, so the manoeuvre would have been tricky enough in broad daylight. Then the lack of light and the incessant rain made it impossible to see more than six inches in any direction, the un-made road was slimy with mud and there were hedges on either side, all of them much too close, obscuring what little vision she had and scratching the side of the car with every turn of the wheel. But eventually, after several sweating, swearing minutes, she saw the entrance to a house of some kind and managed to reverse into it, more neatly than she expected.

She found her umbrella and edged gingerly out of the car into the downpour. She was in somebody's front garden, with her rear wheels on the lawn. Naturally. She would be. And there was a light on in an upper room. Wouldn't you know it? As she fumbled the key into her car's unseen lock, a window squeaked open above her and an Irish voice called out.

'What's goin' on, for the love of God?'

'Road accident,' she called back. 'Sorry about this. The police told me to pull in here. They've got an ambulance coming through.'

The voice changed. 'I'll be down directly,' it said.

'It's pouring with rain,' Lucy warned but she was too late. There was a blaze of light as the front door was opened and a small pale-faced figure trotted out, pulling on a sou'wester as she came.

'Are there many hurt, would ye know?' she asked, her voice and face agog with ghoulish interest.

Lucy confessed that she hadn't asked.

'We'll walk up together and see, poor souls,' the woman said. 'It'll be the weather I daresay. You can't see a hand in front of your face. I've been on and on at them for lights. You wouldn't believe the times. But they don't listen.'

Lucy could have done without her company. She certainly didn't want to be dragged along to look at the casualties, but she couldn't shake her off.

'You could be crashed and killed altogether so you could,' the woman grumbled, 'and no one a penny the wiser. They should do something about it, so they should.'

They'd reached the bend in the lane and there was the police car blocking their way, blue light flashing like Christmas, but no sign of the policeman or anyone else.

'I'm going up to the tower,' Lucy said, edging past the car. The sooner she got out of this and into the warm the better.

'Ah now, I wouldn't advise it,' her unwanted companion said. 'She's a peculiar sort of woman at the best of times, Her-up-the-tower. Most peculiar, so she is. I wouldn't want to cross her on a dark night. They do say she's a witch.'

'For your information,' Lucy said angrily, 'she's my mother.' And she was just taking breath to tell this unpleasant woman what she thought of her and her stupid opinions when she heard a man's voice calling out of the darkness.

'Is that you Miss O'Malley?'

The woman brightened and answered. 'It is.'

'You haven't see a man anywhere about have you?'

'I have not. Have you lost one?'

'The driver's gone wandering off.'

'Ah now, wouldn't you know it!' Miss O'Malley said. 'They've no sense at all some of these drivers.'

Her total lack of sympathy infuriated Lucy even further. If he's wandered off, she thought, he's probably in shock. She felt quite sorry for him, poor man. 'He can't have got far,' she called to the policeman. 'There's nothing at the end of the lane except the field and the tower, is there? You take the field and I'll check the tower.' And she set off at once before either of them could stop her, involved despite herself.

Once beyond the hedges it was marginally easier to see, especially as there were lights in the upper windows of the tower. He'll head for the light, she thought. And sure enough, as she reached the gate she caught sight of a shadowy figure reeling about in the garden, as if he was drunk.

'Hello!' she called, walking towards him. 'Are you all right?'

'Got to get back,' he said, stumbling into the outhouse wall. 'Got to tell boss.'

She was alongside him, put out a hand to prevent him from falling, noticed that he was small-boned and dark-skinned, Indian probably, that he was shaking, that blood was dripping from his right ear, that his eyes weren't focused properly. Then she didn't know what to say.

'Got to get back,' he said, lifting her hand from his arm and stumbling off into the trodden flowerbeds. 'If I do not report back, you see...' But the wind howled his words away.

She ran to the tower and thumped on the door. But no one answered although she knocked and knocked. She ran to the garden wall and called to the policemen. 'Over here! Over here!' But although she could see his outline leaning into the wind, he didn't hear her. She returned to her casualty and tried to lead him to the tower, but he was determined to keep walking and wouldn't follow her. She was soaked to the skin despite her umbrella and blinded by the squalls of rain that kept blowing in upon her and her feet were too cold to feel. 'Oh come on!' she called to her mother, beating on the heavy oak of that great door. 'Let me in! I'm perished out here!'

And then suddenly, the policeman was striding towards her holding the driver by the arm – 'Just a few more steps sir,' – and the door was opened to reveal a total stranger, tall, bulky, with a shock of thick hair and a very square chin, wearing corduroy trousers and a multicoloured jumper and no socks. Who the hell's this?

'What's up?' he said.

And the policeman answered him. 'RTA Mr Langley. Driver's been hurt.'

'Bring him in,' Mr Langley said, as if he owned the place, and called back into the house, 'Gwen! We've had a road accident. Have you got an old towel or something?'

Lucy could see her mother's slippered feet coming down the stairs, then her trousered legs and her familiar hand on the banister. She was vaguely aware that the walls were scarlet, glimpsed a grand kitchen, felt irritated that the room was full of people she didn't know and that the driver, an Indian, was prowling about when he ought to be lying down. Then she realised that the strange man was talking to her. 'Are you all right? Were you in the car too?'

'I'm not a casualty,' she said, quite tetchily. 'I've

come to see my mother. Hello Mum.'

Gwen descended into the onrush of damp night air and raised voices, struggling to pull her thoughts back into focus. She'd been asleep when the pounding on her door began and even now one half of her mind was still resting. But as soon as she saw Lucy's irritated expression and the Indian staggering about with their local bobby beside him, she found purpose and direction in action.

'Hello Neil,' she said to the policeman. 'Bring him here and let's see if we can get him to sit down.' And she addressed her casualty, as she'd addressed so many during her years at the news-agents. 'You're all right now. The ambulance is coming. Can you just hold this against your face?' putting the towel in position. 'That's fine. Just sit down here and I'll make you comfortable.'

'Got to get back,' the man insisted, but he did as he was told, because she was too calm and firm not to be obeyed. 'I got wife you see, four children. I cannot afford to lose job. I must tell boss what is happening.'

'That's all right sir,' the policeman soothed. 'We'll tell him. Don't you worry about a thing. If you could just tell me your name, sir.'

It took a long time for the question to penetrate but eventually it was answered. 'Khan.'

'And your address?'

'Leeds.'

'Whereabouts in Leeds? Can you tell me the street?'

But that was beyond the man and he shook his head, looking so distressed that Gwen instantly told him it wasn't important, and glancing down saw that Jeff had forgotten to put on his socks and sent him a rapid eye message to attend to them. And Lucy, seeing the speed of his understanding and how instantly he moved to obey her, knew that there was something going on. But there wasn't time to wonder about it because Mr Khan was groaning and slipping off the sofa, showing the whites of his eyes.

'Catch him!' the policeman said. 'Don't let him pass out.' And all four of them leapt towards the sofa, grabbing the poor man by the arms and legs and hauling him back into a more or less upright position. 'Open your eyes Mr Khan. Look at us!'

It took several rather fraught minutes before they could haul him back to consciousness and by then there was a siren wailing in the lane and the policeman said he'd have to go and attend to it. 'You'll manage for a little while won't you, Mrs MacIvor? Keep him sitting up.'

'You go,' Gwen reassured. 'Don't worry. We'll look after him.'

But he was gone for nearly a quarter of an hour and Mr Khan was clearly in a bad way and getting worse, even though she did everything she could to keep him talking and conscious. Lucy was full of admiration for her good sense – and cattily pleased to see that the sockless man was ill at ease and didn't know how to handle the situation. Well, serve him right. He shouldn't be here.

'I think I'll go and see what's keeping them,' he said eventually. 'If that was the ambulance they should have been here by now.'

Lucy remembered the scene in the lane. 'I

130

expect they're moving the van,' she told him. 'It was skewed all over the road when I came by.'

'Well why on earth didn't he tell me, the young fool?' he said, relieved to be offered the chance to get out of the house. 'If that's the case I'll go and give them a hand.' And he walked across to the door at once.

But at that moment they heard men's voices at the door and when he opened it there was a rush of wintry air, and two paramedics were in the room, bulky in their fluorescent waistcoats, carrying a stretcher and a full medical kit, with the policeman following on behind them. And at that point everything changed. Their examination seemed horribly slow to Lucy but it was steady and purposeful and when it was completed they strapped their patient onto the stretcher and carried him away into the blackness, leaving an exhausted silence behind them.

'Well I'll be off then,' the policeman said and he turned to Lucy to add, 'The lane's clear if you want to pick up your car.' And then he too was gone, and Gwen was left in the now dishevelled room with a bloodstained towel, a very mud-stained carpet, and her daughter and her lover eyeing one another in a state of bristling and growing hostility.

'What a home-coming for you, Lucy!' she said, stepping between them to smile placation. 'And I wanted you to see it at its best.' Then as her daughter was still glowering at Jeff and he was standing squarely before her as if he were at bay, she introduced them quickly, smiling from one to the other. 'My neighbour Jeff Langley, who's

131

been a great help to me, Lucy. My daughter Lucy, who's an accountant in London and a very good one. Although I'm not sure I can really call you a neighbour can I, Jeff? He lives half a mile away, Lucy.'

Jeff felt he had to make some sort of amends. 'Sorry I mistook you for a patient,' he said. 'Bit of a muddle all this.'

Lucy shrugged. 'That's all right,' she said, wondering when he would leave them alone. 'You weren't to know. I hope you haven't got to walk home in all this rain. I could give you a lift if you like.' And that ought to show him he's not wanted.

He wasn't as abashed as she'd hoped. 'Thanks for the offer,' he said, 'but I've got transport. Fact it would probably be better if I gave you a lift. I gather you had to leave your car in the lane.'

'In somebody's front garden actually,' Lucy said. 'A Miss O'Malley or some such. It was the only place I could find. A horrible woman. She said Mum was a witch.' And was annoyed when he and her mother exchanged a glance that was altogether much too meaningful.

'If that's where it is, I think I'd better give you that lift,' Jeff said to her, 'then you can pick it up before the old besom goes to bed.'

'I don't think that will be necessary,' Lucy said, rather stiffly. 'I can walk down.'

More meaningful glances, much to her annoyance – a raised eyebrow, a decision. Then he went upstairs for his coat – upstairs for heaven's sake – kissed her mother goodbye – and no mere peck either – and left them. Not a minute before time.

'What a night!' Gwen said, trying to sound as if

132

everything was normal. 'Whatever brought you down so late? I'd have thought you'd have been clubbing.'

'I was,' Lucy said, buttoning up her jacket.

The tone of her voice made Gwen suspicious. 'And?'

'I got sick of it. All of a sudden. I don't know why. It all seemed petty somehow. Trivial. Anyway, I had to get out.'

'So you drove down here.' Gwen understood. 'You escaped. Oh Lucy, you're just like me. That's what I did on the day I found this tower.'

'And that's the difference,' Lucy said, 'you find a tower, I run into a road accident.'

'You'd better get out of those wet clothes,' Gwen told her, 'or you'll catch cold. Go and get the car and I'll make some hot chocolate. Oh it is good to see you.'

'Even under these circumstances?' Lucy asked, thinking of the stranger and his lack of socks.

'Under any circumstances,' Gwen said, answering the thought.

And it was nice to have a daughter to fuss over and feed and kiss goodnight, even if it had meant forgoing Jeff's company. They sat up until past three o'clock, nursing the cat and talking of the accident and of life in the village and life in London, while the wind howled about the tower and the rain pattered against the windows. But they didn't say anything about Jeff, although his presence was still in the room, reminding them both, and as she tried to settle to sleep for the second time that night, Gwen wondered how she was going to explain it and how much Lucy had already worked out for herself and realised that her love affair was no longer a simple matter of love and liking but had complicated into problems. But there was no going back on it now. She was committed to him and to this new life of hers. She would just have to try and find a way to make Lucy understand.

Above her head, Lucy was wakeful too. She lay in her unfamiliar bed in her unfamiliar room, listened to the battering of the wind and tried to digest the events of the evening. So much had happened and so quickly that it was as if her brain had been shaken and everything in it muddled up – her flight from the clubbers, that nerve jangling journey, the shock of the accident and finding a sockless man in her mother's house, acting as it he lived there. The more she thought about that, the less she liked it. It wasn't normal or right. But then everything about this evening had been out of skew. In fact the only person who'd been anywhere near normal was the policeman. He'd been the one dependable face on the scene. A touchstone.

She sighed and turned on her side. I shall see things better in the morning, she thought. At the moment she couldn't see anything, for there was no light in the tower at all, just an impenetrable blackness. And how can you see straight in an impenetrable blackness? On which question she fell asleep.

CHAPTER 9

It was well past noon before Gwen woke up the next day. Jet was happily curled up alongside her, the rain was over, the wind had dropped from a howl to a breath and the sky was full of scudding cloud above a peaceful blue-green sea. The events of the previous evening were so far away they could have been a dream.

Lucy yawned into the room as her mother was putting on her dressing gown. 'Whazza time?'

'Mid afternoon,' Gwen joked.

'Is that all? Can I have a bath?'

Gwen considered. 'Yes. I think we could run to it.'

Her daughter was surprised by such an answer. 'Run to it?' she asked. 'You sound like a poor relation. I thought you were loaded.'

'It's not a question of money,' Gwen explained. 'It's the septic tank. A bath's a bit of a treat at the moment, to tell you the truth. I can't have one every day or the tank'd be full in no time. But we'll let ourselves go today because it's a red-letter day and we've earned it. Then I'm going to cook us a brunch. I've always wanted to have brunch.'

'What a lot of light you get here,' Lucy said. 'It must be nice to see the sea every day.' The sunlight was making it shimmer with little diamond flashes of light. And she remembered the blue dazzle of the police car in that dark lane and was reminded of their casualty. 'I wonder how that poor man is.'

They were to find out as they sat down to their heaped platters of bacon, eggs, sausages, tomatoes and beans, for before Gwen could take a mouthful, somebody came knocking at their door.

'Now who's that?' Gwen said, putting down her knife and fork. Not Jeff, surely. He'll have more sense than to come back today. She was quite relieved to find that it was only PC Morrish, off duty and in civvies. 'Oh it's you,' she said. 'There's nothing up is there?'

He seemed ill at ease, which was odd because he was usually so contained and sure of himself. 'No. No. It's all right. There's no problem,' he said, peering through the archway into the kitchen. 'I was just wondering how you were. You and your daughter, I mean. She hasn't gone back has she? I thought I'd just pop in, as I was passing. I didn't really thank you last night, and you were both so helpful. Anyway, I thought I ought to see if you've recovered. Well not recovered. That's not the right word. I mean see if you're all right.'

He's nervous, Gwen thought, and wondered why. But then, tracing his anxious expression across the room to Lucy's averted profile, she was suddenly struck with understanding. Good Heavens! she thought. He's fallen in love, poor boy. He's smitten. Not that it'll do him any good, not with that face and Pete for competition. And she looked at his broken nose and his lop-sided features, at that too-short prickly hair and that

136

too-young vulnerably thin neck, and was suddenly full of sympathy for him. 'Come in,' she said. 'Like I told you, we're just having brunch. Perhaps you'd like to join us? I'll bet you haven't had much to eat today.'

His face brightened. 'Oh! Well yes, I would. Thanks. But not if it's going to put you out. I wouldn't want to be a nuisance.'

By this time he'd followed her into the kitchen and Lucy was giving him a glance of such scowling disapproval he could hardly be unaware of it. 'I've come at a bad time,' he said and dithered in the archway, feeling he ought to leave but too entrammelled by the sight of her to move.

'No you haven't,' Gwen reassured him. 'Sit down and I'll get you a plate. There's more than enough for three. We went mad, didn't we Lucy?'

Lucy was ungracious. She'd been expecting Mr No-socks and had geared herself to be un-welcoming. Now her irritation transferred into vexation at having her meal interrupted and annoyance at being asked to share it, especially with a total stranger in an overstretched jersey and old-fashioned jeans. 'Aren't we going to be introduced?' she asked, putting down her cup.

He smiled. Straight at her. As if he knew her. 'I'm Neil,' he said. 'PC Morrish. We met last night.'

She was momentarily confused. The police-man. Her one sane touchstone from the previous evening. 'Oh!' she said, relenting. 'I'm sorry. I didn't recognise you.'

'People never recognise policemen when

137

they're out of uniform,' he told her, relieved by her change of tone. 'I found that out my first week at training school. When you're on duty they only see the uniform. It's what they look for.'

'How's Mr Khan?' Gwen asked.

So Neil settled to his unexpected meal and told them what he knew. Mr Kahn had concussion and was being kept in hospital for twenty-four hours for observation, the van had been towed away and the hedge was being trimmed. 'Mr Langley's come down himself to see to it. He's there now. I've just seen him. He says it's not as bad as he thought it would be.'

Lucy scowled. Mr No-Socks again, she thought. What business is it of his?

'He owns the land,' Gwen said, interpreting the scowl. 'Which is probably going to turn out to be very useful to me. I want to get connected to the main drainage and do away with that awful tank I was telling you about, and if he applies too, we stand a better chance of it being done. More tea?'

'Actually,' Neil said, pleased to be able to pass on some gossip, 'there's another application gone in apparently. Mrs Smith-Fernley was telling me yesterday. She's none too pleased about it. The feller from the caravan site wants it extended up there. She thinks he's going to expand.'

'Oh how splendid!' Gwen said. 'That is good news.' And she explained. 'Three applications will be even better than two. Have another sausage.'

He dithered again, looking at Lucy.

'Take it,' she advised. 'She always rewards good behaviour with food. It's a wonder Ellie and I didn't blow up like balloons.'

'That's because you were basically badly behaved,' Gwen laughed at her. And Neil said he couldn't believe that and obviously meant it. Oh, he is smitten.

He was a considerate guest too, helping them with the washing up and putting the dishes away. Although that could have been an excuse to stay in Lucy's company. It certainly looked that way, for when he heard that they were going out for the afternoon, he offered to drive them.

But that, as Gwen deftly made clear, was a courtesy too far. So he thanked them for the meal, and after one last look at Lucy, left.

They spent a pleasant afternoon strolling about the village and Lucy had an easy drive home through a now entirely peaceful countryside shaded into deepening colour by the setting sun and without a ghoul or a goblin in sight. We might have kept a few secrets from one another, Lucy thought, but she's still my mum. I wonder what Ellie will say when I tell her about Mr No-socks. Wretched man. I'll bet he'll be back the minute I leave.

But she misjudged him. He stayed away until Monday evening and even then he only visited for a few minutes on his way to a meeting of the local Farmers' Union. Her unexpected arrival had been highly embarrassing and although he comforted himself that he'd covered his feelings immediately and successfully, they were still just under the surface and feeding like tics, needling away at him with small aggravating bites of humiliation and chagrin. Damn it all, they'd nearly been caught *in flagrante*. And he'd been virtually forced to leave. He withdrew into work and solitude, and was consequently more quick tempered than usual and less approachable.

Late on Sunday evening he wondered whether he should phone and decided against it, in case the formidable daughter was still there. Early on Monday morning, he wondered again and decided against it because there was too much work to be done. But by Monday afternoon he'd contrived a good reason for a deliberately limited visit. He would take Dotty's computer over on his way to the meeting and see if she'd like to borrow it. He'd never really approved of Dotty's interest in astrology, although he'd tolerated it, especially at the end when she'd been so ill. His private opinion of it was that it was a load of superstitious nonsense. But it had provided a link between them and now it was linking him with Gwen. Taking the computer over would avoid the necessity for a long visit, remove the possibility of a post-mortem and remind her of one of the things they shared, which was something the daughter couldn't touch. If it went well they could pick up again with their usual meal on Tuesday and no harm done.

So he found the original packing case, the handbooks and Dotty's notes, packed it all up and took it over.

Gwen was on her hands and knees, cleaning the mud off the carpet, when he came knocking.

'It's taken me all afternoon,' she explained, when he looked askance at the mess the room was in. 'It's nearly done now. Just that little bit behind the sofa. I shall have to have a porch built to take the worst of the dirt next time.' Then she saw the cardboard box. 'What have you got there?'

'Thought I'd bring you the old darling's computer,' he said, encouraged by how easy and welcoming she was. And ventured to tease. 'Now you've read all the books.'

'I have not,' she laughed at him, pulling brush and bucket behind the sofa. 'I've got miles to go. It's a very complicated subject. But it might be fun to try a horoscope.'

'I'm on my way to a meeting,' he said, 'but I'll set it up for you if you like. I've just about got time.' He'd have to show willing now that he'd brought the thing over or she'd know it was just an excuse.

So the computer was set up, the book of instructions perused and her own birth details keyed in, the date, time, and place. And seconds later, lo and behold, like something magical, a chart appeared, full of star signs and linked lines. 'Good God!'

'I'll leave you to sort it out,' he said. 'See you tomorrow?'

She was still looking at the screen. 'There's Neptune,' she said, pointing to the trident sign. 'And that's Mars just below it, and that's the sun immediately above it and that's Venus. What a lot of stars were rising when I was born. It's quite spooky.'

'You know more about it than I do,' he laughed at her. 'Must be off or I shall be late.'

She tore herself away from her intriguing chart

and walked to the door with him. 'Incidentally,' she said, smiling at the thought of what she was going to tell him, 'you should have been here yesterday afternoon. You'd have seen something you don't believe in.'

He stopped at the door to smile back at her teasing face, thinking, it is all right. There's no damage done. 'What's that?'

'Love at first sight. Our local bobby's fallen for my Lucy. I watched it happen. It was quite touching.'

His heart fell. 'So now I suppose she'll be down here every weekend.'

'I shouldn't think so,' she said, understanding exactly what he was asking her. 'It all went right over her head. She's in love with someone else. Has been for years. But it was sweet just the same.'

'Well if you'll take my advice, you'll keep right out of it,' he said. 'Let them get on with it on their own.'

She reached up, put her arms round his neck and kissed him. 'You're such an old killjoy,' she teased. 'Just because you've got a good love affair going, you think you've got all rights and privileges to yourself.'

'I do not.'

'You do.'

They were playing at arguments again in their half-teasing, half-joking, intimate way. He could feel the weight of irritability and embarrassment lifting from his shoulders, dissolving and dissipating. 'We'll argue it out tomorrow,' he promised. And left her, feeling light of foot and heart.

How touchy men are, Gwen thought as she watched him go. Even the tough ones. When he'd arrived all his body cues had been wrong, his head turned away from her and his spine so tense he looked like some ramrod sergeant major, now he was his loose-limbed self again, striding off as though he hadn't a care in the world. It pleased her to think that she could soothe him so easily, even though she really didn't know how she'd done it. As she returned to the fascination of her chart she felt she'd earned the right to play with it for as long as she liked. The last bit of the carpet could wait. She gathered her book, settled Jet on her lap and returned to the screen.

Eleanor had spent a lot of her time in front of a screen that week. In fact her Monday had been positively dominated by the wretched thing. Her own fault of course. She'd covered her intended absence on Tuesday by telling the dreaded Ms de Quincy that she was going to work at home for a couple of days to complete the Graham presentation, so naturally she'd felt honour bound to do just that, flow charts, spread sheets and all, and had sat up until past two in the morning to finish it. And then of course, the facts and figures she'd been conjuring onto the screen had jumped in and out of her mind all night, tormenting her while she was awake and confusing her dreams when she finally fell asleep.

Now, as she lay on the examination couch in the ultrasound room, waiting for the sonographer to arrive, she felt decidedly drowsy. She was stripped to her pants and bra, the aertex blanket the nurse had given her was more for modesty than warmth and the mattress was as hard as a plank, but even so she found herself dozing pleasantly, and woke with a start when the sonographer came into the room.

'You mothers!' the young woman said. 'You're all the same. Leave you for a moment and you fall asleep.'

'Actually,' Eleanor corrected, rather crossly, 'I was working till two this morning. I don't usually doze off during the day. You make me sound like an old woman. Anyway I was only closing my eyes.'

'If you take my advice,' the young woman said, 'you'll get as much sleep as you can while this baby's still tucked up inside. You won't get much once it's here.'

That was a view of maternity that didn't please Eleanor at all. And a lot you know, she thought, staring at the girl's nametag. 'My baby's going to be well-behaved, Sandra,' she said. 'I shall see to that from the word go.'

Sandra removed the blanket and gave her a professional smile. 'Well let's have a look at it, shall we?'

Eleanor was rather disquieted to have her belly smeared with jelly and the scanner was smaller than she'd expected. 'Is that it?' she said, looking at the mass of grey lines heaving and swirling on the screen. 'It doesn't look much like a baby to me. It's more like a view of the earth from outer space.'

'We're not quite there yet,' Sandra said. 'But it's not outer space, I can promise you that. It's your

144

inner space. Ah now, that's better. There's the head. Do you see it? And there's the heart.'

It was throbbing. She could actually see it throbbing, sending out little rhythmical pulses that stirred the clouds around it and moved her to sudden and inexplicable tears. 'Oh!' she said, letting them fall. 'It's alive! And there's a foot. That is a foot isn't it? Oh! It's kicking.'

'You've got a nice strong baby there,' Sandra said. 'Nice healthy spine. Lovely head. About eighteen weeks, I'd say. Plenty of movement. Have you felt it yet?'

Eleanor ignored the mistake. She could correct that later. For the moment she simply gazed on enraptured, as the foot kicked and the lovely head turned slowly, like a swimmer. My baby, she thought. My dear little baby. But you're gorgeous. Then she became aware that she'd been asked a question and hadn't responded to it. 'Sorry. What did you say?'

'No problem,' the sonographer said. 'I was only asking if you'd quickened.'

'I don't think so,' Eleanor said, watching the heartbeat. 'I've had a lot of indigestion the last week or so. But that's because I've been working so hard.'

'What sort of indigestion?'

'Sort of ticking. That's the best way to explain it. As if I can feel the food going through. Tick tick tick.'

'That's the baby kicking,' Sandra told her. 'You've been feeling its feet.'

Eleanor was in tears again. 'Really? Have I?' But this is wonderful. Marvellous. It's like a

145

miracle. I've actually been feeling it kick. She felt so close to this hidden child of hers, close and protective and full of love. My baby. My own baby.

'Would you like a print-out?' Sandra was asking.

Oh she would. She would.

She was still clutching the little picture when she climbed into the taxi to take her to the OXO tower and her lunch with Lucy, still stunned by amazement as she lay back against the black leather of the corner seat and let the image wash over her mind, still glowing with the wonder of it when she arrived at the OXO tower and found Lucy already at table and waiting for her.

They kissed cheeks and settled to the menu. After the concentrated peace of the ultrasound suite, the noise in the restaurant was deafening and the print was dancing about.

'You got my call then?' Lucy said.

Eleanor was gathering her wits but she found a cool answer. 'Obviously.' And she quoted. 'Meet me in the OXO tower for lunch. I've seen Mum and I've got some news for you. Right?'

'Right.'

'So,' Eleanor said, buttering her bread roll. 'What is it? What did she say? You did tell her about the baby, didn't you?'

'Well actually, no I didn't.'

'Oh Lucy! Why not?'

Lucy took a second to savour her news before she exploded it. 'She's got a lover.'

The joy of the morning was suddenly deflated. 'Don't be silly. She couldn't have.'

'I've seen him. She has.'

The last of Eleanor's euphoria melted away, the throbbing heart was lost, the perfect head dissolved in annoyance. She was appalled. Absolutely appalled. She couldn't believe it. 'That's disgusting!' she said. 'At her age! I don't believe you. She wouldn't do such a thing. You're making a mistake.'

'I knew you'd be cross,' Lucy said. The horrified expression on Eleanor's face was superb. She'd never seen her so put out. You might have got the man and the baby, she thought, and the Cambridge degree and all the attention but you're not going to get everything your own way now. Not this time. She felt ashamed to have to admit it, but it was really quite gratifying.

'I'm not cross,' Eleanor said, struggling her anger under control. 'I'm gob-smacked. Who is he? What's he like?'

Lucy told her all she knew, which wasn't much. But it was enough to put Ellie into a rage.

'I shall go right down and put a stop to it,' she decided, 'Straight away. Tomorrow morning. Before she forgets who she is.'

Lucy laughed. 'And who is she?'

'She's our mother, 'Eleanor said firmly, 'and we need her. Especially now. She can't go off having affairs. She's got a job to do. I've planned the nursery. I've got the builders coming in next week. How is she going to look after this baby if she's got some stupid lover hanging around after her all the time? It's ridiculous.'

'Well I don't see how you're going to stop her,'

147

Lucy said. 'Not now.'

Eleanor was full of determined energy. 'Watch me!' she said.

Lucy didn't think a direct attack would have any effect on her mother or the farmer, but she could see it would be a waste of time saying so, so she changed the subject. 'Have you told Pete yet?'

Eleanor turned from fury with her mother to an equal fury against her lover. 'Don't talk to me about Pete,' she said, with a flick of her long fingers. 'I haven't seen him for yonks.'

'Doesn't he phone you?'

'Oh he phones but he won't let me get a word in edgeways. He's buying shares ready for this take-over. It's all he ever talks about. Money, money, money. So no, I haven't told him.'

'Where is he?'

'New York. Where else? I expect he's buying up America.'

CHAPTER 10

'So,' Pete's accountant said, 'we've narrowed it down to two options. You either play for safety with option A, which will give you a healthy dividend in the event of a take-over but won't stretch your finances too seriously should it fail to transpire, or you double your outlay and run risks, which is option D, which would give you a very sizeable return but would of course increase the risks proportionately, as we've discussed.' It was a bad line and he was having to shout.

Pete tucked the receiver under his chin and soothed his eyelids with his fingertips. Catherine's party was due to begin in twenty minutes so this had better be quick. 'You'd advise A,' he said.

'Taking all the factors into consideration,' the accountant said, 'yes, I would.'

The hotel room was overheated and poorly ventilated and now that the moment of decision had come, Pete was hot with impatient energy. He knew he was going to take the risky option. Once they'd discussed it, there was really no other choice he could make without losing face. He could hardly expect to buy a foothold into the new company on the cheap. 'I suggest we go for option D,' he said, and was pleased to find that he could take such an enormous risk so coolly.

'OK,' his accountant agreed. 'But like I said, it's

going to take four hundred grand max to be sure of it. And I have to warn you that the value of shares can go down as well as up.'

'Yeh, yeh!' Pete said, brushing the warning aside, 'I know all that. I lost a packet a couple of years back.'

'Right,' the accountant said, remembering.

Even so four hundred grand was an awesome amount to find in a short time and almost double what he'd been expecting. The risks were formidable. The only thing for it was to take out a second charge on the flat and hope to God he could recoup the outlay quickly enough to avoid being crippled by the first repayments. The AGM wasn't until December, so there'd be no dividend till then, but he ought to be able to last out. He'd have to get Staggers to fix up some really good assignments for him while he was still in the States. If the worst came to the worst and he couldn't meet the first repayments – it wouldn't, but just in case it did – he could always let the flat and move in with Ellie for a while. She'd understand. She'd always been very level headed about money. He might make a game of it. Tell her they were going to live like an old married couple for a week or two. Or a month or two. Whatever. She might like that. Women liked a bit of commitment. The risks were becoming easier to deal with as he planned, the cost less prohibitive. 'I could run to that,' he said smoothly. 'No problem.'

'E-mail me if there's anything else you need,' the accountant said. 'We've made the best decision, I think.'

'I know we have,' Pete said with splendid confidence, as he put down the phone. Now for Catherine's party. There was just time to fax instructions to his broker before he had to leave.

It turned out to be one of the most difficult parties he'd ever attended, full of baying businessmen talking big deals, big bucks, investments and the internet, their skinned-lizard wives sharp and shouting in their hideously loud voices about designer clothes and foreign holidays and the benefits of cosmetic surgery, and half a dozen arm-candy bimbos, pouting their collagen lips and flaunting their silicone boobs, flicking their tatty blonde hair and all talking baby-voiced garbage, and no sign of the men from Grossman's. But the champagne was excellent and the food passable and Staggers got drunk and ridiculous and kept them all entertained. And at a little after eleven, when Pete had almost given up hope of them, the team from J.R. Grossman's did finally arrive. He excused himself from the woman who'd been regaling him with a glowing recommendation of some tripe she called the 'latest greatest movie' and eased through the crowd towards his prey, pleased to find that they were drunk enough to be easily charmed.

'Pete Halliday,' he said offering his hand and his television smile.

'Well hi there Pete!' the chairman said. 'Great party!'

He agreed that it was. 'Terrific.'

'You Brits slay me!' the gentleman said, imitating him. 'Terrific! What's your poison?' He

151

turned to bellow at a waiter. 'Bourbon for my friend Pete Halliwell.'

'Day,' Pete corrected.

'Right. My friend Dale Halliwell.'

It's a waste of time trying to correct him, Pete thought, noting the blotched cheeks and swimmy eyes. He's too far gone. 'From Sheldon's,' he said, watching for a reaction.

'Is that right?' the gentleman said. 'How's the world over there?'

That's better, Pete thought, and opened his mouth to tell him, but it was already too late. His quarry was barging across the room, crying, 'Is that my little popsicle? Catherine honey!'

Catherine honey flashed a rueful glance at Pete, which was gratifying even though he knew it wasn't a message he could follow through. Then she allowed the chairman to gather her into his arms for the statutory embrace and was lost to view behind the stretched grey silk of his well-upholstered back, leaving Pete to drift and wait and feel more and more frustrated. Soon he was feeling nauseous too from a combination of rather too much bourbon and champagne and a great deal too much self-control. What he needed was a nice cool glass of ordinary honest water. Now where was the kitchen? He ought to be able to remember that. They'd had a splendid row there one summer afternoon when her husband was away in Eastern Europe. Ended up in bed afterwards. He was still remembering it as he walked into the long white room.

It was clinically empty except for a lone figure swaying beside the double sink, who turned as he approached and complained that he 'couldn't turn the fucking faucet.'

Pete turned it for both of them, found two tumblers and filled them with water. Then they stood side by side drinking like camels parched from the desert.

'Jesus!' the stranger said. 'That's more like it. I was gasping in there.'

'Me too,' Pete said and introduced himself.

'Tom Johnson,' the other man said, shaking hands with the ponderous solemnity of the very drunk. 'Pleasa meetcher. You a company man? Yup. Guess so. We're all company men tonight. I'm the fucking vice chairman of J.R. Grossman's. For my sins.'

What luck! Pete thought, filling his second glass of water. 'Now that's very interesting,' he said. 'You're the man I came to this party to meet. The very man. I've been looking for you all over.' He managed to draw his wallet from his pocket on the third attempt. 'There's my card. Write your phone number on that little card an' I'll phone you first thing.'

'Li'l card,' the man said, giggling as if it was the greatest joke he'd heard all evening. 'Put in a sink!' And he threw the card into the sink and was promptly sick all over it.

I should never have come to this fucking party, Pete thought, removing himself from the stink as fast as his now rather wobbly legs would take him. It's a total waste of fucking time. I ought to be in Chelsea with Ellie. That's where I ought to be. Homesickness washed over him, drowning him in self-pity and making him sweat. He put

153

his hand in his pocket to find a handkerchief to mop his forehead – and remembered his mobile.

Eleanor was so fast asleep when the phone rang that she woke in confusion and it took her several rather frightened seconds to work out what was happening. An alarm? Someone at the front door? Then her ear attuned and she picked up the receiver, her heart still throbbingly disturbed. It had to be bad, whatever it was, at this time of night.

'Yes,' she said. 'What is it?'

'Sweetheart,' Pete's voice said, rather thickly. 'Great to hear you. I've had a fucking awful day. Absolutely fucking awful.'

'Pete,' she said sternly, 'do you have any idea what time it is?'

He supposed it was late.

'Late!' she said crossly. 'It's half-past four in the morning and I've got a big day tomorrow.'

He was sobered by his mistake. 'Oh shit!' he said. 'Look I'm sorry. I forgot about the time lag.' He realised he had to explain, to make her see how necessary this call was, to pull her round onto his side. 'Look, I just had to talk to you. I've had the most–'

'Well you've talked to me,' she said, cutting him off in mid breath. 'Now may I go back to sleep?'

'I'll call you tomorrow evening,' he said, sounding contrite. 'This evening. Whatever.'

'You do that,' she said and hung up on him.

But then of course she couldn't get back to sleep and lying wakeful she realised that she'd missed a chance to tell him about the baby.

Though as the dark minutes ticked past, and she remembered the battle she had ahead of her, she decided that perhaps it was just as well she hadn't said anything. It was too important to be done at a distance and if she tackled this business with Mum first and got the farmer sorted out and arranged for her to look after the baby, she could tell him everything all at once and then he wouldn't feel so bad about it.

Gwen had been awake at first light that morning too. She'd hired a rotovator for the day so that she could turn over the impacted earth of her neglected garden, and it had been delivered at seven o'clock.

It was a perfect day for gardening, cold, crisp and full of energy, with a slight frost on the water meadow and a strong sea running. It was exactly the same blue-grey colour as the base of the long clouds that drifted above it and the surface was ruffled with curls of thick white foam as far out as she could see. It lifted her spirits just to look at it.

'We've chosen a good day,' she said to the cat, 'and we'll have a good breakfast to start us off. What d'you think?'

Jeff arrived just as the bacon was cooking. So naturally they had breakfast together before they tackled the garden. It was very hard work and she was glad of his strength to guide the machine through the more recalcitrant patches but after a couple of hours the area she'd marked off as a vegetable plot had been transformed. She stood beside it, sniffing the rich scent of her newly released earth, and dreaming of what it would be. Neat lines of early vegetables burgeoned in her imagination, daffodils yellowing bright against banks of blue violets, beans spiralling, scarlet blossomed, into summer, peas rounded in the pod, rhubarb unfurling dark leaves to reveal a tenderness of pale pink stems, raspberries ripening against the wall, potatoes swelling to sweetness under the newly dug earth. Oh she couldn't wait to start planting.

'I shall dig the compost in this afternoon,' she said happily, leaning on her fork. 'With a bit of luck I might get some of the turfs laid too, if the light holds. What d'you think?'

And at that moment Eleanor's Espace turned the corner of the lane and drove importantly up to the gate. She watched with the fork still stuck in the soil as her daughter's high-heeled boots swung out of the car, and in a moment of revelation and uncomfortable honesty, she knew she was resenting her arrival and that it was going to be hard to welcome her.

'What's brought you here?' she said, as Eleanor picked her way delicately into the half-dug garden.

'I thought I'd come down and see how you're getting on,' Eleanor said brightly. She was annoyed to be greeted so coolly and furious to find a strange, enormous, unwanted man in her mother's garden. He has to be the farmer, she thought, and held out a firm hand to him. 'I presume you're Mr Langley,' she said. 'I'm Eleanor.'

'So I gathered,' he said, crushing her fingers in

a muddy grip. 'Have you come to give us a hand?'

Eleanor shuddered at the very idea. 'Good God no,' she winced. 'I came to see my mother.'

'Well there she is,' he said, not in the least abashed to be spoken to so coldly. 'Don't you think she looks well?'

Privately Eleanor thought she looked like a gypsy, with that scarf round her head and mud all over her forehead and that awful grubby jersey. And her jeans beggared belief. She'd never seen such an horrendous pair, baggy and stained and caked in earth.

'I've got such plans for the garden,' Gwen told her, admiring her newly dug earth. 'I've bought a whole sackful of daffodils. I'm going to plant them all over that mound there. I thought if I was going to make a splash I might as well make a big one. I'm going to plant clumps of violets in amongst them. The two colours together should be absolutely gorgeous. Don't you think so?'

Eleanor supposed they would, but then her mother switched on some awful machine and, instead of leading her into the tower and making her welcome, went charging off across the garden with it, churning the earth into gobbets and flinging them about. For heaven's sake!

'I'll go inside then, shall I?' she said, shouting above the din.

'What?' her mother shouted back.

'Inside,' she shouted, pointing at the door.

'Oh yes,' Gwen understood. 'I'll just finish this and then I'll be with you. It won't take a moment.'

She was out in the garden for another hour, during which time Eleanor explored the tower from top to bottom, wincing at the colour of the walls, noting with extreme disapproval that there were two sets of dirty dishes on the draining board – so he's stayed to breakfast, bloody awful man – that her mother's bedroom contained a huge new double bed – not a good sign – that there was a black cat sleeping on one of the sofas as if it belonged there, an expensive new computer on an equally expensive stand and some very peculiar books on the bookshelves – what is she doing with them? From the top of the tower, which was actually quite pleasant, or would have been if the walls had been painted white, she had a fine view of the Channel but couldn't see what was going on in the garden. From the ground floor she could see the garden only too well.

Lucy's right, she thought. All the signs were there and much too obvious to be ignored, the meaningful glances, the helping hand when her mother climbed over a mound of earth, the endless talk, the unnecessary stupid laughter. They were more like a pair of young lovers than a middle-aged couple. It was downright disgusting. And it made her feel left out of things, as if she'd been abandoned. How could she tell her mother about the baby when they were carrying on like this?

'Well what do you think of my tower then?' her mother asked, breezing into the room with the farmer alongside her.

Eleanor tried to be tactful. 'Well it's different,' she said. 'You've got a nice view from the top floor.'

'Haven't I just!'

'The walls are a bit lary, of course. They'll be better when you've had a chance to paint them. I mean you can't live with red walls, for heaven's sake, can you.' It seemed a perfectly reasonable observation so she was annoyed when her mother and that wretched farmer roared with laughter at it.

'I chose that colour, I'll have you know,' her mother said. 'I think it's gorgeous. We're not all committed to endless black and white.'

Eleanor was embarrassed. Bad enough to have made such a faux pas, but to be corrected in front of that awful man was much, much worse. 'Actually,' she said, keeping cool with difficulty, 'what I've come down for is to take you out to lunch. Something special somewhere. We haven't seen one another for such an age and there's so much to talk about. What do you think?'

It didn't get the expected response. 'Oh,' her mother said and looked at the farmer. 'That's a bit awkward.'

'She's spoken for,' the farmer said. Oh what a nasty bold face he's got! 'She's having lunch with me. We've booked a table.'

We'll see about that, Eleanor thought, and prepared to fight him. 'Ah but surely,' she said smoothly, 'now that I've come down...'

She was horrified that instead of rushing to change her mind and her plans, her mother actually dithered. And then looked at the farmer as if she was going to ask him what to do. Strike again, she told herself. Quickly. 'I've got so much to tell you,' she said to her mother. 'And of course I want to hear all about the tower and the garden. We could have a little celebration, don't you think? Champagne and everything. All the trimmings.'

The farmer was grinning. Actually standing there grinning at her. 'It's up to you,' he said to Gwen.

'I tell you what,' Gwen compromised, 'why don't you come with us? I'm sure they could find a table for three.'

And share you with him? Eleanor thought. Not bloody likely. 'Oh I don't think so,' she said with heavy sarcasm. 'I can't imagine Mr Langley and I would have very much in common and I wouldn't want to bore him. Besides, three's a crowd.' And she gave him the most venomous look she could produce. Now get out of that.

And he did. So quickly and easily she could have hit him. 'Good,' he said. 'That's settled then. You ready, Gwen?'

No, Eleanor thought in fury. That's not what I meant. And she looked at her mother for support. And didn't get it.

Gwen was in a quandary. She really didn't want to spend hours over lunch when there was so much to do in the garden and she'd only got the rotovator till sundown. But on the other hand, she couldn't just walk out. Not on her daughter. 'What will you do?' she asked anxiously. 'Wait here for us? Or go back? I don't like to leave you.'

'Oh don't worry about me!' Eleanor said. She held herself firmly, head high because she was on the verge of shivering. Not enough heat in this place. 'I've got to be back in the office this

160

afternoon. It's only a flying visit, that's all, to see how you are. I didn't realise you'd be busy.'

'If you'd let me know you were coming,' Gwen worried on, 'I could have cooked for you.'

'No problem,' Eleanor said, as airily as she could. She felt cold, miserable, ignored, defeated but she certainly wasn't going to let them know it. 'I'm off then. I might come down again on Saturday. Is that warning enough?'

'Saturday'll be lovely,' Gwen said, recognising how hurt she was. But Eleanor was already through the door and striding towards her car.

It was a mistake, she thought, as she drove through the village still shivering. But how was I to know I'd got to make an appointment to see my own mother? My own mother for fuck's sake! I can't believe how she's changed. She'd never have gone on like that in the old days. She'd have invited me in and cooked me dinner and made a real fuss of me. It's that fucking farmer's fault. And as there was nobody about to see her she gave vent to her feelings at last in a long satisfying scream. Well fuck you Mum. Fuck you Mr Langley. Fuck you Pete. Fuck the lot of you.

CHAPTER 11

As soon as Eleanor had roared her fury into Mill Lane, Gwen began to feel guilty. It had been such a surprising visit that she'd barely had time to take it in while it was going on but, now that it was over, she knew she'd mishandled it. I should have paid more attention, she told herself, shrinking at the memory of her selfish behaviour, not gone on with the garden. No wonder she was cross. I should have talked to her more. Listened to her. 'Oh dear!' she said. 'I have upset her.'

'She'll get over it,' Jeff said in his trenchant way, 'I'll just wash my hands and then I'll be ready. Five minutes?' And he took the stairs two at a time.

Gwen followed him. 'She came all that way,' she worried, 'and I didn't even give her a cup of coffee. Perhaps I should have said I'd go to lunch with her.'

'Listen,' he said, as he walked into the bathroom. 'She's a tough little thing. I thought she was going to scratch my eyes out when she arrived. If I were you I wouldn't worry about her. You worry too much.'

'The trouble is,' Gwen said, taking off her headscarf and examining her dirty face in the mirror. 'I've spent so much of my life being what other people wanted me to be that I've sort of lost touch with who I really am. I thought all that would sort itself out once I was living in the tower and it has in a way – I wouldn't be here with you if it hadn't. And doing what I want instead of thinking about other people has been wonderful. But you can't do that all the time, can you? Not when it's your daughters you're dealing with. Maybe I've swung too far in the opposite direction.'

He walked out of the bathroom, frowning at her. 'What are you talking about?'

'Being selfish.'

'Why shouldn't you be selfish now and then? Most people are. Just be yourself.'

'But which self?' she said. 'I seem to be several selves all rolled into one. One with you, one on my own, the one I was with Gordon, one with the girls, the one I used to be with the girls. I think it upsets them to see how changed I am.'

'They'll cope with it.'

'I'm not sure they will. They expect more than I'm prepared to give them.'

'So?'

'So perhaps I should make more of an effort.'

'Don't you do any such thing,' he said. 'Unless you want to be a perpetual doormat. Come and have lunch and don't worry about it.'

So, there being nothing she could do to change things now that Ellie was gone, she went and had lunch. But guilt needled her all through the afternoon.

By the time Eleanor finally got back to the open plan offices of Smith, Curzon and Waterbury, Publicity Agents, she wasn't just steaming with anger but suffering excruciating hunger pangs as well. So the first thing she did was to send one of the secretaries down to the nearest Prêt-à-Manger for a baguette – 'brie if they've still got it and a fruits of the forest yoghurt and a slice of apple cake.' Then she dialled her sister to offload her fury.

'I've just seen that fucking fly-in-the-ointment,' she said, 'and were you right or were you right! He's horrendous!' And she launched into a furious diatribe against the man.

Lucy stared at the figures on her screen without seeing them. She'd had a frustrating afternoon and now she ached to be miles away where there were no phones, no computers, no bosses – and no sisters to put pressure on you. But that made her feel guilty because she was only half-listening and Ellie was in a state. 'So you didn't tell her about the baby,' she said, when her sister finally paused for breath.

Eleanor roared with outrage. 'Tell her! You've got to be joking. I couldn't tell her anything. He wouldn't let me get a word in edgeways. I tell you he was in the fucking way all the time. He fucking lives there. Acts as if he owns the place. He wouldn't even let me take her out to lunch, for chrissake. I mean, think of it. My own mother, aching to come out with me, and he wouldn't let her go. He just stood there, Luce, stood there and laughed in my face. It was totally fucking horrendous.' She was so worked up she could have wept if she hadn't been in an open plan office. 'What am I going to do?' she wailed, 'I mean I can't let this go on, now can I?'

164

In the passion of the moment and with guilt to prod her, Lucy forgot that she'd told Ellie that this was her affair and that she'd have to deal with it on her own. 'No,' she said, making rapid plans. 'You can't. We'll go down there together, the first Saturday we have free, next Saturday if it's possible, and we'll tell her together.'

'You're a star!' Eleanor said. 'A total fucking star! I knew you'd help me. But what about him?'

'He won't be there,' Lucy promised. 'Leave that to me. I'll write to Mum and tell her we want to see her on her own. And the minute we're there, you tell her about the baby. Straight out, before he can come in and stop us. It's ridiculous not letting her know. She's going to love being a grandma and it might be just the thing to put Mr No-Socks in his place.'

Eleanor began to cheer up. 'I could get her some brochures,' she said. 'What's on at the theatre. Musicals and that sort of thing. Show her what she's missing. We can't let him dominate her, can we? I'll get them on the way home and make a parcel of them.'

Personally Lucy didn't think a parcel of brochures would impress her mother in the least, but she didn't argue. If Ellie wanted to do it, then let her. The main thing was to tell Mum about the baby and put that farmer in his place. 'Right,' she said. 'You do that.'

'I will,' Eleanor said. And did.

There was a call waiting on her answerphone when she got back to her nice cool apartment with her bag full of glossy paper. 'Pete here,' his voice said cheerfully. 'Sorry about last night.

165

Forgiven? Anyway read your e-mail. Kiss, kiss.'

Kiss, kiss, she thought, half-charmed, half annoyed. He wakes me up in the middle of the night and then says, 'Forgiven?' and expects to be. But she trawled through her e-mail until she found his message.

It was in his usual compressed style and contained a lot of information, some of it incomprehensible, but she picked out the salient facts – now involved in mega deal re Sheldon's – staying in NY three weeks – four assignments – home early Nov – xxx.

'Right!' she said, speaking to her determined expression in the wall mirror. 'You've got three weeks to tell Mum and get this baby organised. So get on with it.' And she went off to her study to pack the brochures.

They made such a large packet that the postman couldn't get it through Gwen's letterbox and was reduced to knocking at her door. It frightened him to bits. Now he'd have to stand face to face with her. Talk to her. Confront her.

Gwen had been sitting at the computer study-ing her birth chart when he knocked and she was loath to leave it. 'Oh!' she said, as she opened the door. 'It's you. What have you got for me?'

'Parcel.' The word came out in a croak, crushed by the awesome sight of a tangle of coloured lines and weird shapes on her computer screen. That's black magic, he thought, if ever I saw black magic. It was worse than he could have imagined. What if she was to drag him in and put a spell on him? How could he stop her? She

166

looked ever so strong.

'That's my magic box,' she said, following his horrified glance. He was such an idiot she couldn't resist the urge to tease him. 'We work on that in the dead of night, me and my black cat. We put our cauldron on the fire and I get my broomstick and we dance round it and chant spells.'

'Oo-er,' he said, and went as quickly as his lanky legs would carry him.

She was still laughing as she opened the parcel. At first she thought it had been sent to her by mistake. What did she want with *What's on at the Barbican?* and *The London Theatre Guide?* Then she read the bright little note that Eleanor had pinned to the front of the *Good Restaurant Guide* and realised that she was being tempted, and laughed out loud. Dear Ellie, she thought. She's so obvious. And she turned to her letters, opening the second because it was from Lucy and the other one looked official and was probably a bill.

Lucy's was little more than a note and disappointingly short. *I'm coming down to see you on Saturday if that's all right. Give me a ring if it isn't. Ellie and I will be travelling down together. We should be with you somewhere between half eleven and midday. We've got something to tell you when you're on your own so you will be on your own won't you? It's quite important.* Does she mean what they've got to tell me or being on my own? *Don't bother cooking for us. We'll go out. It might be a sort of celebration.*

So it's good news, whatever it is, Gwen thought. And picked up the second letter.

It wasn't a bill after all but a polite acceptance of her application to be put onto main drainage. The decision had been taken and work would start in the New Year. So that's the way you hear of a victory, she thought, flushed with triumph. Through the post and quietly. I must tell Jeff.

He'd had the same letter and brought it across to show her, later in the morning. 'Shows you what can be done with a bit of co-operation,' he said. 'I told you Mr Rossi would come across. Now you can put in your application for that garage before your car gets rotted away in the salt air.'

'I'll do it today,' she said, 'before I go shopping. Which reminds me. The girls are coming down on Saturday.'

He frowned. 'Girls?'

'Yes. They're both coming apparently. They've got some good news for me, so Lucy says.'

He wasn't particularly interested. 'Right,' he said flatly.

'The thing is,' she said, 'they want to tell me on my own.'

Now he understood. 'So you're warning me off. Is that it?'

'No,' she tried to deny. 'Not exactly. They just said they'd like to tell me on my own.'

'So you're warning me off,' he repeated. 'OK. OK. I won't come near. They're queering my pitch, I hope you realise, but if that's the way you want it. You're still coming out with me in the evening though. That's a date.'

'Of course,' she said. 'They'll be gone by then. It's Saturday. They'll be off clubbing.'

'Let's hope so,' he said, turning away from her. And as he turned he saw the computer and found an outlet for his irritation. 'Oh for crying out loud! You're not still working on that stupid chart?'

His animosity towards her daughters had upset her and she was glad to turn to a different topic, even though she could see it annoyed him. 'It's fascinating,' she told him. 'Come and see what I've found out. You were right about Neptune. I've gone through it a step at a time, house by house and you see that little symbol there? That's Neptune. Right in the first house, which is where you see the influences that will affect you all through your life. Where you're imprinted. I wrote them all down.'

Despite his bad temper, he was listening.

'Here you are,' she said, finding her notes. 'Neptune in the first house *denotes poor mothering, an absent or ineffectual mother.* And that's spot on. My mother wasn't absent but I hardly noticed her. She never cuddled me that I can remember, and she didn't talk to me much, except to tell me not to do things. And when I got to the twelfth house, there it was again. Right? Venus in the twelfth. *Lonely childhood.* I was an only and living on an island. *Mother self-effacing.* So then I looked up my moon and sun to see what they'd tell me and that was a revelation, it was so accurate. I've got the sun on the cusp between Virgo and Libra which means *a person who wants to serve, to become a useful tool for others.* And the moon shows almost exactly the same thing. It's quite spooky. *Blending and merging. Your*

169

life's work is to serve on an everyday level. And didn't I just? And here it is again. *Relationships are central to you. You have a tendency to martyrdom. An ability to listen and understand. You will realise how strong you are when change comes.'*

'At the risk of throwing cold water,' he said, 'I think you'll find that sort of thing's applicable to rather a lot of people. It's all pretty generalised.'

'But it fits me,' she said. 'That's the point.'

He was reading her notes over her shoulder. 'What's all this?' he said. *Abandoning the self to something numinous, unbounded and divine.* I hope you're not going to be a nun.'

That gave her the chance to tease. 'Fat chance of that with you around.'

'Glad to hear it,' he said and smiled for the first time since she'd told him about the girls. 'I'm off then. I've got work to do. Don't forget you've got a date on Saturday evening.'

'As if I could,' she said. But her mind was occupied with plans for the visit. This time I'll handle things properly, she thought. I'll put the gardening tools in the outhouse, for a start, and scrub all the mud out of my nails, and then I'll make rock cakes for tea and something special for lunch. This time it's going to be different.

CHAPTER 12

Lucy and Eleanor arrived at Gwen's tower on that Saturday morning in a rush and a roar, both scrambling out of Eleanor's car together so that, to Gwen's rather anxious eyes, it looked like a metallic beetle with its wings extended and four long flailing blue-denimed legs. Then they were running towards her, with their arms full of flowers and bottles, and their faces bright. My word, she thought, isn't Ellie putting on weight. She looks quite plump. But then they were on the doorstep and hurling themselves into the room, their arms flung wide, yelling 'Da-daaa!' the way they used to do when they were kids and Ellie's long coat fell open as she spread her arms and Gwen could see what her news was.

'Oh Ellie, my dear chick,' she cried, sweeping her into her arms, flowers and all. 'You're pregnant. How wonderful! Why didn't you tell me before?'

'Your farmer never gave me the chance,' Eleanor said, laughing under the impact of her mother's affection.

Gwen was tossing happy questions at her. 'When's it due? Are you well? You look well. Have you booked in? What does Pete think about it? I'll bet he's thrilled. Oh this is wonderful! Wonderful! What fun it's going to be! We'll have some lunch and then we'll go shopping. How about that?

There's a nice little place in the village that sells baby things and if that won't do we can go to Chichester. It's no distance and they've got a Mothercare there and the Army and Navy. Oh Ellie! This is the best news I've had in ages.'

Lucy felt decidedly out of it. 'I'll set the table,' she said flatly.

I've ignored her, Gwen realised, and rushed to make amends. 'It's all done, chick,' she said, pulling her arms round her. 'You said it was going to be a celebration and I took you at your word. Come through into the kitchen both of you.'

So the champagne was set to cool while the meal was served and the celebration began, with Ellie giggling, 'All we need now is paper hats,' and Lucy doing her best to be happy on her sister's behalf. But it wasn't easy because Ellie queened it terribly – wouldn't you know it? – and trailing round the village afterwards was worse, for by now Ellie and Gwen were arm in arm and head to head, and Lucy felt she was very definitely the gooseberry.

'No,' Ellie said, when they'd examined the window of The Happy Stork Baby Store, 'there's nothing here. I mean it's all pretty gross, isn't it? Don't you think so? Let's go to Chichester.' Then she turned her head sharply. 'There's that policeman again,' she said. 'Is he following us?'

Gwen turned to see who it was. 'Oh that's Neil,' she said waving at him. 'He's our local bobby. Nice chap.'

'That's the third time I've seen him,' Eleanor complained. 'He's like a jack-in-the-box, popping up all over the place. Doesn't he do anything else except walk up and down this one street? What a bore!'

'He's a good copper,' Lucy said, feeling she had to defend him. 'I met him at a road accident and he was first rate.'

'Road accident's right,' Ellie said, disparagingly. 'He's not much to look at, is he? Bit of a gargoyle I'd say. Are we going to Chichester then?'

No, Lucy thought. I'm not. I've had enough of you for one afternoon. 'You two go,' she said. 'I'd like to stay here and explore.'

'There's not much to explore,' Gwen warned her. 'You'd better have my spare key and then you can get back in the warm when you've finished.' And she took it off the ring and handed it over.

Then she and Eleanor strolled off to the car park, arm in arm, and Lucy was left in peace.

Her mother was right, of course, there wasn't much to see, but she walked from one end of the street to the other and looked at what little there was. Then she followed the road south, exactly as her mother had done, until she found the sea, and decided to take a walk on the beach.

The sea was coldly green and heaved long ominous waves towards her, which broke with such force against the pebbles that the white spume flew high into the air, and the beach was totally empty and extremely cold. Even huddled into her thick jersey, with her jacket buttoned to her chin and her scarf mounded about her neck, she felt the chill of it. And how grubby it was, the pebbles strewn with flotsam – old plastic bottles, fish heads, a battered shoe grey with salt, several tangled lengths of dirty orange rope – the narrow promenade marked by trails of long-dead black weed and sticky blotches of tar. It was a long way from the beaches of summer.

Nevertheless, having decided on a walk she determined to go through with it. It was very hard going, even in boat shoes. The stones hurt her feet, the wind made her eyes water and the great view she'd hoped for was obscured by clouds and darkening skies. This is a mistake, she thought, as the pebbles slipped away from under her feet. And it's getting dark. I think I'll go back to the promenade and head home.

But when she'd climbed up the beach there was no promenade, only a rough flint wall enclosing a scruffy expanse of grass and, beyond that, a row of equally scruffy shops and flats with flat roofs and peeling paintwork. It was so run-down she was quite alarmed by it and, now that she was inland and away from any sea-reflected light, she was aware that darkness was descending fast. The clouds above the flat roofs were already blue and purple and a pale moon was out. No place for me, she thought, and quickened her pace to get back the village as soon as she could, head down against the wind and looking straight ahead. She was walking so fast she didn't notice the car until it slowed down alongside her, headlights menacing. She was seriously alarmed. Oh God! Now what?

'Are you lost?' a voice said.

And she looked up and it was the policeman, dressed in civvies and driving his Mondeo. The headlights were friendly. Thank God for that.

'No,' she answered. 'I don't think so. I've been walking on the beach. I think I came too far.'

She looked so cold that he dared an offer. 'Would you like a lift back?'

'Yes,' she decided. 'I would. If it's not putting you out.'

'Hop in,' he said, and opened the door for her.

It would have been hard to tell which of them was the most surprised, she because she was accepting a lift from a man her sister called a gargoyle, he that this gorgeous girl was actually sitting in his car, the way he'd dreamed she would ever since he first saw her.

They drove through the village and turned into Mill Lane, where the tower rose above the hedges, black and forbidding.

'You'll be all right now,' he said.

She was thinking what a relief it would be to be indoors in the warm with a nice pot of tea and one of Mum's cakes. And that gave her an idea. It was nice of him to bring me home and I'll bet it's taken him out of his way. Besides, it'll make Ellie really wild. 'You could come in and have tea with me, if you'd like,' she said. 'Mum's made some cakes.'

His face lit up so markedly, she could hardly miss noticing it even in the half-light. 'Well yes, I would,' he said. 'Very much.' And then felt he ought to explain himself for fear of giving the wrong impression. 'Your mum's a very good cook.'

So they had tea in the kitchen, all very proper, one on either side of the table, and they talked. She told him about her job and what hard work it was, he told her how much he enjoyed being a village bobby.

'You get to know people in a place as small as this,' he said. 'You get to be part of it. Takes time of course. They're rather cagey. They don't accept you straight away.'

'How long?' she asked, thinking of her mother.

'Couple of years. Year maybe,' he told her, knowing what she was thinking. 'Depends.'

'Have they accepted my mother?' she asked.

He decided to tell her the truth. 'Not yet, but she's only been here a couple of months. It's early days yet.'

'The reason I ask,' she said, 'is that that funny old woman – the one at the accident, right? – well she said she was a witch. I took a poor view of it and told her so. But it made me think. I wouldn't like her to be unhappy here.'

'I'll keep an eye on her, if you like,' he offered.

'The majesty of the law,' she laughed. 'But seriously, yes, I wish you would. Have some more tea.'

'Is that a reward for good behaviour?'

'What?'

'You said your mother used to feed you as a reward for good behaviour. Last time I was here.'

She was impressed. 'What a good memory you've got.'

'Trained to observe,' he said, warmed by her praise. This was going so well. Better than he'd dared to hope. 'Look,' he said. 'Say no if I'm out of turn but you wouldn't like to go to the pictures with me I suppose? If you're staying overnight. But I expect you're going back aren't you? Bound to on a Saturday night. I *am* out of turn.'

'Actually,' she said, thinking how much *this* would annoy Ellie, 'I am staying over as it happens. What's on?'

His throat was suddenly so full it was all he could do to answer. 'What about *Elizabeth?*'

The choice surprised her. 'Yes,' she said, smiling at him. 'I'd like to see that. It's had some good reviews.'

They had a date! A date! He was so happy he wanted to jump about, thump the table, yell, kiss her. But he controlled himself with a great effort, told her he'd call for her at seven, said he'd better get going or her mother would wonder what he was doing lounging about in her house, and made as dignified an exit as he could, to roar and whoop in the fastness of his car all the way back to his flat.

Eleanor and Gwen returned twenty minutes later, cheerfully flushed and with their arms full of shopping.

'You must see what we've got,' Eleanor said and unpacked all the bags for her sister's inspection. 'These are called babygros. Aren't they just too cool? Mum's coming up to Chelsea next weekend. It's all arranged, isn't it Mum? She's going to see how my nursery suite's coming on and then we're going shopping in Harrods. God! Is that the time? I've got to be in Bayswater by eight. Quick cuppa, Mum, and one of your cakes and then we'll be off.'

'Actually,' Lucy said. 'I'm staying here, if that's all right with you Mum.'

Eleanor was amazed. 'Staying here? You mean

not going back to London?'

'I've got a date. I'm going to the pictures.'

Amazement gave way to disbelief. 'Who with?'

'Your gargoyle. Our local policeman.'

'Oh Luce,' Eleanor protested, 'for heaven's sake. You can't go out with him. He's hideous. Besides you don't know him.' And she called through the archway. 'Talk to her Mum.'

The appeal put Gwen into a difficult position. She didn't want either of them to stay the night, not after she'd given her word to Jeff, but she could hardly say so, not when she'd spent the entire afternoon lavishing Ellie with presents and leaving Lucy to her own devices. 'Well of course you can stay, chick,' she said, and sounded as though she meant it, which she did in a way. 'I'd love to have you. I'm going out this evening too but we've both got keys.'

'Well I think you're being ridiculous,' Eleanor said, folding up the babygros. 'But it's your lookout.'

'That's right,' Lucy agreed. 'It is.'

So they prepared for their various engagements. Eleanor tripping to her car with her arms full of presents, still protesting that her sister was making a big mistake, Gwen off to take a shower and try on the new dress she'd bought that afternoon, Lucy to wash and attend to her make-up because that was all she *could* do, not having brought a change of clothes. In a doubtful moment before the mirror she wondered whether she really *was* making a mistake but decided it was too late to go back on it now.

He arrived exactly on time, dressed in a new

blue shirt, open at the neck, chinos, an old-fashioned jacket and black shoes. Black shoes, for heaven's sake! And he looked horribly uptight, shoulders hunched, brown eyes glaring, mouth too tightly set. Oh God, this is a mistake.

But she greeted him cheerfully, 'Hi there!' And called up the stairs to her mother as if this were just an ordinary date. 'I'm off now, Mum. Shan't be late.'

'I thought we might go for a drink afterwards,' he said as they walked to the car. And when she didn't answer, 'If you'd like to, I mean. Or something to eat. You've only to say.'

'Possibly,' she temporised, thinking, it all depends how we get on.

They got on better than she expected, for the film gave them something to talk about, and when they arrived in one of the local Indian restaurants they met up with a gang of his friends, most of them PCs and all of them slightly drunk and extremely chummy, so the outing became a party, which was a definite improvement on an awkward twosome.

'From London eh?' they said when she was introduced. 'So what d'you think of us then? Are the natives friendly?'

'Some of them,' she told them, taking a long draught of her lager. 'Not all by any means.'

'Name 'em,' a burly man said, 'and we'll feel their collars for you, won't we boys?'

After that it wasn't long before they were amusing her with exaggerated tales of the villains they'd apprehended, and the dirty deeds they'd uncovered, and what with hot food, warm

179

company and well-spiced stories the evening passed with light-hearted speed. It was past two in the morning before they finally decided they should all go home.

The countryside was oppressively dark and after the lights of the town the sky seemed black. She remembered her long drive down and the horrors that lay behind the ghostly grey of the hedges. And shivered.

He was concerned that she was cold.

'It's not that,' she said. 'It's just I hate the dark. Always have.'

'I'm used to it,' he told her, happy to be able to brag a little. He'd been rather overpowered by all the macho talk in the restaurant. 'I spend a third of my time driving about at night. Your eyes adjust after a while.'

'It's not my eyes,' she said, 'it's the thought of all the awful things that could be lurking. Take no notice. I'm just being silly.'

'Well you're quite safe with me,' he reassured. 'I shan't let anything lurk or have us off the road or anything like that.'

'I know,' she said. 'You're a good driver.'

He was pleased by her praise. 'I try to be.'

'You don't drink and drive.'

'I've seen too many RTAs for that.'

She thought of Henry who made a point of driving no matter how drunk he was. And remembered Mr Kahn and the lorry in the ditch. I'm in safe hands, she thought, and looked at them, held in exactly the right position on the driving wheel. Good strong hands. And her brain began to play word games. Touchstone hands.

Will they touch me? God, I hope not. I'll have to find some way to put him off.

They were approaching the tower for the second time that day and now it was merely a black hulk with a faint light in one of the upper windows.

'Your sister's not back yet, I see,' he said, as they got out of the car.

'My sister's in London,' she told him.

'But didn't you come down with her?' he asked. It was a rhetorical question for he'd seen them arrive. 'How will you get back?'

'By train I expect.'

'It'll be tricky,' he warned. 'They do repairs on Sundays. You get driven all over the country in rotten old coaches. It takes hours.'

'Oh great! I can't wait.'

They'd reached the door. 'Tell you what,' he offered. 'I'll drive you back if you like. You'll have to wait till the afternoon because I'm on duty till two, but if you don't mind that...'

'Well it's very kind,' she said, tempted by the offer, but not wanting him to think she was encouraging him.

'It would be a pleasure,' he said and wondered if he could kiss her.

'I'd better get in,' she said briskly, easing the key into the lock. 'Don't want to wake Mum. It's been a lovely evening.'

'See you tomorrow,' he said. The door was open, she was gentling inside. 'Good night.' Good night you wonderful, gorgeous girl, I shall see you tomorrow.

CHAPTER 13

Although Lucy tip-toed across the first landing and eased up the second flight of stairs as quietly as she could so as not to wake her mother, she needn't have bothered, for Gwen was wide awake. Ellie's news had put her into a state of such happy excitement that sleep was impossible. I'm going to be a grandmother and a lover, she thought, lying beside Jeff's warm, peaceful bulk, in their comfortable double bed. What an amazing thing! A grandmother and a lover. Even the words sounded extraordinary, like a contradiction in terms. And it's all happened in the space of a few short months. Who'd have thought that when I was nursing Gordon, back in the summer? I wouldn't even have thought it myself. And now here I am, so happy I'm almost too happy. I shall need to take care or I shall start making mistakes.

She'd almost made one at the start of the evening, when she'd bounced her news at Jeff the moment he arrived. 'What d'you think? My Ellie's expecting.'

'Is she?' he said, but with so little interest that she knew she had to change the subject and asked where they were going.

He'd chosen a different restaurant that evening, because he'd heard good things of it and thought they needed a change. 'We've eaten so much fish

182

it's a wonder we're not growing scales,' he said. 'I fancy a nice juicy steak for once.'

It was a bad decision. The steak was tough and her pork fillets were little better although she tried to pretend they were all right. In her present state of cheerful contentment it didn't matter what they were like.

But Jeff was in a bad mood and called the waiter over to complain. 'This steak won't do,' he said, 'and neither will the fillets. Take them both away and bring me back the menu.'

The waiter didn't seem particularly surprised and he certainly wasn't apologetic. 'We shall have to charge you for them sir,' he warned.

Jeff grew bull-massive with instant temper. 'Indeed you will not,' he said.

'That is the house policy, sir.'

'Bugger the house policy. Go and get the manager.'

The waiter drifted off, insolently casual.

'It's all right,' Gwen said. She was aware that the other diners were watching them and was afraid of a scene. 'They're not that bad. I don't mind. I'm not terribly hungry!'

'They're bloody revolting,' he said, 'and they needn't think I'm paying for them.'

The manager tried a different tack, assuring them that the steak was from the best Scottish beef and that the pork was local produce and the best available, but he was wasting his breath.

'Don't tell me about local produce,' the farmer said. 'I know about local produce. I'm one of the locals who produce it and that lump of cag mag is no more local than you are.'

183

'I assure you–' the manager tried.

'Or if it is, you've got a bloody awful chef. You tell him from me I've eaten better shoe leather. Come on, Gwen, we'll go somewhere else. This is no place for anyone with a discerning palate. And don't give me any rubbish about paying. You'll be lucky if we don't sue.'

'Of course, sir,' the manager said with an attempt at sarcasm, 'there will no question of asking you to pay. Only gentlemen pay.'

Jeff stood up to his full and anger-swollen height, brushing sarcasm and manager aside. 'Good,' he said. 'That's settled then.'

They went straight to The Lobster Pot. But even here they were in for something of a disappointment for the place was crowded, their favourite table was occupied and they were too late for the lobster thermidor.

'Never mind,' Jeff said, trying to make the best of it and to show that he'd recovered. 'We'll make do with the trout, eh, and have a superb evening next Saturday to make up for it.'

She wanted to agree with him but the truth was leaping up and down in front of her, waving semaphore flags. 'I'm ever so sorry,' she said, 'but I've promised Ellie I'll go to London next Saturday. She's booked a matinee for us and we're going to have supper before I drive back.'

'Oh that's great!' he said, anger flaring again. 'Why did it have to be Saturday?'

'Because she's working the rest of the week. Oh come on, Jeff, it isn't every day your daughter tells you she's pregnant.'

'Thank God for sons, that's all I've got to say.

They grow up quietly, go to college, get qualified, find a job, no problem. You don't find boys making a fuss, giving you grief.'

'It isn't grief,' she said. 'I love it.'

'I know,' he said crossly. 'That's the trouble. Oh well, I suppose it can't be helped. Just so long as you don't go making a habit of it. What do you want for dessert?'

When they got back the tower was still dark except for her one guiding light on the landing, so in a stupid but loving moment she decided not to tell him that Lucy was staying overnight. He'd had enough disappointments for one evening and with luck she wouldn't get back until long after they were in bed and asleep. So the final disappointment was hers and could be kept decently private. It was a disappointment nevertheless, for it was the first time they'd made love and she hadn't felt anything. But there you are, she thought, lying awake afterwards, you can't hit the heights every time and it was inevitable really, knowing Lucy could come home at any moment. It didn't matter in the long run. It was just one night among many. What was important was that they were lovers and she was going to be a grandma.

She fell asleep abruptly, as though she were falling down a deep hole, and was plummeted straight into a nightmare. She was back in Fulham nursing Gordon, who complained and groaned and was so heavy she couldn't move him, although she tried and tried, heaving and straining, afraid that he would develop bedsores. And the girls were in the house too and tiny,

185

needing more attention that she could give them, falling over and grazing their knees and howling, tumbling off the swing, quarrelling over a teddy bear with Pete's handsome face. She woke with a start as they were tearing it in half and, for a few startled seconds, she couldn't think where she was. Then she heard the sea, and saw daylight streaming in through her window, and realised that it must be quite late. Jeff was gone, leaving one of his notes propped up on the dressing table. *6.00 am. Cloudy. Will ring later.* It sounded a bit cool but there wasn't time to think about it because she could hear Lucy clinking cups in the kitchen.

'What must you think of me?' she asked, as she came downstairs. 'Sleeping on like this.'

'I've only just got up myself,' Lucy told her. 'There's tea in the pot.'

Gwen turned her mind to a more immediate difficulty. 'How are you going to get back to London?' she asked as she poured the tea. 'Will you take the train?'

'Neil's offered to drive me, actually.'

'That's nice,' Gwen said. 'What time's he picking you up?'

'Half-past two,' Lucy said. 'When he comes off duty.'

Half-past two it was and she carried it off with such aplomb that neither her mother nor her escort had any idea of the doubts that were plaguing her now that they were all in sensible daylight and Ellie wasn't there to be annoyed. Whatever else, she decided, he mustn't be allowed to think that there's anything in this beyond friendship.

So she made sure that they chatted cheerfully all the way and never allowed the conversation to get personal. They discussed films, she told him Ellie was taking her mother to a theatre matinee and talked about the poor quality of the shows in the West End.

He was cast down to realise how many shows she'd seen and how cosmopolitan she was. But he hung on gamely and tried to make a joke of it. 'Is there anything you haven't seen?' he asked.

'Not much,' she said, lightly. 'Except *Les Mis*. That's supposed to be very good.'

He made a mental note of it. 'I suppose you'll come to Chichester in the summer,' he said. 'The shows there are supposed to be pretty good too.'

If I say yes, he'll offer to take me, she thought, and sidestepped the possibility by changing the subject. 'There's a supermarket just up here. Do you mind if we stop off?'

She bought enough fresh food to last the week and when they arrived in Battersea it took the two of them to carry it to the door. By the time she put her key in the lock, Helen and Tina were watching from the bay window.

'That's the lot then,' he said, setting down the last two bags. And dithered. 'I expect you'll be coming down to Seal Island again soon, won't you?'

'Oh yes,' she said lightly. 'Bound to.'

'Next week-end?' he hoped.

'No. Not then. Mum's coming here. I told you.'

He retreated from disappointment into rigid formality, that being the only defence he knew.

'Right then,' he said. 'I'd better be off.' And went quickly.

'Who was that?' Tina wanted to know.

'Friend of my mother's,' Lucy told her.

'There you are,' Tina said to Helen. 'Told you. I knew he wasn't shag-worthy.' And explained. 'We were having bets.'

Lucy unpacked the salad. 'You were wasting your time. It's not like that.'

'He's gay. Is that it?'

'Quite possibly,' Lucy said. It was likely and would explain a lot – the kindness, the lack of girl friends, the all-boys-together atmosphere in that Indian restaurant, the rather distant air. Everything except the lack of kissing. All the gays she knew in London were very kissy-kissy. But then that's London for you, and it takes all sorts.

Back In Seal Island, Gwen was making the most of the afternoon sunshine, hard at work in her garden with Jet in her favourite spot on the outhouse roof and Jeff sitting rather impatiently in her new lounger.

'How much longer are you going to be?' he asked.

'Five more minutes,' she told him, stooping to pull out a weed. 'Why? Are you getting hungry?'

'You could say that,' he said, daring her with his eyes. 'Why don't you come here and kiss me.'

'I'm covered in mud,' she warned.

'I don't care,' he said and pulled her down onto his lap to kiss her long and pleasurably. 'Now that's better,' he said, when they finally stopped. 'Now you're interested. Which you weren't last night, were you?'

She was thrown to have been so transparent. 'How did you know?' Was that why he'd left such a cool note?

'You were too quiet.'

'It was the thought of Lucy...'

'The sooner those girls get used to us, the better,' he said trenchantly. 'You mustn't let them think they can run your life.'

She accepted the rebuke and decided to clown, saluting him as if he were an officer. 'Yes, sir. I'll see what I can do next time, sir.'

'Tell you what,' he said, giving her his lazy smile. 'Let's see what we can do now.'

So they left the cat and the garden to get on by themselves.

Eleanor brought all her business training to bear on her mother's visit to Chelsea. The flat was spotless and extravagantly lit, brochures for furniture and fittings were laid out in order on the dining room table, with swatches of curtain material set beside them like hands of cards, the plan of the new nursery suite was displayed right at the centre of it all and held in place with white scented candles.

At her first sight of it, Gwen thought it was a shrine. Walking into the dazzle of all that white and chrome always disorientated her. It was so vast and impersonal, more like a clinic than a home. She felt out of place there and never knew how to respond. Now she stood by the door in her black and purple cape and her crazy hat, like a refugee in a foreign sanctuary, and wondered why she'd agreed to come.

Fortunately Eleanor didn't notice her uneasiness. 'Let me take your coat,' she said holding out her hand for it, 'and then I'll talk you through. Everything's ready.'

At that point, Gwen realised that she'd been invited to a presentation and noticed that her cool daughter was glowing with excitement. Which made her feel better, excess of feeling being preferable to no feeling at all.

'I thought I'd take you round first,' Eleanor said. 'Clear the ground, so to speak, and then we can get down to details afterwards. This is going to be the bathroom at this end, with a nice curved archway leading through. I know how you like archways. And there'll be plenty of room here for beds and cots and so forth. Fitted wardrobes of course. So much more convenient – don't you think so? – and they give you so much more space. And then in this corner I'm going to have a kitchen bar, for the baby's bottles and cups of tea and so on. What do you think?'

Gwen thought it was an extravagant idea but she tempered her opinion and said it sounded sensible.

'That's what I thought,' Eleanor said in her decisive way. 'Now come into the dining room and let me show you the furniture. A white bathroom I thought. More hygienic. Don't you think these tiles are gorgeous?'

Personally Gwen thought they were horribly plain but she managed to find something to praise. 'White's always clean,' she said, blinking round at the dazzle of white that surrounded her.

'What colour are the curtains going to be? Babies like a bit of colour.'

But the only trace of colour that Ellie had entertained was a thread of pale green in one curtain swatch and the possibility of a small pale green design in one or two of the bathroom tiles. 'We don't want to overdo it.'

Gwen was remembering the mobile she'd made when Ellie was a baby, all bright reds and blues and yellows and greens. It had dangled over her cot and she'd squealed with delight every time she saw it. Even Gordon had approved of it.

'What do you think?' Ellie was saying.

She looked so anxious that Gwen lied. 'It all looks lovely.'

Ellie sighed with relief. 'I'm so glad you like it. Now is there anything I've left out? Anything I've forgotten?'

'No,' Gwen said and asked. 'What does Pete think of it?'

'Oh he hasn't seen it,' Eleanor said, speaking lightly with considerable effort.

'He's not still away?'

'He is. Doing a voice-over in LA or something. He says he'll be back in time for the de Quincy fireworks but I'm not holding my breath.'

Which accounts for her tension, Gwen thought. She's missing him, poor girl. 'High time he came home,' she said. 'You tell him from me. You need looking after when you're pregnant.'

'Oh come on!' Eleanor said. 'This is Pete we're talking about. When have I ever been able to tell him anything?' The question tugged her heart into a spasm of distress. If only he would come home. If only she could tell him. 'Time for a little drink,' she said briskly, 'and then we'll be off to the theatre.'

Lucy had decided to go clubbing again that evening. She'd had a hideous week at work and needed something loud and crazy to redress the balance. She'd dressed to let herself go, in black halter-neck top, skimpy orange skirt and clompy boots, she'd sprayed orange colouring on her hair and painted her lips to match, and she was highlighting her cheeks with glitter, shouting at her flatmates over the racket of the radio, when the phone rang.

'Yes?' she shouted, holding her right ear closed with her fingers. 'Who is it?'

'Me,' Eleanor's voice said. 'I've had a marvellous afternoon. Done really well. She likes it.'

Lucy was very surprised. 'She's agreed?'

'Well not in so many words. But as good as. I mean we didn't need to spell it out. She was thrilled with it. Said it was lovely. Good eh?'

'Incredible,' Lucy agreed. 'Look, I can't talk now. I'm just on my way out. Call me tomorrow.'

'Will do,' Eleanor said happily. And hung up.

Lucy returned to decorating her face, feeling a bit stunned by such an easy victory. But she'd barely started on her right eye before the phone rang again. 'Not now Ellie,' she shouted into the receiver. 'I'm on my way out. I told you.'

There was a breathing silence. Then a strange voice spoke – hesitantly. 'Er – um – could I speak to Lucy MacIvor please?'

'Who's that?' Lucy said sharply, but recognised

him as she spoke. 'Is that Neil?'

The voice was still hesitant. 'Could I speak to Lucy?'

'This is me.'

'Oh. Sorry. I didn't recognise you for a moment. I hope this isn't a bad time. Only I've got two tickets for *Les Mis* and I wondered if you'd like to come and see it with me.'

'What?'

He repeated himself.

'Good God!' she said. 'When for? You'll have to shout. I can barely hear you.'

'Next Friday.'

Lucy wasn't sure whether she wanted another date with him but the thought of seeing *Les Mis* was a temptation, and she was in a rush to get out, and there wasn't time or peace for a long conversation, or for any proper consideration, and anyway, if he was gay, there was no risk in it. 'OK,' she shouted. 'Yes. I'd like that. Ring me tomorrow.'

'Who was that?' Helen shouted.

'My gay policeman,' Lucy shouted back. 'He's got tickets for *Les Mis*.'

'Oh him!' Helen said and lost interest. 'Give us a lend of your glitter, will you.'

By the time Gwen got home to her tower that evening, she felt quite weary. It was a relief to take off her shoes, slummock into slippers and flop down on the sofa. Emotional wear and tear, she thought, as Jet jumped onto her lap to welcome her home. It's hard work finding the right things to say. It had surprised her to find her confident eldest in such an uneasy state, fussing over curtains and fittings, and needing approval all the time. It's not like her to be unsure of herself, she thought. The baby must mean more to her than she's letting on. Still I've done my duty and now I can get on with all the other things I've got to do, like getting the cat doctored and planting the flowerbeds and improving the tower.

Work began on the porch the following Wednesday and the next morning a letter arrived from the council to tell her that her application to convert the outhouse to a garage was being considered and to request that she should display the enclosed planning application notice in a prominent position on her property.

She pinned the gaudy orange sticker to the outhouse door, pleased to think that her plans were proceeding so well, 'Not that anyone will see it there,' she said to Jeff. 'I'm too far away from the village for anyone to be interested.'

CHAPTER 14

The Seal Island Parish Council met religiously every first Monday in the month in the new village hall, whether or not there was anything for it to discuss. It was – or considered itself to be – an august body, consisting of a chairman and eight members, four of whom had been persuaded to stand and had then been duly elected – in a proper bona fide election what's more, even if the turn-out had been a mere eleven per cent. The rest had been co-opted from friends and relations. Being at the very bottom of the electoral scale, both in terms of that derisory vote and in the general lack of impact their debates actually achieved, they were naturally sticklers for protocol, careful to speak through the chair and to request a show of hands on every matter that could even remotely require one. All of them, that is, except for Mrs Agatha Smith-Fernley.

She went her own way in the council as she did in Ye Daynty Tea Shoppe, speaking her mind in that trenchant booming voice of hers and compelling obedience with the certainty of a Centurion tank. The Chairman was horribly in awe of her, although he did what he could to appear fair. He was a short, dapper, soft-spoken man, who looked like an old-fashioned bank manager but had actually been the local florist until he retired. As mere Mr Perkins he was no match for Mrs Agatha Smith-Fernley.

On that particular Monday evening, he was feeling rather pleased with himself because the council had two new planning applications to consider and, as this was the one area in which they actually had any real influence on local affairs, it raised the importance of the occasion to pleasing heights.

'Item four on your agenda, ladies and gentlemen,' he announced happily. 'Planning application from Mrs Barnes for the felling of one diseased elm tree in her front garden. I assume we are agreed on this.'

They were but it took ten minutes before they voted it through and could move on to Item five.

'Planning application from Mrs MacIvor of West Tower,' the chairman said, 'for permission to convert her outhouse cum garden shed into a garage with a hard standing for two cars.'

'I think we should consider this very carefully,' Mrs Smith-Fernley boomed. 'There is more at stake here than a mere garden shed.'

Teresa O'Malley understood that the application was to be opposed. 'If you can call it a garden shed, Mr Chairman,' she said, 'which I do not, for that's a misnomer for a start. A thoroughgoing misnomer, so it is. That is a brick and flint single storey dwelling, that's what, and not a stone of it that you could you call a shed.'

'Precisely,' her mentor approved. 'But more to the point, it's a provocation.'

The word rang alarm bells in every head about the table – with the exception of old Mrs Gallagher who had fallen asleep with her head on her chest and was making cheerful bubbling sounds into her lambs-wool jersey.

'We have to bear in mind, Mr Chairman,' Mrs Smith-Fernley went on, 'that this – um – Mrs MacIvor is a newcomer. She doesn't know our ways and what's more, which is worse, she hasn't made the slightest effort to find out what they are. Not the slightest effort. She rode roughshod over poor Mr Makepeace in the matter of that fitted kitchen. Refused to pay the poor man. Which is not the way we behave in this village, as I'm sure you'll agree.'

Oh they did, indubitably.

'I won't comment upon the rumours that she is a witch,' Mrs Smith-Fernley said magnanimously, 'although they are rife I believe.'

'She told Mrs Gurney's son she was,' Miss O'Malley reported. 'Right out with it. You know young Kevin the postman. "I'm a witch," she said to him. Can you believe that? And she has the most peculiar things on her television. Kevin saw them only the other morning. Unnatural charts all full of occult signs. Mrs Gurney was telling me. If you ask me, that's weird and sinister altogether. Weird and sinister altogether. Quite upset him so they did, poor boy. And she's got a black cat.'

Mr Perkins tried to be fair. 'I cannot see what bearing the lady's – shall we say, proclivities – have upon her application,' he said. 'Which is the matter under discussion.'

'Of course, Mr Chairman,' Mrs Smith-Fernley said, smiling upon him. 'The point we have to consider is the impact this proposed development will have upon the environment. And I have to say that I think we should oppose it on the following four counts. That it would be an unjustified change of use. Number 35. That it would damage the environment. Number 97. That it would constitute a traffic hazard. Number 68. That it would set a bad precedent. Number 102. Of itself it may well appear to be a fairly harmless alteration, but we have to consider its impact not just upon the present environment, which we are duty bound to protect, but also upon future applications, which could be endless.' And she spread her jewelled hands on the green baize cloth with the air of one who had already delivered her verdict.

'I open this matter to debate,' Mr Perkins announced. And noticed that Mrs Gallagher was asleep. 'Could you – er?' he suggested to her neighbour.

The lady woke with a start. 'I always hang my washing out on a Monday,' she said.

It was a long and vigorous debate, in which all Mrs McIvor's sins were remembered and elaborated, and at the end of it, all four of Mrs Smith-Fernley's objections were voted upon and passed unanimously.

'And now,' Mr Perkins said, shuffling away an embarrassing suspicion that they might have been a trifle unfair, 'there only remains Item 6, preparations for this year's firework display. Which I must say looks as though it is going to be the best yet.'

'The posters are up already,' Mr Vetch reported happily.

'Indeed they are,' Mr Perkins said, 'and most eye-catching, wouldn't you agree?'

They had caught Gwen's eye that very morning, as she walked down to the main street to buy one of the baker's nice fresh cottage loaves. Maybe I'll invite the girls down, she thought. If I could get them both here for the weekend, it might be easier for them to cope with Jeff staying overnight and a firework party could be just the thing. We never had one for them when they were little. All we ever did was stand around in the living room holding sparklers, and that wasn't any fun at all. She remembered Gordon, smoothing his moustache and oppressing them with his approval. She could hear his voice, 'This is much better, isn't it girls? We don't want to mess with a lot of nasty fireworks. Nasty dangerous things, fireworks.' Well now they can mess with whatever they like, she thought. I wonder whether there'll be a bonfire.

'Oh yes,' the baker told her. 'We always have a bonfire. Great big thing. They build it up for days beforehand. Right by the sea. All the old wood from the farms and the building sites. People bring it in from all over the village. Great big thing. When it's lit you can see it for miles.'

All the primitive elements together, Gwen thought, picturing it. Earth and air and fire and water. 'Sounds great,' she said, taking her loaf.

That night, she waited until both her daughters would be home from work and phoned to tell them.

Lucy already knew about it. 'Neil told me,' she

said, 'when we went to see *Les Mis*. He says it's going to be spectacular.'

Gwen was encouraged. 'He could be right,' she said. 'It's generating a lot of excitement. So what do you think? Will you come down?'

'I might,' Lucy said. Actually she'd almost made up her mind about it. She'd got nothing better to do and her conscience was troubling her because she'd sent him straight home after the show. They'd had a fantastic evening and she could at least have invited him back for coffee or something. It wasn't as if he'd put any pressure on her. He hadn't even dropped hints. 'Depends on the work situation.'

'Take an evening off,' her mother advised. 'You work too hard and I'd love to see you. They're going to have a bonfire.'

Lucy laughed at that. 'Oh well, that settles it,' she said. And teased, 'You and your bonfires!'

'See you Friday week then,' Gwen said. And dialled her elder daughter.

Eleanor sounded fed-up, which was sad when she'd been so thrilled about the nursery. 'Oh,' she said flatly, 'it's you.'

'Have I phoned at a bad time?' Gwen worried.

'No, no. It's all right. I was just hoping Pete would phone.'

'Is he still away?'

'Yes,' Eleanor said, 'he is and I'm getting fed up with it. Anyway,' she tried to make her voice sound brighter, 'you'll be pleased to know they're getting on with the nursery suite. The kitchen bar went in this morning. It's a bit of a mess at the moment but you can see it's taking shape. It should be ready for your inspection by the end of next week. How about that?'

'Guy Fawkes Day,' Gwen said. 'That's why I'm ringing.' And explained.

'Well it's a lovely idea,' Eleanor allowed, 'but I've got the de Quincy party. I told you.'

Gwen had forgotten. 'Yes. So you did.'

'Why don't you come up here?' Eleanor suggested. 'The suite'll be ready by then and I'm sure I could swing an invitation for you. It's more party than fireworks actually but they're having a display on Clapham Common and we're going to watch from the drawing room.'

'I can't say I'm tempted,' Gwen admitted. 'I wouldn't know anybody there and besides I don't like the sound of your Mizz de Quincy. Never have. We wouldn't get on.'

'She's the Great White Chief.'

'I know. And a bit too much of a good thing, if you ask me. What if you were to tell her you're coming to a family party on Guy Fawkes Night?'

'She'd fire me,' Eleanor said and she was only half joking. 'And I can't afford to be unemployed. Not with my mortgage, and the nursery to pay for and everything. The job's important to me. Very important.'

'I hope you don't let her know that,' Gwen said. 'If your job's too important the bosses feel they've got you over a barrel. They gave your father a dog's life.'

'They have got us over a barrel, believe me,' Eleanor said heavily. 'That's the way big business works.'

The tone of her voice was so world-weary that

201

Gwen decided not to press her. 'Cheer up chick,' she said. 'He'll come home in the end.'

But that's the problem, Eleanor thought as she put down the phone. He'll come home and I still haven't told him and he'll see the state I'm in straight away. He can hardly miss it. Even my face is getting fat now. And then what'll happen? In honest moments, she had to admit that she'd been cowardly and silly not to tell him at the start, but the longer the situation went on the more difficult it was to know how to deal with it. I ought to say something next time he phones, she thought. But she didn't have any idea how to do it. She stood indecisive before the looking glass, gazing at her distraught expression in the mirror and trying to smooth out the worst of the lines that were spoiling her forehead. Oh, why is life so complicated? she mourned. I've got Mum sorted out and the nursery built but there's still this. And I'll bet he's having the time of his life stateside. I'll bet he hasn't thought of me for weeks.

But she was wrong. Pete was having an extremely difficult time and he'd been thinking of her at stressful moments, day and night, for the last fortnight.

The voice-over had been a nightmare. It had gone wrong from day one when the producer had requested 'one of your fancy English voices, clipped enunciation, right?' and then, instead of leaving him to get on with it, had interfered with every other phrase, insisting on combining an English accent with American terminology. By

202

the time it was finished it was absolutely grotesque. But at least, once it was over, it could be put behind him as one of the irritations of the job.

Finding the cash to finance his enormous loan was much more difficult. He'd had an e-mail from his London bank only last week to inform him that the first monthly repayment on his second charge was now 'somewhat overdue'. He mailed back at once assuring them that payment was on its way and that the oversight had been unintentional, but it was a nasty moment. Even when he put all his recent earnings together he could only just meet the first repayment and the next one was already bearing down upon him, jaws gaping. There was nothing for it. He would have to let the flat and go and live with Ellie.

The thought of living with Ellie gave him heart. Whatever their differences – and they'd had their differences – who wouldn't have done after all this time? – she always supported him when he was down. Well not down. He never allowed himself to be down. Low maybe. Whatever. It would be good to see her again, have a meal together, a bottle of bubbly, some good sex, wake up in her nice cool flat with everything neat and well-ordered. Yes, he decided, that's what he'd do. Put the flat up for rent and live with Ellie.

That afternoon he sat in his New York hotel suite and composed a glowing description of his 'superb London penthouse, a dwelling for one of the international elite, now vacant'. Then he ran off copies for his new buddy the junior accountant to display on the company notice boards, and another to post through the company e-mail, and waited for results.

Luckily they weren't long in coming. By mid morning the following day he'd had four replies and one, a phone call from a certain Walter B Hackenfleur II, who said he was the president of a subsidiary firm attached to 'the parent company', was particularly pressing and interesting. 'Could be just what I'm looking for,' he explained. 'My wife and I fly to England on Monday week and we'd rather live in our own apartment than a hotel room. That's rather short notice I guess.'

'No problem,' Pete assured him.

'What's the rental?'

Pete asked the full price of his repayments plus another two hundred dollars for wear and tear. And after a nerve-wracking pause while Mr Hackenfleur thought about it, the terms were accepted, 'for a calendar month to see if we like it, and if we do, for a further two. How does that grab you?'

Pete's relief was so acute it made him feel sick. It was a godsend.

But the struggle to put himself forward as one of the possible senior executives in the post takeover company was becoming more and more pointless. He'd dropped coded hints into so many deaf ears it was demoralising. I'll take in one more party he decided, and then I'll book a flight and go home. The cost of this suite is just a drain now. It's not getting me anywhere. And I ought to be in London soon, in any case, to see Mr Hackenfleur into the flat.

So he took very little notice when he found a message on his answerphone from 'the office of J.T.R. Johnson' with an invitation to lunch. The name meant nothing to him, and after so many disappointments he had little hope of anything more exciting than the offer of another modelling assignment, but it was a prestigious restaurant and he had nothing else to do, so he accepted the invitation, taking care to arrive late by a quarter of an hour.

His host was already seated and stood to greet him. And Pete recognised who he was. The drunk from Catherine's kitchen. Tom Johnson, the Vice Chairman of J.R. Grossman's no less.

'Glad you could make it,' he said as they shook hands. 'What are you drinking?'

The meal got under way, after hospitable attention to the menu and the wine list, pleasantries were exchanged and food commented upon, but it wasn't until the sweet trolley had been wheeled away that the real business of their meeting began.

'Now then Pete,' Mr Johnson said, lighting his post-prandial cigar. 'I got one or two things to ask you. In confidence, you unnerstand.'

Pete kept his expression suitably blank.

Mr Johnson puffed cigar smoke sideways out of the corner of his mouth. 'To tell you the truth Pete,' he said, 'an' I believe in the validity of telling the truth, it's been my byword in the company, my byword, I been hearing some mighty queer rumours about your company.'

'Oh yes?'

Mr Johnson leaned forward across the table.

'So tell me Pete – in confidence you unnerstand – what's your opinion of Lord Fossway?'

Pete assumed his most honest expression. 'He's a fine man,' he said loyally. 'Lots of experience. He's been with the firm a quarter of a century. Knows our history inside and out. You can't fault him on it.'

Mr Johnson grimaced. 'Out of date would you say?'

Pete pretended caution. 'Well not exactly.'

'That's not what we've been hearing Pete. Sure as hell, it's not. So put me in the picture.'

'Well...' Pete said. 'He's a bit old-fashioned but there's no harm in that.'

Mr Johnson blew smoke like a dragon. 'Let me be the judge of that, Pete,' he said. 'In what way old-fashioned?'

'Well,' Pete said again. 'He still believes that advertising should be aimed at a family audience. He sees the family as the principal consumer unit. It's rather charming really.'

'D'you share that view Pete?'

'Well no,' Pete said. 'I must admit I don't. But that's no reflection on Lord Fossway. It's just that times have changed. We have to pitch our recommendations at the client and the product and the market these days. Key into the current research and use it before the opposition.'

'So what's your buzz-word?'

'Speed of communication, good research, adaptation,' Pete said smoothly, thinking, now tell me that's not exactly what you're looking for.

It obviously was, for the cigar was put aside. 'Go on.'

It was the chance Pete had been angling forever since his arrival. 'Well,' he said, 'as I see it, the three consumer groups we should be aiming at are the teenage market, which has enormous spending potential, the pre-teen market which is getting younger and younger, and the twenty, thirty-something singleton market which has even greater potential, and a definite and recognisable lifestyle for us to key into and has doubled in the last five years. These are all market areas in which you find there is less resistance to change, where new products would be open to trial and taken on board – providing they're advertised in the right language and use the most powerful images.'

'Most interesting,' Mr Johnson said. 'You should have a seat on the board.'

'Or the new board.'

'If all goes according to plan. Your shareholders might take a bit of persuading.'

'I'm quite a sizeable shareholder myself,' Pete said. 'And I think I can say they're a pretty shrewd bunch.' He steadied himself by finishing his coffee. It was time to make his pitch. 'Trouble is, I've taken on so many modelling assignments these last few years, my committee work has been a bit marginalised. Maybe it's time for a change. Time for me to stop sitting on the sidelines.'

Mr Johnson nodded. He'd found out all he needed to know for the moment. Hints had been dropped. They understood one another. The interview was over. 'Right,' he said, and signalled for the bill. 'It's been great talking to you, Pete. You must keep in touch.'

'I will,' Pete promised. Oh wouldn't he just!

It was all he could do to walk out of the restaurant without doing side kicks in the air. 'You should have a seat on the board,' he thought. Wait till I tell Ellie.

She was very pleased for him and congratulated him warmly. 'It's no more than you deserve after all this time,' she said. 'You ought to have a say in what goes on. I'm all for it. Especially now when you're going to be—'

'A member of the board,' he said. 'Yes, I think I just might. If I get my way. What do you think of that?'

I can't get through to him, Eleanor thought. He's too high to listen. 'Great,' she said. 'When are you coming home?'

'Monday,' he said.

'You'll miss the fireworks,' she said. 'De Quincy's giving a party. You could have come with me, if you were coming home sooner.'

'No problem,' he said, and dropped his voice into its most seductive register. 'There'll be mega-fireworks when I get back. Mega. I promise.'

CHAPTER 15

Rockets screamed into the air in a banshee chorus to explode one after the other in long dazzling cascades of artificial stars, flame red, tinsel gold, neon green, ice white. They spread as they fell, hurtling outwards as if they were stretching the sky. Below them the water meadow was full of dark figures, bundled into heavy overcoats or padded anoraks, standing with their faces upturned, mouths agape to squeal or sigh, foreheads, cheeks and noses bronzed by the dazzle of descending stars. In the middle of the field the bonfire rose ten feet into the night sky like an elongated pyramid, balanced and woven and waiting to be lit, and all round the edges of the field barbecues were cooking and burning, puffing out smoke and the cloying smell of charred meat to mingle with the stink of cordite and the faint odour of churned mud and trampled grass. The gossips had gathered by the footpath to Mill Lane, ready to observe and comment, most of the men were by the bonfire drinking canned beer, and the children ran from group to group, burgers in hand, shrieking and eating as they ran.

'Wonderful!' Gwen said, watching the latest golden star-burst. 'Oh look at that one! Aren't you glad you came?'

Lucy shivered. She wasn't sure whether she was

enjoying the fireworks or not. It had all been very well organised with barely three seconds between one display and the next, and it was good to see her mother so relaxed and happy, but there was something about this event that alarmed her. When the rockets fizzled out they left an ominous void in the night sky, and she was pricklingly aware that she was out in the open, where ghouls lurked and anything could happen. 'Yes,' she said, trying to be sensible, 'it's very nice.'

'I read my chart this morning,' Gwen told her happily, 'and it all fitted.'

That was a surprise to Lucy. She'd taken her mother's initial enthusiasm for astrology as a sign of homesickness, a need for comfort, an intellectual clutching at straws, certainly something that would pass as she settled. 'You're not still doing that, are you?'

'Course,' Gwen said. 'It's fascinating.'

'But you don't believe it?' It was only just a question.

'You sound like Jeff,' Gwen laughed. 'He doesn't approve of it either. How can I explain it to you? It's not a matter of believing. I mean, the sun and the moon and the planets are where they are, unalterably. There's no changing them. You can look up and see them.' Which she did. 'It's like looking at a map. It shows you the road you're on but you don't necessarily have to follow it. Oh look at that one! Isn't that splendid! I love fireworks.'

'So I suppose you saw fireworks and bonfires on tonight's road, is that it?' Lucy teased.

'As far as my chart's concerned it's all to do with the planet Mars tonight,' Gwen explained. 'That's the main influence. Fire, danger, excitement, something illicit, a tendency to take risks, speak out of turn, that sort of thing.'

'Fireworks aren't illicit,' Lucy said practically.

'No,' Gwen allowed. 'They're not. They just feel illicit to me. I suppose it's because your father wouldn't countenance them. Well you know what he was like about them, fireworks and bonfires.'

Neil Morrish materialised out of the smoke, bulky in a blue and yellow anorak, his black boots spattered with mud. 'Would either of you like a hot-dog, or chicken or something?'

He's so happy to be beside her, Gwen thought, watching his face. I've never seen anyone so obviously in love. 'Let me ponder,' she said.

But while she was pondering Jeff arrived, looking every inch the farmer and landowner in his green wellies and his expensive flat cap and his Barbour, to tell them it was time to light the bonfire. 'Ready to do the honours?' he said to Gwen.

She was thrilled by the question. 'You mean I'm going to get to light it?'

'You, me and Mr Perkins,' he told her. 'It takes a concerted effort.'

'Barbecue later,' she said to Neil. 'Fire first. What are we using? It's hardly going to be a paper and matches job, is it?'

It took three tar torches with extra long handles. They caught fire slowly but once alight they blazed strongly, even when their flames were blown sideways by the night breeze, and they

211

gave off a powerful smell of tar and burning wood. Gwen held hers before her face, glowing with warmth and delight, and listened while Jeff warned that they had to be plunged into the mass at exactly the same time so that the pile would burn straight. 'On the count of three. One, two, go!'

The joy of setting off a bonfire as big as this one, to watch the inner flames catch and curl, to smell the wood smoke as it rose and gathered, to see the great flame-tigers leap, and hear the wood spit and crackle and roar as it dried and caught ablaze. It was magical, powerful, pagan, this winter ceremony of fire. Earth and air and fire and water, she thought. Mars conjunct with Mercury.

'Good?' Jeff asked at her elbow.

'I wouldn't have missed it for worlds,' she said.

He asked his next question although he already knew the answer. 'Happy?'

'Totally.' And it was true. They'd weathered their first row and now they were here together with a great fire warming their faces, and more fireworks to come, and Lucy here to share it all. It was better than anything she could have imagined. It only needed Ellie to be here too and it would be perfect.

Down by the footpath to Mill Lane, where the slight rise gave her a clear view and she could retreat to Teresa's house if the rain set in, Mrs Agatha Smith-Fernley was holding court, with her friend and echo at her elbow.

'Look at that!' she said. 'And you tell me she's

212

not got her hooks in. Poor Mr Langley. He's just no match for her, poor man. No match at all. Just look at the way she's gazing at him. She's making a proper exhibition of herself.'

'She is,' Miss O'Malley agreed.

'Lighting the bonfire!' Mrs Smith-Fernley said scathingly. 'If you ever heard of such a thing. That should have been done by the Parish Council, the way it always has been, as he very well knows.'

'He does.'

'It'll end in tears,' Mrs Smith-Fernley predicted. 'You mark my words.'

The bonfire had drawn the rest of the crowd and was now completely surrounded by shifting figures, dancing darkly behind the flames and looming through the smoke, their faces grotesqued by firelight. The sight of them made Lucy shiver, as she stood beside Neil Morrish holding a chicken burger in both hands and eating hungrily.

'Are you cold?' he asked, wondering whether he could put an arm round her.

'No,' she said. 'It's just... Oh I don't know. There's something about these people... The way they look at my mother. The way they sort of edge away from her. I've been watching them. Something ... well, hostile. I'm probably being silly. Take no notice. Are the fireworks finished?'

'Oh no,' he told her. 'There's the grand finale to come yet.'

'What's that?'

'It's the set piece. That's it over there. See? They

213

all go off at once and make a pattern. It's a hell of a row. The kids love it.'

He was right. The noise of so many rockets all screaming upwards at the same moment was ear-splitting. But when Lucy turned to tell him so he wasn't looking at the sky but sideways at the tower, scowling and stiff-spined.

'What's up?' she said. And then she heard the screams, high pitched, sharp, terrified, and was instantly and horribly afraid. Hadn't she known something awful was going to happen? 'My God! 'What is it?'

He was pounding towards the tower. 'Bloody Dion!' he called back.

She ran after him, her heart pounding, could see dark shapes leaping about in her mother's garden. Three of them. Men? Boys? Male certainly, she could see their shaven heads, and darting between them, down on the ground, a small flashing light. She saw boots swinging and then there were more screams and she knew it was an animal and that it was afraid and hurt. A small animal. A cat? Is it a cat? Oh shit! It is! It's Mum's cat.

Neil was leaping the wall, hurtling towards the three figures, had seized one of them by the throat and was pushing him against the outhouse wall. A skinhead in a denim jacket and huge boots, fighting and yelling 'Fuck off! Leave it out!' And the other two ran away, pushing past her, so close that she could smell their sweat. And the flashing light disappeared.

'Where's it gone?' she yelled.

Neil was too busy struggling with the skinhead

to answer her. 'This is well out of order!' he was shouting.

'It's a witch's cat,' the skinhead shouted back. 'That's what you do to witch's cats.'

'Not on my patch you don't.'

That's right, Lucy thought, give him hell. But she could see her mother and Mr Langley running across the field towards them and she knew she had to find the cat and quickly. Now that her reason had caught up with her legs, she realised that they must have tied a firework to its tail, poor thing. And now it had gone to earth. But where? Not to the tower or she'd have seen the light heading that way. The outhouse then.

It was pitch dark inside the little building and smelled of must and stale drink and dirt, and it was so full of junk that she could barely move an inch without knocking something over, but she could hear the cat swearing somewhere nearby.

'It's Jet, isn't it?' her mother said beside her. 'Is she hurt? It's all right Jet. We're here. Don't swear.'

Someone was pushing at the door with both hands, shoving it wide open. Jeff, a bulky shape stooping amongst the clobber, with a piece of sacking in his hands. 'If she's injured she'll scratch,' he explained to Gwen. 'If we can wrap her she'll be easier to hold.'

Lucy's eyes had adjusted to the darkness. 'I think she's in the wheelbarrow,' she said.

They approached cautiously, stumbling among the rubbish, could see the glint of the cat's eyes, hear its panting breath.

Gwen leant towards the wheelbarrow, but Jeff

was before her, lifting the animal clear, all four paws held in the sacking although it was struggling frantically. Then they were all out in the garden again, Neil and the skinhead were gone and the display was over. In the light from that great beacon of a bonfire, they could see that there was a spent firework tied to the cat's tail with a twist of wire and that the tail was cut and badly burned.

Gwen was torn with pity for it. 'What a wicked, wicked thing to do!'

Jeff was already on his way to the tower. 'We'll get her safe inside,' he said, 'and then I'll go and get Ed Ferris.'

The cat was still growling and plainly in shock, her mouth open and her eyes dilated, even though he was carrying her very tenderly. Lucy remembered the kicks and wondered what other damage the thugs had done. But she decided not to say anything about it until the vet arrived.

She and her mother sat side by side on the sofa with the cat panting on Gwen's lap and waited.

'It's so cruel,' Gwen said, stroking the animal's head. The fur at the end of her tail was so burnt and shrivelled that it looked more like threads from a brillo pad than fur, and the flesh was charred and split to the bone. 'I can't understand the mentality. To hurt a little cat. Poor thing. What's she ever done to deserve this? They must be really sick. I do wish Jeff would hurry.'

It seemed a very long time before Jeff returned with Ed Ferris but then action was quick and decisive. 'She'd better come into the surgery,' the vet said. 'The sooner this is dealt with the less chance of infection. I've brought a cat basket.'

There was just time for Lucy to catch his attention as her mother gentled the loaded basket through the front door. 'They were kicking her,' she warned. 'I saw them.'

'Don't worry,' he reassured. 'I'll check every bone.'

Out in the field, the bonfire was still blazing but the sky was dark, the true stars had returned and the crowd had diminished. People were drifting back home along Mill Lane in chattering groups. They stood aside to let Jeff's Land Rover pass and one or two waved at him. But Gwen barely saw them. 'What made them do such a thing?' she said, over and over again, her mind stuck in incomprehension. 'I can't credit such cruelty.'

Left on her own in the tower Lucy waited and worried, as much on her mother's behalf as the cat's. She wished Neil would come back and tell her what was going to happen to the yobs. She wished Ellie could be there with her. She even wished there was some housework she could do to keep her occupied. But as there was nothing, she climbed to the top of the tower and sat in her mother's favourite chair in the dark and looked out at the night sky. The stars were clear and bright in an indigo sky but she couldn't see the sea at all, and wouldn't have known it was there if it hadn't been for its rhythmical edging of white foam. There was something mesmerising and calming about that rhythm, so she sat on in the darkness and watched it. And eventually she heard the Land Rover return and her mother's key in the lock and was on her feet and half-way downstairs, eager to find out what had happened, when she realised her mother was crying and Jeff Langley was comforting her.

'She's in good hands,' his voice said.

And her mother's voice answered, muffled and indistinct and full of tears. 'Yes I know. It's just...'

He was murmuring, comforting and steadying. 'I know what it's just, my lovely.'

'It's so unfair,' her mother wailed. 'It's not as if she's ever done anything to them. She's a gentle little cat.'

The timbre of her voice kept Lucy still at the top of the last flight of stairs. It was the first time she'd ever heard her mother in distress. She never cried, never had, not even when Dad died. And yet there she was, weeping on Jeff Langley's chest with his arms round her and one big hand tenderly stroking her hair. And that was a first too. When had she ever seen her mother being comforted? Comforting, yes. She comforted everybody. But being comforted herself? It was unheard of.

She must have made a shuffling sound on the stairs, for the farmer looked up over her mother's bowed head, saw her and opened his eyes wide in question. For a few seconds she looked down at him, unsure what to do, then he mouthed, 'She's all right' and signalled with his head that she was to go back upstairs and leave him to cope. She surprised herself by obeying him. It annoyed her to think that he could manage things better than she could, and she was upset to realise that her mother needed him more than she needed her

218

own daughter, but she had to accept it. It was a peculiar situation and it kept her awake for a very long time as the voices below her murmured on and on.

It was a restless night for all three of them and they were glad to get up in the morning and start a new day. Gwen had been told to phone the vet at nine o'clock and she sat by the phone until it was exactly on the hour, according to Jeff's watch.

The voice on the other end of the line was professionally calm. The cat was fine. She'd had part of her tail amputated but she'd come through it well. 'You can collect her this afternoon. Any time after two.'

'What did I tell you?' Jeff said. 'Right, that's it then. We can get on with the rest of the day.'

Which they did, he to the farm, promising to return for lunch, Gwen and Lucy to some gentle cooking.

'Shall you come with us to collect her?' Gwen asked, as she peeled the potatoes.

When she'd thought about it, Lucy decided she'd rather not. 'I think I'll just take a walk down by the lagoon,' she said. 'If that's all right with you.' She needed time on her own to digest the events of the previous evening and to try and make some sense of them.

It was a restless, disturbing afternoon. As Lucy left her car and walked down the little lane to the lagoon everything seemed to be on the move, worrying and fretting and whispering, from the dead beech leaves swishing and swirling at her feet, to the tops of the bare trees flailing and creaking in the force of the wind. There was nobody about, which was hardly surprising on such a blustery day, and when she emerged from the enclosure of the trees to the dark mud flats that edged the lagoon she found herself in the bleakest of landscapes, with a strong tide rolling grey waters and the sky heavy with cloud.

She walked automatically, head down against the gale, her thoughts seething. After taking against Jeff Langley so strongly it was hard to have to face the fact that she could have been wrong about him. But now that she'd seen how gentle he could be and watched how well he'd handled her mother's distress, she knew her opinion had been drastically altered. And then there was the menace she'd sensed at the firework display. She certainly hadn't been wrong about that. 'A witch's cat' that hideous boy had said. 'That's what we to do a witch's cat.' And she remembered that horrible old woman on the night of the accident. She'd called Mum, Her-up-the-tower. And she'd said she was a witch too. There was something going on, an undercurrent of gossip and suspicion, and tormenting the cat was proof of it. But knowing it was one thing, knowing what her mother ought to do about it was another. She strode on, following the long sand ridge, denimed legs striding rhythmically, hands in her pockets, scarf flapping behind her, in a scowl of hard thinking.

Which was how Neil saw her when he too emerged from the footpath, and the sight of her trudging alone on the edge of the harbour, silhouetted against the darkening sky, with only dried sedge and a flock of wild duck for company, roused him to a tenderness of protective affection. He pounded after her, boots crunching on the gravel, calling her name.

At first the wind blew his voice away, but on the third attempt she heard him and turned to wait for him, hunching her shoulders against the buffeting of the wind. She wasn't particularly surprised to see him, nor particularly pleased. He'd come to tell her what had happened to the yobs, which was only right and proper, but she hoped he'd be quick about it because she wanted to get back to her thoughts.

'Did you catch them?' she called.

'I did.'

'All three of them?'

'Nathan's a grass,' he said as he caught up with her. 'Always was. Push him and he'll tell you anything.' Now that they were face to face, he could see that her nose was pink and her face peaked. 'You're cold,' he said.

She didn't want to talk about her feelings. 'So,' she said, 'what's going to happen to them?'

They walked side by side and so close he could smell her perfume. 'Well,' he said, trying to be professional, 'they've been cautioned for a start.'

The answer didn't please her. 'Is that all?' she said crossly. 'They should have been locked up. Why didn't you charge them?'

'That's up to your mother,' he explained.

That didn't please her either. 'She'll let them off,' she predicted. 'She's too soft.'

He wanted to placate her, to stop her scowling,

to make her feel better about all this, to pull her into his arms and kiss her. But of course he couldn't do that. It wasn't the time or the place. 'At the moment,' he said, offering the only comfort he had, 'they're clearing last night's litter from the water meadow.'

'Good!' she said, grimly. 'Whose idea was that?'

'Oh theirs,' he grinned. 'Once I'd persuaded them a bit. And after that they've got to meet me at the tower and apologise to your mother face to face.'

'I don't think much of that for a punishment,' she said. 'Anyone can apologise. It's only words.'

'I don't think there'll be a repeat performance,' he tried to assure her. 'I told them we'd hand them straight over to the RSPCA if they ever did anything like that again and they would prosecute.'

'But they don't need a repeat performance, do they?' Lucy said bitterly. 'They've made their point. That's what they do to a witch's cat. You heard what that Dion creature said. A witch's cat. This goes deeper than three brainless morons kicking an animal about. This is about scape-goating.'

'Well yes,' he admitted. 'It does look that way at the moment.'

'Never mind look. It is that way and it makes me furious. She came down here for a new life, not to be called names and have her cat attacked. She's a good woman. Always has been. Not a witch.'

Her anger pained him. 'I know. I know.'

'I'd like to see them with fireworks tied round

their tails with a bit of lousy wire. See how they'd like it. I'd light them myself. No problem.'

He was sure she would but he didn't have the faintest idea how to answer her. 'Well yes,' he said. And was annoyed with himself for sounding inadequate.

'Well yes, nothing,' she snorted. 'Think how you'd feel if it was your mother. You'd turn the world inside out. Well you would, wouldn't you? It wouldn't just be an apology. You'd want blood. Like I do.'

'Actually,' he said. 'I haven't got a mother.'

The confession checked her anger, made her remember her father, roused instant sympathy. 'Oh Neil. I am sorry.'

He rushed to reassure her. 'It's all right. She isn't dead. I mean I'm not bereaved or anything. She put me in a home, that's all. That's what I meant.'

Her face creased with pity for him. 'Oh Neil! That's awful. How old were you?'

'It's all right,' he said again. He hadn't meant to play for sympathy and getting it was embarrassing. 'I can't remember it. I mean I was two. You don't remember things at that age.' And he tried to change the subject. 'It's coming on to rain. I think we should be making tracks. I don't want them to run off and not say sorry.'

'Yes,' she agreed, recognising his embarrassment. She'd have liked to have questioned him and found out more. Being an orphan would account for all sorts of things. I'll bet that's why he went into the police. But this wasn't the time to prod him. 'I suppose we'd better. Do you want

223

me to be there when they grovel?'

'Oh yes,' he told her. 'The more people who hear them the more they'll get the message.'

Jet's three tormentors were lurking by the outhouse, picking out chunks of lichen with their grubby fingernails and kicking at the flints with their equally grubby Reeboks. In the chill daylight they looked smaller than they'd done the previous evening, as Lucy was delighted to notice. The oldest, who was pale-faced and covered in pimples, couldn't have been more than fourteen, the other two, one pudgily overweight and the other skinny and sharp-eyed, were even younger. As Neil drew up alongside them, all three shuffled away from the wall, looking sheepish.

'Right,' he said to them, 'is the field clean?'

It was the smallest boy who answered. 'Yes sir.'

'Has Mr Langley seen it?'

'Not yet sir,' the boy said. 'He's, like, with Her-in-the-tower.'

Neil's thick eyebrows descended with dis-approval. 'She has a name, Nathan,' he said. 'Same as you do. Her name's Mrs MacIvor.'

What a face he has, Lucy thought. That broken nose makes him look really fierce.

'Yes sir,' the boy said. 'Mrs MacIvor. He's, like, in with her sir.'

'Then we'd better get, like, in with her too, hadn't we?'

All three were now profoundly uncomfortable. They shuffled to the door, not looking at one another, knocked and were admitted by Jeff

Langley, sternly.

Gwen was sitting on the sofa with the cat asleep on her lap. It had a stumpy bandage on the end of its tail and what looked like a white lampshade round its neck, and Lucy could smell the anaesthetic from where she stood.

'It's to stop her pulling the bandages off,' Gwen explained, as the boys looked at the lampshade. 'To give it a chance to heal. She had to have the end of her tail amputated, poor thing. It was so badly burnt it couldn't be saved. That's what you did to her.'

'This is Dion Casterick,' Neil said, pushing the oldest boy forward. 'And this is Ryan and that's Nathan. They've got something to say to you. Haven't you lads?'

They muttered that they were sorry, standing in line together and not looking at her.

'So I should think,' she said.

'And?' Neil pressed.

'We, like, didn't mean to hurt her,' Nathan offered. 'We were, like, mucking about.'

Gwen was angered. 'Mucking about!' she said and looked down at the cat's bandages. 'You call this mucking about?'

'It was, like, a bit of fun,' the fat boy said, his face impassive.

'Fun?' Gwen shouted, rounding on him. 'So you think it's fun to torment an animal! Is that it? She must have been in agony, poor little thing. They had to cut off part of her tail. She was cut and burnt and terrified and you think it's funny! You wouldn't find it so funny if somebody was doing it to you.'

'It was only for a joke,' the fat boy said. 'We didn't think she'd get hurt.'

'You didn't think at all,' Gwen said. 'Any of you. Well you'd better start thinking now because if I want to I can have you charged and brought up before a magistrate. You know that don't you?'

They mumbled that they did and, although Dion was still sullen and Ryan still plumply impassive, Nathan began to cry.

'Please miss, don't miss,' he begged, wiping his nose with the back of his hand. 'I won't do it again. I promise. Please miss. My Dad'll go ape.'

'I shouldn't think any of your parents will be particularly pleased,' Gwen said. 'Will they?'

The fat boy shrugged. 'I don't care,' he said. But then he had to pull in his mouth so that they wouldn't see it was trembling.

Dion sneered. 'If you really want to know, miss,' he said, 'mine won't give a toss.'

'And that's enough of that sort of talk,' Jeff said, menacing him with his greater height and bulk. 'You just remember where you are and who you're with.'

Dion looked away from him. 'Sir,' he said, sullen faced.

There was a pause and more shuffling of feet.

'Right. That's it,' Jeff said, opening the door. 'You've apologised. We've all heard you. Remember that. We've all heard you. Now there's a man waiting for you in the field to see if it's properly clean, and if it isn't he'll tell you what else you've got to do. You can go.'

They pushed one another through the door in such a panic to escape that it shut with a bang that woke the cat.

'It's all right,' Gwen said, stroking its black head. 'They've gone.'

'So what are you going to do?' Lucy asked. 'You will prosecute won't you? They ought to be punished or they'll think they can do it again.' She looked at the two men for support.

'If it was up to me, I'd have them in court before their feet touched the ground,' Jeff said. 'But it's your cat. Your decision.'

'Neil?' Gwen asked.

He considered it carefully. 'Well,' he said, 'if it was just Dion I'd say throw the book at him. But if you take him to court you'll have to take the others too and I think they'd be better left to stew for a day or two and then let off the hook. I mean, no matter what you do to them you can't undo what they've done. You can't bring back the cat's tail. And they know it'll be straight to the RSPCA if they ever do anything else. But like Mr Langley says, it's up to you.'

Gwen had made up her mind while he was speaking. 'Well,' she said. 'We all know what they've done and they know we know. I think that's enough. The skinny one was frightened. And I think the fat one was too. All that hoity toity *I don't care* business was a front.' Then having made her decision she changed the subject. 'Just listen to that wind.' It was making the oddest noise, as if it were howling round the tower. 'It sounds like a wild thing.' She smiled, first at Lucy to mollify her – dear Lucy, she was so cross – then at Jeff and Neil with an invitation. 'Let's have tea, shall we?'

CHAPTER 16

The strong sou'westerlies howled against the tower all through the weekend. Gwen was quite glad to stay indoors with Jet but the continuing gale made Jeff restless.

'Always does,' he explained. 'It sets something off in me. I get the fidgets as soon as it starts and when it really blows I can't settle to anything.'

On Sunday evening he drove over to tell her that he'd decided to go to the midlands for a day or two to look at some new tractors and visit his brother. 'It'll get me away from the wind,' he said and he was only half joking.

'I'd come with you if it wasn't for Jet,' Gwen said. There was another reason too but she'd decided to keep that to herself for the time being. Ellie had phoned on the day after the fireworks to say that she was coming down on Monday afternoon, and she'd been so loving and concerned Gwen was quite looking forward to her visit.

It began really well, for she arrived clutching a huge bunch of white chrysanthemums and rushed to hug her mother, flowers and all.

'Poor little cat,' she said as they walked into the tower. 'How is she now?'

She was lying on the sofa in her customary place with her bandaged stump on a cushion, and didn't even open her eyes as her sad story was told.

Eleanor gave the stump a cursory glance, just to show willing. 'Gruesome!' she said. 'Shall I put these in water for you?'

'So how are you?' Gwen asked, as Eleanor busied herself at the sink. 'You look blooming.'

'Coming along very nicely according to my midwife.'

'You've got your own midwife?'

'Oh yes,' Eleanor said gaily. 'There have to be some advantages to going private. The caesarean's going to cost me an arm and a leg.'

Such a casual mention of a caesarean operation was alarming. There must be something wrong, Gwen thought, and she isn't telling me. 'Have they decided on a caesarean already?' she asked anxiously.

'Oh God yes,' Eleanor said. 'I should just hope so. It'll either be that or an epidural. I don't want to go through all that pain. Not if I can help it. I said to them *Just put me out*, I said. *I don't care what you do so long as I'm not conscious to feel you doing it.*' She gave her artless laugh. 'You know me. I'm a coward to my bones.'

Oh dear, Gwen thought. I hope she knows what she's doing. But there was no point in arguing. If she's made up her mind she'll go through with it no matter what I say. 'How's the nursery?' she asked.

Eleanor carried the flowers through into the living room and set them on the side table against the wall, primping them until they were arranged to her satisfaction. 'Finished and furnished,' she said. 'The bed came on Thursday. Isn't that good? So if you want to come and stay with me for a few days it's all ready for you. I thought you might like to get away from it all, after all you've been through. We could take in a theatre or something. What do you think?' And she sat down on the sofa, arranged her clothes more comfortably and looked up at her mother with affection.

Gwen was touched. 'Well that's really kind, chick,' she said, sitting on the other sofa and stroking the cat's back. 'I wish I could. But I can't leave Jet. Not yet anyway. I have to take her to the vet's twice a week to have her dressings changed.'

Eleanor frowned. 'You could take her to a vet in Chelsea, couldn't you? I mean, there are vets everywhere.'

'Well I could,' Gwen allowed, still stroking, 'but I'd rather not. She knows this one. And besides it's a long journey.'

'Well, when she's better then,' Eleanor said, struggling to be reasonable. 'Say next week. The week after. Whenever. But you will come, won't you?'

Gwen was beginning to feel pressurised. She stopped stroking the cat and put her hands in her lap. 'I'll come up for the day,' she said.

'Well a day would be nice, of course,' Eleanor said, still determinedly reasonable, 'but it's not the same as a week, is it? I want you to settle in, get the feel of the place, live there. I mean it's all ready for you now. The bed's top of the range. Really comfortable. You'll love it. And there's all sorts of good shows on at the moment. Or concerts if you'd prefer. Come for a week.'

'Who'll look after Jet?'

Eleanor was getting heartily sick of that cat but she kept her cool. 'Bring her with you,' she offered. 'I mean, she'll have to come up when you move in, so she might as well start getting used to it. It won't be a problem, so long as she's house-trained, and she is, isn't she? I don't mind cats if they're house-trained and she'll be nice for the baby. Babies like pets, don't they? Of course I know you'll want to get back here for the week-end sometimes, just to keep an eye on the place, but that won't be a problem. She can stay with me while you're gone and it won't be for long will it, because you'll have to be back by Monday morning at the latest. Sunday evening would be better. Anyway, I'll feed her. So it's all sorted.'

Gwen heard her out but with a growing and uncomfortable suspicion that her life was being taken over. 'What are we talking about?' she asked when her daughter paused for breath. 'You make it sound as if I'm going to live in your flat.'

'Well not now you're not,' Eleanor said patiently. 'No. Of course not. I mean when the baby's born. When I go back to work.'

For a few seconds Gwen sat quite still looking across at her daughter's pretty complacent face as a gulf opened between them like the fissure of an earthquake. 'Let me get this clear,' she said, deliberately calm. 'You're expecting me to come up to London and look after the baby while you go back to work?'

'Well I did think about driving it down here to you every week,' Eleanor admitted. 'But that would mean a three hour drive, here and back, and that would be difficult – well horrendous really, especially when I'd got a rush on at work. And you've no idea how often that happens. It would be easier for you to make the journey. I mean you must see that. I'll pay for the petrol and everything, and have a meal ready for you when you get in. And you love the nursery, now don't you? You said so.'

'As a nursery, not as living accommodation.'

'If there's anything you don't like, I'll change it for you,' Eleanor offered. 'You've only to say. I want you to be comfortable.'

'I'm perfectly comfortable here,' Gwen said.

'Yes, I know,' Eleanor agreed. 'But it would be easier if you came to me.'

'I don't think you understand what I'm saying,' Gwen said. 'I'm not coming up to London and the baby isn't coming down here. I'm not going to look after it.'

The shock of hearing her say such an awful thing stopped Eleanor's breath. 'But I've got it all arranged,' she said, her face crumpling with distress.

Her stricken expression made Gwen feel un-comfortable. But she held on. 'Then you'll have to un-arrange it,' she said.

The fissure had reached Eleanor's expensive boots and the ground was disintegrating under them. 'But you agreed,' she wailed.

'No Eleanor,' Gwen said sternly. 'I didn't agree to anything. I said I liked the nursery, that's all. I never said anything about looking after the baby and neither did you.'

'But you're such a good mother. Wonderful. Everyone says so. I thought you'd love to do it.'

'Well you thought wrong. I've done my stint and very hard work it was. Now it's your turn. If you want this baby you must look after it. That's the way things are.'

'You don't understand,' Eleanor said. 'That's not the way things are at all. Not now. You can't afford to give up work and stay at home. Not in this day and age. Nobody does. If you lose out on your career you're finished, and it isn't just the job either, it's your prospects, promotion, pension, status, everything. You never get back.'

'Then you've got a choice,' Gwen said firmly, 'haven't you? You either have a baby or a career. You obviously can't have both.'

'Yes you can,' Eleanor told her. 'People do. It's a matter of finding good child care, that's all.'

Gwen was stung by the selfish assumption behind the words but she stayed calm. 'And that's how you see me, is it?' she said. 'Good child care.'

Eleanor gave her an honest answer. 'The best,' she said. 'I mean what can be better than the baby's own grandmother?'

'The baby's own mother.'

The fissure was a gulf, a chasm, gaping and growing, unbridgeable.

'You're not hearing me,' Eleanor cried. 'I can't do it. It's out of the question. You must help me. I need the money.'

Money, Gwen thought. It's always money with this generation. 'Let Pete provide for you. That's what fathers are for.'

The confession came blurting out before Eleanor could stop to think. 'Pete doesn't know about it. I haven't told him.'

'Oh Eleanor! For heaven's sake!'

'Don't for heaven's sake me!' Eleanor yelled. 'He's been away. I have tried. He won't listen.'

Gwen shook her head and grimaced. 'I don't believe this!'

The grimace gave Eleanor some hope. She'd seen it before, many times, when she was little, and it had always meant she was going to get what she wanted. 'So you will help me, won't you,' she cajoled. 'I mean I don't know how I shall cope if you let me down. This is the hour of my greatest need.'

'Don't be melodramatic.'

'It's true. It is. I've never needed anything so much. I'm depending on you. So you will, won't you? You won't let me down.'

Gwen hesitated. The wind was snuffling under the door and she could hear the roar of the sea even through the double-glazing. 'How can I make you understand?' she said. 'I'm not going to do this. No matter what you say. I spent thirty-six years living for other people, thirty-six years looking after you and Lucy and letting your father live the life he wanted. That's a hell of a long time. Half a lifetime. And now I've got the chance to live my own life in my own way, and it's a good life. I enjoy it and I'm not going to give it up. If you want somebody else to look after your baby, you must find somebody else. It's not going to be me. I've done it once and once is enough.'

Eleanor began to cry. She couldn't help it. 'How can you be so fucking selfish?' she wept. 'I thought you loved me.'

'I do love you.'

234

'Well then. Be a grandmother to my baby.'

'Grandmother I can cope with,' Gwen told her. 'Grandmother I shall enjoy. I'll take it to the zoo and the pictures and have it here for holidays and teach it to swim and all that sort of thing but you mustn't expect me to be its mother, you really mustn't. I'm too old for it.'

'I thought you'd stand by me,' Eleanor cried. 'I'm your daughter for chrissake. Who else are you supposed to turn to if it's not your mother? Your mother's the one person in all the world you can really trust. The one person. But no. You're no mother to me. You don't love me. Not when it comes down to it. Oh I can see what it is. It's that fucking farmer, isn't it? He's been giving you ideas. He wants you all to himself. We don't stand a chance.'

'No,' Gwen said, staying calm with an effort. 'It's nothing to do with him. He doesn't know. How could he? I've only just found out myself. This is my decision. And I'm not going back on it.'

Eleanor sprang to her feet, gathered her handbag, blundered to the door. 'You've never loved me,' she wept. 'And now I know it. You're a hard selfish woman. You haven't an ounce of love in you. You didn't love Dad and you don't love me. You don't care what you're doing to me.'

It was another childhood ploy and Gwen recognised it with a lurch of misery because it wasn't going to help her. 'You're wrong of course,' she said sadly. 'But if that's what you want to think, I can't stop you.'

Eleanor abandoned herself to weeping. The

door was stiff and hard to open but she struggled with it as tears ran down her elegant nose and dripped onto her elegant coat. 'Don't bother to see me out,' she said wildly. And left.

After she'd gone Gwen sat where she was on the sofa, automatically stroking the cat's head and feeling too miserable to move. Now that the tower was quiet, all sorts of awkward questions intruded themselves. Am I being selfish? she thought unhappily. Should I have given in? Perhaps I should, if only for the baby. If I don't look after it, she'll hand it over to a stranger. And God knows what'll happen to it then. She won't look after it herself. Oh how stupid I've been all these weeks. Fancy not seeing what was coming. All that business about the nursery and wanting to know whether I liked it or not. It was right under my nose and I missed it. How could I have been so blind? If I'd paid more attention, I could have been better prepared, handled it better.

The car started up and drove away, tyres skidding against the gravel. 'Ah well,' she said sadly to the cat, 'we shall just have to wait and see what happens next, won't we puss?'

What happened next was the sound of the car returning. She was so relieved she got up at once and rushed to the door. If we can just make up, she thought, it won't be so bad. It's dreadful to quarrel. I won't give in to her but we needn't quarrel.

It was a Renault but not Ellie's. A strange young woman was easing out of the driving seat and walking up the garden path towards her, tall, dark haired, with horn-rimmed glasses, wearing a dark trouser suit and carrying a clipboard in her hand.

'Mrs MacIvor?' she asked, holding out her hand. 'I'm Kate Fenchurch. From the council. About your application. I've come to inspect the site.'

It took a second or two for Gwen to pull her mind back to such a mundane thing as a planning application. Then she found her cape and hat, and she and the young woman walked across to the outhouse.

It was a thorough inspection. She checked the state of the flint walls, measured the length of the building, asked about the roofing, took a close look at the area Gwen intended for the hard standing, and finally pronounced it satisfactory. 'No problems as far as I can see,' she said. 'Except for the local opposition.'

It was the second surprise of the afternoon and almost as upsetting as the first. 'What local opposition?' Gwen asked.

A file was found and handed over. It made no sense to Gwen at all. There were no letters opposing her, just a small, badly printed form, headed 'Seal Island Parish Council' on which someone had written four bald numerals – 35, 97, 68 and 102. If this was the opposition it was very peculiar. 'Is this it?' she said. 'What does it mean?'

'Oh those figures,' the woman said. 'That's the shorthand they use in parish councils. I've no idea what they mean. You'll have to see the chairman or the secretary about it. Their names are on the form.'

'I'll go there tonight,' Gwen said. It was absurd for her garage to be opposed, and especially by a set of figures.

It was dark enough for headlights by the time she set out that evening but that didn't deter her. From her walks about the village she knew that the chairman's house would be somewhere on the new estate on the easternmost edge and she found it easily, a small neat bungalow with a regimented garden and a well-swept drive.

It didn't surprise her that the man who opened the door was small and neat himself. Yes, he agreed, he was Mr Perkins, and yes, he was the Chairman of the Parish Council. 'Do come in. How may I help you?'

'You can tell me what these numbers mean,' Gwen said, noting the chintzy neatness of his living room, the size of the television set, the absence of books, the row of china ornaments on the windowsill. Then, watching for the effect she would have, she told him who she was. She didn't know whether to be pleased or cross to see how embarrassed he became.

'If you'll just wait a moment while I find the rule-book,' he said. 'Do sit down.' It was all a nonsense. He knew perfectly well what the numbers meant. He could remember how they'd been chosen. But he could hardly admit that. Especially if she'd come to give him a wigging. If only county hadn't started all this nonsense about open government. It had been asking for trouble from the beginning. 'Ah yes,' he said, spreading the book out on the coffee table in

238

front of her. 'Here we are. 35 – unjustified change of use, 97 – environmental damage, 68 – traffic hazard, 102 – setting a precedent.'

Now Gwen was very cross indeed. 'How can it be an unjustified change of use?' she asked him. 'We're talking about a dirty old outhouse, full of empty bottles left there by the man who lived in the tower before me. You did know he was a drunk I suppose? I want to turn it into a nice clean garage. What's unjustified about that? Where's the environmental damage? Surely a clean garage is preferable to a bug-hutch. You should come and see it, Mr Perkins. It's an eyesore.'

He was squirmingly uncomfortable. 'I'm sure it is,' he said.

'Then why are you opposing me?'

'I think it was the garage door that was objected to,' Mr Perkins told her. 'It's all a matter of taste of course, but there were those who felt that a modern garage door would look out of place in an old brick and flint building.'

She snorted. 'And dirty old bottles don't?'

'Well like I say, it's a matter of taste.'

'All right then, let's look at the others. Traffic hazard, wasn't it? You do know where it is I suppose. Right down the end of Mill Lane. There's no traffic there except for cars that are coming to visit me.'

'There have been rather a large number of builder's vans I believe.'

'Well of course there have,' Gwen said, dark with anger at his obtuseness. 'I've literally had to rebuild the place. It was rotting when I moved in.

Your drunk had let it run down so badly it's a wonder it was still standing. You should come and visit it and see what I've done, instead of scribbling numbers on a bit of paper.'

'We were asked to comment, Mrs MacIvor,' the chairman said rather stiffly. 'That's the function of a parish council. And that's what we did. And I might add, the numbers were not scribbled. They were neatly written. I wrote them myself.'

Gwen ignored this for the petty irrelevance it was. 'Why didn't any of you come down to the outhouse and look at it?'

'We saw the plan. We listened to the arguments.'

'You took against it,' Gwen said, understanding this just a little too clearly, 'because I'm a newcomer. That's why you were against establishing a precedent. Newcomers have to be kept in their place. I'm right, aren't I?'

'Oh, no, no. My dear Mrs MacIvor, you mustn't think that.'

'There's nothing else I can think,' Gwen told him, standing up and pushing away her chair.

'It's nothing personal,' he tried to assure her.

'Yes it is,' she said on her way to the door. 'It's personal and vindictive and bloody unkind. You ought to be ashamed of yourselves. Good evening to you.'

'Who was that?' Mrs Perkins asked, coming into the room as Gwen drove away. 'I could hear her shouting in the kitchen.'

'That,' her husband said, shuddering, 'was Mrs MacIvor and I'm afraid she's taken offence.'

240

By the time the offence-taking Mrs MacIvor was back in her tower it was completely dark and her anger had seeped away. Now, she felt beleaguered and depressed. It was demoralising to have to face the fact that her new neighbours disliked her so much they'd deliberately blocked a perfectly reasonable proposal, worse to have the suspicion that Jet had been attacked and injured as a way of getting back at her. If that was what had happened, it was evil. But much much worse was the memory of her dreadful row with Ellie. If only Jeff wasn't away. She did so need to talk to him.

But away he was and away he stayed. She didn't like to call him on his mobile and he didn't call her. For that matter neither did anyone else, so it was miserably lonely in her tower. It wasn't until late on Wednesday evening that her phone finally rang. She picked it up with such relief she felt quite agitated.

'I'm back,' Jeff's voice said happily. 'I've bought a new tractor. First rate. Even old Martin approves. It'll make a real difference when we plough the set-aside. Wait till you see the brochure.'

She tried to enthuse. 'That's nice.' But she couldn't bring herself to care about a tractor and her voice was flat.

'What's up?' he asked, his voice instantly tender.

'It's a long story,' she told him wearily. 'Well, two long stories and not very pleasant ones. Did you see your brother?'

'I'm on my way over,' he said. 'Get the glasses

out. I bought some malt too.'

It took a long time, an outburst of tears and a considerable amount of whisky before she'd told him what had happened and answered all his questions. But once he'd heard her out, his advice was instant and sound.

'You can ignore the old biddies for a start,' he said. 'They're just being petty and spiteful, which is what you'd expect from a gang of two-bit local politicians with nothing else to occupy them. They're not worth a row of beans. The final decision's up to the planning committee and they'll pass it. There's no real reason why they shouldn't.'

'Perhaps I should just give up,' Gwen said, 'and leave it as it is.'

'That would be the worst thing to do,' he told her. 'That way they'll think they've won and they mustn't be allowed to think that. It would be bad for their souls.'

'But what about my Ellie?' she mourned. 'I should have said I'd help her, shouldn't I? She was so upset. I've never seen her so upset.'

'Your Ellie's as tough as old boots,' he said. 'I've told you that before. She's been badly spoilt. OK. OK. I'm not saying you did it, but somebody did. She expects to get her own way, every time, and that's not healthy.'

'You're making her sound selfish.'

'She is selfish. And you were absolutely in the right to refuse. Good God woman, you don't want to be looking after a baby at your age.'

That was true and she had to admit it. 'But if I don't take it, she'll hand it over to someone else,' she said. 'Some awful au pair who'll knock it about and shout at it. I really couldn't bear that.'

'She's not a child,' he said, taking both her hands and holding them firmly. 'She's got to make her own mistakes and you've got to let her do it. You're not responsible for her. Just cut the apron strings and let her get on with it.' Then, when she sighed and pulled a face, he paused and gave her a long level look. 'OK. I've got a better idea.'

She was intrigued by his expression and his sudden change of tone. 'What?'

'If you sit around here with nothing to do but think about it, you'll end up giving in. You will. You know it. All right then. I think you should have something else to do. Something more important.'

'Like what?'

'I think you should marry me.'

Caught by surprise she gave him an instant and honest answer. 'But I don't want to marry you. I like things the way they are.'

Her candour hurt his pride and made him irritable. 'Well thanks very much.'

She saw the damage she'd done and hastened to soothe him. 'I don't mean I don't love you. I do. Very much. It's just... Well if you want the truth I don't want to be a wife. I like being independent.'

'At least think about it,' he urged. 'There are some real advantages. You wouldn't be Her-up-the-tower, you'd be the farmer's wife. Much higher status. It'd put paid to the old biddies at a stroke. And we could be together all the time instead of all this coming and going. You could keep the tower. You wouldn't have to give it up or anything like that. We could have two homes and run them both. One for work and one for fun.'

'We do that already.'

'I know. But think about it. We'd make a great team.'

She was remembering Ellie's stinging words. 'It's that fucking farmer. He wants you to himself.' Was it true? Did he? Was that what this was about? And did she want to be part of a team? He made them sound like a couple of farm horses.

'Sleep on it,' he advised. 'See what it looks like in the morning.'

So she promised to think about it, although she knew she wouldn't change her mind.

The promise restored him a little. 'And while we're on the subject,' he said. 'How about spending Christmas with me? It's my turn to host the family and we always have a big party on Christmas evening. You'd love it.'

That she could agree to, 'Providing you don't mind Lucy and Ellie tagging along as well. They'll probably have Christmas with me – or part of it anyway – if Ellie's forgiven me.' But then she might not. I might have lost her. Oh no! I couldn't bear that.

He saw her expression change and spoke quickly to sweep her along. 'The more the merrier,' he said. 'There's so many of us two more won't notice.'

That sounded rather daunting. 'How many?'

'I'm one of five,' he told her. 'Two boys and

three girls and we've all got families, so there'll probably be about twenty-six or so, if both my boys come too.'

'Good God! It sounds like a tribe.'

'That's better,' he said. 'I've made you laugh. Just sleep on all this, eh? Now I must go. I should have been with old Kit Voller half an hour ago. We can solve most problems together, believe me.'

But not this one, she thought, as she waved goodbye to him. You've just made this one more complicated. Now that he'd gone she felt uncomfortable to think how much she must have hurt him by refusing him, but what else could she have done? She really didn't want to marry him. Being a lover was wonderful – she should have told him how wonderful – but even the thought of being a wife made her shudder. Once was enough. Still, she thought, as she walked back into her nice red living room – fancy him thinking I'd want to leave all this – he's right about one thing. It would be easier if I had something to do. If I sit around thinking about it, I shall give in. Maybe I ought to get a job. There were plenty advertised in the local paper. She'd seen them only yesterday afternoon, when she was reading the ads for the local garden centres and planning her vegetable plot.

She found the paper and opened it almost idly, wondering if there was anything that might suit. A job was only a job. If she didn't like it she could leave and no harm done. This one might do, for a start, doctor's receptionist in Chichester, 'good telephone manner'. And so might that. School secretary in Little Marsden, 'used to handling the public and with some accounting'.

The old Gwen MacIvor would have dithered about it, the new one wasted no time in unnecessary thought. Nor was she modest when she started to compose her CV. If she wanted a job she knew she had to sell her talents. She was a graduate, after all, she was used to handling 'the public', she had a very good 'telephone manner', she'd done all the accounts in the shop in Fulham. Very well then.

It took her over an hour to compose both applications but when they were written she felt quite pleased with herself. I'll post them first thing tomorrow morning, she decided, and then we'll see.

CHAPTER 17

Mr Walter B Hackenfleur II stood beside the picture window in Pete's Pimlico apartment and looked out over the Thames. It was late afternoon and the river was dusk-dark and shimmering with reflected light. Tower blocks reared blackly before him, windows blazing, the bridges to right, and left were sooty shapes etched with small bright lights, and as he watched, a river boat slid past, hung about with fairy lights, its prow carving two wings of moon-white water as dark figures danced and drank below decks. 'This is one helluva view, Pete,' he said. 'One helluva view.'

'I'm glad you like it,' Pete smiled, but he was thinking, so hurry up and sign the agreement, why don't you, and give me my cheque. The flat was ready for them to move in, all his things were in the car waiting to be taken to Ellie's. There was no need for all this faffing about.

But Mr Hackenfleur II was waiting for his wife to give her approval and although her inspection seemed to be going well, it was slow. The kitchen had been pronounced 'cute', the en suite bedroom 'neat', the living area 'great for parties', and now the lady was examining the guest room, opening the fitted wardrobes and running her fingers along the window sills for dust. And you won't find any, Pete thought, watching her.

Eventually she wafted back into the living room. 'You've got a great little place here,' she said regally. 'We'll take it.'

'You won't regret it,' Pete assured her, as her husband signed the agreement and that necessary cheque. 'I know you'll both be very happy here.' Now he could cut off to Chelsea at last. Good old Ellie, he thought. He couldn't wait to see her again.

Eleanor was on the phone. She'd had a hideously busy day, dragging from one horrendous meeting to another and ending up with a long gruelling session with Ms De Quincy, who was now a blonde with a startling white quiff and looked like a cockatoo. But by the end of their meeting she dropped into gushing praise for Eleanor's latest presentation – 'Mr Young was most impressed' – and even asked how she was keeping.

As if I'm a carton of milk, Eleanor thought, and likely to go off. But she smiled politely and said she was fighting fit.

'I trust everything's still in order for after your maternity leave,' Ms de Quincy said, as Eleanor stood to leave. 'Your mother's still available.'

'Naturally.'

Ms de Quincy was into her caring executive mode. 'No problems then.'

The memory of her mother's perfidious treatment dragged Eleanor right down. But she maintained her poise and answered gaily. 'Of course not. You know me.' I'll find someone else, she thought. You see if I don't.

So now back at home in her nice cool flat, she

248

was ringing round. She'd tried the three most likely people but they were useless and when Pete rang the bell, she was speaking to Monica Furlong. 'Hang on just a minute,' she said. 'Someone's at the door.'

He was in the room, had swept her into his arms and was kissing her passionately before she could even say his name.

'When did you get back?' she asked as he paused for breath, her arms still round his neck 'Oh it is good to see you. Why didn't you phone?'

'I like that!' he said happily. 'Your fucking phone's been off the hook for fucking hours. I've been trying all the way here. Have I got news for you! It's been a helluva trip. Absolutely, totally, fucking marvellous. Wait till I tell you. You could be looking at a senior executive of the London branch of J.R. Grossman UK. What d'you think of that? Great or what?' And he kissed her again, ecstatic with success and homecoming. 'Hey!' he said when he finally pulled apart. 'Let me look at you.'

It was a palpable shock to see how fat her face was. 'For Christ's sake Ellie!' he said. 'What have you done to yourself?'

She was so thrilled by their rapturous reunion that she thought he was teasing and teased back. It was all right. He loved her. Wasn't he showing it? 'Well that's nice,' she said, smiling at him. 'It takes two to tango.'

But then he looked from her plump face to her swollen belly, and his expression changed from surprise to horror. 'Jesus on a bicycle!' he said. 'You're pregnant.'

She was alarmed and afraid. It was going wrong. Oh God! What could she say? She tried to pretty her way out of it. 'Congratulations would be nice,' she said and pouted at him, that being the most successful trick she could think of.

It didn't work this time. He was reeling with shock, turning away from her, pacing the room in agitation. 'Congratulations?' he shouted. 'Have you gone out of your head? It's nothing to be congratulated about. Whose is it?'

'Don't be silly Pete,' she said, standing where she was but still smiling at him brightly. 'Whose do you think it is?'

'Well not mine,' he blazed. 'I never run risks. Never. You know that. Did you forget to take the pill? Is that it? Oh Ellie! You fucking idiot.'

She remembered that the phone was still off the hook and listening to every shouted word. 'Just a minute,' she said, and went to deal with it. 'Hello. Monica? Pete's home... Oh! You heard... Yes he is. You know what a paddy he gets into. Got carved up on the way here apparently... I'll ring you back.' Then she turned to face her lover. If he was going to make a scene the sooner he got it over with the better. 'Now,' she said; 'let's make one thing clear. I didn't forget to take the pill. I came off it.'

He was aghast. 'You mean deliberately?'

She was cornered now and nothing else would do except the truth. 'I mean deliberately,' she said. 'I did it once before, for a month, to see what would happen. And nothing did. So I tried it again.'

He threw his hands in the air in theatrical

250

despair. 'Fucking madness!' he said. 'Total fucking madness.'

'No it wasn't. I wanted a baby. I've wanted one
for years. I just didn't think it would happen.'

'You didn't want a baby. Don't talk such
bollocks.'

'I did. I do.'

His face was suffused with anger. 'You should
have told me.'

'I tried to. Only you wouldn't give me the
chance. I kept saying, "I want a baby", and you
kept saying, "No you don't".'

'You should have told me,' he corrected, 'the
minute you came off the pill. That's what you
should have told me. I can't believe this. It's so
fucking underhand.'

'It wasn't underhand,' she said, pouting in
earnest now because his words were stinging. 'I
was going to tell you. But you went away. You
wouldn't listen.'

'I'd have listened if you'd said, "I'm coming off
the pill." I'd have listened to that right enough.
You realise what you've done?'

'I've got pregnant,' she said, facing him boldly.
'And I know you're cross but I'm glad.'

'You played Russian roulette with my sperm,'
he said. 'You stole my sperm. And that's a
criminal offence. I could take you to court. There
was a case in the States while I was there. Exactly
the same. She came off the pill and didn't tell
him and he sued her for half a million fucking
dollars.'

'Oh how ridiculous,' she said frightened by the
very thought of a court case. 'I suppose I held

251

you down and forced you, is that it? Chained you to the bedpost. Oh come on, Pete. I didn't steal anything. You gave it to me. Willingly as I recall. Very very willingly.'

'I gave it for fun,' he said furiously. 'That's what we agreed it was for. Not to make a fucking baby. We're not cut out to be parents. Parents are bad news. Oh, how could you be such a fucking idiot? We must get you booked in to a good clinic. The Marlborough maybe.'

'I'm booked.'

'Thank God for that. When are they going to do it?'

'Easter,' she said. 'It's all planned.'

'But that's months off.'

'Four and a half months, to be precise. I'm half-way there.'

'We are talking about an abortion?'

She was horrified. 'No we are not. I'm not having an abortion.'

'Oh for chrissake Ellie, you're not going through with it. You can't. Think what it'll do to your career. To us. We're not cut out to be parents. Just get rid of it. I'll foot the bill.'

She turned away from him, feeling sick with misery, her heart trembling in the most alarming way, the baby's foot ticking in her belly. 'You sound just like my rotten mother,' she said. 'That's all she could say. Get rid of it. You can't have a baby and a career. Well let me tell you something. This is my body and my baby and if I want to have it, I shall have it.' And she put her hand over the spot where baby's tremulous foot was kicking and rubbed it gently. 'Don't you worry my darling,' she said to it. 'I won't let anyone hurt you.'

Her complacency was so infuriating he couldn't bear to be with her another second. 'You're fucking mental,' he roared. 'I'm off home.' And he strode out, banging the door behind him.

She was perfectly calm, standing in the middle of her white room, stroking the tiny throbbing feet under her hand, surprising herself by how sensible she was being. 'Don't worry,' she said to the baby. 'I'll look after you. Your Daddy and your Nan can be as foul as they like, but you've got me. You're going to have the best of everything. Designer clothes. A trip to Disneyland. Your own PC. I won't let anything beastly happen to you, I promise. I'll find you the best au pair in the world.' Then she began to cry.

Pete was half way down the King's Road before he remembered that he couldn't go home. For a few seconds he was completely thrown, not knowing where to go but so enmeshed in traffic that he had to keep driving. Not to Staggers' or he'd have to tell him he'd quarrelled with Ellie, and he'd prefer that to be a secret. Carolyn was a possibility but she was too clingy. Susie What's-her-face was too thick. If Mrs M had still been living in Fulham he could have gone there. She'd have taken him in, no questions asked, the way she did when the God-awful parents cut off to India and left him behind. But it was no good thinking of her. She was too far away and he'd got a business appointment at nine o'clock tomorrow morning.

Then, with the clarity of sudden sunshine he thought of Lucy. Dear old Lucy. Always there, always loving, just like her mother. She might be just the one. He took a right turn and headed for the Albert Bridge.

Lucy was in the bathroom washing her hair. She'd been at work until seven o'clock that evening and had come home tired and sweaty and aching to be clean again. When Helen called up to her that she had a visitor, she wasn't pleased to be interrupted.

'Who is it?' she called back.

'Pete,' his voice answered her.

She ran from the bathroom, water cascading from her wet hair, to lean over the banisters and see him, at once and for herself. 'What are you doing here?'

He stood in her blue and cream hall, and smiled his lovely slow smile straight into her eyes. He was so devastatingly handsome it made her heart beat quicker just to look at him. 'Luce!' he said. 'You don't know how good it is to see you.'

'I'll just get a towel,' she said. 'Go through into the kitchen. I won't be a jiff.'

By the time her hair was rinsed and combed, he'd settled into the kitchen and was entertaining Helen and Tina with tales of his adventures in the Big Apple. 'And then guess what he did. Took the card, dropped it in the sink, for Chrissake, and spewed up all over it. Vice president of the company. Can you credit it?'

The two girls were listening avidly. 'Ugh!' they said. 'How revolting! You must have been livid.'

254

'You get used to it,' he told them casually, and turned as Lucy walked in. 'So how's my best girl? You look absolutely fucking gorgeous.'

'I feel absolutely fucking knackered.'

'No,' he said, 'I mean it. I've never seen you look so good.'

'How's my sister?'

'Your sister,' he said, 'has turned me out of house and home. I'm an orphan of the storm come to fling myself on your tender mercy.'

She laughed at that, the way she'd laughed when they were all young together and he'd clowned to entertain them. 'Don't muck about.'

He was suddenly and disarmingly serious. 'I'm not mucking about my lovely Lucy. I only wish I were. I've let my house to a rich American. Fucking inconvenient but it's a sound business move. Had to be done. I thought I could stay with your precious sister for a week or two. Home from home, sort of thing. Be a live-in lover for once. But no. She's shown me the door. Doesn't want anything to do with me, so she says. She can be bloody hard when she likes. So there you are. I've got nowhere to lay my poor old weary head.'

'And you'd like to stay here,' Lucy said. 'Is that it?' There was something unreal about this conversation, something she couldn't quite believe, although she yearned to accept it. After all these years wishing he'd leave Ellie and turn to her, he was doing just that, suddenly, in the middle of an ordinary evening, when she wasn't expecting it. It was a dream.

'Could I?' he said, looking at her with such dazzling intensity that she would have given him

255

anything, just to prolong the look. Oh those blue, blue eyes, those white teeth, that handsome, sunny face. He was like Phoebus Apollo, filling the room with warmth and sunshine, a god of love and hope and all things beautiful, her dearest, dearest Pete, the only man she'd ever wanted, and he was here, turning to her for help, calling her 'my lovely Lucy' as though he meant it.

'You'll have to sleep on the sofa,' she said, annoyed because her voice sounded so flat and practical. 'There's nowhere else.' Except my bed. Oh God! Except my bed. Will you want to sleep there or are you just a refugee?

'You're a star,' he said. And caught her hands, lifting them to his lips to kiss them. 'I knew I could depend on you.'

He was turning her on so strongly she was afraid she would blush and they would all notice. 'You know me!' she said lightly. 'Always the friend in need.'

'Do I?' he asked earnestly, still holding her hands. 'Do I really? Or are there hidden depths?'

'Well I'm off out,' Tina announced, 'or the others'll go on without me.'

He turned to charm her too, sensing the disapproval in her voice. 'I'm holding you up,' he apologised. 'I've chosen a bad time. You've got places to go. Naturally.'

'Yes,' Tina told him, standing so that she could look down at him. It irritated her to see him coming on so strong to Lucy, poor cow. You might be Mr almighty TV ad, she thought, but you're not the only pebble on the beach. 'We have. Haven't we Helen? Lucy?'

Helen was going out too and said so. But Lucy shrugged.

'My social life's shot to ribbons,' she admitted. 'I'm always at work.'

'You're not working now,' he pointed out. 'I tell you what. Let me wine and dine you. It's the least I can do after barging in like this. What d'you say? I know just the place.' And he took out his mobile to book a table. 'Hi there. Peppi?... Yes it's me. Look, can you find me something special?... Tonight, for two?... Great! You're a star. We'll be there in an hour.'

It was a magical evening and luxurious in every way.

'We'll take a taxi,' he said, when she was dressed and ready, 'then we can drink as much as we like. Right?' So they began their evening sitting side by side in the leathery darkness of a black cab, with his arm draped casually along the back of the seat within two embracing inches of her shoulders while the lights of the city roads dazzled past them. Then came a star-struck arrival at the restaurant with all the other diners looking at them with admiration and recognising him. 'Take no notice. It happens all the time.' Then champagne and a meal served at a table where pink candles warmed their faces, and there were flowers scenting the air between them, and food was served that she ate and barely noticed and she drank so much champagne that she was soon giddy and giggling.

They talked and talked, of days in the garden at Fulham, of the daft games they'd played and the

257

dreams they'd shared, of how wonderful her mother had been to take him in when he was left behind by the 'obnoxious parents'.

'Is that how you still see them?' she asked, moved to sympathy by the bitterness on his face.

'Yep,' he said. 'Beyond the pale, the pair of 'em. More interested in themselves than their own son. "We're off to India," for fuck's sake! You don't just walk out on your own son.'

Champagne was swimming her thoughts in and out of focus but she wondered whether Ellie's baby would be a son and how he would feel about that. But he was speaking again, leaning across the table to catch her hand, gazing at her with that intense look of his. She was so dizzy with rising desire that she couldn't speak. I am here, she thought. Here with you. My dearest dearest Pete.

'Now where?' he said, smiling into her eyes. 'How about a club?'

It was past three in the morning before they finally decided to call a cab and go home and this time as they settled into their seats, he pulled her into his arms and kissed her long and expertly. 'Oh my little Lucy!' he murmured into her hair. 'Why has it taken us so long?'

The house was dark and very quiet, her flatmates in bed and either happily occupied or asleep.

'I haven't really got to sleep on the sofa have I?' he asked, one arm amorously about her waist.

'It's only a three-foot bed,' she warned.

'Ah, but it's got you in it,' he said.

So she took him to her bed and they were both

richly rewarded by lovemaking better than he'd expected or she could ever have hoped for. He was her sister's lover and the baby's father and she knew, in the reasonable depths of her mind, that her mother wouldn't approve, that Ellie would be monstrously upset, that it probably wouldn't last, but she didn't care. He was here, in her bed, the scent of his skin in her nostrils, his tender hands caressing her nipples, his long splendid legs wound about hers, his beautiful mouth kissing and kissing. If she had no more than this one magical, passionate extraordinary night it would be enough.

CHAPTER 18

When Gwen slipped her two applications into the post box on Thursday morning she was surprised to realise that she was feeling adventurous. The thought of what Ellie would do with that poor baby still stuck in her mind like a burr, and she was grieved to think how much she'd hurt Jeff's pride by refusing his proposal, but nothing dimmed her optimism.

She walked home slowly, wondering how long it would be before she had a reply. Ages probably because there were bound to be scores of applications to sort through. She would have to be patient. But as it turned out the phone call came the very next morning.

'My name's Mrs Fenchurch,' the caller said. 'I'm the deputy head at Little Marsden Primary. About your application for the post of school secretary here.'

That was quick, Gwen thought. And as an answer seemed to be expected she said, 'Yes?'

'Would you be free to come for interview today?'

Quicker and quicker. 'Today?'

'I know it's short notice,' 'Mrs Fenchurch said, 'but we're very keen to appoint. Our previous school secretary retired at the end of the summer term and we haven't had a proper secretary since, only temps, and Christmas is rushing down on us like a steam train.'

Gwen liked the sound of that sort of Christmas. It was just what she needed. 'No, that's fine,' she said.

So they arranged that she would arrive at two o'clock and that Mrs Fenchurch would meet her 'at reception'.

'And I thought jobs were hard to come by,' Gwen said to the cat as she put down the phone. It was rather exciting. Things happen so quickly here, she thought. I spend years in Fulham just festering along doing nothing, and now I rush from one thing to another, first the tower and then meeting Jeff and now Little Marsden Primary School. I can't wait to see what it'll be like.

It was a bungalow school built of brick and flint in what she now recognised as the old Sussex style with tall gabled windows at each end and a porched entrance in the middle, and it stood in considerable grounds, with a playing field to one side and a garden and a playground to the other. There was someone waiting for her in reception, just as she'd been promised, a small slender woman with straight greying hair cut very short and a huge pair of round red-rimmed glasses.

She stepped forward at once to shake Gwen's hand and introduce herself, this time as Beatrice Fenchurch. 'We're not a very big school, as you can see,' she said, as she led Gwen into the building. 'There are eleven classes besides the reception class, sometimes two a year, sometimes one, so we have two huts. But then don't we all these days?'

261

They walked along a corridor hung with children's bold pictures and a line of posters about birds and wild flowers, and glanced in at the classrooms to left and right. There seemed to be hordes of children wherever Gwen looked, all of them in bright red jerseys and most of them sitting at low tables, some reading, some writing, some painting with huge brushes, some with their hands in the air offering answers, just as she remembered from the time when Lucy and Ellie were at primary school. They passed an inner hall where there were shelves full of brightly coloured books and a table holding a display of geometrical shapes. There were three small children sitting at one end of the hall reading aloud to a young woman in a long denim skirt and a chunky jersey. She looked up and smiled at her visitor and Mrs Fenchurch said, 'This is Kim. She's one of our classroom assistants.' And turned to ask her briefly, 'Everything all right?'

It's a friendly place, Gwen thought, as she and the deputy progressed. There's a happy buzz about it. I'd like to work here.

They'd reached a door labelled Staff Room. 'If you'll just wait in here,' Mrs Fenchurch said, 'I'll tell Mr Carter you've arrived.'

Now I shall meet the other applicants, Gwen thought, as she walked into the room. But there was nobody there, just an untidy circle of easy chairs, four notice boards covered in paper and a row of tables scattered with piles of exercise books and dirty coffee cups. Being asked to wait made her feel nervous so she walked to the window and looked out at the playing field and the distant roofs of the village. And after five minutes or so, Mrs Fenchurch returned to say that the headmaster was ready to see her. 'Where are the other candidates?' she asked, as they walked out into the corridor again.

'They're not here today,' Mrs Fenchurch said. 'We wanted to see you first.'

Well, well, well, Gwen thought. So I'm the pick of the bunch. How about that? And she walked into the headmaster's study feeling so confident that she actually smiled at him and held out her hand to greet him as he rose from his seat.

He introduced the other two people in the room. 'Mr Coles our chairman of governors, Mrs Fenchurch, our deputy head, whom you've met already.' In his brown suit and badly knotted tie, there was an untidy diffidence about him that Gwen found rather warming. He's a medium man, she thought, medium height, medium age. I'll bet he's middle of the road in everything.

But he ran a searching interview and as it progressed she saw that there was more to him than met the eye. He wanted to know her typing speeds, if she could use a word processor and run a filing system, if she could withstand the pace of a school. 'It's non-stop. I ought to warn you. There'll be times when you'll be doing three things at once.' And finally and most particularly, how much accounting she'd done.

'We have to keep to a very tight budget here,' he said, 'or we lose Brownie points. I gather you did the accounts for a shop.'

She told him what had been involved. 'The boss hated doing the accounts, so after a while I took the whole thing over, invoices, orders, returns, stock checks. It was easier that way.'

'So you don't mind taking responsibility.'

'I enjoy it.'

He smiled. 'You'll get plenty of it here,' he said. 'It's a demanding job.'

'That's the sort I'm looking for,' she told him. 'I was in and out of primary schools when my children were young and the secretaries always seemed to be on the go.'

He paused, considered, looked down at the paper on the desk before him. 'Well then, are there any questions you would like to ask me?'

She felt she could be frank with him. 'Are there any new duties that have come in recently that I wouldn't know about and we haven't mentioned?'

'There's the Ritalin kids,' Mrs Fenchurch said. 'The secretary usually looks after their medication. You know about Ritalin kids I expect.'

'No. I'm sorry. I don't.'

'They're massively hyperactive,' Mr Carter explained. 'If they weren't on Ritalin they'd be a real problem. Most of them are OK on one dose a day, but some need topping up and those are the ones you'd be responsible for. They bring their medication to the office and you keep it and give it to them when they need it. They're usually quite good about it. They know they need calming down.'

It sounds horrible, Gwen thought, like something from a sci-fi film. Fancy having a child who had to be perpetually calmed down by drugs. But there was bound to be a downside to the job and she felt she could cope with this one. 'Thank you for telling me,' she said.

'It shouldn't be a problem,' Mrs Fenchurch said. 'Not once you know the kids.'

They're going to offer this to me, Gwen thought. She's talking as though they already have. And she looked at Mr Carter.

'I have to discuss this with my colleagues,' he told her seriously, 'as you will appreciate. So if you wouldn't mind waiting?'

It took them a minute and a half. She timed them. And then she was recalled and offered the position, 'if you would care to accept it.'

She would love to.

'Splendid,' Mr Carter said. 'When could you start?'

'When would you want me to start?'

He grinned at her. 'How about Monday?'

'This Monday?'

'As ever is.'

So Monday was agreed upon. It had all been so quick she could hardly believe it. I shall have to get my domestic life organised, she thought, as she drove back through the peninsula towards the island. Late afternoon appointments for Jet for a start and I shall have to do my week's shopping on Friday evening now and fit the housework in as and when, the way I did when I was at the shop. And I'll have to tell Jeff and the girls. The thought of telling Jeff made her quail a little so she decided to tackle Lucy first because she'd take it best. I'll wait till she's home from work, she thought, as she pulled up outside the tower, and then I'll ring.

She waited until eight o'clock. But there was no answer, only a taped message which was a disappointment. So she left her name and her love and said she had some good news and that she'd ring back later. And tried again after supper. But it was still the answerphone. And there was no answer on Saturday morning either nor in the afternoon. Off for the weekend somewhere, she thought, as she got ready for her dinner at the Lobster Pot. I shall have to try and catch her during the week. It was a nuisance because it meant she'd have to break the news to Jeff without the benefit of a trial run.

Luckily he seemed to be in a good humour, full of news about his proposed golf course, which he talked about all through the first course and well into the second. 'I've seen the plans and it's looking good. Kit's really enthusiastic. Could be a winner if we put our backs into it. Might even be up and running by the summer.'

'I'm glad to hear it,' she said, eating her chocolate mousse and thinking, at least while he's happy about this he's not taking me to task for turning him down.

'Old Mr Rossi's come down,' he said, as he finished his apple and apricot tart. 'Saw him this afternoon. Wants to buy another parcel of land for four more caravans. Says he's going to let two of them to a couple of local families for the winter.'

Gwen tried to show an interest, although she was growing steadily more apprehensive as the meal progressed. 'Oh yes?'

'I've pointed out the risks, but he reckons he

266

knows what he's doing. Says they'll be caretakers.'

'Well they could be, I suppose.'

'Not that lot,' he said with feeling. 'They'll trash the place. They're cousins to your cat-torturer, Dion. Or half cousins or something. I wouldn't touch 'em with a bargepole. Still it's his lookout. As long as he pays the ground rent it's up to him what he does with the caravans. So what have you been doing with yourself?'

She looked straight at him and told him quickly before she could lose her nerve. 'I've got a job.'

He was instantly massive with anger, his face realigned into a completely different shape, cheeks elongated, mouth taut, eyebrows knitted, eyes glaring. 'A what?'

'A job,' she said, keeping her voice steady with an effort. 'School secretary at Little Marsden. I start on Monday.'

He looked at her with undisguised anger. 'What do you want to go and do a thing like that for?'

'Because you advised me to.'

'I did not. As I recall I asked you to marry me.' The firelight was painting curves of flame along the shining sides of her wine glass and her breath was making the candles flicker and smoke. It was turning him on to look at her. Which was bloody unfair. 'As I recall you turned me down.'

'As I recall,' she countered, 'you said I needed something to occupy me or I'd sit at home and brood and give in to Ellie.'

'I made you a bloody good offer,' he said, 'and you're telling me you turned it all down to go and work in some crummy school. It's beyond belief. A school secretary, for crying out loud! You're out of your head.'

She sighed. 'I knew you'd be cross.'

'Cross?' he said. 'I'm gob-smacked.'

She leaned across the table to touch his hand, her face placatory. 'I didn't mean to hurt you. You must believe that. It's just I've got to live my life my own way. I'm sorry but that's how it is.'

'Even if it means turning your back on me.'

'I'm not turning my back on you.'

'That's sure as hell what it feels like.'

'I'm not. Really. It's just that I don't want to be a wife. I want things to go on as they are.'

He was growling. 'Fat chance of that now.'

The coffee arrived but it didn't comfort either of them. He was still massive with disapproval and irritation.

'I'll take you home,' he said, as he signed the bill. 'I shan't stop.'

She felt she was being abandoned but she managed to stay calm. There was nothing to be gained by arguing. 'No.'

'I've got things to attend to.'

'Yes.'

It was as if they had frozen one another out, broken all contact, become strangers. He drove back to the tower without saying another word to her, brooding over the wheel, and when they'd walked to her door, he turned on his heel as soon as her key was in the lock, grumbled, 'Well good night then,' and was gone into the darkness.

She didn't cry until she was indoors and the lights were lit and the curtains drawn. But then she sank into the sofa and wept with abandon, because that was what it was. We had such a good thing going, she thought, it can't just be over. Not like this. Not so quickly. Jet crept into her lap, clumsy in her cardboard collar, eager to be stroked and comforted.

'We all need loving, don't we cat,' she said. 'And now I've thrown my chance away.' Even to think of it made her bleak. This is what comes of being selfish, she thought. First I upset Ellie and then I ruin my love affair. And I really didn't mean to. I don't know how I could have been so silly. Still it's no good crying over spilt milk I've done it now and it's my fault and I shall have to face up to it. Just as well I've got a job to go to. But she was so cast down she wasn't even sure about that.

Monday morning was dispiritingly cold. Long dank clouds of sea mist rolled off the beach to envelop the tower, and the sea was half hidden and stone grey. Typical November, Gwen thought, as she set off for Little Marsden. Or a neat example of the poetic fallacy.

But once she reached the school she was enveloped by warmth and activity and cheered up at once. The work was too demanding to leave her time to brood. She took two phone calls before she'd had a chance to take off her cape, both from parents reporting that their children would be absent, and after that the day bowled her along. Class monitors, all proudly badged, arrived to collect the registers, the phone rang endlessly, a mound of mail was delivered and the first of her Ritalin kids arrived shyly at her window to ask for his top-up.

'You're new ain'tcher Miss,' he said. 'Are you

269

gonna stay?'

'Oh yes,' she reassured him. 'You won't get rid of me for a long long time. I'm a fixture.' And by the end of the afternoon she really felt she was. She and Mr Carter had dealt with all the mail and caught up with a pile that had been outstanding since the middle of the previous week, she'd eaten sandwiches at her desk and drunk so many cups of tea it was a wonder she wasn't waterlogged, and she'd made a start on the filing.

'How d'you get on?' Beatrice Fenchurch asked, as they were putting on their coats in the staff cloakroom.

Gwen grimaced. 'It's been quite a day.'

The deputy grinned. 'We did warn you.'

But it was a rich life even if it was fraught. By the end of the first week she knew all the monitors by name, had befriended some of the teachers and quite a lot of the children and was running off carol sheets for the nativity play. By the middle of the second, she'd seen a child bawled out for misbehaving, had heard two of the women teachers yelling at one another because they'd booked the hall at the same time and was beginning to understand the tensions inherent in school life. That Thursday Jet had her bandages and collar removed and was signed off as perfectly recovered. And by Friday Gwen had begun to pace her new life and managed to take time to stand in the hall and listen to the sixth year singing their special carol, warmed by the pride of their teacher and the innocent passion of their voices.

'I love Christmas,' the teacher said. He was

270

young and scruffy and obviously enjoying himself. 'Don't you?'

'When it's like this,' Gwen told him. 'Yes I do.'

In fact it was only the weekends that were difficult and that was only to be expected. She could keep herself busy on Saturday morning and for most of the afternoon by shopping and catching up with the housework but the evenings were lonely. She couldn't deny it.

By that second Saturday she'd phoned Lucy so often she'd lost count of the times, but all she ever got was the answerphone and it was beginning to dawn on her that her daughter had either gone away for a long holiday or was deliberately making herself unavailable, which was worrying. Has she been talking to Ellie? Is that it? Are they both cross with me now? In the normal course of events she would have phoned Ellie to find out what was happening, but that was out of the question because Ellie was obviously still angry or she'd have been in touch. She'd have liked to have phoned Jeff, but that wasn't possible either after the way they'd parted. If either of them were to make the first approach it had to be him. She had some pride.

So the days passed and there were no calls and no letters and the second weekend crawled by as slowly and silently as the first. There was nothing to do on a dark evening in her tower except listen to the radio or watch TV and there was nothing on the bookshelves that she wanted to read. Not even Dotty's books on astrology. But at least they gave her an idea.

I'll look up Ellie's birth chart, she decided, and

see if that can tell me anything about the mess we're in. Even if it doesn't, it might be interesting.

She keyed in the details, date, time and place of birth, and waited for revelation. And there it was. Leo in the ascendant. Of course. Leo to give her confidence and self-importance, the golden child with her beautiful sunny face and that mane of thick fair hair, the child born to succeed. Impatient and imperious. Yes. Self-centred. Yes, I'm afraid so. Determined. Very definitely. Then she noticed that the fifth house, which she now knew was the house that influences your relationship with your children, was empty of any planets at all and that seemed a very ominous sign. However, she'd read enough of Dotty's books to know that there were other influences on the houses besides the planets, so she took down the pile from the shelves and set about finding out what they were.

It was a fascinating study, but not because of what she found out about Ellie or her horoscope. In fact after ten minutes she'd forgotten all about them, for what she discovered was a series of annotations in Dotty's neat handwriting, written at the head and foot of nearly every page and sometimes all along the margins too. The first was above the rather daunting statement that what the moon foretold would happen whether you would or no. *True*, she'd written, *as I know. My death swims upon me fast and I must endure it, whether I will or no.* Then she'd crossed out the word *endure* and written *accept* instead.

What courage she had, Gwen thought, and

turned the page.

This time the relevant passage had been underlined in red. *This conjunction marks a time for farewells, for putting your house in order and settling your affairs.* And *How can I bear this?* she had written at the top of the page. *I must say goodbye to my boys. It will break my heart and if I do not do it well it may break theirs. I can see no strength here for me to draw upon. Where can I find strength? It slips from me hour by hour.* But at the foot of the page she'd written, *Come on Dorothy. Show some spunk. Look with both eyes. There is always good as well as bad.* And on the next page she seemed to have found it, for she'd underlined the words, *There is comfort in acceptance, even if what is accepted is adversity.*

Gwen ached with admiration. To be able to write like that when you're dying of cancer, she thought, with such concern for other people, and so little self-pity. Gordon couldn't have done it. She remembered his daily complaint. 'Why me? What did I ever do to deserve this?' and how cantankerous and self-centred he became. And she yearned towards this unknown woman, wishing she could have met her. And read on.

'Jeff is so good to me,' the next entry said. 'He does everything for me now. Three score years and ten would not be enough to repay his tenderness.' She's right, Gwen thought. He is tender. And now I've lost him. Haven't I?

Three pages on, Dotty had underlined the words, 'a time of contrasts, strength and weakness, advance and retreat,' and had written below them. 'Pain and joy. When the pain comes there

273

is nothing but pain, when it recedes life is so good. Oh my darling Jeff.'

At that point Gwen began to weep but she went on reading, following the comments from page to page. She was still sitting with the book in her lap when there was a knock at the door. She put down the book, flicked the tears from her eyes and went to see who was there.

It was Jeff, bulky in his Barbour and looking very ill at ease. But his expression changed to concern when he saw her face. 'What's up?' he asked. 'Is something the matter?'

'No, no,' she said. 'Come in. It's just – something I've been reading.'

He strode into the room. And saw the screen.

'It's not those damned charts again?'

'No,' she said. 'Actually I've been getting to know your wife. Did you know she'd written notes in these books?'

This wasn't the sort of answer he expected but he was glad of the neutrality she'd offered and made the most of it. 'She left notes all over the house,' he said. 'Reminders of things she had to do. Messages for me when she went out.'

'These are rather particular,' Gwen told him, picking up the book. 'They're a sort of diary, following her last illness. She was a very brave woman.'

He took off his coat, slung it over the back of a chair and sat down on the empty sofa, facing her. 'She was,' he said. Were they on safe ground? Could they talk? It felt possible.

'I wish I could have known her,' Gwen said.

He relaxed into a smile. 'You'd have got on

274

well,' he told her. 'In many ways you're two of a kind. Only she wasn't a fighter. I wish she had been. I kept wanting her to fight the cancer. But she wouldn't. She said she had to let it happen. Would keep telling me it was easier to go along with it. I suppose it wasn't in her nature. She was a supporter.'

'Yes,' Gwen said. 'You can see that. It comes through in all sorts of things. Worrying about you. And your sons.'

'Mind you,' he said, 'she gave me a black eye once.'

That was a surprise. 'I can't believe that.'

'It's true. Took a swing at me when we were in the middle of a row. Caught me just under the eye. A real shiner.'

'Did you row?'

'Course,' he said. Now they must face their own division. 'All couples row. Unless they're dead from the neck down or they don't give a damn for one another. They row and then they make up. Usually.'

'I'm sorry I upset you,' she said.

'I'm sorry I took it so badly. That's what I came to say.'

'Are we making up?'

'I hope so,' he said seriously. 'Look, I know it's raining cats and dogs, but would you like to go to the Lobster Pot?'

'Yes,' she said, putting the book on the table. 'I'd like that very much.'

It was a deliberately happy evening because they were both determined to make it so and although deliberation stifled their spontaneity it smoothed away any possible awkwardness. Gwen didn't mention her job, he didn't mention his proposal, and both of them took care not to say anything that would remind them of their quarrel. At the end of the evening they splashed back over the causeway, which was now partially under water, and arrived wet and happy in the shelter of her porch, both of them feeling that the evening had been an achievement.

'Am I to stay the night?' he hoped.

'Oh I think so, don't you?' she said, taking care to treat the offer lightly. 'I can't have you drowning on my doorstep.'

At that he kissed her at last. 'Thank God for the rain,' he said.

CHAPTER 19

Lucy had been in a state of such rapturous happiness since Pete moved into her life, that she hardly noticed anything or anyone else. At work she crunched figures automatically, careless of whether they were right or wrong, at home she lived for the moment when he would come home and consequently forgot her bills, left letters unanswered and didn't hear the phone. Each new day was the extension of a miracle, proof that the love she'd yearned for was possible, happening, continuing. Occasionally minor irritations would push past into her contentment. The insistent pulse of red light on her answerphone was one of them, especially when the call minder revealed that it was her mother who was ringing. Then she felt guilty because she knew she ought to return the call, and worse when she didn't do it.

Once or twice she was afraid that it would be Eleanor on the line and wondered how on earth she would answer her, but Eleanor didn't ring and, after a while, she decided not to worry about it. There were too many other and delightful events to take her attention.

On their third evening she asked Pete what he would do if Eleanor arrived at the same place and saw them.

The question didn't faze him at all. 'Ask her to join us, I expect. We're all grown up.'

He's so cool, she thought, admiring him. It's fantastic. But then everything about her new life was fantastic. Or almost everything. She was irritated when he hogged the bathroom and filled the wardrobe with his clothes and made such a fuss over his shoes but she excused him because she knew how important it was for him to look his best in public; it annoyed her that he didn't always tell her when he would be late home but she made allowances because he had such a busy schedule and she knew he was pushing to be elected to the board; and she didn't really like his habit of leaving dirty clothes all over the place for her to gather up and launder, but forgave him because that was Eleanor's fault. She should have had him better house-trained.

But for the most part she was simply and carelessly happy, content to live from one pleasure to the next – red roses delivered to their table, chocolates on her pillow, rich meals, gallons of champagne, frequent and delectable sex – to enjoy her new life and not ask too many questions.

Which was how she suddenly found herself in the middle of a phone call with her sister, just when she least expected it. It was Wednesday evening and she and Pete were getting ready for a meal at Quanto's, he brushing his hair and admiring his reflection at her dressing table, she sitting on the bed applying her second layer of mascara. The call came through on her mobile, which was lying on the duvet beside her, and she was so sure that only business colleagues would use that number that she picked it up and answered it without thought.

'Hi there,' Eleanor said brightly. 'Long time no see. How are you?'

It took a few seconds for Lucy to recover from the surprise and she had to cough to get her voice under control. 'Too much work,' she said, calming herself by putting her mascara away and closing her mirror. 'You know how it is.'

'So what's new?' Eleanor sympathised. 'They're running me ragged too.'

'How are you? Apart from that.'

'Fit as a flea. No problems. Except... Have you heard from Mum?'

'Well no. I mean, she's rung me, several times, actually, but I've been so rushed I haven't had time to ring back. I feel a bit guilty about it to tell the truth.'

'Well don't,' Eleanor said. 'She doesn't deserve it. She's been absolutely foul to me.' And told her tale in full and dramatic detail. 'Refusing her own daughter! It's just too abysmal. Don't you think so?'

Put on the spot, Lucy didn't know how to respond. 'I can't say I'm surprised,' she ventured. 'I mean, she's really settled into that tower of hers.'

'Well yes, I know she has, but it wouldn't hurt her to leave it for a few days. I mean, it's not as if I'm asking her to stay in London forever. It's only during the week, for fuck's sake. She ought to be able to manage that. I am her daughter.'

'Yes,' Lucy said and mouthed 'Ellie' at Pete who had raised his eyebrows in query.

'It's so selfish,' Ellie went on. 'I mean what else has she got to do with her life? It's not as if she's holding down a job or anything. I'd have understood that. But no. She just won't help me. Refused point fucking blank. Said the most dreadful things to me. "You can't have a baby and a career. Get rid of it." I mean, it's not as if I've got a choice. I'm over half way now. It's kicking all the time. I mean you can't get rid of a baby that's kicking. It wouldn't be natural.'

'I'm ever so sorry, Ellie,' Lucy said struggling to be sympathetic but non-committal. 'It must be awful.'

'It's not your fault,' Eleanor said warmly. 'You haven't been vile. You're the best friend I've got.'

Lucy squirmed with guilt, looking over her shoulder to where Pete was putting on his jacket and admiring himself in the mirror. 'I wish I could do something to help you,' she said. 'What will you do now?'

'Find an au pair, I expect,' her sister said. 'Or a nanny. I've got some addresses. It won't be the same for it as its grandmother, poor little thing, but beggars can't be choosers. You haven't seen Pete about anywhere have you?'

Even though she'd been holding herself ready for it, the question made Lucy feel afraid and ashamed. She looked across the room to where he stood, smoothing his hair, adjusting his tie, smiling at her through the mirror. And mouthed at him again, 'She wants to know where you are.'

He shook his head and frowned to urge her to silence, and she nodded at him before she answered. 'He's back then.'

'Been back a fortnight,' Ellie said and went on, 'up to his ears in some business deal,' feeling she had to explain or Lucy would wonder why she

280

was asking. 'I suppose I could call him at work. It's just I don't like to ring his mobile. He's a bit touchy about it.' And then as Lucy listened but didn't answer, she went on again, speaking in her lightest, brightest way, 'We had words. Nothing serious. You know the way we are. I thought he'd gone back to his flat but apparently not. Seems he's let it to some American couple. Quite nice actually. I've just rung them. Anyway, they've been re-directing his mail. I've got a stack of it here and he's bound to want it. So I thought I'd ask around and see if anyone knows where he is.'

'I can't help you,' Lucy said, trying to sound as though she meant it. But it shamed her to be devious.

Ellie sighed. 'Ah well. I've done my best. I shall just have to leave it. I'm off to Paris tomorrow, giving a presentation to Jean-Paul Renaldo. They're launching a new perfume. I'll ring you when I get back.'

'Take care,' Lucy urged and was relieved again to realise that she meant it.

Pete was standing before her, looking impossibly handsome. 'You're a star,' he said. 'Thanks.'

'We shall have to tell her in the end,' she warned. His insouciance was making her feel rather cross. It wouldn't hurt him to show some concern. 'I mean, she'll find out sooner or later. She's got your mail. Your Americans are re-directing it.'

He'd forgotten all about it. 'No problem,' he said easily. 'I'll send someone over to get it. Right? Are you ready?'

As she checked her handbag it occurred to Lucy

281

that now Ellie had finally phoned she wasn't reacting in the way she expected. For years she'd dreamed of how she would steal Pete away, of how he would turn to her and love her, of what a triumph it would be and how it would serve Ellie right and pay her back for all the years when she'd had everything her own way. It had all seemed so simple then, probably because she'd always accepted that it was totally impossible. Now reality was proving a great deal more complicated than her easy fantasy. For underneath all the pleasures, grumbling away like appendicitis, was the knowledge that she actually felt sorry for Ellie, left alone to bring up her baby with no one to help her, and sorry for herself because she was being underhand and selfish – and enjoying it..

'Don't you feel anything for this baby?' she asked as she eased into his BMW.

'Nope,' he said. 'It's her lookout, not mine. I don't want anything to do with it. I told you.'

'Yes. I know you did. But don't you want to know how she is?'

He slipped the car into gear, assuming his haughty expression, not wanting to be drawn in. 'Not particularly,' he said. 'She'll be all right. Don't worry about her. This is a big night. The last before the shareholders' meeting. I've got a lot of persuading to do.'

It was the first time she'd seen how uncaring he could be and it evaporated her happiness, for she knew he would be just as indifferent if she were the one who was pregnant. Poor Ellie, she thought. I know she should have told him she was coming off the pill, but she's paying a heavy price for it and it'll get worse when the baby's here. I hope she has a huge success in Paris. Something really mega.

'Food first,' he said as they walked into the restaurant. 'Then we're all going on.'

'We all?' she asked. 'I thought this was just you and me.'

'Good God no,' he smiled. 'Like I told you. This is business. This is when we wow the share-holders. Best foot forward. Big bright smile. That sort of thing.'

She was shrinking, appalled that she was expected to be on display, especially when she'd been expecting a romantic evening for two. 'How many shareholders?'

'Didn't count 'em,' he said, carelessly. 'Two or three. Don't worry. We'll have 'em eating out of our hands.'

There were over twenty and they descended on him en masse as soon as he set foot in the bar. He moved into public mode immediately, giving them his most dazzling smile, greeting them all individually as they shook hands. 'Great to see you.' 'How's the kids?' 'Did you get your cruise then Jerry?' 'This is my girlfriend, Lucy. Luce, this is Mr Tempest, one of our major share-holders.' Giving her a rapid eye-message that the man was to be buttered up.

It was a brilliant display, slick, showy and entirely artificial, like a well-rehearsed play. Even in her now rather jaundiced state Lucy couldn't help admiring it, although she noticed that for all their false bonhomie, the shareholders were a shrewd-eyed lot and were plainly estimating the size of the profit they could make from their takeover, even while they were talking to him. Except for one elderly lady who said she did so hope he would get a seat on the board 'Once all this business is settled. He's such a personable young man. Don't you think so my dear?'

Lucy agreed with her and did her best to make small talk with the others but it was very wearing and by the time her long evening was over and she and Pete were finally back in Battersea she was aching with exhaustion and, which was worse, her longstanding, unalloyed love for him was beginning to show signs of tarnish.

'That went well,' he said, flinging himself backwards on her bed. 'If they don't vote for this takeover after all this, I shall be very surprised. We made a good team. Don't you think so?'

'I wouldn't know,' she said, kicking off her shoes. 'It's not my scene.'

He was rosy with triumph. 'Come and kiss me,' he ordered.

She wasn't in the mood but she did her best to obey orders. And was then cross – with herself and him and the evening – because she didn't feel a thing.

She was still down when she woke next morning. He was already up and splashing about in her bathroom. 'Big day today,' he said, as he emerged, towel wrapped and glowing. 'Be a sweetie and bring my breakfast up will you?'

She wrapped her dressing gown around her as if she was shielding herself. 'If you want a tray, I'll put one out for you but you'll have to come down and collect it. I'm not running up and down stairs.'

He gave her his most glamorous smile. 'For me?' he coaxed.

'No time,' she told him and added rather cattily, 'I've got a big day too.'

It was a bad start and worse was to follow. As she walked into the kitchen, Tina was standing by the sink fluffing up her hair with both hands, looking thoughtful.

'Look,' she said, abruptly. 'I wasn't going to tell you till the end of the week, but I might as well now he's not here. I'm moving out.'

The news gave Lucy quite a shock because they'd bought the house between them, splitting the mortgage three ways, and the cost would be prohibitive if there were only two to share it. But she kept cool, sipped her tea and merely asked, 'When?' as though it wasn't important.

'Third week in December,' Tina said. 'If that's OK by you. It'll give you a month to find a replacement and for us to get the agreement sorted out and the mortgage and everything. My cousin's just got a flat in Kensington, and she wants me to share. So I thought I would. I mean, this place was OK for three of us but it's a squash with four. Even you've got to see that.'

'He's not permanent,' Lucy said, feeling she ought to defend him. 'He'll be back in his own flat in Chelsea in a month or two. This is only to tide him over.'

'Hum,' Tina said, raising her plucked eyebrows in disparaging disbelief. 'Well you'll see won't you? He's broken the ground rules, permanent or temporary. You remember the ground rules. No live-in lovers. It was the one thing we all agreed

285

on.' And when Lucy opened her mouth to defend him, she swept on. 'Anyway it's all academic now. I've said I'll go. If he does move out, you'll soon find someone else. Place like this.'

If she moves out, he can pay the mortgage, Lucy thought, feeling decidedly sour towards him. It's about time he made a contribution. But there wasn't time to say any more for at that moment Helen drifted back into the kitchen, yawning, with the day's post in her hand.

'Don't tell me,' Tina said, flicking her hair with her fingers again. 'More damn bills.'

'It's mostly junk,' Helen said, tossing the pile on the table. 'You've got a real one though Luce.'

It was from Neil Morrish.

'*Reporting as promised,*' he wrote. '*I have seen your mother several times during the last few days and you will be glad to know there have been no more incidents. The cat has been signed off and looks fine except for not having all its tail. The garden is now dug over and planted. Your mother is well and happy in her new job.*

We've had a lot of sea mist recently but apart from that the weather has been fair. It can be quite warm down here even in winter.

I don't suppose you will be coming down at this time of year but I might see you at Christmas. Your mother told me she is inviting you. Perhaps you would like to go to the theatre. They have some pretty good shows at Christmas time and I know how you like the theatre.

Anyway must rush. I am on duty in twenty-two minutes.

Regards,
Neil, your neighbourhood copper.

She was filled with a surge of unexpected

286

affection towards him. He's honest, she thought, and unassuming and uncomplicated. If he gives you a promise he keeps it. I shall write straight back and thank him. But then she digested what he'd told her and was alarmed. What new job? she thought. She never said anything about a job. And what's all this about inviting me down for Christmas? I can't go there for Christmas. She'll invite Ellie too. If she hasn't already. And then what will happen? It'll all come out and there'll be such a row. I'd better phone her and make some excuse. She couldn't think what it would be – but something.

'I'm off then,' Pete announced, materialising beside her, flamboyant in his best Gieves and Hawkes suit. 'Wish me luck!'

'I shouldn't think you'll need it after last night,' she said.

'Don't you believe it,' he told her seriously. 'You can dot every I and cross every T and you still need luck, especially when it comes to a vote.' He gave her a far too mechanical kiss, took a swig from her teacup and left.

Gwen was chopping potatoes and onions for a soup when the phone rang. She'd gone shopping in Sainsbury's on her way back from school that afternoon and the variety of potatoes on the shelves had given her an appetite for something home-cooked and old-fashioned. But she set her chopping knife aside at once when she heard Lucy's voice.

'Well hello!' she said. 'It is nice to hear you. How are you? Did you get my messages?'

'I've been working all hours,' Lucy said, diplomatically answering the first question and ignoring the second. 'We've had a rush on. I hear you've got a job.'

'That's right,' Gwen said and told her about it, briefly and happily. 'No two days are the same,' she said. 'I really enjoy it.'

How clever she is, Lucy thought. She's making it clear that she isn't going to look after Ellie's baby and she's doing it in the language Ellie's bound to understand. 'So I gathered.'

'Who from? How did you find out?'

'Neil told me. You know. Your neighbourhood copper.'

'Everybody knows everything down here,' Gwen said. 'So what have you been doing with yourself, apart from working?'

'Nothing much,' Lucy said, and managed to laugh as though she was joking.

'It's all Christmas preparations here,' Gwen told her. 'They've got the lights up in Chichester ready to be lit. I saw them this afternoon. And the shops in the village are all tinsel and fairy lights. It's quite pretty.' Then she paused to give Lucy a chance to react. If she shows an interest, she thought, I'll invite her down.

The very word Christmas made Lucy feel exposed, but she felt pressurised to answer, so she said she could imagine it, and then steeled herself to break her bad news.

It was enough to give her mother hope. 'This'll be my first Christmas in the tower,' she said. 'I can't wait to cook a turkey in my nice new oven. I've made two lovely puddings. I thought we could have one on Boxing Day. You will come down won't you? You and Ellie. And Pete too, if he's here. It would be lovely to have you. Jeff's giving a party on Christmas evening. He's got all his family coming down. He's one of five brothers and sisters, so he tells me. I shall need a bit of support to keep my end up with all that lot.'

'You're spending Christmas with him then?' Perhaps that's the solution.

But her mother's answer increased the problem. 'Only Christmas evening. We'll have the rest of the holiday to ourselves. You will come won't you? I know everything's different since last Christmas but it would be lovely to be together again. Don't you think so?' Oh say yes, Lucy. This could be the chance to put things right. Say yes.

Lucy had a sudden vivid memory of that last Christmas, of the four of them sitting together round the dining room table in that buff and porridge room, listening while her father ranted about the electoral system and how it ought to be put right. 'Dad was alive then,' she remembered. 'And Pete was in Hawaii. It doesn't seem possible it was only a year ago. I suppose it's because such a lot's happened.'

'Yes,' Gwen said. 'Hasn't it just. So what do you think? Could you fancy Christmas in a tower?'

I can't say 'No' straight out, Lucy thought. Not when she wants a yes so much. I'll have to say it in the end but not now. 'Well maybe,' she temporised. 'I haven't thought about Christmas yet. Too much work. Have you asked Ellie?'

The mention of her name made Gwen feel anxious. 'Not yet,' she admitted. 'I've been so

289

busy.' For a second she wondered whether she ought to tell Lucy what had happened but decided against it. It wasn't a thing to be discussed over the phone – if at all.

'She's in Paris at the moment,' Lucy offered.

'Is she all right?'

'She said she was fit as a flea the last time I spoke to her.'

'Well I hope she is,' Gwen said. 'You never know with Ellie. She puts a bold face on things. Always has.'

'Yes,' Lucy said, remembering. But what sort of face will she put on when she finds out that Pete's living with me?

'Anyway, give her my love when you see her,' Gwen said. 'When's she coming home? Do you know?'

'No,' Lucy said, more or less truthfully. 'Could be weeks yet. It's some sort of campaign. For one of the big fashion houses.'

'They work you girls too hard,' Gwen said, 'that's the trouble.'

It was the cue to say goodbye. 'My boss is coming,' Lucy said. 'I'll have to go. I'll ring again soon.' And she made a kissing sound and put the phone down.

The office was littered with paper, the desks crowded with dirty coffee cups, the air stale and sour, the screens insistent. I made a right pig's ear of that, Lucy thought, and was ashamed to have been so cowardly. But it's one thing to make up your mind to say something hurtful and something else to actually say it.

CHAPTER 20

For a company reputed to be one of the most respectable and stolid in London, the Annual General Meeting of Sheldon's UK was an exceptionally excitable affair. Most of those who attended had been shareholders since the original company had been founded and many were old friends with formidable portfolios, so the talk before the meeting was knowledgeable and self-assured. They were all aware that the firm's profits had been merely steady for the last three years, which hadn't pleased them, and although share prices had jumped since rumours about this American takeover began, most of them felt that there was plenty of room for improvement and hoped that the takeover would deliver it, the way 'that young Halliday feller' predicted.

They were impressed with Peter Halliday. 'A young man to trust,' they told one another. 'Gives one pretty sound advice.' 'He'd make an excellent member of the board, don't you think?' Lord Foss-Wellington spoke particularly well of him, declaring that he was 'a stout feller' and pointing out how well he knew the trade and how valuable his international experience was. And of course many of them had been wined and dined by the young man himself and had discovered how charming and generous he was. An asset to the company, without a doubt.

The asset had made a suitably timely entrance to the gathering and had been charming them since his arrival, smiling until his jaws ached, although he was secretly in a turmoil of anticipation and anxiety. Come on, come on, come on, he urged silently, as his fellow shareholders ambled into the hall, get a move on for fuck's sake.

He needn't have been anxious, for the takeover was virtually decided. It only remained for the last votes to be counted and for the result to be announced. Yes! he thought as he listened to the applause and gazed round at their gratified faces. Yes! Yes! He couldn't wait to tell Ellie. She'll be really chuffed. Now I can move into management. He could already see himself driving a new Mercedes convertible, hosting prestigious dinner parties, dominating the board, raking in the shekels.

But then his memory caught up with his excitement and he remembered that it was Lucy who was waiting at home to be told the news and felt foolish to have made such a mistake – even if it was private.

A hard-faced man was holding out his hand. 'Congratulations! Mr Halliwell. Or may I call you Pete?'

'Well thank you,' Pete said, pulling his thoughts away from his embarrassment. 'Pete. Yes. Of course.'

'We shall expect to see some changes now, Pete,' the man continued. 'Jimmy Foster. Member of the board. We met at Peggy's.'

Pete couldn't place him but said 'Ah yes!' as

though he remembered him intimately. So, he thought, the political alignments are beginning already.

'I'm giving a little dinner party on Saturday week,' Mr Foster said, 'to discuss tactics. This firm's needed a shakeout for years and now we can get moving. Your internet idea is first rate. I hope you can join us?'

He could and would. He'd like to see anyone stop him.

'Eight for eight-thirty,' Mr Foster instructed, handing over his card. 'Bring your good lady.'

His good lady had spent that afternoon in a peculiarly volatile mood. After her near quarrel over that wretched tray and Tina's bad news at breakfast, she'd had a pig of a day at work. The senior accountant had thrown one of his wobblies right at the start of the morning and the entire office had been prickly with temper and tension ever since. It was very late by the time she left for home and she knew she would be returning to an empty house because Helen and Tina both had dates. The traffic was appalling, her back ached, it was the first day of her period and she was tired and hungry.

Shopping first, she thought, and then straight home. The metro-store was only a few hundred yards away and they usually had a good fillet steak and their vegetables were fresh. Just don't let him be late back

But he was, of course, breezing into the kitchen so full of himself he never gave her a chance to say a word. He kissed her – briefly and roughly –

and then spread his arms in triumph, shouting, 'Ta-daaa! Am I a success or what? Ask me how it went.'

It was stupid to be so easily upset, and she knew it. 'I can see how it went,' she said. 'You've got it written all over your face.'

'Absolutely fucking marvellous,' he chortled, kissing her again, even more roughly. 'What's for dinner?'

She told him and was praised for her choice but the atmosphere was sour. He's so self-centred, she thought, watching him eat. He's not paying any attention to me at all. And she wondered why she'd never noticed it before. And decided to set him a problem.

'What are we going to do about Christmas?' she asked.

'Let it happen I expect,' he said easily.

Oh no, she thought. You're not pushing it aside like that. You've annoyed me and you can answer. 'Mum's invited us all down to the tower.'

He smiled. 'Good idea,' he said. 'I haven't had one of your mother's Christmases for ages.'

She was stunned that he could be so thoughtless. He must know the implications. 'All of us,' she said sternly. 'You and me and Ellie.'

He refused to be worried. 'So?'

'Oh come on Pete. We can't all go. Unless you want her to find out about us.'

He shrugged. 'She'll have to find out sooner or later,' he said. 'She's a big girl. She'll handle it. I can't see the problem.'

'I think,' Lucy said, picking her words carefully and speaking slowly, 'you should make an excuse not to be there and let Ellie and me go down together and try and sort things out with her and Mum.'

'And I think,' he said, speaking equally slowly, 'you should leave well alone and let them sort it out for themselves. It's none of your business.'

Her annoyance with him was growing with every word. 'This is your baby we're talking about.'

'Now look,' he said glaring at her, 'if your sister wants a baby, that's her affair. Let her get on with it. It's nothing to do with me. Right. Absolutely fucking nothing. Parenthood is a stinking rotten business and I'm not being drawn into it. Not by her, or you, or anybody. Right?'

She was upset by such a violent attack. We haven't been together three weeks she thought, and we're quarrelling already. I knew it wouldn't last for ever but this is awful.

He pushed away his empty plate. 'That was first rate,' he said, wiping his mouth with her white napkin and smiling at her. 'You're a great cook. What's for afters?'

The old childish word eased her a little. 'Strawberries and cream,' she said.

'Sounds great. And that reminds me. We're invited out to dinner on Saturday week.'

'Oh yes,' she said clearing the plates. Maybe quarrelling like this is normal to him, the way he goes on. Maybe I'm reading too much into it. 'Who by?'

He explained. 'Jimmy Foster. One of the big bugs on the board. You and your good lady he said.'

She was so irritated by the belittling description

that she simply had to sting him. *Good lady* for heaven's sake! She put down the dirty plates and looked him in the eye. 'I expect he meant Ellie, don't you?' she said.

He recovered his balance. 'Never met him,' he told her coolly. 'He's new in my life. Very influential. We shall need to keep in with him.'

She had a sudden and unpleasant sense of déjà vu. This was what Ellie had said. 'We shall have to tell Mum.' They're so alike, she thought and asked, ominously, 'Who's *we*?'

'You know who's *we*,' he said – inelegantly because he was still rattled despite his apparent calm. 'You and me. I've accepted for both of us.'

'Has it occurred to you that I might not want to go?'

'Of course you want to go,' he said, giving her his slow smile. 'You'll love it. This is one rich man we're talking about. It'll be a helluva party.'

His charm didn't work. For the first time his charm didn't work. So this is what happens when we quarrel, she thought, I go cold on him. 'No,' she said, stubbornly. 'I don't want to go. It's not my scene. I shan't know anybody there.'

He tried again, still smiling into her eyes. 'You'll soon meet people.'

'Your sort of people, not mine.'

'This is my career we're talking about here,' he pointed out, the smile fading. 'It's important.'

'To you maybe. Not to me.'

'I thought we were an item. I thought you loved me.'

'Look,' she said, feeling she had to make this clear to him, 'you live in my house – rent free, I might add and we shall have to do something about that because Tina's pulling out – and you sleep in my bed–'

He decided to joke his way out of that one. 'So I'm back on the sofa. Is that it?'

'You can't be back on the sofa,' she pointed out. 'You were never there in the first place.' And was annoyed because that sounded petty.

'I see what it is,' he sympathised and gave her his charming smile. 'You've had a hard day and it's the wrong time of the month. Right?'

That was so crass she boiled into anger. We're discussing really important things here, she thought furiously, like how we're going to live our lives together, whose needs are going to dominate, and he's not getting his own way and he's going to blame it on my hormones. 'Don't patronise me,' she said. 'That's cheap.'

'Actually,' he said, feeling miffed again, 'I was sympathising with you.'

'Well don't. I don't want sympathy. I want a bit of financial support.'

'And you shall have it. The minute my dividends come through.'

'And when's that likely to be?'

'Another month I should say. You can manage till then can't you?'

'Well no,' she said. 'I can't. Like I told you, Tina's pulling out. I can't afford to pay two-thirds of the mortgage.'

'OK. OK. I'll pay my way just as soon as I've got some cash.'

'And what am I supposed to do in the mean-time?'

'I don't know,' he said. 'It's your house. I mean she's your tenant or co-owner or whatever. Get somebody else.'

It was such a glib answer she moved into the attack. 'Don't you ever feel any responsibility for anyone?'

It was more than he could endure and much too near the knuckle. 'Right!' he said, standing up. 'That's it! I didn't come back here to quarrel. I'm off out.'

The thought of being left alone in the middle of an argument threw her and for want of something better to say, she offered, 'What about the strawberries?' And was then cross with herself because it sounded fatuous.

'Fuck the strawberries,' he said. 'I'm going.' And left her.

After he'd gone, she ate both portions of strawberries liberally washed down with cream – even though it made her feel rather nauseous, cleared the table, washed up, cleaned the work-tops and made herself a strong cup of black coffee. It was either that or weeping and she was damned if she was going to cry. They were bound to quarrel sooner or later. She'd known that from the beginning. But not like this, she grieved. Not storming out and leaving me. That's cruel.

The rest of the evening spread out its emptiness before her. She drifted into the television room but there was nothing on worth watching, so she drifted out again. Phone someone? But who? Write a few letters? But who to? The only person who'd written to her in the last week was the policeman. Now she thought of him warmly. Neil the Touchstone. OK then. She'd write to him. Now where had she put his letter?

It took her several minutes to find it but no time at all to start to write, for she simply put down the first thing that came into her head, glad that she had something to occupy her and didn't have to think about anything else.

By the time she'd thanked him for looking after her mother and given him what titbits of London gossip she thought would interest him, she felt so amiably disposed towards him that she signed off, 'See you soon,' as if he were one of her London friends and seeing him soon was possible.

And that gave her another idea. There was no way she was going to that wretched dinner party. Even if Pete came back and was as sweet as pie, he had to understand that she wasn't his property, and certainly not his *good lady*. OK then. She'd simply be away for the weekend. And the obvious place to be was Seal Island. She folded Neil's letter and put it in an envelope and wrote a second, shorter, letter to her mother.

Can you put up with a little one the weekend after next? I can't stay for very long because of driving in the dark but I could be with you by lunchtime on Saturday and stay till about three on Sunday. If that's OK. Ring me if it isn't. Otherwise I'll see you then.

All love. Luce.

Then since she still had time to kill and it was a clear night even if it was cold, she walked to the postbox.

As she pushed the letters through the slit into the tinny darkness of the box she looked at Neil's address, 'PC Neil Morrish, 6 East Beach Parade, Seal Island,' and wondered idly what East Beach Parade was like. It sounded rather romantic and a great deal better than Abercrombie Road, Battersea, where you had to worry about paying two thirds of the mortgage – and quarrelling with your lover.

In fact, the flat where Neil Morrish slept and ate when he wasn't on duty was a nondescript apartment above a terrace of tatty shops on the outskirts of the village. It consisted of two small, square, magnolia painted, identical rooms, one with an ice-cream pink bathroom alongside it, the other adjoining a kitchen fitted with a frowzy sink, an elderly cooker, a battered fridge and a row of cheap units which even to his rather unobservant eyes looked decidedly naff. The one good thing about the place was that the living room had a fine view of the sea, although it also overlooked a litter-strewn green where the local rowdies gathered of an evening to brag and smoke and horse around and show off on their motorbikes. The environment hadn't worried him when he'd first rented the place. It was cheap and functional, he only needed it for bed, breakfast and dreams, plus the occasional take-away meal, and he thought it would be useful to be living among the more troublesome members of his manor. Now, with Lucy's letter in his hand, he was having second thoughts. It was hardly the sort of flat you could bring a girl back to, and especially a girl like her. He remembered the solid affluence of that house in Battersea – even from the outside you could see what an expensive place it was – thought of the rich colours and beautiful furniture in her mother's tower, of the stylish clothes her sister wore and the swanky car she drove, and felt himself outclassed.

It wasn't a new feeling. He'd lived with it for most of his life, mocked at his comprehensive school for not wearing the right trainers or the right designer jeans, teased at the police training school for not knowing the right things to say or the right clubs and pubs to visit, always the outcast, always on the edge. Even now he only felt comfortable when he was camouflaged by uniform, and he was privately aware that it's a bit too easy to make mistakes and show yourself up when you're offered a free choice.

And now choice was burgeoning before him. A chance to move into the life he'd yearned for all through his childhood, the chance to love a beautiful girl who would love him in return, to marry and have a family, a real family in a real home. When he'd first met her, on that amazing night back in November, he'd known at once that she was the girl he would love if it were possible. He'd thought of nothing else ever since, although always with doubt and a dragging lack of confidence, convinced that he was too ordinary and too ugly for her to notice, let alone consider. When she went to the pictures with him and allowed him to drive her back to London, and when they saw *Les Mis* together, he was happy beyond words and even began to hope for an hour or two. But then days passed and he didn't hear from her and after a while he grew despondent again, sustained by dreams but shunning hope, knowing from bitter experience how dangerous it could be. And now she'd written him this wonderful letter and the best hope of his life had risen to roar in his head. He couldn't believe his luck.

Gwen MacIvor had received some significant mail that morning too, although, when the bundle of envelopes flopped through the letterbox onto her doormat, she hadn't been impressed by it.

'It'll all be junk,' she said to the cat as she gathered it up. But as she sifted through the special offers with their coloured envelopes and screaming slogans, she found a proper letter for once and saw that it was from the council. It was positive, polite and to the point, telling her simply that her planning application for 'a garage with hard standing' had been granted.

'Well how about that!' she said, showing it to Jet as though the little animal could read. 'They're going to let me build my garage after all. Isn't that great! Wait till I tell Jeff. He always said they'd pass it. Won't the old biddies be annoyed. Serve 'em right for being spiteful.'

After that she went through the rest of her mail with more interest and to her delight found a picture postcard of Monet's garden at Giverny, addressed in Pete's beautiful handwriting. What it said made her heart jump with hope.

Dear Mrs M, he'd written.

Lucy gave me your message. Christmas at the Tower sounds pretty cool to me. What would you like me to bring? How about champagne? Can't wait to see you again. Seems an age since last time.

What good news, Gwen thought as she put the card down beside her plate. If he's going to come down it must mean Ellie's coming too. Now we can kiss and make up and find some sort of compromise over the baby. It only needs a little push to get us going. Dear Pete. He must have talked her round. I wonder whether Lucy knows. She must do. They'd hardly have made a decision like this without telling her. And she's always phoning Ellie about one thing or another. Or Ellie's phoning her.

She tossed the next piece of promotional junk onto the pile of rejections and there, immediately underneath, was a letter from Lucy herself. Oh such a lovely letter. Dear, dear Lucy. Of course I can find 'room for a little one.' So I was right. You do know and you're coming for Christmas too. You and Ellie and Pete. All at once. Oh I can't wait to see you all again.

But meantime there was work to be done and if she didn't look sharp she'd be late for school. 'Better get a move on,' she said to the cat.

It was a lovely morning, the sun too pale for warmth but strong enough to enrich the bare branches of the village trees with unexpected colour. Until she lived on Seal Island, she'd always assumed that winter trees were dull and lifeless, grey when if was dry and black when it rained, because that was how they'd appeared in London. Now, as she drove through the village, she saw that many of the bare branches were actually ginger and looked spectacular against the pale blue of the sky. And what a lot of green there was, in neat lawns, holly bushes, evergreen shrubs and more cypresses than she could count.

Presently she saw Neil Morrish cycling along the street towards her in his slow, deliberate way, and drew up so that she could wind down the window and speak to him.

'Isn't it a lovely day,' she said. 'I've had such good news this morning.' It wasn't his business but she was so happy about it she had to tell someone. 'My girls are coming down for Christmas. I had a card from Pete this morning.' Then she saw that he was looking puzzled and realised that he didn't know who she was talking about. 'He's the baby's father,' she explained. 'Ellie's partner. Anyway, they're all coming down. We're having Christmas in the tower.'

Neil felt suddenly and miserably lonely. On the outside again. 'I suppose she's not coming down beforehand or anything?' he asked. 'Lucy I mean.'

She was touched by his expression. 'Yes,' she said. 'Actually she is. Saturday week. For the weekend.'

His ugly face reddened with pleasure. 'Great!' he said, and then tried to disguise his feelings by adding. 'I mean. You must be pleased.'

'I am,' she said. And noticed that a familiar coat was walking towards them. Well, well, well, it's that horrible Miss O'Malley. What luck! 'Actually I had another piece of good news this morning,' she said, speaking loudly so that her adversary would hear. 'I've had a letter from the council. They've given me planning permission for my garage after all. I can build it whenever I want.

Isn't that great?'

'Terrific,' Neil agreed. 'When will you start?'

'After Christmas, I expect,' Gwen told him. She was gratified to see that Miss O'Malley was lurking at the entrance to the supermarket, pretending to examine the goods in the window and plainly listening. 'It'll be a relief to clear out all the junk that horrible old man left behind him. It makes the place such an eyesore, an outhouse full of empty drink bottles. Now I can get it all tidied up and put a nice new roof on it and it'll be a credit to the community.' And put that in your pipe and smoke it, Miss Gossip.

At which point, Miss Gossip turned her head, looked sheepish and scuttled into the shop.

Neil made a grimace. 'Now you have put the cat among the pigeons,' he said.

'Good,' she said 'I hope I have.' And, she thought, they'll be spitting blood in Rose Cottage this evening. 'Must rush or I'll be late for school.'

'Bold as brass,' Teresa O'Malley said as the card players settled at their tables. 'Chatting away to our policeman, so she was. Poor feller. And in the loudest voice you could ever imagine. You wouldn't believe how loud it was. That's how I came to hear, so I did.'

'I can't think why they bother to ask for our opinion if they don't take it when it's given,' Mrs Jenkins observed acidly. 'All the trouble you went to. My Clarence sat up all night over it. It's not right.'

'That's the weakness in the system,' Agatha Smith-Fernley explained in her magisterial way.

'I'm afraid they're free to ignore our advice however sound it might be. Which is immeasurably foolish, because of course they don't know the reality of the situation as it affects local people, and we do. But there you are, planning officers are distanced from what is happening on the ground and planning officers have the ultimate power.'

'They have,' Miss O'Malley agreed. 'More's the pity of it.'

'The main thing,' Mrs Smith-Fernley said, stripping the wrapper from a new deck of cards. 'The main thing is that we have made our position clear. Mrs MacIvor can hardly be unaware of it. And that's the main thing.'

'It is,' her echo agreed.

'She may think she has the upper hand now,' Mrs Smith-Fernley went on, nodding the auburn waves of her latest hairdo, 'but times can change and she'd do well to remember it. We none of us know what's just around the corner, believe me.'

CHAPTER 21

Eleanor came back from Paris in a bad mood. Despite her usual meticulous preparation, the presentation had been a failure. The great designer had been away supervising some wretched show and, although his underlings had gushed that the package was *divin* and *superbe* and *incroyable*, when it came to the crunch none of them had the power to accept it. It would have to be left to Jean-Paul, they explained. His was the final word. Which meant, as she was far too experienced not to know, that they were sifting through plenty of competition.

To make matters worse she was swelling up like a balloon. She'd actually grown out of her new skirt in the three days she'd been in Paris and her return journey was downright uncomfortable, even in one of Eurostar's nice wide seats. Worse, there'd been no word from Pete in all that time. No phone-call, no email, nothing. She was beginning to think they'd come to the end of the line, that he really meant what he'd said about the baby, that she really was on her own.

But she gave a good report of her trip to the great Ms dc Quincy, admitting that no decision had been made but stressing how impressed the underlings had been. 'They have a leisurely approach to these things,' she explained. 'Very annoying, I agree, but I think you'll find they will accept our offer. I can't see any other company producing anything to top it.'

'Let's hope so,' Ms de Quincy said, shaking the ash blonde feathers of her hair. 'There's a lot riding on it.'

That felt uncomfortably like criticism, especially as one of the things riding on it was Eleanor's hope of promotion, and it left her more demoralised than she cared to admit.

It was a relief to get back to her nice cool flat and kick off her shoes and flop into her nice white sofa with a cup of tea to hand while she sorted through her mail. Nothing from Pete, of course, although she noticed his mail was still being re-directed to her. Where is he? she thought crossly. And what's he playing at? He could at least have told them where to send all this instead of leaving it for me to deal with. But even when she'd hidden the offending letters in a drawer along with all the others, she was still annoyed with him, and annoyed with herself and the underlings and Ms de Quincy. It's not kind to send his letters on here, she grumbled to herself. He must know they'll remind me. If he's left me he should make a clean break of it, not trail letters all over the place for me to find.

She had half a mind to ring Lucy and see if she knew where he'd got to. Yes, dammit, she would ring. It would be nice to talk to her even if she didn't where he was.

But Lucy was out that evening and all she got was the answerphone. Typical, she thought. Well that's it. They've all deserted me. I'll have a nice warm bath and an early night. God knows I've

308

earned it. And she remembered how she'd eased her teen-aged miseries with scented baths at Crescent Road. And felt bleak with loss.

It was now five days since Pete had stormed out of the house in Abercrombie Road and, as he hadn't come back or phoned, Lucy was making it her business to be out more often than she was in and had switched on her answerphone to demonstrate her unavailability. It still infuriated her that he had left her so abruptly, so she certainly wasn't going to sit around at home waiting for him to deign to contact her. Let him draw a few blanks too. So nobody who rang her got an answer, although many of them tried several times. The first thing she did when she came home from work was to listen to her messages but she never heard the voice she hoped for and the longer she waited for it the more miserable she became. It was the same on that fifth evening – Mum twice, sounding happy, Ellie saying she was back and would call again, nothing from Pete. Where the hell is he? she thought, as she switched off the answerphone. And as if to answer her, the phone rang.

'Yes?' she said breathlessly. Oh let it be Pete. Please let it be Pete.

'Neil here,' his voice said. 'Thought you'd like to know I've seen your mum again.'

She swallowed her disappointment. 'I'm in rather a rush,' she warned.

'I won't keep you long,' he said and then paused, uncertain what to say next.

'Is she all right?' she prompted.

309

'Oh yes. She's fine. Thrilled to bits to have you all coming down for Christmas.'

She couldn't believe what she was hearing. 'Sorry?'

'She's had a card from Pete,' he explained. 'She was really chuffed.'

Lucy was so cross that for a few seconds she simply sat where she was, scowling and speechless. How dare he write and say such a thing! What was he playing at?

'Lucy?' Neil worried. 'Is that wrong?'

'Well let's put it this way,' she said. 'It's news to me. I haven't made my mind up about it yet.'

'Oh,' he said, feeling demoralised. 'I hope I haven't put my foot in it or anything.'

She tried to reassure him. 'No, no,' she said. 'It's not your fault. You're just telling me what you know.'

'I suppose you're not coming down on Saturday either then?' he said.

I'll have to go now, she thought. I'll have to explain. 'Yes,' she said, 'actually, I am.'

'The thing is,' he said, 'I was wondering whether you'd like to come out for a meal or something Saturday night. I mean, I wouldn't want you to be on your own and they're bound to go out – your mum and Mr Langley I mean – it being Saturday. But you might have something planned.'

She'd forgotten about the farmer. 'Yes,' she said. 'Thanks. I'd like that.' It would be pleasant to be wined and dined, even by a policeman with a face like a gargoyle. Better than clubbing. And much much better than sitting around waiting for Pete to phone. How dare he say they were all going down for Christmas.

'I'll see you then,' Neil said. 'Seven o'clock, if that's all right.'

There was somebody thumping down the stairs, banging against the banisters and giggling, making so much noise she could hardly hear what he was saying.

'I'll have to go,' she said. 'This house is bedlam. See you then.' And went out into the hall to see what was happening.

It was Tina, arriving at the bottom of the stairs, pulled sideways by the weight of a huge suitcase in one hand and clutching a battery of bulging carrier bags to her chest with the other. 'I thought I'd take a few things over to Kensington,' she explained from behind the pile. 'Sort of pre-liminary move. Valuables and that sort of thing. It's got a bit out of hand.'

'You can say that again,' Lucy said, catching two of the carrier bags just before her burdened friend lost hold of them. 'Why didn't you make two trips?'

Tina was giggling again. 'I thought I could manage. It's the story of my life.'

They blundered out of the house and staggered off towards her car, which was parked three houses away. And the phone shrilled again.

'Answer it,' Tina said, moved by the expression on her friend's face. She might not think much of the Great I Am but she was fond of Lucy. 'I'll manage.'

But Lucy insisted on carrying the bags to the car. If it's Pete, she thought, he'll wait a little while. He must do, after all this time. And if it

311

isn't, it doesn't matter. Oh let it be Pete. Surely I've earned it now. Tina was opening the boot. It was still ringing. They were easing the bags in. It was still ringing. It was still ringing as she hurtled back into the hall. By this time she was so breathless with hope and running, that as she picked up the receiver it was all she could do to say 'Yes?'

'Do you know what that rotten bugger's done now?' Eleanor's voice said furiously.

Disappointment, followed by surprise and an anxious suspicion. 'What rotten bugger?'

'Pete? Who else? He's only gone and written to Mum and told her we're all going to her place for Christmas.'

He's gone back to her, Lucy thought and was crushed with jealousy. 'You've seen him,' she said.

Ellie's voice was dismissive. 'No. Course not. I told you. He's buggered off.'

Relief. Guilt. Curiosity. 'Then how do you know? Has Mum...?'

'She wrote him a letter. I steamed it open.'

'Oh Ellie!'

'Don't "Oh Ellie" me. I had to know. I mean, she wouldn't have written to him if there hadn't been something going on, now would she. This is serious.'

'Right,' Lucy agreed. 'It is. What are you going to do?'

'Well I'm not going down there for a start. Not after the way she's treated me. And not if he's going to be there. He needn't think that. Oh I can see what he's up to. Artful bugger. I've got his number, don't you worry. I know how he ticks.'

312

'More than I do,' Lucy admitted – with perfect truth.

'He's trying to force my hand,' Ellie said. 'That's what he's doing. And it won't work. I won't be bullied. And he needn't think it.'

'Look,' Lucy said, 'I'm going down to see her on Saturday. How about coming with me? I mean, it's silly you two quarrelling and not seeing one another.'

'No way,' Ellie said firmly. 'Not after last time. But I tell you what. How about you persuading her to look after baby for me?'

'Can't be done,' Lucy said and smiled to think of the sting she was going to deliver. 'She won't be looking after anybody now. She's got herself a job.'

Ellie was shrill with fury. 'She's what?' And when Lucy had told her all she knew, 'Oh for fuck's sake! She's so selfish. How can she be so selfish? She knows how much I need her. I mean, I made it quite, quite clear. She doesn't need a job for fuck's sake. She's got me and the baby. Oh I can't believe this.'

'Don't shout at me,' Lucy said. 'I'm only the messenger.'

To her credit, Ellie made a great effort and controlled herself. 'Right,' she agreed. 'You're right. Must rush. I've got a dinner party.' And hung up.

Typical! Lucy thought crossly. She flies off the handle and roars and shouts and then runs away. Pete writes bloody stupid cards and then buggers off and doesn't phone. And I'm the one who's left to pick up the pieces. How am I going to tell her?

Poor old Mum. She'll be shattered.

But in fact, when she arrived in Seal Island, she found her mother in high spirits. The living room was full of brocade curtains, spread out on the carpet, draped over the sofa, folded up and piled on a chair, and all in very rich colours, scarlet, gold, sky blue, peacock green.

'What are you doing?' she said, trying to take it all in.

'It's the nativity play,' Gwen told her happily. 'I'm making the costumes for the kings. Sorry it's such a mess. Just step round it. Lunch is all ready.'

'I thought you were the school secretary,' Lucy said as they settled at the kitchen table.

'I volunteered,' Gwen said. 'It's such fun. We've got belly dancers and Roman soldiers and camels and I don't know what. I wish you could be here to see it. The kings are a riot.'

She's in another world, Lucy thought, as she wielded the salad spoons. I can't tell her now. Not when she's so happy. I must choose a good moment. But the moment didn't present itself. They were still sewing costumes and talking about the school when Neil Morrish arrived for his date.

He was dressed in his usual unfashionable mufti and very nervous, apologising because he was too early.

'No problem,' Lucy said, to reassure him. 'It's better to be early than to miss the start of the film.'

There was a problem, of course, and she

314

carried it with her all through the evening. It weighed down the film until it was mere noise and shadow and leached away her appetite even though he took her to their original Indian restaurant and did his best to provide her with food he knew she liked. By the time they were driving back to the tower, it reduced her to a sigh she couldn't control.

He felt criticised and inadequate. 'I'm sorry the film was such a dud,' he said.

She dragged her attention away from her thoughts. 'It wasn't,' she said. 'I mean, it was all right. It's not the film. It's me. I'm – well, a bit worried.'

He took his eyes from the road to glance at her. 'What about?'

'Ellie and Mum.'

'Your Mum's OK isn't she?' he asked. 'I mean there hasn't been any more...'

'No,' she said quickly. 'She's all right as far as that's concerned. Matter of fact I've never seen her so happy. That's the trouble.' And as he waited, she went on, 'It's that card from Pete. The one you told me about. Remember? It's made her think we're all coming down for Christmas and we're not.'

He could actually feel his heart sinking. 'None of you?'

'Well I'm coming, and Pete probably will, although there's no knowing with him, but Ellie definitely won't. And now he's written that stupid card and she's as happy as a sandboy thinking we're all going to be together for Christmas and we're not and I've got to tell her.'

315

'You've been lumbered,' he understood. 'Is that it?'

'That's about the size of it,' she agreed and made a grimace, fed-up with herself and Ellie and Pete and the whole tricky business. 'Piggy in the middle. That's me.'

The car made gentle speed between the grey hedges. They were alone in the upholstered darkness, cut off from the rest of the world in a warm private space where confession was not just possible but easy. So having started, she told him all about it – or nearly all about it. She didn't say anything about Pete moving in with her, naturally, because that was private, but she gave a pretty clear account of her mother's dilemma, and told him how sick and tired she was of being a go-between, 'I've done it all my life and I don't see why I should. It's not my problem.'

When she finally stopped talking she felt a bit guilty to have off-loaded so much. It wasn't his affair and she might have embarrassed him.

But he answered her seriously and didn't seem embarrassed at all. 'I think you're right,' he said. 'If your sister wants a baby she should be prepared to look after it. I don't go along with all this stuff about child care and how women ought to go back to work the minute the baby's born and how babies don't know who's looking after them. That's just rubbish. They do. But then I'm biased. I've got an axe to grind. I don't think anyone should hand their baby over to someone else. If you're not prepared to bring it up yourself, you shouldn't have it. And if you do have it you should look after it.'

316

He spoke with such passion that she was surprised and shamed. 'I'm sorry,' she said. 'I should have thought. I mean, you being...'

'It's all right,' he reassured. 'You weren't trying to upset me or anything. I know that. You were just speaking your mind. Quite right too. It's just I've got a viewpoint and I thought you ought to know it.'

'I share it,' she told him seriously. 'I think it's awful to walk out on a baby. Well on any child actually. I know what it does to you.' And when he looked a question at her, 'Pete's parents walked out on him when he was fifteen. Buggered off to India and left him in a boarding school and never came back. He's never forgiven them. He calls them the obnoxious parents and the objectionables and things like that. Really hates them.'

'Quite right too,' he said trenchantly. 'If that's what they did, they deserve it.'

They were talking so intimately that she questioned him without bothering to think about the consequences. 'Do you hate yours?'

He gave her a lop-sided smile. 'I never knew them,' he said, 'so no, not like that. I just hate what they did to me. Or what she did. I don't think my father knew I was born. Fat lot he cared.' Then he changed tack and tone. 'Now your mum's a good woman.'

'Yes,' Lucy agreed. 'She is. And now I've got to upset her. It's not fair, is it?'

If he hadn't been driving he would have put an arm round her to comfort her. As it was his help had to be practical. 'Seems to me,' he said, 'you've got three options. You can keep quiet for the rest of the weekend and not say anything. Which is putting off the evil hour. Or you can tell your sister to fight her own battles. Which is what I'd do. Or you can tell her tomorrow and hope for the best.'

He's so sensible, she thought, looking at his broken nose and that lop-sided mouth. So steady. 'That's probably what I will do,' she said. 'If I can find the right moment.'

'That's always a problem,' he said, turning into Mill Lane. 'Finding the right moment.'

The tower was dark except for the courtesy light in the porch. Mum and the farmer must have gone to bed, Lucy thought, and was glad that she wouldn't have to face them.

'Thanks for the evening and everything,' she said to Neil. 'You've been a star.' And on a sudden impulse she leant forward and kissed his cheek.

'A pleasure,' he said and for a wild second wondered whether it would be all right to kiss her properly. But she was already opening the car door, swinging those long blue legs out into the chill of the night air, standing beside the car, saying goodbye.

'I'll ring you,' he said. 'To see how it went. Good luck.' And watched, with heart still pounding, as she walked away and disappeared into the hazy half-light of the porch.

CHAPTER 22

It was such an easy domestic morning. Tea and toast at a sunlit table, the clock ticking towards eleven, her mother happily sewing up the hem of the second completed costume, the cotton rasping through the thick brocade. The peace of it all made Lucy's heart sink. How can I tell her on a day like this? she thought. It isn't possible.

'Good eh?' Gwen said, holding up the finished tunic. 'What d'you think?'

'Magnificent,' Lucy said. And so it was. 'You must have been working all night.'

'Some of us get up in the morning,' Gwen teased. 'Besides, I like being busy. It makes me feel virtuous. I've done all my Christmas shopping. Did I tell you? I've got a gorgeous shawl for the baby and some lovely earrings for Ellie. I'll show you presently. Oh I can't wait for Christmas, Luce. You and me and Pete and Ellie all round this table for the first time. It'll be a real occasion.'

Lucy's moment had arrived, unbidden, inopportune, sharp-edged, but too immediate to be avoided. The words were out before she could think about them. 'Not all of us,' she said. 'We're not all coming.' And when her mother looked puzzled, 'I am and so is Pete, as far as I know, but Ellie won't. I am sorry.'

The news struck ice into Gwen's brain, freezing

her happiness, congealing the ease of the morning. She fought against it, willing it not to be true. 'No chick,' she corrected. 'You've got it wrong. She is coming. Pete told me.'

I've got to go through with this now I've started, Lucy thought, and pressed on. 'You had a card from him, right?'

'A lovely card,' Gwen said. 'I'll show you.' She got up to find it. 'There you are, you see what he says. 'Christmas at the Tower sounds pretty cool to me... Can't wait to see you again.'

Lucy took the card and read it slowly. 'It's a message from him,' she explained. 'Just him. He doesn't say anything about Ellie. Read it again and you'll see.'

Gwen didn't want to read it again, didn't want to see. The pendulum that had kept her swinging between hope and apprehension ever since that awful quarrel was broken and useless, spinning away from her. She put out a hand as if she were trying to catch it. 'No,' she said. 'That's implied, surely. If he says he's coming, she'll come too. I mean he'd hardly come without her, now would he?'

Lucy took her time to answer. 'Look,' she said eventually, 'I wish it wasn't me having to tell you this, but they've split up. He doesn't know what she's doing.'

What is she talking about? Gwen thought. It can't be true. Not after all these years. 'They can't have,' she said and her tone was stubborn. 'It's a tiff. That's all. The way they go on. They always have, right from the beginning. They fight like cats in a bag. Usually over nothing. Then he

320

flounces out, she sulks. And after a day or two he comes back and they make it up and they're all lovey-dovey again. That's all it is. One of their tiffs.'

'No,' Lucy said, as gently as she could, putting out a hand to touch her mother's arm. 'It's not. This time it's different. He really has left her.' And when Gwen still looked disbelieving, she went on, 'It's because of the baby. He says she cheated him. He doesn't want it. Never did, so he says.'

Gwen felt as though she was drowning in bad news. 'It's his child,' she said, 'whether he wants it or not. You don't walk out on your child. Of all people, he should know that. What's the matter with him'?'

'He's a commitment freak,' Lucy explained. 'Some men are these days. Lots of them actually.'

Anger rose in Gwen MacIvor strong as a tide. 'He's selfish,' she said. 'That's what you're saying. The baby can go hang providing he can go on living the way he wants to. Selfish. That's what it comes down to. And so is your sister, I'm sorry to say. It's a selfish world. Me, me, me all the time. And the selfish have got the rest of us over a barrel. If you're prepared to compromise you can do it all the time. If you give in, you never do anything else. When I came here, I thought I'd earned the right to a life of my own. I thought I could be irresponsible for once, go my own way, do my own thing. I was a bloody fool. I haven't any rights at all. Once you've taken on responsibilities you can't step away from them. I tried to and this is what comes of it. She knows I'll

321

take this baby. She's only got to stick out for it long enough and she knows I'll give in. She isn't thinking about the baby at all. I'm doing that. All she's thinking about is her bloody rights. That's the trouble. Everybody banging on about their rights all the time. Women's rights. Consumer rights. The right for mothers to go back to work when they've got babies they ought to be looking after. Nobody mentions responsibilities. They all walk away from responsibilities.'

In the face of such fury, Lucy was lost. 'Not everybody,' she said. 'Some of us...'

Gwen wasn't listening. She was thinking of Ellie, walking out through that door, with tears glistening on her cheeks, leaving her, not writing, not phoning, not coming for Christmas, planning to dump her own baby. 'It's dreadful,' she raged. 'Unnatural. Babies should be with their mothers instead of being left with some poor little au pair to look after; fathers should support them instead of walking out on them. There are thousands of single mothers in this country living on state handouts and costing the rest of us a fortune because the men who fathered their babies just bugger off and won't take responsibility for them. It's a disgrace. And look at what happens on dairy farms. That's unnatural if you like. Calves should feed from cows. It's what they're both designed for. But no, they take them away as soon as they're born, poor little things, and feed them on some ghastly mash and then wonder why they suffer from diarrhoea and horrible infections. Did you know that? No. I didn't until I watched it happening. And they feed the poor cows on pellets made from animal carcasses when everybody knows that cows eat grass. Is it any wonder they get mad cow disease and then pass it on to us? And foot and mouth. It's all totally unnatural. And all done in the name of cheap meat and milk, because we must have cheap meat and milk, and bigger profits for the wholesalers. It's all wrong. If you're not prepared to look after your baby, you shouldn't have it.'

'That's what Neil says,' Lucy remembered. 'We were talking about it last night.'

'He's got his head screwed on,' Gwen approved. But then she sighed, her anger suddenly evaporating, exhausted by her long outburst. 'Oh dear, Lucy. I don't know! I thought this Christmas was going to bring us all together. I thought we could find some sort of compromise. And now...'

Lucy leant forward across the table to pat her mother's arm. 'I'm so sorry,' she said. 'I knew you'd be upset.'

'It's not your fault,' Gwen sighed. 'You're just the messenger.'

'If it's any consolation, I think she's selfish too.'

'It won't stop her dumping the baby though, will it?'

'Are you really going to look after it? I mean it would mean leaving here and giving up your job, wouldn't it?'

'I don't know what I'm going to do,' Gwen admitted, wearily sad. 'I don't want to leave my tower. Not now, when I've got it just right. And I'd hate to leave the job because it's such fun – and I'm good at it. But if she's going to hand the baby over to an au pair or some awful nanny, I don't have much choice, do I?'

'Not put like that,' Lucy said. 'No.'

'I've got all those presents for her too,' Gwen remembered. 'Her and the baby. Now they'll all go to waste.'

Lucy tried to cheer her. 'No they won't. You can post them.'

Gwen was too down to be cheered. 'Maybe.'

'Post them,' Lucy urged. 'It'll show her you still love her. Because you do, don't you, despite what she's doing?'

'You never stop loving your children,' Gwen told her. 'Not once you've started. That's half the problem.' She looked through the archway into her scarlet living room to where Dotty's computer sat blank-eyed on its table. 'I think the stars are against me,' she said sadly. 'That's what it is. I'll bet if I were to look up today's horoscope I'd see all this on the chart.'

'You might not,' Lucy said, glad of a diversion. 'It might show that you're having a wonderful day. That would be interesting, wouldn't it?' She'd always been sceptical about horoscopes, and it would be cheering to see the stars proved wrong. 'Have a look.'

'Shall I?'

'Why not?'

'Yes,' Gwen said, seeing the sense of it. 'Why not?' It would be something else to think about. Something different. And God knows they both needed that.

The computer was switched on, the day's date keyed in and within seconds the magical circle of the astrological chart swam into focus, its familiar symbols shining like the stars they were. Gwen was soothed by the sight of it. She knew that nothing would be changed by it, that the mistakes she'd made were still hurtful and would go on being divisive, that Christmas was going to be a mess and couldn't be altered, but she felt she was stepping back into some sort of control. She could read a chart quite well now – or at least she could recognise the symbols and knew where to look for interpretations that weren't immediately obvious.

'Fifth house to start with,' she said, settling before the screen, 'because that's the house for home and family. There it is. And that's the planet Uranus, that little sign there, the one that looks like a television aerial on top of a globe.'

'Yes,' Lucy said, looking over her shoulder. 'I can see it. What does it mean?'

'I don't know,' her mother confessed. 'I shall have to look it up.'

According to Dotty's books, when Uranus was in the fifth house it showed unexpected things to do with children. 'Well how about that?'

Lucy looked from the symbol to the words on the page, alert and fascinated, because she certainly hadn't expected it to be as accurate as that. 'And what else?' she asked.

The rest of the chart was rather a disappointment. It said much the same things in several different ways and Gwen couldn't see her situation in any of them, for they were all to do with what the books called her relationship with her environment. She read them aloud as she found them in the books, 'This conjunction indicates a period when your identity within your environment will be undergoing radical change. Well that's not right. This represents team-work, working with other people, starting a new cycle. That could be the school I suppose. This shows an expansion of your sense of authority. And so could that. But it's wrong if it's referring to my life in this village. I'm not working with other people here at all. I'm keeping out of their way after all that horrible business with poor Jet and the way they blocked my application.'

The chart was intriguing her daughter. 'I didn't expect it to be right about anything,' she admitted. 'I mean I thought it was all a sort of con trick. Something to fill up a corner in the papers. But it's not, is it? It's actually very complicated. All this could be referring to your job couldn't it. And if it is, it's spot on. I tell you what. See what it has to say about Christmas.'

More of the same apparently, which wasn't at all satisfactory to either of them. Gwen had had enough of unexpected things to do with children and Lucy wanted a prediction.

'Try the New Year,' she suggested. 'Maybe it'll tell us how that's going to turn out.'

So Gwen moved on in time and as she did she began to realise that something significant was happening. 'Well look at that,' she said. 'That's a transit, or I'm very much mistaken. Uranus is in transit and right through my stars. Do you see? And look there. Jupiter's on the move too, heading for Pisces. I've never watched that happen before.'

Lucy was following the movement too. 'What does it mean?' she asked.

'I've no idea,' her mother said. 'I don't know enough about it. I shall have to look it up. Transits bring change. I do know that. I should say there's some sort of disturbance on the way. Not at Christmas. Or the New Year. Nor in January, as far as I can see. No, not January either. They're getting closer but they're not there yet. I think they're heading for a position where they'll be square to one another. And that's really significant. It's quite exciting.' And at that point she reached 26th February and saw that there was going to be a solar eclipse in Pisces. And there was Jupiter right alongside the sun and moon in the same sign, with Uranus and Neptune immediately beneath them.

'There you are,' she said to Lucy, 'this is when it's going to be. End of February. And it'll be a major change with all this going on.'

'What sort of change?' Lucy asked. 'Does it tell you? I mean, can you work it out?'

'Possibly,' Gwen said. 'It'll take a bit of time though. I'll have to look up every single planet to really make sense of it.'

'So what are we talking?' Lucy wanted to know. 'Hours? Days?'

Gwen looked at her excited face. 'Longer than we've got anyway,' she said. 'You'll need to be going soon, won't you, if you're not to drive in the dark. Tell you what. I'll phone when I know what it is. How would that be?'

It was agreed. Happily. 'And Christmas is going to be all right,' Lucy said as they kissed goodbye.

'I promise. Don't forget that parcel.'

'I'll wrap it up the minute you've gone,' Gwen promised.

And did, having found an old chocolate box as a container, and sufficient string to make a neat job of the packing. The baby's shawl was lined with tissue paper and folded into a neat bundle, the earrings packed in their own little box and laid carefully on top of the book of sonnets. Then, as there was still room inside the box for something else, she added a box of marrons glacés, and having wedged everything in neatly and securely with more tissue paper, she turned her attention to the message she wanted to send.

It took a lot of thought and several rough attempts before she found the right words, for if this was to be a peace offering it had to be subtle. She didn't mention the break-up, in case she wasn't supposed to know, or Lucy had got it wrong, and she was careful not to leave a trace of rebuke in her final draft and to drop the merest hint that she would like to know how Ellie was, for the door must be left open as though it were of no importance whether it were open or shut. That way they might be able to move on – if Ellie wanted them to. There was an unforgiving streak in her eldest, as she knew only too well, because it was so like her father's. Once he'd quarrelled with somebody he never spoke to them again. Even his mother and his sister. Oh God! Even his mother! Still, as she read through that last rough draft, disentangling the words from the black spikes of all her anxious rewriting, she felt she'd made contact possible, even if it wasn't likely, and she'd done it delicately. She hadn't given the impression that she was expecting it or hoping for it.

Dear Ellie, she wrote eventually,

I am so sorry you won't be able to join me at Christmas. Lucy told me about it. I shall miss you. I am sending you these presents by courier so that you will have them for Christmas morning, wherever you are. I couldn't resist the shawl and I could just see the earrings in your ears. I thought the marrons glacés would make a nice addition to the feast, wherever you are having it.

I hope the pregnancy is going along all right and that you are keeping well.

Have a very happy Christmas.

Your ever loving Mother.

She pinned the letter on top of the folded shawl and tied up the entire parcel with brown paper and string, feeling that she'd been virtuous and sensible – and probably foolish as well. Then she went back to her needlework.

Lucy's journey back to London was dark and uncomfortable. Even though she'd left her mother in a better state, thanks to those charts, her conscience began to tweak her as soon as she'd driven through the village. Now she was miserable to think how much she'd upset her mother and cross with Eleanor for using her as a cat's paw and furious with Pete for sending that card. The only person she could think about without feeling angry was Neil Morrish and even he presented her with a problem because it looked as though he wasn't gay after all and that would take a bit of getting used to. The more she thought about her weekend, the more difficult it all seemed. I told her so clumsily, she thought. I should have been more gentle instead of blurting it out like that. And that's only the start. Sooner or later I'll have to let her know about me and Pete. And what will happen then? She was still worrying about that, when she turned into Abercrombie Road.

Hardly anywhere to park, of course. There was a brand new Mercedes convertible blocking her rightful parking space so she had to squeeze in between a lorry and a mini right down the road. A suit with attitude, she thought, as she walked past the Mercedes, bristling against its opulence. Come here slumming and thinks he owns the road.

But it was great to be back, despite the weekend and the suit, to stand secure inside her own nice solid Victorian porch, to open her own nice solid door with her own familiar key, to step back into the scents and sights of her own familiar house.

The lights were on in the hall and the kitchen and she could hear the TV playing in the front room and see the flicker of its blue shadows through the chink of the half-open door. 'Who's home?' she said as she walked into the room.

It was Pete, sprawled in the big armchair with his feet on her little coffee table, watching football.

'Hi there!' he said, turning his head lazily to smile at her. 'Your housemates are out. Did you see my new Merc? Great or what!'

For a second or so she couldn't think what to say, partly because she was so surprised to see him, partly because he was impossibly handsome in a magenta tee shirt and jeans, sprawled out in her chair, with his long legs stretched before him, and the wall lights darkening his eyes and making his hair shine like gold. It was turning her on just to look at him. 'Well hello stranger,' she said at last and as coolly as she could. 'Where have you been all these weeks?'

'Days actually,' he corrected. 'Going up in the world. My dividend came through. You're looking at one rich man my lovely Lucy. Great or what? Come and kiss me.'

She tried to freeze him. Wanted to freeze him. 'So you'll be able to pay your share of the mortgage,' she said.

'No problem,' he said. 'Name your price. I'm a fucking millionaire. A fucking millionaire.' It wasn't quite true. But as near as dammit. A little judicious investment would take him over the top in no time. 'Come and kiss me.'

'No,' she said, standing before him and scowling at him.

'Why not?' he asked, smiling at her.

'Because I don't want to,' she told him sternly. 'I've just come back from Seal Island. Mum's really upset and it's all your fault.'

He laughed. 'I don't see how you make that out. Was I there?'

'No but your card was.'

He shrugged. 'Oh that.'

'Yes,' she said furiously. 'That. It's done a lot of damage. She thought we were all going there for

Christmas and I've had to tell her Ellie's not coming.'

His interest was instant and sharp. 'Why not?'

'They had a row. Over the baby. Ellie wants Mum to look after it and Mum won't.'

'That fucking baby again.'

'It's not the baby's fault. You wrote the card.'

'Well I'm sorry it upset her,' he said easily. 'Naturally. I didn't write it to upset her. I wrote it to tell her I'd be seeing her at Christmas. I said I was looking forward to it, as I remember. I'm very fond of her. Always have been. But if it's let Ellie's cat out of the bag so be it.'

'How can you say that?'

'Because it's the truth. Oh come on Lucy, she had to know sooner or later. It's no good putting things off.'

'You provoked it,' she said, enraged by his insouciance. 'Deliberately. I don't call that being fond of her. I call that being unkind. Cruel.'

He wasn't a bit fazed by her attack. 'Actually,' he said coolly, 'if I was being cruel – which I don't admit, but if I was – I was being cruel to be kind. You three are all the same. You can't face difficulties. Never could, any of you. If it's tough, you look away and don't say anything. You all think if you keep quiet the nasties will go away. Well let me tell you my lovely Lucy, they never do, ever. They just lurk under the carpet getting nastier and nastier. The sooner you face up to them the easier they are to cope with.'

It was true – look at Mum when she went to the island and didn't tell them till the last minute, and Ellie not telling him about the baby – but she wasn't going to admit it. And she wasn't going to stop in mid-attack either. 'Right!' she said. 'Then here's something for you to face up to. I told her you'd walked out on Ellie.'

She was delighted to see a spasm of distress on his handsome face. But he recovered very quickly. 'Well, like I say,' he shrugged, 'she had to know sooner or later.'

'She was furious with you.'

He shrugged again. 'Very likely. Can't be helped.'

'So you don't care that you've upset her,' she said crossly. 'Is that what you're saying?'

'You know perfectly well what I'm saying,' he told her. 'You're just not listening. I wouldn't hurt her for the world. You know that. Not deliberately. She was the only one to stick up for me when the fucking Impossibles went haring off to fucking India. The only one. She's been as good as a mother to me. Better actually, when you think what a cow my real mother was. So I tell you what I'll do. I'll send her a huge bunch of flowers to tell her I'm sorry she was upset and then I'll go down to her tower on Christmas Day and make a humungous fuss of her. If Ellie's quarrelled with her she'll be feeling low. Right? So it's up to us to cheer her up. Isn't it?'

She was softening towards him because he did have a point. It wouldn't solve the problem of Ellie not going, but at least he was being positive. And loving. And unexpected. Although she should have expected it after knowing him all these years. 'Yes,' she agreed. 'I suppose it is.'

He stood up and put his arms round her,

333

changing his expression from earnest explanation to tender concern. 'Still love me?' he asked.

It was so right to be in his arms, even knowing all she knew and feeling guilty about two-timing Ellie and miserable because she'd upset her mother. 'You know I do,' she said. 'I've always loved you.'

He nuzzled into her neck, kissing the scented skin of her throat. 'Sweet!' he said.

It is, she thought, enjoying the kiss, but it's not right. 'Look,' she said, gathering strength to stop him.

'I'm looking,' he told her and kissed her long and amorously.

'That's cheating,' she said breathlessly. She knew she should go on being cross with him, should make him listen and understand how upset her mother had been, how upset she'd been, but he was turning her on so strongly she couldn't think straight.

'Yes,' he agreed, kissing her neck again. 'Isn't it. Tell you what. Let's go to bed first and eat after.'

She was caught between a residual loyalty to her mother and the roaring insistence of her senses. Naturally her senses won. But afterwards, as they lay side by side in the half-light from the street lamps, guilt and doubt returned to make her feel uncomfortable.

CHAPTER 23

Gwen's peace offering was delivered to her daughter's flat at six o'clock on the evening of the Smith Curzon and Waterbury Christmas party. Eleanor had just arrived home. Late of course. She was late for everything these days. Too dammed fat, that was the trouble. She was easing the key into the lock, yearning for privacy, when her neighbour from across the landing came smiling out of his door, parcel in hand.

'Came by special delivery this morning,' he explained. 'I thought you'd like to have it as soon as you got in.'

She opened it as she was taking her much-needed rest on the bed, with her feet on a pillow for comfort and tea at her elbow for sustenance. They were nice presents. She had to admit it. The shawl was sweet. And so were the earrings. I'll wear them this evening, she decided. Then she could say 'Another pressie!' when people noticed them and they'd all think she was having a wonderful Christmas.

She'd been putting on the same act non-stop for the last fortnight, ever since she'd faced the brute twinned facts that Pete wasn't coming back and that she was going to have to spend Christmas on her own, and it was beginning to wear her down.

At home and privately, she allowed herself to

335

weep – although not for long in case she made her face look puffy. In company she was the shriek and soul of every party, larger than life in every sense of the word and privately determined not to have a minute to spare for the entire holiday. By dint of giving two prestigious dinner parties, and manipulating several skilfully artless conversations, she'd managed to fill her social calendar almost to capacity, although it had taken considerable guile to inveigle an invitation anywhere for Christmas Day. Everyone had naturally assumed that she would be with her family, as usual, and it wasn't until she took the dogged and indefatigable Mr Cuthbert to lunch, that she managed to correct the impression.

'My dear old Mum's gone off on a cruise,' she explained. 'Left us all high and dry. Not that I blame her. As a matter of fact I told her to go. She needs the rest after all she's been through. But of course it means no family Christmas this year, which is rather sad. And of course Pete's up to his ears in work these days, what with the takeover and everything.'

'You don't mean to say you're going to be on your own?' Mr Cuthbert asked, eyebrows raised.

'Yes,' she admitted, laughing. 'I'm afraid I am. Ridiculous isn't it?'

'But that's dreadful,' Mr Cuthbert said. 'Look here. Would you mind if I told Helen?' Being the great lady's office lieutenant he felt it incumbent upon him to keep her informed. 'I'm sure she'd invite you down to Clapham. She does so like her staff to be happy. Especially at Christmas. It's one of the things she's really hot about. She looks upon us all as family at Christmas time.'

So, after Eleanor had protested that really she didn't want to be any trouble to anyone, and she'd only told him because it was such a joke, the message was passed on, the invitation given and accepted, and Christmas was accounted for. Thank God. Now it was just a matter of living through the season and trying to dress appropriately – which wasn't easy because she felt uncomfortably bulky in everything she wore, even her new flowing tunic and trousers.

I shall be glad when this baby's over, she thought, as she eased the grey silk over her head, standing sideways to the mirror so that she could examine the size of her belly. I'm as big as a house and I've still got another three months to run. The idiots at the hospital were still insisting that she was due in February and there were times when she did wonder whether they might be right. But for the moment that was a problem she was happy to leave to one side. Sufficient unto this evening to find the right shoes to wear with the silk and to be sure to make the right impression at the party, which would be easy enough as it was bound to be a crush.

As it was. 'Wonderful to see you!' she cried, swooping from colleague to colleague, champagne flute in hand.

'You're looking so well,' they said, squinting at her bulk. 'How do you manage it?'

'Strength of character,' she joked, 'and plenty of vitamins.'

But then just when she was feeling really pleased with herself, that awful Sally from accounts bore down upon her, wearing a black jump suit that made her look disgustingly skinny and smiling in that horrible false way of hers. Obviously out to make mischief. 'Hi there Eleanor!' she cooed. 'Where's your handsome Pete?'

'Worked off his feet,' Eleanor said, coolly. 'His firm's just been taken over by J.R. Grossman's. I expect you've read about it. It was all over the papers.'

'I don't read the business pages,' Sally said. 'They bore me out of my skull. I like the gossip columns. I saw him yesterday in Quango's, having lunch.'

Here it comes, Eleanor thought, turning back to face it out, smiling brightly. Now she's going to dish the dirt. Didn't I know it? 'Well naturally,' she said. 'He's always lunching someone or other. That's the way he does business.'

Sally opened her big blue eyes and gave her the full beam of her spiteful innocence. 'She was a lovely girl,' she said.

'That's par for the course in the city,' Eleanor told her. 'Look around you.'

'Lucy, her name was. At least that's what he was calling her. My lovely Lucy. They were holding hands.'

Eleanor could feel her heart shrinking as if it had been struck. Oh God! she thought. Not Lucy. He couldn't do that to me. Not my little sister. But she maintained her composure and her smile and answered as brightly as ever. 'Well how nice. Lucy's my sister. I'm so glad he's remembered. I thought it might have slipped his mind with all the work he's been doing. He always takes her out at Christmas, you know. It's a brother and sister thing. We all grew up together when we were little, you see. My mother sort of adopted him.' Then she saw Monica Furlong wobbling towards her in a boob tube that was several sizes too small and swooped off to greet her before the hideous Sally could make matters worse by telling her something else she didn't want to hear. 'Monica darling! You look stupendous.'

From then on she redoubled her efforts to be the centre of happy attention, admiring every unsuitable outfit, telling risqué stories, laughing uproariously at every joke, as her thoughts ricocheted around her brain, buzzing and stinging. He couldn't have taken up with Lucy. He simply couldn't. It was obscene. Incestuous. Perhaps he's just staying there, while the flat's let to those Americans. But then if that's what it is, she'd have told me, surely. I asked her if she knew where he was and she said she didn't know. A lie! It had to be. And if she's lying they're guilty. Oh God how could he do this to me? After all these years. I thought he loved me. No. No. Don't jump to conclusions. It could be just a hunch. No more than that. But if it was, why did she lie to me? Oh God I can't bear this.

By the time she got back to Chelsea she was worn with the need to retaliate. Sleep was out of the question. She found the most impressive Christmas card left in her depleted bundle and settled down to write to her mother.

Lovely pressies. You are kind. Many many thanks. I

hope you have a wonderful Christmas with Lucy and Pete. I've got so much to do I'm rushed off my feet. I've never been to so many parties and then in January I'm off to Birmingham to give a presentation to Vixen Brothers and after that I'm going to Edinburgh and after that I've got to go back to Paris to clinch the deal with Jean Paul Renaldo. It's all go. I barely have time to breathe.

Much, much love, Ellie.

Perfect, she thought, when she'd read it through. Grateful, affectionate, but keeping my distance. The presents are nice but she needn't think I've forgiven her.

Then she found another even larger envelope, slipped her mother's card inside and wrote her really barbed message all over the front of it. *Dear Pete and Lucy, The enclosed card is for Mum. I'm sure you won't mind delivering it when you go down and I'm sure you'll have a wonderful Christmas together. E.*

The next morning she made a detour on her way to work and delivered it to Battersea in person. It was past ten o'clock and she knew the house would be empty. But the moment the envelope disappeared through the letterbox her anger evaporated and she had second thoughts. She dithered on the doorstep, wishing that Lucy was at home and that they could talk. What if she'd jumped to the wrong conclusion? What if it had been just a hunch? What if she'd misjudged them?

I need to know, she thought, as she walked back to the Espace. But how could she find out, short of phoning them and accusing them directly?

And at that point she remembered his redirected mail. But of course, she thought, as she edged out of the line of parked cars. I'll phone his flat. His mail must be going somewhere, now it's not coming to me, and they'll know where.

It took three calls before she got an answer and by then she was so tense her neck and shoulders were aching. But the voice that finally spoke to her was female and friendly, if brassily American. 'Miriam Hackenfleur,' it said, and when Eleanor asked if she could speak to Mr Halliwell, 'I'm afraid he's not here, honey. We're renting the place.'

'I suppose you don't have a forwarding address do you?'

'Well now honey, I do believe we do. I have it here somewhere if you'll just hold. Yes. Here it is. 26 Abercrombie Road, Battersea. Does that help you any?'

Eleanor thanked her politely and told her she'd been very kind but anger and hurt pride were provoking such tears that she had to pretend she had an eyelash in her eye and run to the loo before anyone in the office could see the state she was in. How could he do such a thing? Well serve him fucking right if that envelope fucking upsets him. And her too. Serve them both fucking right.

In fact neither of them saw the envelope until late that night, when they got back from his office party and she decided to open the last of their Christmas mail before they crashed out. 'We'll never get time in the morning,' she said, gathering up the pile and beginning to sort it through.

341

'Not if you want to go rushing off at first light,' he joked, throwing himself into the sofa.

'I don't call ten o'clock first light,' Lucy said, tossing him a crimson envelope. 'That's from Staggers isn't it? And this one's Carla. And that's...'

'From the Hideous Parents,' he said. 'OK. Hand it over. I don't care.' He ripped the envelope open with his thumb, leaving it jagged. 'Let's see where they are now. Well wouldn't you know it? Sri Lanka. Bless! I should have guessed. Lots of work for them to do, apparently. Isn't that sweet! I wonder they had time to remember me.'

His face had changed so much that if it hadn't been Pete she was looking at, Lucy would have said he was ugly. His mouth was twisted completely out of shape, brow drawn, nose pinched and narrowed. Even his lovely blue eyes seemed small and furious, like an animal at bay. 'Oh Pete!' she said, full of sympathy for him. 'I am sorry.'

'No problem,' he said, shaking her hand away. 'How many more of those dammed things have you got to open?'

'Three,' she reassured. 'That's all. I'll leave them till morning if you like.' But then she saw the writing on the second one and covered her mouth with her hands.

He was so caught up in misery that he almost ignored the telltale flutter of fingers. But he looked up at her instinctively, and then he too saw the handwriting and understood at once, with a shrinking of the heart that was so strong it was painful.

'Ellie,' he said flatly.

Lucy's eyes were wide with distress. 'She knows,' she said. 'Oh God! This is getting worse and worse.'

He was determined not to be thrown for a second time. Once was quite enough. 'So?' he said, as coolly as he could. 'She knows. It's no big deal. She was bound to find out sooner or later.'

Lucy held the envelope in both hands, as if it were alive and would run away from her if she let go. 'This is awful,' she said. 'What if she rings? What can I say to her?'

'Don't say anything,' he advised, now icy-cool. 'If she asks you a question, answer it. Otherwise leave well alone.'

'I can't do that,' she cried. 'She's my sister.'

'Look,' he said, 'she brought all this on herself by cheating over that fucking baby. She knew the score. Now she's just got to face the music. It's not your problem.'

She knew she shouldn't shriek at him, that he'd hate it and react against it, that it wouldn't do any good, but she couldn't help it. 'How can you say such a bloody stupid thing?' she roared. 'Of course it's my problem. She's my sister, for fuck's sake. She was your lover...'

He was furious with her. 'And now she's not,' he said. 'No love lasts forever. Look at the fucking Objectionables. They couldn't even love their own son for five fucking minutes. Don't talk to me about love. She was then. You are now. Unless you don't want to be. Is that what you're saying?'

Her heart contracted at the very thought of

343

losing him, stung with fear by his angry face. 'No,' she said passionately. 'You know I'm not.'

'Well then, just leave it. I don't know about you but I'm knackered. I want a good night's sleep and a clear drive down tomorrow. We'll think about all this later. Right.'

Christmas, she thought. We've got Christmas to face on top of all this. It saddened her to realise how much she was dreading it. 'On one condition,' she said. 'We don't say anything to Mum about us.'

He was too tired to argue. 'OK,' he said. 'I think you're being stupid but if that's what you want.'

'That's what I want. And we sleep in separate rooms while we're there.'

'All I want is to sleep. Now,' he said, yawning. 'I'm dead on my feet.'

She persisted. She had to be sure about this. 'Agreed?'

'Yes. Yes. Anything you say.'

So their bargain was made and they went to bed, where he turned his back on her and fell asleep easily and within seconds. But she was too upset to settle. It was all very well saying they'd think about it later. Shelving their problems wouldn't solve them. Whichever way they looked at it they were two-timing poor Ellie and now Ellie knew it, so eventually they would have to face her and it was bound to be horrendous. And they couldn't keep it from Mum for ever. In fact Ellie could have told her already. Oh God! What if she has? She'll be so upset. Poor old Mum. It really isn't fair on her, all this. Oh why does love have to be so fucking complicated?

Had she known it, her sympathy was wasted, for Gwen had made her own decision about Christmas. Her awful anger still shamed her whenever she thought about it, but it had washed her into a curious state of acceptance and tolerance. She'd made up her mind to enjoy the days leading up to the holiday, as much as she could, and to set her problems aside – for the time being at any rate. She had plenty to do and plenty to enjoy. The excitement at Little Marsden was bubbling everybody along and she was happily part of it, from the splendour and importance of the nativity play to the cheerful noise of the sixth year Christmas disco. And at home there was the chart to keep her mind occupied.

She spent her time in the run-up to Christmas cooking by day and studying Dotty's books in the evening. By Christmas Eve the cupboards were full of good things, the chart had revealed most of its secrets and she'd sent Lucy a Christmas card to tell her what she'd found out. Jeff might mock but there was no doubt now that something unusual was going to happen at the end of February and that she was going to be in the thick of it, whatever it was. It was really quite exciting and in an odd way it put her present problems into perspective, demonstrating that life rolls on regardless. She wasn't at all sure how she felt about Pete now that she knew how selfish he was being, but one thing was certain. She wasn't going to bawl him out, as she explained to Jeff when they were driving to the Lobster Pot on

Christmas Eve.

'I'm not going to let him be a martyr,' she said, 'that would only make him feel justified in what he'd done. I'm going to take his apology at face value – did I tell you he'd sent me flowers? – and I'm going to make him welcome and treat him exactly the same way as I always have and see how his conscience can stand that.'

'Very clever,' Jeff approved.

'I'm learning. How are the party preparations?'

'All in hand. How are the stars?'

She told him in happy detail.

'It'll be a flood,' he said when she'd finished. 'There's usually a flood in February. I expect you're going to take a witch's broom and sweep the water back into the sea.'

'One of Dotty's books says this sort of transition is a sensitive point for – what was it? – *powerful, unexpected, transpersonal events.* Unexpected. So it won't be a flood because you're expecting it. It's supposed to be unexpected.'

'And what do the stars foretell for this evening?' he asked as he parked the car.

'Oh all sorts of good things,' she told him. 'Good food, good wine, good fire, good environment. I'd say good company too but that might give you a swollen head.'

'No fear of that with you around,' he grinned.

Oh it was good to back to their easy, happy teasing. And it was a good evening. A good normal evening. Just what she needed. And when they reached the coffee stage, it got even better.

'Pour out,' he said. 'I've left something in the car. Won't be a minute.'

He was back in seconds carrying a small oblong parcel. 'Thought I'd give you this tonight,' he said. 'It'll be chaos tomorrow. Happy Christmas, Neptune's daughter.'

It was a gold chain with a gold charm hanging from it, a special and extraordinary charm, made in the shape of the glyph for Neptune, the three-pronged trident rising above its neat cross and suspended from the cross a blue opal set in gold. She took it from its box and held it on the palm of her hand, turning it so that the opal flashed fire.

'It's gorgeous,' she said. 'I've never had such a lovely present.' Which was perfectly true. Gordon had always given her the dullest things, like sensible slippers and aprons and even, on one dismal occasion, a set of oven gloves. 'Can I wear it now?'

He was beaming at her, rewarded by her pleasure. 'Wear it whenever you want,' he said. 'I thought it would remind you, in case things got rough over Christmas.'

She hung the chain round her neck. 'I'm not expecting an easy ride,' she told him, 'but I think I shall manage.'

'And there's always the flood to think about,' he teased. 'You mustn't forget that.'

'Whatever it turns out to be,' she said, touching her charm.

CHAPTER 24

Christmas Day dawned grudgingly in a squall of sleet, the sea lead-grey and pockmarked under a pewter sky. Fortunately Gwen was too busy to notice or she might have taken it for an omen. Preparing Christmas dinner had always been something she enjoyed, even in the darkest days at Crescent Road, for she was a good cook and had the entire process down to such a dependable routine that there was little anxiety about it. Now, in her new kitchen with everything she needed to hand, it was a steadying pleasure – whatever the day might bring.

She was happily at work and ready to serve when she heard a car crunching across the gravel. It annoyed her that the sound made her heart tremble, but she set the baster on its stand and went to open the door, determined to welcome them, no matter what state they might be in.

Lucy looked cold and understandably apprehensive but Pete was at his most exuberant, rushing towards her with his arms full of presents, calling 'Merry Christmas, Mrs M! Where shall I put them?'

She ushered them in, suggested that he put his parcels down by the bookcase and watched as he rushed off to the kitchen to put two bottles of champagne on ice.

He was so happy and excited she found herself

laughing despite herself. 'We'll never drink two bottles,' she protested.

'D'you wanna bet?' he said. 'Well how are you? You look fabulous. Sea air suits you. I like the new hairstyle. What do you think of my new car?'

She hadn't noticed it.

'I'll take you for a spin later,' he said. 'My God, that smells good.'

From that moment on, he carried the day before him, praising her cooking, plying them with champagne, entertaining them with ridiculous stories and finally, when the meal was over, driving them down to the lagoon for 'a bit of fresh air'. He was still telling extravagant tales when it was time to dress for Jeff's party.

'This is the first big family party I've ever been to,' Gwen confessed as they went upstairs to get ready. Now that it was upon her she was beginning to feel daunted and unsure of herself – although she certainly wasn't going to tell them that. Urged on by Jeff, she'd treated herself to a new dress for the occasion, long and straight in wine-red jersey, but now she was afraid his sisters might think she was playing for attention in such a colour. He'd been so insistent that she should dress up that she knew she being put on display and the knowledge worried her.

'It's a first for me too,' Lucy pointed out. 'It was only ever us when I was little.'

'That's right,' Gwen remembered. 'Your father didn't believe in parties.'

'The Objectionables believed in non-stop parties,' Pete told them as they reached the first landing and Gwen's bedroom door. 'Life was a party. We used to have our Christmases in communes. They were all out of their heads most of the time.'

'What was the food like?' Gwen asked, intrigued by the thought of Christmas in a commune.

'No idea,' Pete laughed. 'Never got to eat any. Trampled under foot most of it.'

He's doing this so well, Gwen thought, admiring him despite herself. She was still cross with him for running out on Ellie, but she had to admit she was glad of his company and his style. Even when he discovered that he wasn't to drive them to the party in his new car, he laughed it off and set out across the fields carrying Gwen's party offering, which was a tin full of mince pies, as though he were one of the kings in the nativity play.

Lucy was admiring him too, as she followed him through the dark fields arm in arm with her mother. He's just going to blaze confidence all the time, she thought, and she was caught between relief that he was handling the situation so boldly and irritation to see him so self-possessed when she was feeling down. It's easy for him, she thought, like switching on a light.

The farmhouse rose bright as a cruise liner from the dark sea of the fields. Lights blazed from every window, and hung in neon-coloured profusion on the bare branches of the garden oak to flick and bounce in the wind, the front door was obscured by an enormous wreath of holly and ivy, and the entire ground floor seemed to be swelling and thumping with loud music. They could see people dancing in the long drawing room and when Jeff opened the door the hall was

350

a blur of movement and bright colour.

The impact of it was so strong that Gwen was too entranced to move. She stood on the doorstep absorbed in the happy confusion before her, her apprehension melted away, enjoying the warmth and excitement of it, savouring the blend of scents, the white arms waving and gesticulating, the army of striding legs, mostly blue-jeaned, the excited eyes, glowing skin, mouths laughing and shouting. As far as she could see, there was only one person there who wasn't on the move and that was a small child who stood next to Jeff with its arm round the neck of a large and extremely shaggy Alsatian. So this is a family party, she thought. This is what it's like. And in that brief second as the door opened and she took it all in, she knew that it was what she'd been missing through all those arid years with Gordon, and that she was going to enjoy every minute of it, no matter whether his family accepted her or not, no matter what Lucy thought of Jeff, no matter what she now thought of Pete, no matter what any of them might say.

'Come in!' Jeff said, stooping to kiss her. 'If you can find a space. You must be Pete. Right? Are those the mince pies? Stick 'em on the table for the moment. Hello Lucy. Would you like some punch? I can vouch for it. I made it myself.'

There was a soup tureen full of it, steaming in a corner of the hall. It was very hot and very strong.

'Great stuff!' Pete approved. 'Just the thing on a night like this.' He turned to give Gwen a hug, explaining, 'This awful woman made us walk

351

here. Can you imagine? We're chilled to the bone, aren't we Lucy.'

'This'll warm you,' Jeff told him, handing over a beaker full. 'Guaranteed.'

'What have you put in it?' Gwen laughed, when she'd tasted hers. 'You'll have us all drunk.'

'That's the object of the exercise,' he told her happily. 'Come and be introduced.' He caught at the arm of a passing teenager. 'This is my niece, Sandy. Say hello to Gwen, Sandy. She's my new neighbour. This is my brother Nick and that's my little sister Peggy and this is her daughter Jenny. And that's Sam over there being a pain.'

There were so many of them it wasn't possible to distinguish one from the other, but Gwen said hello and shook hands and said she was pleased to meet them and told them how alike they all were.

'It's the Langley nose,' brother Nick said. 'It's quite handsome when it's not broken.' And he grinned at Jeff.

'As the best noses are,' Jeff said.

Noses and eyes, Gwen thought, looking at the sweeping eyelashes of the girl called Sandy, and the same way of talking and looking straight at you. It's a real clan. And she felt rather over-whelmed by them.

There was a roar from the other side of the room, and a man's voice bellowing. 'Peg! Peg! Where are you? Your bloody dog's eaten my trifle.'

Peggy pushed through the throng in the direction of the yells. 'Well if you will put it on the floor, of course he did. What d'you expect, you great pillock?'

'You can't leave anything for two seconds,' the man complained. But he was laughing, Gwen noticed, as if complaining was a joke. 'Why don't you control the bloody thing?'

'He's got a sweet tooth,' Peggy said. 'He can't help it. Can you Sugar?'

Sugar was a golden retriever who was lying beside the licked dish, keeping his head perfectly still but following the conversation with anxious eyes.

Guests swirled around them, laughing and shouting, and cutting off Gwen's view, although she could hear Peggy's voice saying, 'There you are. There's a clean plate. Now get yourself another helping and don't make such a fuss.' Then she noticed that Pete and Lucy weren't beside her and looked around to see where they were.

Pete was holding a plateful of ham sandwiches and preening because he'd been recognised by Sandy and her cousin, who were tossing their long hair at him and giving him the eye.

'I hope you don't mind me saying,' Sandy ventured, standing close to him, 'but you look just like the man in the coffee ads.'

'The same,' he said, bowing to them and giving them the full benefit of his charm.

'You mean you are?'

'I mean I am.'

'Cool!' Sandy said, much impressed.

Lucy was on the other side of the room talking to one of Jeff's sisters. Watching her, Gwen was pleased to see that she'd relaxed a little and was smiling almost happily. She waved at her briefly across the crowd and Lucy waved back and was obviously explaining who she was, for the sister looked across and waved too. So far, so good, Gwen thought, returning her smile. But she'd relaxed too soon. Jeff was beside her again and had brought a young man with him, a young dark-haired, dark-eyed man with a disapproving expression.

'This is my son Simon,' he said, 'the one who's an airline pilot. Simon, this is Gwen MacIvor.'

They shook hands, made the right noises, said they were pleased to meet. But the young man's spine was too stiff, his face too stern, his animosity towards this woman who was taking his mother's place too palpable. I must be very very careful, Gwen thought, and decided not to smile but to talk to him as seriously as he would allow.

'I'm rather a gatecrasher at a family party like this,' she said.

'No you're not,' Jeff protested. But his son merely looked at her coldly.

'My daughters are in the same position as you are,' Gwen said, looking back as steadily as she could. 'It gave them quite a shock to find me befriending your father.' But he didn't respond at all so she had to press on. 'We none of us like change,' she said. 'I think that's what it is. At least we don't if we're happy in our situation. We'd all like to turn the clock back to better times when things go wrong. I know I would. I sometimes think it would be nice to find a new time zone altogether.'

'I fly from one time zone to another all day long,' Simon said, his face still cold. 'All you get from that is jet lag.'

Oh dear, Gwen thought, noting the stern line of his mouth. But at least he'd given her the chance to show an interest in him that was nothing to do with her relationship with his father. 'How do you cope with it?' she asked.

'I wear two watches.'

'You have your mother's good sense,' she said, and added, quickly, because she could sense his disapproval increasing, 'She was an extraordinary woman.'

That wasn't what he'd expected and it annoyed him. 'Did you know her then?'

'We never met, if that's what you mean,' she told him, 'but I do feel I know her. Not the way you and your father knew her, naturally, but in another way. I suppose you'd call it a literary way.' That intrigued him enough to remove a little of the condemnation from his face. So she explained. 'I think I'd have admired her anyway, because of the way your father speaks about her, but I've been reading some of her books too. He lent them to me, to cheer me up when I first came down here. I enjoy books as much as she did.'

Now it was Jeff's turn to receive the disapproving stare. 'Which books were they?'

'The astrology ones.'

They could be dismissed. 'Oh those!'

Gwen smiled. 'Yes, those!' she said. 'Actually I find them fascinating. And touching. It's not the books you see, it's the things your mother wrote in the margins, things about her illness and how she was facing up to it. Some of them are quite extraordinary.'

355

Simon turned an accusing face to his father. 'Did you know about this?' he asked.

'No,' Jeff told him. 'None of us did. I wouldn't have known if it hadn't been for Gwen.'

The young man turned back to Gwen. 'I hope you realise they were private.'

'Yes,' Gwen said, standing her ground. 'I saw that at once. They're a sort of diary. Which is why I felt so honoured to be able to read them.'

Outright hostility now. 'Perhaps you shouldn't have read them. Did that occur to you?'

'Look,' Gwen said. 'There's something you ought to know. I'm not trying to take her place. I'm not going to marry your father.'

He didn't believe her. 'If you say so.'

His hostility was so open that Gwen didn't know how to counter it and while she was thinking what, to say, the boy with the Alsatian shuffled into their circle, dragging the dog beside him. 'Mum says I can't have any more trifle,' he complained. 'I can, can't I?'

'Not if your mum says not,' Jeff told him, ruffling the dog's head. 'Try some ice cream instead. That's not so rich.' He turned to Gwen and Simon. 'I haven't fed you two either. Or Lee. Where is she?'

'Over there,' Simon said, looking across the room to where a pretty Chinese girl was talking to Pete.

'Take her a selection,' Jeff instructed, 'before Sugar clears the table. Go and find out what she fancies. Now then Gwen, what would you like?'

She allowed him to lead her to the food table, even though she knew she couldn't face any more food, not after all she'd eaten already and not when she was feeling so defeated.

'Oh God!' she said, when they were more or less alone. 'Wasn't that awful!'

Jeff shrugged. 'He'll get over it.'

'He didn't believe me.'

He was bold with drink. 'That makes two of us. I still think we should get married. I shall go on thinking it.'

'Please don't start that again,' she begged. 'Not now. It's all I can do to cope with so many new people.'

Someone was beaming at them from the other side of the table. Oh no! Gwen thought. Not now. It was Neil Morrish, dressed in his best and smiling like sunshine.

'Is Lucy...?'

'Over there,' Gwen told him, getting rid of him as quickly as she could. 'Next to the golden retriever.' And was relieved as the policeman went leaping away to find her. 'Now,' she said turning back to her lover. 'Look...'

But there was a rush of people flocking towards the table, joshing and shoving, and, knowing he'd annoyed her, Jeff was making it his business to attend to them. And pushing in beside Gwen were all his sisters, the one called Peggy, the one who'd waved to her across the room and a third one she hadn't met before.

'Come and eat with us,' Peggy said to her. 'You mustn't let him monopolise you all evening.'

'I like that,' Jeff protested. 'I've hardly had a chance to say three words to her.'

His sisters were as determined as he was.

'Come on,' Peggy said, tucking her hand under Gwen's arm. 'We'll find a peaceful corner.'

'No such thing,' Jeff told them. But they were already leading the way, pushing through the waving arms of the teenagers who were still gyrating in the drawing room and finally heading out into a little conservatory. It was lit by a single blue bulb, and smelt of damp earth and must, but they cleared a space among the potted plants for their plates and glasses, found three rather unstable wicker chairs to sit on and settled to what was plainly going to be an interrogation.

Having introduced her sisters, 'This is Madge and this is Sis,' Peggy plunged straight in. 'So when are you two getting married?' she said.

Here goes, Gwen thought, and answered her honestly, watching her face in the half-light to see how she would respond. 'We're not. As I've just been telling Simon.'

The sisters looked at one another shrewdly. 'Very sensible,' Madge said. 'He was very fond of his mother. But you can tell us. We're all for it. He's been like a lost soul since Dotty died, poor old thing. 'Course, we've been up and down to keep an eye on him, Christmas and summer holidays and so on, whenever we can, but it's not the same. Not like being just up the road.'

'No,' Gwen agreed and went on. 'Actually that's quite a good place to be. Just up the road. Close enough for company and not too close for comfort.'

Her hint was too subtle for them. 'So when's it going to be?' Sis insisted.

'It's not,' Gwen told her. 'We're very happy

together but we're not getting married. I've got a home of my own and a full-time job and he's got this farm and a dairy to run. Marriage would only complicate things. Anyway, we're happy as we are.'

'That's not what he says,' Madge told her, biting into a mince pie. 'He's mad keen to get married. He was telling us last night.'

Gwen was caught in a spasm of anger against him. What a stupid thing to do, she thought. Was he drunk then too? 'Well maybe he is keen,' she said. 'But I'd rather stay as we are.'

'It's a beautiful house,' Sis said. 'Queen Anne.'

'My tower's pretty stunning too,' Gwen said, fighting back. 'You must come and see it. Tell you what. Come tomorrow. For tea.' If she was going to correct his false impression befriending them was the best way to do it.

Peggy raised her eyebrows. 'All of us?'

'Why not? You'll have to bring your own cups. I've only got enough for twelve.'

'You're on,' Peggy said.

There were people moving furniture about in the drawing room and the boy with the Alsatian appeared in the doorway. 'Uncle Jeff says to tell you it's charades,' he announced.

'We'll be along,' Sis told him, popping the last piece of mince pie in her mouth.

So they joined the crush in the drawing room where a huge dressing-up box was being dragged into place in front of the French windows and Jeff was setting out a semi-circle of chairs. He looked a question at Gwen as she and his sisters came in, but she was still cross with him and wouldn't respond to it, keeping her face empty and looking away from him. And as soon as they were all gathered, the clamorous business of choosing teams began and that made conversation impossible.

It was a complicated game because they argued over every other word and disputed every other syllable. And as it progressed it became steadily more riotous and ridiculous, for they rewarded all the actors by plying them with drinks and throwing sweets at them. Neil Morrish contrived to be in the same team as Lucy and although he was such a wooden actor that they ended up casting him as a policeman and simply requiring him to say ''Ello, 'ello, 'ello, what's goin' on 'ere?' no matter what the word might be, he enjoyed himself thoroughly, caught sweets like a champion, and gradually relaxed into such happy confidence that they let him play a clergyman in a paper dog-collar giving advice to Lucy's bride in full if tatty veil. It was the final scene and the word he had to slip in was 'matrimonial', so they gave him a list of four-syllabled virtues as a smoke-screen, told him to read it and let him loose.

'I am glad you have come to me for advice and information,' he read. 'The matrimonial estate is an honourable estate, instituted for mutual help and comfort, the one of the other, and not to be entered into lightly. You will need to be responsible and act intelligently and...' But then he looked into Lucy's eyes and the list was lost. 'An honourable estate,' he said. 'The best in all the world, the strongest and finest. Two people who will be all in all to one another for the rest of their lives, no matter what happens to them. They'll look after one another when things get rough, and have fun with one another, and trust one another, and share everything, the things they think and dream about and hope for, because your husband is the one person in all the world who'll always be there, who'll never let you down, never run away, never rat out on you, the one you can always depend on.' At which point he ran out of breath and inspiration and stopped, blushing deeply, as his audience burst into applause.

'Well said that man!' they cried. And 'If only!' And 'Quite right!' And Jeff looked straight at Gwen and called out, 'My sentiments entirely.' At which most of his family turned in their seats to look at her.

She was irritated to be under such public pressure, particularly as she couldn't think of a way to deflect it and she could feel that it was making her blush. Oh for heaven's sake! But as she was struggling for control and inspiration, Pete rose to the rescue.

'Matrimonial,' he called. 'Easy-peasy. Mat, rim, own. I don't see how you got 'nial' though. That was stretching it.'

'Neil!' the players yelled at him. 'Neil Morrish!'

'Oh dear, oh dear!' he mocked. 'No sweeties for them.' And everybody laughed as the sweets were thrown and he and his team stepped up for their next offering.

He was the star of the show. Naturally. It didn't matter what he did, he was applauded rapturously. He played a teletubby, a lovelorn swain gazing into Sandy's spellbound eyes, a disruptive child at school, even, having donned a white wig and a doleful expression, Inspector Morse, foot-flicking limp and all. And as if that weren't enough he produced the most admired word of the evening. Ad-mini-stray-shun.

'Isn't he brilliant,' Madge said to her new friend Gwen. 'You can see why they chose him for that coffee ad.'

Gwen was content to agree. He'd treated Ellie scandalously but he was wonderful company.

Eventually someone discovered that the boy with the dog was fast asleep at the foot of the stairs, using his pet as a pillow, and at that point they looked at their watches and were surprised to find that it was a quarter past one.

'We must go,' Gwen said.

'Seems wicked to stop,' Peggy said, 'but you're right. These kids should be in bed. We'll see you off.'

So the entire party trooped out into the garden to say goodbye. There wasn't a glimmer of light anywhere. The streetlights down in the village had long since blinked out, the moon was obscured by cloud and, pretty though they were, the fairy lights simply dropped their dappled colours into the branches. Gwen shivered and felt in her pocket for her torch, knowing it would be im-penetrably dark out in those long empty fields.

'Good party?' Jeff said, coming up behind her.

'It would have been very good,' she said, speaking quietly so that the others couldn't hear, 'if you hadn't told your sisters we were going to get married.'

'They asked,' he explained. 'I told them what I was hoping.'

He's so bloody determined, she thought, looking at that jutting jaw and the strength of his neck and shoulders, so certain he'll get what he wants, so sure I'll give in. She remembered how he'd talked about it right at the start, when he'd bullied Mr Makepeace for her. 'It's easy. You make up your mind you're going to win and you just keep on.' And now he's playing the same trick on me. Well it won't work. I won't be bullied. Not now. 'You made assumptions,' she said.

They were on the cusp of a quarrel, gathering breath for it, but at that moment Lucy emerged from the shadows to hold her mother's arm and interrupt them. 'Where's Pete?' she said.

There was no sign of him among the dark figures milling about on the blackness of the lawn and it was several minutes before he finally emerged from the house. Naturally his exit was staggeringly dramatic. He lurched and stumbled, to delighted cheers, missed the path, fell over his feet and finally ran straight into the side of the oak tree landing with such force that the lower branches swayed and the fairy lights tossed into clinking agitation.

'Beg a' pardon,' he said thickly. 'Li'l trouble with the old legs. Gotta siddown.' And fell sideways onto the lawn where he lay flat on his back while his audience applauded.

'He's drunk!' Lucy hissed to her mother and strode off at once and angrily to haul him to his feet.

It was a serious mistake. 'Who'ssat?' he said, as

her face swam towards him. 'Ellie is it?'

'No, it's not,' she said, and put out a hand to drag him to his feet. 'Get up! You're making a fool of yourself.'

He looked at the scales of coloured light swimming across her face, was puzzled, tried to focus his eyes. ''Snot Ellie,' he said. 'I'd know my Ellie anywhere. Tell you who it is. 'Smy lovely Lucy. My lovely luscious Lucy. Tha's who is it. Bes' girl in the worl'.' He turned his head to shout at his audience. 'This is my Lucy. She loves me. Issen that right, my lovely Lucy? She's my girl. Bes' girl in the worl'. Do anythin' for me.'

Oh God! This is awful, Lucy thought, looking at the ranks of faces behind her laughing and grinning, aware that her mother was one of them. I've got to stop him. 'Shut up for fuck's sake!' she spat.

But now he'd begun he couldn't stop. 'My lovely Lucy,' he said. 'She's always loved me. Always. Not like the other one. Took me in. Orphan of the storm. My lovely luscious Lucy. Bed an' board.' He began to giggle. 'Well bed anyway. Didden you my lovely.' He didn't seem to notice that she was kicking him, nor that her face was frantic. 'Bed an' board and never boring,' he said. Then without any warning, he turned his head to one side and was instantly asleep.

She was infuriated by the crass stupidity of this man she thought she loved. How could he be so thoughtless, so unkind, such a total fool? But there was no time for questions or answers or even to acknowledge her own distress. Feet were running towards her over the black grass and looking up she saw her mother's face, fraught with disbelief, and Jeff's, gazing down at his drunken guest as though he were amused. It's not funny, she thought, avoiding her mother's eye.

'Out for the count,' Jeff laughed.

'What are we going to do with him?' Gwen said, stooping over the sleeping body.

'Put him in the conservatory,' Jeff said. 'Let him sleep it off. You can hardly carry him back to the tower. Don't worry. There's enough of us here to lug him indoors.'

It seemed a sensible solution but there was still the dark walk back through the fields and no one to escort them. She looked round for Neil but there was no sign of him and she could hardly expect Jeff to leave his guests, especially when they'd come so close to a quarrel.

The body was rolled into an old curtain and carried indoors by a contingent of mocking men and superior teenagers. Lucy stood under the tree watching, her face drawn in the faint light.

The sooner we get home the better, Gwen thought, and she switched on the torch, looking at her daughter. 'All we've got to do is follow the beam,' she said and set off along the path. 'We shall be all right. Don't worry.'

But how can I not worry, Lucy thought, as she walked obediently behind her mother's flowing cape, after all that?

CHAPTER 25

After the pulse of the party, the tower was hissingly quiet. Even when Gwen switched on the light and she and Lucy stood blinking at one another in the sudden brightness, the tide of silence swelled between them, heavy with questions.

'Right,' Gwen said, striding into the kitchen to switch on the central heating. 'Let's have a bit of truth now shall we. I take it that wasn't just drink talking.' Her anger with Jeff had given her an unexpected strength.

Lucy stood in the middle of the room, as though she were in the dock. 'Well no,' she admitted and rushed to explain, 'but not in the way he said it. I mean, that was the drink talking.' It was embarrassing her to remember it. 'I mean, he made it sound sordid and it's not like that at all. Really. We love each other.'

'Oh Lucy!' Gwen mourned, as she walked out of the kitchen. 'How could you be so silly?'

Lucy turned her head aside and looked at the floorboards, just as she'd done when she was rebuked as a child. 'Please don't be cross,' she begged. 'I know I shouldn't have but I really couldn't help it.'

'I'm not cross,' Gwen said truthfully, 'I'm sad. Well no, that's the wrong word. It's much more than sad. This is such a mess and you're all going

366

to get hurt by it.' And she led the way upstairs. 'I must get my make-up off. My face feels as though it's cracking. Come with me and we'll talk in the bedroom.' She'd feel less exposed up there, poor kid.

Lucy was still looking away, face averted and shoulders drooping but she followed her mother up the stairs. 'I know it's not sensible,' she said. 'You don't have to tell me. I love him too much. That's the trouble. I always have. You don't know how much.'

They'd reached the little landing on the first floor and Gwen could see her nice comfortable bed waiting to welcome her. She stood in the open doorway, limp with fatigue, aching to be absolved from this confession, knowing absolution was impossible, yearning with pity for both her daughters. 'I do,' she said. 'I've always known.'

That came as a shock. 'Have you?'

'Yes. It was written all over your face, every time you looked at him.'

'Oh God!' Lucy said. 'It wasn't! Did everyone know?'

'Only me,' Gwen assured her. 'I don't think anyone else noticed. Your father certainly didn't and Ellie was always too wrapped up in her own emotions to be aware of anyone else's.' Then because Lucy's stricken face was making her feel uncomfortable and she wasn't sure how they were to proceed, she gave them both the chance to recover by walking into the bedroom, standing back slightly so that Lucy would follow. Once there she sat down at her dressing-table and began to remove her make-up, working the cotton wool across her forehead so that she had something to occupy her and could watch Lucy's face in the mirror with the ease of a little distance between them.

'So much for secrets,' Lucy said bitterly.

'I don't think you can have secrets from your mother,' Gwen said. 'Not when you're a twelve-year-old anyway. Although saying that, my mother never knew what I was thinking so maybe I'm talking out the back of my neck.'

Lucy sat down on the bed, wearily, and seemed to be gathering her strength for another confession. I'll make it easier for her, Gwen thought, and looked at her through the mirror again. 'Can I ask you something?'

Lucy's sigh was as touching as her averted head had been. 'I suppose so.'

'This wasn't why he left Ellie, was it?'

That could be denied and with relief. 'No,' Lucy said. 'We ... our ... that happened afterwards. He'd let his flat to some Americans and he didn't have anywhere to go when he and Ellie split up, so he came to me. That's all it was to start with.'

'Does she know about it?'

'Oh God,' Lucy remembered. 'I've got a card for you. She left it Christmas Eve.'

'So you've seen her.'

'No. We were out,' Lucy said. 'Hang on a tick and I'll get it.' And she went up to find it, glad of the chance to escape for a minute or two.

'She's keeping herself busy,' Gwen said when she'd read it. 'Don't you think so?' She handed the card to Lucy. 'Still I'm glad she's written. It gives me the chance to write back.'

Lucy was looking at the message on the enclosing envelope. 'You'd better read that too,' she said. 'It's...'

'Pointed,' Gwen said when she'd read it. 'So she does know. Oh Lucy! What a mess!'

Lucy's face was strained with the need to cry but she struggled to control herself. 'I never meant all this to happen,' she said. 'I didn't mean her to be hurt. I thought we could keep it private.' And when her mother raised her eyebrows. 'Yes I know. I must have been crazy. I think I was in a sort of way. It was a dream come true, you see. After all those years, fantasising about him, imagining how it would be if he left Ellie and turned to me, and there he was. I never imagined it would actually happen. Never, ever. You must believe that. It was a fantasy. That's all. I knew that. I'd always known it. And then suddenly...'

Gwen was so upset by her distress that she deliberately turned her attention away from it. 'I had this fantasy that I'd live in a cottage by the sea,' she mused, finding common ground between them, 'roses over the door and everybody welcoming and no problems and always summer.'

'Right,' Lucy understood. 'It's not the same is it? Not when you're living it.'

'No it's not,' Gwen said, relieved that she'd responded so quickly and understood so well. 'Better in some ways, worse in others, but never what you dream. You can shape a fantasy any way you like, but when it's real, you have to adapt.

369

Then it's workmen being bloody-minded, and yobs injuring your cat, and,' she smiled at Lucy through the mirror, 'daughters muddling up their lives.' And lovers determined to marry you when they know quite well you don't want to get married.

'Right,' Lucy said again. And she made a wry grimace. 'The awful thing is, when it all began, I was so happy I didn't care what happened. It was enough just to be with him. To have him say he loved me, to know he was part of my life. He's too good-looking, that's the trouble.'

'Always was,' Gwen said. 'Even as a boy. And vulnerable, of course, which is another attraction.' She surveyed her face. 'That'll do to be going on with,' she said. 'Do you want to do yours?'

They changed places and Gwen sat on the bed, took off her shoes and went on with her thoughts. 'He was very unhappy of course, and that's another thing.

Lucy was removing her mascara. She looked at her mother with one eye make-up bold and the other half-cleaned and greasy. 'Still is sometimes,' she said. 'You'd never believe how touchy he can be.'

'I would,' Gwen said, drifting into the bathroom to clean her teeth. 'I remember how he was when they first left him. Off to his room to hide at the least little thing. Never talking anything through. Always too bright. It was heartbreaking.'

'He does that now,' Lucy realised. 'If things get tough, he walks out and stays away for days.'

'And gets drunk.'

370

Lucy winced. 'Wasn't he foul! I couldn't believe he was saying all those awful things. And then to pass out on us like that.'

Gwen spat toothpaste. 'I've seen him worse. At least he's not been sick. He drank himself silly on cider when his parents walked out. He was so sick I thought he'd never stop. I felt really sorry for him.'

'I feel sorry for him too,' Lucy confessed, looking at her reflection. 'He's like a little boy lost sometimes. And he talks to Ellie in his sleep.'

Gwen didn't know how to respond to that, so she put on her nightdress and walked back into the bedroom where she could see Lucy's face. 'Don't let him hurt you too much,' she warned.

'I don't think he knows when he's hurting people,' Lucy sighed.

'Ah! So he's hurting you already.'

'Sometimes. Yes,' Lucy admitted. Then she paused and brooded, plainly thinking hard. 'Look,' she said, 'it's not going to last. I know that. I've known it all along. But it's no good saying end it because I can't. Not yet.'

'I wasn't going to say anything,' Gwen told her. 'I've never seen the point of offering advice unless it's asked for. I'm not even sure it's much good then.'

Lucy grinned at her, the old grin, half teasing, half daring. 'Thank God for that!'

Now it was possible for Gwen to hug her. 'I'll love you whatever you do,' she said, as she put her arms round her daughter's thin shoulders. 'You know that, don't you?'

'Yes,' Lucy said huskily, 'but I'd rather you

371

didn't tell me or you'll have me in tears.'

'Time you were tucked up in bed,' Gwen said, smoothing Lucy's hair. 'We've got a houseful for tea.'

'I wonder how he'll face us,' Lucy said.

'You and me both,' her mother said.

On the other side of the village, in the chill of his spartan bedroom, Neil Morrish was shivering. From the moment that obnoxious man had started his drunken rant, he knew he was defeated. Within seconds, depression had congealed in his veins, dragging him down and down into an all too familiar sense of rejection and failure. He'd left the party instantly, without looking at Lucy or Mrs M, or saying goodbye to Jeff, and retreated into the darkness, striding through the empty village at impossible speed, lungs straining and calves aching. And eventually his brutal activity lifted him from his misery into a blaze of anger.

He'd never really stood a chance with Lucy. How could he have done, when she was surrounded by media types like that arrogant Halliday with his flashy Merc – oh, he'd seen it speeding through the village – and his dyed hair – he might fool those silly girls but he doesn't fool me – and that god-awful mouth always open, yak, yak, yak, showing off and dropping names.

I was fooling myself, he thought, gazing out at the impenetrable blackness that hid the beach. I read more into it than I should. She went out with me but it didn't mean anything. She wrote to me but that didn't mean anything either. But oh, how well he remembered those letters. He knew them by heart. 'You are good. I knew I could trust you the minute I met you.' And all the time she'd been having sex with that foul Halliday. Her sister's lover. How could she do such a thing? Well, I've learnt my lesson now. I'll make sure I never see her again, or him, or any of them. I'll put in for a transfer. That's what I'll do. Go somewhere else. I can't go on working in Seal Island after this. I'd be a laughing stock.

He glanced at his watch and registered that it was four twenty-five and that he would be on duty in an hour and a half. There was no point in going to bed. He might as well wash and change and get a bit of breakfast. The thought of going to work without sleep didn't worry him. It was simply something he had to do. He knew the job would carry him along once he was back in the station. The job and his anger.

At four o'clock in the darkening afternoon, when Neil had finished his Boxing Day stint and was back in his flat and fast asleep, Gwen's guests drove to the tower in convoy to join her for tea. Pete wasn't with them, and nor were Simon and his wife – 'they're flying tonight' – and nor was Jeff.

'He's at the milking,' Peggy told her as they all came trooping into the tower, 'and then he's driving over with the cups and saucers. He's packed our big teapot too. We thought it might come in handy, didn't we Madge? We left the dogs behind 'cause he says you've got a cat. My stars! What a gorgeous room! I love that red.'

'Wait till you see my look-out post,' Gwen said, leading the way upstairs.

The sisters were impressed. 'I can see why you don't want to leave this,' Madge said, as she stood by the window. 'It's stunning.'

'Which is not to say we don't want you to marry our Jeff,' Peggy pointed out. 'Just that we can see why you won't.'

The tower was a-swarm, as the family trailed in and out of all the rooms, approved of the kitchen, exclaimed at the view from the look-out, and jostled one another on the stairs. When Jeff and Pete finally arrived, carrying two cardboard boxes full of china and the biggest teapot Gwen had ever seen, the kettle was on the boil and she was cutting up the Christmas cake. Well now Pete Halliday, she thought, as he strolled towards her, let's see what you've got to say for yourself.

It annoyed her that he didn't seem to be the least bit abashed. His skin had the translucent pallor of a hangover and his eyes looked decidedly weary, but apart from that he was his charming self, bending to kiss her cheek as though there were nothing the matter between them. 'You look a treat, Mrs M,' he said. 'Can I give you a hand with anything?'

She opened her mouth to say something biting, but at that moment Peggy breezed into the kitchen behind him. 'Is it OK if we move your sofas back a bit?' she asked. 'It's rather a squash with all us lot.'

'Leave it to me,' Pete told her and went off at once to organise it. 'Let's have that one up against the bookcase, right?' Soon he was flirting with

Sandy. 'Hello Gorgeous!' and flattering Jeff's three sisters, 'Plenty of room for you here. You're all slim. I mean, look at you, there's nothing of you. Slender as wands.'

'I bet you say that to all the girls,' Peggy teased.

'Only the good-looking ones.'

When Lucy came downstairs with the last of the kids, he was busy distributing tea and cake, and the tea party was loudly under way.

She greeted him coldly. 'Oh there you are. I'll bet you've got a thick head.'

He gave her the full beam of his most charming smile. 'You know me,' he said. 'More tea, Sis?'

Lucy walked past him into the kitchen to talk to her mother. 'Did he say anything?' she asked, speaking quietly so that the others wouldn't hear.

'No. Did you think he would?'

'Not even sorry?'

Gwen looked through the archway to where he was distributing smiles and cake. 'No.'

'Well I shall have something to say to him, even if you don't,' Lucy said. 'He needn't think he can just bounce back. Not after shooting his mouth off like that.'

'But you'll leave it till after tea, won't you,' Gwen said and strode off into the living room carrying a plate in each hand. 'Who's for a biscuit?'

All in all, it was a successful tea party. By the time it ended, the friendships that had begun rather tentatively the previous evening were beginning to establish, and all three of Jeff's sisters had invited Gwen to come and stay with them.

'You must bring her with you next time,' Peggy told her brother as she and her husband left the tower. 'Make sure he does, Gwen. That's a date. Even if you don't marry the man.'

'Forgiven?' Jeff asked as his relations tumbled into their estate cars shouting goodbye.

'Not quite,' Gwen said. 'You really dropped me in it yesterday.'

He held up his hands to forestall a wigging. 'I know. I know. I'm sorry. I shouldn't have said anything.'

That's the nice thing about him. Gwen thought, smiling at him. He can apologise and mean it.

He knew himself forgiven. 'OK for Thursday then?' he said cheerfully.

'If you promise not to say a word about us getting married.'

He had relaxed enough to joke. 'Would I?'

'Yes,' she said seriously. 'You would. You think I'm a softie. You think you've only got to keep on long enough and you'll wear me down. Well you're wrong. You won't.'

'OK,' he said, as if he was agreeing with her. Was he agreeing with her? Neither of them were quite sure. Change of subject indicated. 'How long are your two staying?'

'Two or three days I think. Two anyway.'

But she was wrong. As she closed the door on her departing guests, Pete walked down the stairs with the suitcases.

'We're off then,' he said.

She was surprised and cross. 'What now?'

''Fraid so,' he said easily. 'I've got a meeting

first thing tomorrow morning. Crack of dawn stuff.'

'I think we ought to talk,' she said.

'So do I Mrs M,' he agreed smoothly. 'Can't be done though. You ready Luce? Right. I'll be in touch.' He bent his handsome head to kiss her cheek, briefly and rapidly, moving away from her even as he kissed. 'Thanks for everything. It was a super Christmas.'

There was barely time for Lucy to grimace at her mother before they were gone. It was so quick it left Gwen breathless. And extremely angry. Running off like that, she thought. What cowardice. Well you needn't think you've got away with it. I shall catch up with you eventually and then there'll be even more to say.

Lucy was as cross as her mother, although she didn't say anything until they'd left the island and were speeding along the A27. Then she asked a pointed question. 'You haven't really got a meeting tomorrow have you?'

'Nope,' he said. 'I was just getting us out of harm's way.'

'Us?' she mocked. 'You, you mean.'

He agreed easily. 'Me then. I didn't want to spoil things when it had all gone so well.'

She echoed him in amazement. 'Gone so well? I don't believe I'm hearing this. You roll around on the grass telling everyone we're an item, when I specifically askcd you not to, and you say...' Words failed her. 'You're unbelievable.'

'Look,' he said, 'if there's one thing the Impossibles taught me by running out on me, it's that you're on your own when the chips are down and the best way to cope is to get out of trouble as fast as you can.'

There are times, Lucy thought, looking at his determined face, when I simply don't like you, Pete Halliday. But she didn't want to start a full-scale row when he was driving. She was a little too aware that people have accidents if they row when they're driving. So she deferred all the things she wanted to say to him, turned up the collar of her jacket and went to sleep. It was the only sensible thing to do.

CHAPTER 26

After such an unexpectedly difficult Christmas, Gwen was relieved to go back to work. Christmas had always been a bit of a letdown, even in the Fulham days when she hadn't expected much of it. Too much cooking, she thought, and too many preparations, that's the trouble. And too many hopes. Why do we always hope so much of it – as if it can work some sort of tribal magic – when the reality is just more of the same – and worse. I'm no nearer to knowing what to do about that poor baby than I was at the beginning, and how Lucy and Pete will make out I cannot imagine, and even Jeff's a problem now. She felt she was treading water, waiting for the next breaker to knock her off her feet again. Still, she thought, as she set out on her first morning back to work, at least there's the school.

Mr Carter had asked her if she wouldn't mind coming in for two days before the start of term because there was so much to do.

'I do appreciate this,' he said, when she arrived in his study, 'We're due to be Ofstedded in ten days' time so every minute counts.'

'Is it as bad as we read in the papers?' she asked.

'It is,' he told her, scratching his scruffy hair. 'Most of the staff have been in a lather about it since we broke up.'

That seemed rather extreme. 'Oh dear!'

'It's enough to put anyone in a lather,' he said. 'If we're not very very careful, we're going to be judged and found wanting, and we all know it. That's what Ofsted inspections are about.' He was gathering papers as he spoke, his fingers stiff with sudden anger. 'In the old days inspectors were ex-teachers. They knew the score and they were usually fair and helpful. But this lot are shop-keepers and local businessmen and a different kettle of fish altogether. They're not looking to praise any of us, they're looking to find fault and cut us down to size.' And when Gwen raised her eyebrows, 'It's true. I wish it weren't. We have to look for ways to stay out of trouble. I'm going to dazzle them with statistics. They love lists. I'm going to make sure we're well supplied with everything we could possibly need and rub their rotten noses in our good organisation.'

'It sounds like a war,' Gwen said.

'It is,' Mr Carter told her grimly, 'and they've got all the big guns.'

'Well I'm on your side,' Gwen said, annoyed to think that her teachers were being upset. 'Just tell me what to do.'

She spent the first day chasing up stock that hadn't been delivered, catching up with the mail and printing lists of all the school's achievements in large black print for an eye-catching wall display that their critics couldn't miss. From then on she was endlessly and rewardingly busy, for there were letters to be sent out for a parents' evening on top of everything else, the usual daily snowstorm of mail to be opened and answered, and a steady procession of parents and visitors arriving at her window each with a different request. By the end of the first week she was played out and when the dreaded inspection finally began it got worse, for then she spent a lot of her time dispensing comforting cups of tea and on two occasions providing tissues for her pressurised teachers.

'I can't see what anyone gains by putting teachers under such stress,' she said to Jeff on the final evening of the Little Marsden torture. 'It's so negative.'

He had little sympathy for the trials of the teaching profession. 'They've got to be inspected,' he said reasonably, cutting into his Dover sole. 'How else would we know whether they were doing a good job? The best thing they can do is put up with it and try not to be such wimps.'

'Nobody likes being told how to do their own job,' she pointed out, sipping her wine. 'Look how you feel about set-aside and milk targets.'

She had a point and he had to admit it. 'Well possibly,' he said. 'I just don't like to see you getting so involved. It's their problem. Let them get on with it.'

'I like getting involved,' she told him. 'It keeps my mind occupied.' There had been no word from Ellie since her thank-you letter and nothing from Lucy either.

'You could have been involved with me,' he said, giving her one of his stern looks.

'I am involved with you,' she laughed, deciding to pass it off with a joke. 'Or haven't you noticed?'

'Well don't go knocking yourself out, that's all,'

381

he warned. 'I know you. You'll run yourself ragged looking after your precious teachers and then you won't have any energy left to enjoy yourself.'

'Which I shall need next week,' she told him.

He looked up from his fish. 'What's happening next week?'

'They're starting on the drains.'

By New Year's Day Eleanor was exhausted. She didn't wake until two that afternoon and even then she was still so tired she didn't grumble from her bed until it was past four o'clock and the room was darkening.

'I'm turning into an owl, I hope you realise,' she said to her squirming baby, as she switched on the lights. 'And I'm about the same shape too.'

When she was on her own and had time to consider it, she was quite alarmed by the size of her belly, especially as she still had another two months to go, according to her own private mathematics. Her midwife was determined that the baby was due in four weeks and had booked her in for a weekly check-up, which was very inconvenient and another reason for her exhaustion. Rushing from the clinic to the office and then having to pretend that she wasn't tired when she got there was very very wearing. In one way she'd be quite glad if the midwife proved right and the baby came earlier than she'd intended, but in another it would make hellish difficulties, now that she'd trumpeted her intention of giving birth over Easter and coming back to her desk immediately afterwards. 'I can't win,' she said to the small spine shifting under her soothing hand.

In the meantime there was the Vixen Brothers presentation to prepare, Mum's letter to answer, a nanny or a child-minder to find – she'd interviewed six so far and they'd all been horrendous – and this business with Pete to be dealt with. She hadn't had a word from him over the holiday and she was horribly upset about it. Lucy'd sent a card, the way she always did, with kisses all over it and a loving message, but that was no comfort after Sally's revelation. I shall have to face her with it, she thought, and see if I can get at the truth. It's silly to let it drift on. But I'll get Birmingham out of the way first.

The presentation was even worse than she'd dreaded, with horrendously late nights, horrendously demanding clients and a series of anxious phone-calls in transit that left her feeling totally drained. For the first time in her pregnancy she called in sick on the day after she returned, attended the clinic at leisure and spent the afternoon lying on the sofa with her feet up – her ankles were swollen – eating chocolates and reading magazines as though she was brain-dead. But at teatime she bestirred herself and finally phoned her sister.

Lucy had had a very difficult morning. Pete was away. He'd been away a lot since Christmas. In fact he'd left her as soon as they got home on Boxing Day and although he'd returned with his arms full of presents and whisked her off to a New Year's Eve party, he'd left again two days later, this time to visit some business friends and in a mood so ruthlessly determined that he made her feel quite uncomfortable. Apparently the

Chairman was due for the chop. 'Grossman's are putting in one of their own.'

'Poor man,' she said, feeling sorry for him. 'What's he done to deserve that?'

'Nothing,' Pete said, casually. 'That's the whole point. He's a drag and we want to move forward. Anyway he's old.'

'And that's a crime?'

'He's yesterday,' her lover told her. 'We're today. End of story.'

She was upset to find him so heartless. But, sadly, not surprised. 'Power corrupts I see,' she said.

'Don't be like that,' he grinned, swooped to kiss her and was gone.

And then, as if that weren't bad enough, Helen had come down to breakfast that morning to tell her that she would be moving in with her current boyfriend as soon as they got back from their skiing holiday.

'It's not been the same since Tina went,' she explained. 'I mean we were such a good team. I thought I'd better let you know. Proper notice and everything. You'll soon get someone else, won't you? Bound to with a house like this. I mean it's so roomy and everything.'

And so costly, Lucy thought. But she thanked Helen for giving her good notice and said she hoped she'd be really happy and poured them both another cup of tea as if they were celebrating instead of parting company.

So when she heard her sister's cheerful voice on the phone suggesting lunch next day she was halfway to agreeing before she stopped to think about it.

'I haven't seen you for an age,' Eleanor said. 'We've got quite a bit of catching up to do.'

Lucy decided to ignore that as a tad too dangerous for the moment. But she had to admit it would be a relief to be out of the office and away from all her problems – providing they didn't talk about Pete. If she was careful and handled it delicately they might get away with it. 'How are you?' she asked.

Eleanor was vague. 'Oh you know me. Soldiering on. Oxo tower at one then. I can't wait to see you again.'

As soon as she put the phone down, Lucy had second thoughts and as the taxi took her to Blackfriars Bridge next day, she was gathering safe topics for them to talk about almost as if they were business rivals. But the minute she saw her sister all plots and plans dissolved into irrelevance. She looked absolutely dreadful, so bloated and puffy she was barely recognisable, even though she was dressed in a stylish grey suit and had her hair layered and streaked, and was waving to her with immaculately painted fingers. But those fingers were unmistakeably fat and her face was like a full moon and there was something wrong with her eyes. They seemed to be open too wide, as though she was staring. Poor Ellie, she thought, as she walked towards her.

'Yes,' Ellie said, acknowledging her shocked expression. 'I know. I'm as big as a house. This is what pregnancy does to you, little sister. Just as well it doesn't go on for ever.'

Lucy bent to kiss her, full of pity and affection.

385

'I think you're lovely no matter how pregnant you are,' she said.

'Do you hear that, Sprog?' Ellie said to her bulge. 'You've got a lovely aunty.'

So they settled to food and office gossip and didn't mention their mother or Pete until the coffee had been served. Then Ellie's question was asked so casually there was no difficulty in answering it.

'Did you go to the tower at Christmas?'

'I did.'

'And Mum was all right?'

'Well she missed you, naturally, but she was OK. We went to a party at the farmer's place.'

'Bully for you,' Eleanor said, grimacing. And added artlessly, 'I suppose Pete was there too.'

'Don't talk to me about Pete,' Lucy said, relieved that she could start by criticising him. 'He got drunk and rolled about in the garden when it was time to go home. Couldn't stand up. We had to leave him there to sleep it off.'

'In the garden? That must have cooled his ardour a bit.'

Lucy recognised the jibe for what it was but decided to ignore it and concentrate on her story. 'They put him in the conservatory I think. I suppose he slept on the floor. Anyway they got a blanket and lugged him indoors somewhere. We left him to it. If he was uncomfortable it served him right. It was very embarrassing.'

Ellie gave her a look that was as shrewd as she could make it, given her swollen cheeks and pop-eyes. 'And how is he now?'

Here it is, Lucy thought, but she kept calm,

with an effort. 'I've no idea. I haven't seen him for ages.'

Again the shrewd look. 'I thought you were an item.'

It was necessary to deny it. Outright. With a good strong lie. 'Good God no. What gave you that idea?'

'Oh quite a lot of things actually,' Ellie said coolly. 'The Yanks said they were forwarding his mail to your address, for a start, and that awful Sally from accounts said she'd seen you having lunch together. Several times, she said.'

'Quite right,' Lucy agreed, heart pounding. 'So she did. He's been staying with me off and on – mostly off I might say – ever since you sent him packing. He came straight to Battersea that night. Said he hadn't anywhere else to go and he was an orphan of the storm and would I take pity on him.'

'And you did?'

'And I did. Tina was leaving so I had the room.' Did that sound plausible? 'And I wasn't going to say no to a bit of extra rent. I was a third down on the mortgage with Tina going. But I've no idea where he is now.'

'Well, well, well. And here's me thinking... Well never mind what I was thinking. He's never been what you'd call faithful. I mean we've always had an open relationship. I expect you knew that. But I'm glad he didn't add you to the list. And I'm so, so glad I was wrong. Dear old Luce. I knew you wouldn't do the dirty on me.'

'You're my sister,' Lucy said feeling desperately uncomfortable. 'Blood thicker than water and all that sort of thing.'

Eleanor was looking at her watch. 'Oh my God,' she said. 'Look at the time. I shall have to go. I've got a meeting with the Big White Chief. Don't you rush though. Finish your coffee. I'll pay the bill on the way out.'

She was gone in a swish of silk and a waft of her expensive perfume. It's over, Lucy thought, watching her as she waddled towards the desk. I can't go on with it now, not after this, not after lying to her. I must make it true. It's the only thing I can do. If she finds out it was a lie it'll ruin everything for everyone, her, me, Mum, Pete. I can't do that to her. Not when she's on her own and looks so awful. I must finish it as soon as I see him again. Her heart was still throbbing most unpleasantly and her shirt was damp with sweat but the decision was irrevocable. And that's the way the world ends, she quoted to herself, not with a bang but – in a pool of perspiration. I'll take a shower the minute I get home, she promised herself, and then I'll work out exactly what to say to him.

But there wasn't time for shower or thought. His Mercedes was parked at the kerb and the man himself was draped across the sofa in the living room watching a quiz show.

'Hi there!' he said, turning down the sound. 'You're late.'

She had to make an effort to steady herself. 'I had lunch with Ellie.'

He treated it as a joke. 'What, all this time? Now that's what I call a working lunch. So what are we doing with ourselves this evening? How about taking in a show?'

'Actually,' she said, speaking at once while her resolve was still strong, 'I think it's time for a show down.'

He was perfectly cool. 'Is that a fact?'

There was such a strong pulse in her throat that she found it hard to speak and had to cough before she could begin. 'I don't think we should go on with this any longer,' she said. 'She asked me if we were an item, right out, and I told her we weren't.' And when he raised an eyebrow, 'Well I could hardly say yes could I? Not when she's pregnant and all on her own and everything. Anyway, that's what I said, and now I think we ought to split up and make it true, because it's never been right and we never ought to have started.' And she took a step backwards away from the wrath that she knew would follow.

He was so cool he didn't even widen his eyes. He lay where he was, looking up at her with a faint smile on his face. 'OK,' he said easily. 'If that's the way you want it. I think you're being silly but that's up to you.'

Apprehension was instantly replaced with anger. How dare he just lie there and accept it, when she expected him to fight, wanted him to. 'Don't you care?' she said.

'It's immaterial whether I do or not. You've made up your mind. So OK, that's it.'

'Don't I mean anything to you?' she said. She was unreasonable with anger. 'You said you loved me.'

He mocked her. 'And you want to end it?'

She was so angry with him she would have

thrown him out bodily if it had been within her power. 'Yes I do,' she said furiously. 'You're unkind and selfish and heartless and shallow and conceited, and you've walked out on your own child, and you don't care that we've been fucking incestuous, and you hog the bathroom and I'm sick of your fucking shoes and all that stupid polishing, and ... and ... you don't love anyone except yourself.'

He smiled at that but it was a tight smile and there was venom behind it. 'Well I'm glad we got that sorted out.'

Her anger suddenly deflated, leaving her defeated and hopeless. 'I don't think I ever really knew you,' she said. 'I thought you were wonderful when we were kids. You were my hero. And now...'

He uncoiled himself from the sofa. 'So when have I got to leave?' he asked. 'Am I allowed to take you out to dinner first?'

She felt bleak with approaching loss. 'What for?'

'Old times' sake?' he suggested. 'Look, I'd like to part friends. OK, it was a mistake. I'll admit if it'll make you feel any better. We shouldn't have started. I've been thinking the same thing. For quite a long time actually. But we did, and it was good while it lasted, and if we can handle this well, there's no need for either of us to get hurt. If we part on bad terms we shall never see one another again and I wouldn't want that. Not after all these years. And not when I'm really very very fond of you. Always have been.'

He had walked towards her as he spoke and now they stood face to face. 'And what about

Ellie?' she asked, turning away from him.

'Ellie's a different matter altogether,' he said. 'But she doesn't need to know about it, if that's what you're asking. We're the only ones who know and if we don't tell her, it can be our secret.'

'I can't bear the thought of hurting her,' she said. 'If you saw the state she's in...'

'Don't let's talk about her,' he interrupted. 'We'll only quarrel. Let's have a good meal and then I'll pack my bags and leave at midnight like a noble Cinderella.'

He'd made it sound charming and friendly and harmless. So, rather to her surprise, that's what they did. She even helped him pack his clothes and waved goodbye to him from the bedroom window. But when the road was quiet again she felt bereaved and lonely and wondered whether she'd made the right decision after all.

For the rest of the week she spent as much time at work as she could and all her evenings clubbing and pretending to enjoy herself. But when the weekend began she was too lonely to sit it out in an empty house any longer and that Friday evening she phoned her mother to beg an invitation to the tower.

'Of course,' Gwen said. 'I'd love to see you. But I'd better warn you, they're laying the drains and it's all mud and mayhem here. There's not much road left either. You'll have to park at the other end of Mill Lane and walk up. And I'm clearing the outhouse.'

'I'll help you,' Lucy said. 'Mud and mayhem I can stand.'

Her voice roused Gwen's sympathy at once. 'What's up chick?'

'Nothing much,' Lucy said, trying to sound careless. 'It's just we've split up.'

'Ah!' Gwen understood. 'Come here first thing tomorrow morning. Bring some old clothes. It's filthy in the outhouse.'

It was like the set of a horror movie. Long swathes of white mist rolled off the sea to drift in the hollows of the water meadow and obscure the empty flowerbeds in Gwen's sea-damp garden. The road was a deep trench full of evil-smelling mud and petrol-stained puddles, the mechanical diggers stood where they'd been left, grotesque and alien, shaggy with wet earth and showing ugly teeth. There was a skip full of ancient rubbish stinking beside the outhouse, a set of vicious looking rakes and spades beaded with black moisture stacked against the garden wall, and her mother's right arm was draped in cobwebs that clung to the wool of her jersey and floated behind her, trailing dirt and dead flies, as she walked across the garden smiling and calling.

'Isn't it a tip! I did warn you.'

But in an odd way working in the dirt and dust seemed right to Lucy, like an expiation. It was very cold even inside the outhouse and after a while she felt chilled to the bone and her hands were black with grime, but she worked doggedly, needing the satisfaction of cleaning and clearing, wanting to see what this little ancient building would look like when it was empty. And Gwen, glancing at her from time to time, as she carried the next wheelbarrow load of old crates and

392

broken flower pots out to the skip, was touched by her closed face and her determination and took care not to question her. So they spoke rarely and simply allowed themselves to be carried along by their labours.

Midday passed and they didn't notice it, the church clock struck two as they were throwing another load of broken tools on to the skip, but although they told one another they were beginning to get hungry, they decided to work on.

'We'll just get rid of those sacks,' Gwen said, striding towards them, 'and then we'll call it a day.'

The sacks were decaying and so full of dust that lifting them raised a cloud and made them both cough and choke. 'Drop 'em in the wheelbarrow quick,' Gwen said, spitting to clear her mouth. 'Let's get out in the air before we suffocate.'

'There's something underneath,' Lucy said. 'A lamp or something. Shall we take that too?'

'It'll be some dirty old standard lamp,' Gwen said.

But it wasn't. It was an old fashioned storm lantern, and even in its present filthy condition, coated with dirt and dust, sticky with cobwebs and with all the glass in its four windows sulphur-yellow with grime, they could see that it had once been a rather splendid object. It was made of iron with elaborate scrolls above and below the frame and the long handle was a stout piece of oak.

'I've half a mind to keep it,' Gwen said. 'It might come in useful.'

Lucy laughed. 'I can't think when,' she said. But she helped her mother carry it into the tower, spread newspaper on the kitchen table for protection, put the lamp in the middle and set to work to clean it.

In the privacy of the kitchen it was possible for Gwen to ask a tentative question. 'I gather you've seen Ellie.'

And equally possible for Lucy to give an honest answer, which led to a full account of their lunch in the Oxo tower, her need to lie and the subsequent split with Pete. 'I couldn't do anything else, could I?' she said.

'No,' Gwen agreed. 'You couldn't. Not really. And are you all right?'

'Better than I thought I'd be actually,' Lucy admitted and tried to make light of it. 'It's funny how things turn out. I have the love of my life served up on a plate for me and then after all that I find I don't want him.'

She's got style, Gwen thought, admiring her, even if she does make mistakes. But then don't we all? 'There,' she said, turning the lamp on its side and giving them both something else to concentrate on, 'that's one side done. It's going to look good when we've finished it.'

They were still hard at work on it when Jeff arrived.

'It's a good age,' he said, examining it. 'You can tell by the size of those reflectors. It should give a very strong light. There used to be lots of them about the village one time. We had one. What are you going to do with it?'

'Fill it with oil and hang it on that old hook by the door,' Gwen said, 'and light it of an evening as a guide to weary travellers. Or take it to school for the History table. The kids'ud love it.'

'Or use it to face the Great Unexpected,' Lucy suggested.

'That too,' Gwen agreed. 'You never know.'

'You and your great Mumbo-Jumbo,' Jeff teased. 'You're not still on about that are you?'

'Wait till the February 26th,' Gwen told him darkly. 'That's all.'

'When do your builders start?' Jeff asked.

That made her laugh. 'No. Not on February 26th,' she said. 'They're not going to be the Un-expected, if that's what you're thinking. I've got everything planned down to the last detail. No. They start Wednesday, if the drains are down and they can get through. Why do you ask?'

'I've got to cry off tonight,' he said. 'Mr Rossi's taking delivery of his new caravans in half an hour and then we're going off for a drink to sign the new lease. I was wondering if Wednesday would do for us instead.'

'Wednesday'd be fine,' Gwen told him. 'We'll have fish and chips, won't we Luce?' It was actually quite a relief to find that she hadn't got to cook a meal for three.

'Fish and chips is fine by me,' Lucy said. 'It'll give us a chance to get out in the air and have a look round. I haven't seen your village for weeks.' Or your village bobby.

So they set off for the High Street arm in arm. And as they were strolling along in the dark trying to decide whether they would have cod or huss, there was the familiar blue uniform, trundling towards them on the familiar bicycle.

'Look who's coming,' Lucy said, nudging her

mother's arm. And she turned her smile to greet him.

The person who loomed out of the darkness was a total stranger, a tall stringy-looking man with a beard. As he was being smiled at, he greeted them cheerfully. 'Evening ladies.'

Lucy felt she had to explain her smile. 'I thought you were PC Morrish,' she said.

'No, ma'am. I'm his replacement. PC Duckworth.'

'You mean he's gone?'

'Long since. Like I said, I'm his replacement. I've even got his flat. Quite nice all things considered. Right on the front.'

Gwen was surprised and rather annoyed but Lucy was flattened with disappointment. It didn't seem right for him to have left without a word. Not when they'd been so friendly and he'd been keeping an eye on her mother and everything. He might at least have written.

'Did you know he'd gone?' she asked her mother as they walked back along Mill Lane.

'No I didn't,' Gwen said. 'That was news to me too. I suppose he got posted somewhere. They do shift policemen around.'

'Nearly home,' Lucy said, changing the subject. They were passing their two cars standing forlornly in line beside the wet hedge.

'It'll be a good thing when I can put that car in the garage,' Gwen said. 'If it stands there much longer it'll rot away.'

'Let's hope everything goes according to plan next week,' Lucy said.

Which rather to Gwen's surprise it did,

396

although slightly more slowly than she would have liked. By the time Lucy arrived for her third flying visit, the road was restored, the lamp was hanging from its hook beside the porch, the outhouse was sporting a new garage door – and the Great Unexpected was a mere four days away.

'Do you really believe something will happen that day?' Lucy asked, as they sat in the kitchen over tea on Saturday afternoon.

'Sometimes I do,' Gwen said. 'When Jeff's been teasing me about it, I do. He makes me defensive. But sometimes I don't. I mean I don't really see how the planets can affect what goes on in a tiny little place like Seal Island. Still it gives me something else to think about when I'm worrying about the baby. Ellie doesn't write, you know, or phone.'

'No,' Lucy said. 'I know.'

Gwen looked a question at her.

'She phoned me yesterday,' Lucy said. 'We talked about it.'

'Is she all right?'

'She said she was. She's off to Paris again apparently. Trying to clinch the Jean-Paul Reynaldo deal.'

'Has she got a nanny or an au pair or anything?'

'No,' Lucy said. 'Not yet. She's still trying. Time enough. It's not due till Easter is it and that's ages away.'

'Five weeks,' Gwen said. 'That's all.' Five weeks and nothing settled. Anxiety nipped her brain in a sudden vice. Five short weeks and nothing settled.

CHAPTER 27

February 26th turned out to be an ordinary wintry day, the kind of day Gwen had come to expect since she lived on the south coast, cold and grey with a strong sea running and a strong wind blowing. Gulls and crows flew inconsequently against the force of it, tossed about like scraps of paper, the naked trees rustled and groaned, and out in their wind-chilled pastures the cows lay in the grasses, chewing and flicking their ears.

'So where's the Great Unexpected?' Jeff teased, when he arrived for their mid-week dinner.

Gwen lifted the joint from the oven. 'The day's not over yet,' she said.

'It is as near as dammit,' he laughed, 'and all you've got to show for it is the usual gale force wind.'

'The kids have been manic,' Gwen said, testing the potatoes. 'Beatrice says this sort of weather always gets them worked up. A bit like you. I wonder you're still here. I thought you'd be off to the Midlands.'

'No chance of that,' he told her. 'I've got six heifers ready to calve.' He tossed a bundle of glossy brochures onto the table. 'I brought these over. Thought you might like to take a look.'

She was too busy to do more than glance at them. 'What are they?'

'River cruises,' he said. 'As you won't marry me I thought the next best thing might be a holiday.'

He'd put her on the spot again. She could hardly say no when he was so eager and he'd asked her so cleverly, but how could she agree to a holiday when she might be looking after the baby? 'I'll look at them later,' she promised, carefully diplomatic. 'When we've had dinner. I'm starving. Aren't you?'

'That's the gale,' he said. 'Gives you an appetite.'

'It's a peculiar sort of sky,' Gwen said, looking through her kitchen window. 'Look at the way it divides. It's in two separate halves, summer on one side and winter on the other.'

It was an accurate description, for the sky in the east was still sharp-lit, its dusky blue patterned with long high ripples of very white cloud, while the western sky was already dark and heavy with oppressive storm clouds.

'There's a storm brewing,' Jeff said. 'That's all. Batten down the hatches and let's eat while we can.'

So they dined as the wind gathered force and read through their brochures as it tossed the trees like flails and made love as it howled against the sides of the tower and whipped the Channel to a force 9 gale. Jeff slept instantly as he always did, but Gwen lay awake for a long time, listening to the drama outside her window, too busy with her thoughts to sleep. Now that her predicted day had come, she was disappointed to have been proved wrong, but that was nothing to the problem of what was to be done about that baby.

I've only got a month now, she thought, and then I shall have to decide. And what am I to do about this holiday? It would be lovely to have a holiday but how can I agree to it when I might be baby-sitting? She was still turning the facts over and over in her mind when she finally drifted into darkness.

She was woken by a reverberating crash. It was so loud that for a second she thought it was an explosion and sat up at once, thoroughly alarmed and alert.

Jeff woke too. 'What the hell was that?' he said and rolled over to switch on the bedside lamp and look at the clock. It was just before one o'clock and outside the window the wind was rushing and pounding and roaring so loudly they could barely hear one another speak. 'Well you've got your storm and no mistake,' he shouted at her.

And at that the light went out and there was a series of explosive bangs, all very loud and close by, and the window began to rattle.

'This is more than a storm,' Gwen shouted and got up to feel her way across the room to switch on the main light. There was no response and when she eased out onto the landing, the lights were dead there too.

'You mind what you're doing,' Jeff called to her.

'We've lost power,' she called back.

'Stay where you are,' he yelled into the black-ness. 'I don't want you falling downstairs. Wait till I've opened the curtains.'

But when he'd groped his way to the window and pulled the curtains back as far as he could, they were still in darkness. The air outside seemed to be full of dust, swirling and very fast moving and carrying the smudged shapes of tumbling debris, twigs and branches and what looked like pebbles or pieces of tile. It was pressing in so hard upon the tower that he couldn't see anything else at all, and he remembered a tornado he'd seen in the states and in a moment of stunned disbelief realised that he was in the middle of another one, that the windows could be blown in or sucked out and that they were both in danger.

By now his eyes were accustomed to the lack of light and he could see Gwen's outline as she walked back to the bed. 'Get down!' he shouted. 'Lie on the floor.'

'What?'

There was no time for explanations or gentleness, only instincts, and his instincts were roaring. His mind was flailed with images of bodies gashed by flying glass, he imagined her tender flesh gored and opened, and he was furiously afraid. He threw himself at her, grabbed her by the shoulders and pushed her onto the carpet, covering her body with his own and pulling the duvet down to smother them both. And as they fell the window cracked as though it had been hit by a shell.

She was awed with terror. 'Oh Jeff. What is it?'

'A twister,' he said, his mouth close to her ear. 'A tornado. Stay still.'

They lay together in the darkness, hearts pounding and ears painful with pressure as the wind buffeted the tower, screaming like a jet at full throttle. It seemed a very long time before the

401

pressure began to diminish, although in fact it was less than a minute.

He sat up carefully, listening. And it was moving on, still roaring and accompanied by explosive crashing sounds, loud bumps and thuds, a crackle of glass, the creak and thump of a tree falling. There was marginally more light and it had started to hail, the stones pattering against the windows in white lumps as big as mothballs. Now that the extreme darkness had passed they could see that the window had been dented as though it had been punched by a great fist.

'My God!' she said, staring at it. 'Look at that!'

'That's nothing,' he told her. 'Last twister I saw smashed every house in the street.'

'We must go and see what's happened in the village,' she said. 'People could have been hurt.'

They searched for their clothes, dressing as quickly as they could, in a fumble of shocked fingers. 'I'll go,' he said. 'You stay here.'

'I'm coming with you,' she said. 'If there are people hurt they'll need all the help they can get. I shall light my lamp. It's just the thing.'

He was peering out of the landing window, struggling to penetrate the darkness. 'It's heading for the village,' he said. 'I can see the top of it. Do you see? The thing like a black funnel. Must have come off the sea. I hope to God it missed the farm.'

'We'll go there first,' she said.

They groped down the sightless well of the staircase, following the wall with their fingers, found a torch in the kitchen drawer and were reassured by its light and stepped out into a

402

sharpness of hail and freezing air. The wind was still pounding around them. They could hear the clatter of tiles falling, and nearer to hand something banging, clomp, clomp, clomp, in an oddly rhythmical way. Gwen turned her torch towards the sound and saw that her new garage door had been blown open and bent sideways and was now banging against the upright. The air throbbed with movement and prickled with dust and strange smells and unfamiliar sounds. It took quite an effort to fight their way through the weight of it to the Land Rover and they were both relieved to climb inside and switch on the headlights and have the power of an engine to propel them forward.

But they only managed to inch as far as the first bend in Mill Lane and there, suddenly and totally, their way was blocked by the striated trunk of a fallen tree.

'Buggeration!' Jeff said, glaring at it through the flurry of the windscreen wipers, his fear and anger finding expression at last. 'How the hell am I going to get through now? I shall have to drive over the bloody fields.' But Gwen wasn't listening to him. She'd opened the door and was swinging her feet out into the rain. 'Gwen! For Christ's sake. Where d'you think you're going?'

'There's someone there,' she shouted. 'On the other side of the tree. I can hear them.' And was gone, running through the beam of the head-lights at full tilt, climbing over the trunk, boots and raincoat shining in the wet.

There was a small figure on the other side of the tree, cowering against the trunk and

403

whimpering, a small shivering figure in a long wet nightdress and sodden carpet slippers, with her hair in old-fashioned curlers. 'Holy Mary Mother of God! Holy Mary Mother of God!' It was Teresa O'Malley.

Gwen stooped towards her, concern obliterating every other emotion. 'Are you all right?' she said.

She didn't seem to be hurt. There was no sign of blood or broken bones, but she was soaking wet and gibbering and when Gwen tried to lift her, she refused to budge from her perch among the fallen boughs. 'There are ghosts in the house, so there are,' she wept. 'I've seen them. They've come for to get me. Oh Jesus, Mary and Joseph! That I should live to see such a night. Great big terrible ghosts. Big as a room, so they are. 'Tis the end of the world. Holy Mary Mother of God.'

Jeff loomed out of the darkness. 'Is she hurt?'

'I don't think so. She says there's ghosts in the house.'

'Go back indoors,' he shouted at Miss O'Malley. 'You'll catch your death of cold out here.'

But at that she burst into frantic tears and declared that she couldn't do such a thing, not if it was ever so, not if the world was to end that very minute, not with all the ghosts of hell come to torment her.

'She's off her head,' Jeff said in exasperation. 'Leave her. I've got to get to the farm.'

'No. Wait,' Gwen said. 'I'll get her some dry clothes and we'll take her back to the tower. We can't leave her here like this. I shan't be a minute.' She turned to Miss O'Malley. 'I'm going in the house,' she shouted. 'If there are any ghosts I shall chase them away.' And torch in hand she swept off to the cottage.

It was exceedingly dark in the front garden but the beam from her torch was sufficient to show that part of the thatched roof had been ripped away, the front door was off its hinges and the garden full of debris, most of it broken thatch. Inside the hall it was all confusion. The runner lay squashed and crumpled against the far wall, a mirror had been slammed to the floor and smashed into vicious shards of glass, the hall-stand was on its side, coats and scarves bundled beneath it, and swirling all around her, rising from the debris to curl against the walls and writhe up the stairs were thick columns of grey-brown dust, turning and twisting through the beam of her torch, like huge ethereal snakes – or long swathes of ectoplasm – or ghosts. No wonder the poor old thing was afraid.

She found a long coat and a pair of shoes, and underneath them, a gardening jersey and an old skirt, all blessedly dry, bundled them under her raincoat and ran back to the fallen tree.

'Come on,' she said to Miss O'Malley. 'We're going to the tower. There aren't any ghosts there. I've got you some dry clothes.'

And although she protested, 'Oh now I don't know. I don't know at all', Miss O'Malley stood up, followed her to the Land Rover and was reversed to safety.

The tower was still in total darkness, the garage door still banging, the trees still creaking, the surrounding fields susurrating but unseen. But now that she'd started her mission Gwen wasn't deterred by any of it. She found candles and matches and an old blanket, and instructed her refugee to get out of her wet clothes and into the dry ones she'd brought from the cottage.

'We're going to see what's happened to the people in the caravans,' she said. 'I've set the central heating to come on as soon as we get our power back. Wrap yourself in this blanket and keep as warm as you can. We shan't be long.'

Teresa O'Malley was beginning to recover. 'You're a saint so you are, Mrs MacIvor,' she said gratefully. 'Don't you worry about me. You just go where you have to. There could be people killed out there, so there could, and they'll be wanting you to save them.'

So the storm lantern was taken down from its hook beside the door and laid in the back of the Land Rover and Gwen and Jeff set off into the howl of the night. Neither of them said much, he because he had to concentrate on driving safely over the bumpy grass of the water meadow, she because she was caught up in the most unexpected and extraordinary emotion. The event had happened, just as she'd predicted, and she was involved in it, just as she'd known she would be, and despite past terrors and present uncertainties, she realised that she was triumphantly happy, bumping along in the Land Rover, tossed from side to side, ready for anything.

'This is as far as I can get,' Jeff said, stopping the van. They'd reached the stile and the long rows of hedges that marked the top of the long meadow. 'Now we'll have to walk. Still up for it?'

Of course she was up for it. What did he expect? She lit the lantern and was impressed to see what a strong dependable light it gave. Then they climbed the stile and set off towards the milking shed, arm in arm and carrying the lantern between them, saying very little because they were anxious about what they would find when they arrived. Once Jeff asked if she was all right and she shouted back that she was fine. Once she stopped to hold the lantern aloft so that he could see that the cows really were as settled as they sounded. But apart from that they simply battled forward.

The milking shed didn't appear to have been damaged at all and the farmhouse hadn't been touched either, although there was a tree uprooted at the end of the lane. But when they'd struggled across the fields to Mr Rossi's caravan site, what they found there left them in no doubt about the size and strength of their tornado.

It looked like the aftermath of a battle. One of Mr Rossi's new expensive caravans lay on its side with its roof caved in and all its windows smashed, the original vans were spun about as if they'd been kicked out of the way, or had fallen backwards into the hedges, and, when they held the lantern aloft, they could see that there were strips of twisted metal, broken spars and spears of glass all over the field.

There was a dark figure picking its way towards them through the debris, a man's voice calling 'Are you the police?'

407

They called back, identifying themselves, and presently the figure stepped into the light and became old Fred Casterick, panting, unshaven and dishevelled, telling his tale in a rush of stammered words and baffled distress.

'We thought we was a-goner... Evenin' Mr Langley. We was swayin' like a ship at sea... I said to the missus, "Get out fer fuck's sake!" Pardon the French Mrs MacIvor. The kids are soaked to the skin... The rain come in the winders like seawater. What we shall do now I do not know.'

'I do,' Gwen said, putting a calming hand on his arm. 'First of all you'll find a black plastic bag and put as many warm clothes in it as you can find, and then you'll pack up your blankets or your duvets – anything to keep you warm overnight – and then if you've got waterproofs or raincoats or wellingtons put them on, and then we'll take you back to the tower. It's warm and dry there.'

'You wasn't blown over then?'

'Not in that tower,' Gwen said happily. 'They built it storm proof.'

Jeff had been examining the new caravan. 'I'm going back to the farm,' he shouted over the wind. 'For the milking. To see my heifers. You'll be OK with your lantern, won't you?'

'Yes. Course,' Gwen shouted back. 'You go. I'll manage.'

They made a bedraggled procession back to the tower, Fred, his wife and their three children, Rachel Carnaby and her two, subdued for the first time in their exuberant lives and like all the others carrying bulging plastic bags on their backs, and bringing up the rear their terrified, rain-tattered dog who slunk along with his belly close to the ground and his tail between his legs as if he were carrying the blame for everything that had happened. But once there they had a pleasant and warming surprise. The lights were back on and so was the central heating and Teresa O'Malley was sitting on the sofa with Jet on her lap looking quite herself again.

'Shall I be after making tea?' she asked brightly. 'I've laid out a few things.'

Light and warmth restored them all. Even the air inside the tower felt normal. But Jet took one look at the bedraggled dog and slithered up the stairs out of harm's way.

Fred's eldest was intrigued by her stumpy tail. 'Is it a manx?' he asked.

It gave Gwen a moment of malicious pleasure to enlighten them. 'No,' she said, speaking to the child but looking at Fred. 'She was attacked by a boy with the same name as you. Dion Casterick I expect you know him. He and his friends tied a firework to her tail with a bit of wire and set light to it. She was so badly injured the vet had to cut her tail off.'

They were horrified and rushed to tell her so, eager to distance themselves from their cousin's cruelty.

'He's a bad lot that Dion,' Fred said staring at her earnestly. 'Always was. 'E needs a good seeing-to. No good saying nothing though, 'cos he's nothing to do with our side of the family. We keep out the way, don't we, Maeve? Best thing. I hope you're gonna sue him, Mrs MacIvor.'

'No,' she said, feeling splendidly magnanimous.

409

'PC Morrish dealt with him. Let's have you out of those wet clothes and into something warm. Then you can have a cup of tea. There's the caddy Miss O'Malley. I'm going down to the village.'

In the stress of their own trauma they'd forgotten that other people could have been hurt too. 'Course,' Rachel said. 'If it's knocked our vans for six, you think what it'll have done to all that thatch.' And she turned an earnest face to Gwen to promise, 'The kids won't be no bother or nothing, Mrs MacIvor. I'll see to that.'

So Gwen left them changing their clothes and spreading duvets on the floor, and set out into the darkness again, the lantern radiating a comforting brightness around her. The rain had stopped but it was impossibly dark and the wind was still blowing so violently that it was hard to make headway, especially as Mill Lane was a treachery of scattered thatch and broken branches that now lay heaped against the hedges and tossing across the roadway. But the path of the tornado was easy to follow. It had obviously cut across Windy Corner, for she could see a garage there with one wall smashed open and two cars at the crossroads with their windscreens shattered. It had missed Manor Farm Road entirely and then seemed to have veered east into Seadrift Lane. There was a police car parked diagonally across the top of the lane, fluorescent stripe glowing and blue lights flashing dramatically, and beyond it she could see the lights of four or five fire engines, one with its ladder extended against one of the houses, and all about them the busy movement of the firemen, purposeful in their yellow jackets, and the small smudged shapes of a crowd of people, standing about in the wind and talking in the hushed murmur of sudden shock. Only one voice was recognisable above the hubbub, and that was the boom of Mrs Agatha Smith-Fernley, who was standing importantly in the middle of the road, huge in a massive yellow raincoat and a very wet sou'wester, shouting at their new community policeman.

'I've sent Mr Jenkins to commandeer the school hall,' she was saying as Gwen's light swayed towards her and he was nodding and saying 'Good!'

'Hello!' she called, squinting into the beam. 'Who's that? Oh it's you Mrs MacIvor. This is a bad business.'

Now that she was in the lane Gwen could see that the tornado had struck here with such force that it had demolished all the roofs on one side of the road, punched in all the windows, and removed the gable wall at the end of the terrace, exposing the incongruous private domesticity of a rumpled bed and a chair piled with discarded clothes above a tumble of dusty bricks and broken roughcast. Most of the cars by the kerbside were covered in dust and tiles and one had a chimney embedded in its roof, but bizarrely, none of the houses on the other side of the street seemed to have been touched at all, although their gardens were piled with the wreckage from the storm, broken gates and fences, smashed garden chairs, heaps of bricks and tiles, dustbin lids rolling in the wind, dustbins spewing garbage. In the long strobes of light from the fire

411

engines it looked unreal, like a scene from a film.

'It just came out of nowhere,' one man said to her. 'One minute we was in bed asleep and the next the roof was sort of sucking in and out and then there was this great hole and all the hail was coming in on us.' He'd thrown a coat over his shoulders but his feet were bare and he was shivering despite valiant efforts to control himself. 'We're not allowed in,' he said. 'The fireman says it's dangerous.'

An ambulance was making careful progress from the southern end of the lane, windscreen wipers squeaking against a new flurry of rain. 'Who's hurt?' Gwen asked the policeman.

Connie from the Post Office and her daughter apparently. 'Only cuts,' the policeman said, 'but they'll need stitching. Flying glass you see. They were blown against the wall.' The medics were walking towards them and the road seemed to be full of fluorescent jackets.

'Look,' Gwen said to Mrs Smith-Fernley, 'these people shouldn't be standing out here in all this rain. Specially the kids. If you can gather them together I'll take them back to the tower. They'll be warm and dry there.'

'Capital!' Mrs Smith-Fernley boomed. 'Just the thing. It could take hours to sort that hall out. I'll see to it.'

And did, producing a loud hailer and assembling the refugees in very quick order. 'Follow the lantern!' she instructed. 'You're to go to West Tower. Mrs MacIvor will show you the way. Don't worry. Everything's under control.'

Lucy had been to Helen's first dinner party that evening, in her new flat in Wimbledon, and what with the wine being so plentiful and the talk so wickedly witty, she was still there at two in the morning. It was the first time she'd really enjoyed herself since she and Pete had split up, and the first time she'd spent an evening with Helen and Tina, so naturally she didn't want to bring it to an end. When the two girls retired to the kitchen to collect more wine, she went with them, gossiping all the way.

The sink was heaped with dirty dishes and, in a moment of helpfulness towards her old flatmate, she offered to load the dishwasher. So Helen turned on the radio for background noise, and they started work

When the news flash began, none of them paid much attention, although they grimaced at the mention of a tornado on the South Coast. It wasn't until the newscaster said Seal Island that they turned and took notice.

'Isn't that where...?' Helen began.

Lucy held up her hand, shushing her to silence.

'...swept through the village at one o'clock this morning,' the newscaster said, 'destroying several houses. There are no other details as yet but we will bring you more in our next bulletin.'

'My God!' Lucy said, instantly in denial. 'It's got to be wrong. I mean, it can't be Seal Island. They've made a mistake.'

Helen was already offering her the phone. But Lucy was in such a state that it took several struggling seconds before she could remember the number, and then the phone rang and rang and nobody answered. 'Oh come on! Come on!'

'She could be asleep,' Helen said. 'Give her time to wake up.'

But the phone just rang. Uselessly.

'She's not there,' Lucy said at last, her face stricken. 'Oh my God! She's not there. She's been hurt. I must go down.'

'You can't drive,' Tina pointed out. 'Not after all that wine.'

But panic was roaring Lucy on. Common sense was disregarded, the strictures of the Highway Code immaterial, the terrors of night driving shrunk to insignificance. 'Damn the wine,' she said, looking about her wildly. 'I'm going. I've got to. I've got to know.'

'Black coffee,' Helen said, reaching for the cafetiere. 'And you'll need a warm coat and a blanket. You always need blankets in emergencies. Stay there and I'll get them.'

Half an hour later, partially sobered by coffee, wearing her friend's sheepskin jacket and with two thick blankets on the back seat and a thermos flask in the glove compartment, Lucy set off into the dark. The night had become unreal. There was no traffic and the streetlights seemed to be melting in the rain, their neon colours slipping and faltering. The sweep of her windscreen wipers fractured the road ahead like a migraine and she could see the rain in the beam of her headlights, as thick as a grey curtain. She was driving much too fast and she knew it and didn't care. She knew it was just the sort of night for an accident but she didn't care about that either. If there were daemons in the dark fields

414

and ghosts ready to spring from the hedges, she no longer gave them credence. There was only the monstrous need to know and to be there. Please God, she mustn't be hurt, she prayed, pressing her foot to the floor. I'll do anything if you'll let her not be hurt.

When she reached the village it was obvious that something extremely serious was going on, for there were fire engines and police cars wherever she looked and the end of one road was blocked by two silver TV vans. She could see a stout woman in a yellow raincoat holding forth to a damp reporter. But there was no sign of her mother, or anyone else she knew for that matter, so she pressed on to the tower, her heart juddering.

Mill Lane was impassable, but by then it was what she expected. She left the car at the end of the lane, struggled through the debris in the buffeting darkness, climbed over a fallen tree, turned the bend and at last, at last saw the tower, intact and dependable and blazing light from every window. She was so relieved that she ran the rest of the way and fell against the bell, ringing it loudly until the door was opened.

Her mother's fine red living room was packed with dishevelled people, and they all seemed to be rushing straight at her. For a few seconds she was unbalanced after the long panic of her drive, but then she saw her mother pushing through the throng towards her, and realised that she was calling her name and obviously all right.

'Lucy my dear girl!' she said, and turned to explain to her refugees. 'This is my daughter.'

They dragged her into the room and found a seat for her on the nearest sofa, while a woman with orange hair went off to make a fresh pot of tea.

'We've been drinking it by the gallon,' Gwen said, sitting beside her. 'I've never known such a night. How did you get here?'

'I drove.'

'All this way? In the dark?'

It was a moment of some pride. 'All this way in the dark. Was it really a tornado?'

'It was. How did you know about it?'

'It was on the news.'

'Hear that,' Gwen called to the crowd all around her. 'We've made the national news.'

'And so I should think,' Miss O'Malley said stoutly. 'You don't get a tornado every day of the week and that's a fact. I was blown right out of my house into the road so I was.'

'Good heavens!' Lucy said.

At that they all embarked upon their own stories, happily outdoing one another, some playing their experiences down, some making as much of a drama of them as they could, but all of them eager to tell her what a wonderful woman her mother was and how grateful they were that she'd come out to rescue them. 'She's a saint so she is. A blessed saint.' 'My mum says she's the Lady of the Lamp, don'tcher Mum.' 'I don't know what we'd ha' done if she hadn't come to find us. You should ha' seen the state we was in. There was glass all over the place. Connie from the Post Office got cut to shreds.'

Lucy listened vaguely because she was too tired

416

to take it all in. She smiled and sipped her tea and nodded, but really she was watching her mother, marvelling at how calm and controlled she was. She's a power here, she thought. A leader. They're looking to her to tell them what to do.

At that moment the phone rang into her thoughts. 'Now what?' Gwen said happily, heading off to the kitchen to answer it.

It was Pete. 'Hi there Mrs M,' he said. 'Are you all right?' And when told she was. 'I had to ring you. You're on breakfast TV.'

'Which one?'

'Channel 3.'

'Someone switch on the television,' Gwen called. 'Thanks for telling us, Pete. I'll ring you back. OK?'

Watery pictures swam into focus and were greeted with delighted importance and renewed horror. 'There's the Sailor's Arms. It missed that then.' 'That's your place issen it, Henry?' 'Blimey! Look at that!'

Then the scene changed and Mrs Smith-Fernley filled the screen with her yellow raincoat and her booming gravitas. 'I have to say,' she intoned, 'that the citizens of Seal Island have acquitted themselves quite admirably tonight in appalling conditions, as is invariably the way when we British have our backs to the wall. It's the Dunkirk spirit you know. Never downhearted.'

'I believe one of your neighbours has turned out to be quite a heroine,' the interviewer prompted.

Gwen raised her eyebrows wondering what on earth her adversary would say. But Mrs Smith-

417

Fernley wasn't fazed in the least. She rose to the occasion as smooth and imperturbable as a yellow whale.

'Yes indeed,' she agreed. 'She came out with a storm lantern in the worst of it all and led the homeless back to her tower.' There was a shot of the tower, very black and with yellow light in every window. 'A fine woman,' Mrs Smith-Fernley's voice declaimed. 'The sort of neighbour to depend on.'

'I understand she's quite a newcomer,' the interviewer said.

'Relatively speaking,' Mrs Smith-Fernley said. 'But we took her to our hearts from the first day. Yes, indeed. We knew at once that she was just our sort of person.'

The effrontery of it was so irritating that Gwen burst out laughing. It was either that or yelling. But the occupants of the tower burst into a spontaneous cheer and those who were near enough to manage it patted their sort of person on the back and the knees.

'Wasn't she the one who...?' Lucy asked under cover of the racket.

'Wasn't she just!' Gwen said. 'And now she has the gall to...'

'You've arrived,' Lucy laughed. 'Neil always said you would.'

'Yes,' Gwen agreed, as the cheers went on. 'I suppose I have.' It was a sort of triumph in a way, just as the night had been. A vindication. But there was still the problem of Ellie and the baby. Even a tornado hadn't solved that. I wonder where she is and what she's doing.

CHAPTER 28

Over in Paris, in her comfortable hotel room, Eleanor had been watching the moon all night.

She'd stayed in the office until late the previous evening briefing her campaign team and checking that all their display material was ready. She'd been so absorbed and busy that she hadn't had time to go out for a meal but had sent out for sandwiches to eat where she stood, so it was no surprise that she was awake most of the night with indigestion. At first she thought she'd eaten something that had disagreed with her and half hoped it would make her sick so that she could get rid of it and go to sleep. But the hours passed and she wasn't sick and the griping pains came and went and anything more than a catnap was impossible. In the end she got up, put on her bathrobe and sat in the armchair by the window to look out at the roofs and the stars, hoping that a new position would ease her discomfort.

The moon was full and unusually bright, its white orb dazzling and every crater clearly visible, and after a while she was intrigued to realise that it wasn't simply hanging there all the time, but that it was actually moving. She could see it tracing a long slow parabola across the patch of sky in the window of her hotel bedroom. It's so close, she thought, watching as a long cloud moved across its face, concentrating on it to take her mind off another dragging pain. You can see why it pulls the tides. If she'd been superstitious she could have said it was pulling at her, making the pains come and go.

She must have fallen asleep in the chair, for the next thing she knew was she was opening her eyes with a start, the moon had moved a considerable distance and somebody was knocking at her bedroom door and calling to her in French. 'Breakfast Madame.' It was still dark but the day was beginning. She eased herself out of the chair, stiffly, switched on the bedside lamps and lumbered to the door, feeling fat and clumsy, aware of the weight she was carrying, eager for the comfort of coffee and croissants.

The chambermaid was middle-aged and motherly. She insisted on carrying the breakfast tray to the table, gave Eleanor a look of conspiratorial sympathy and asked if she was unwell.

'*Je suis fatigue*,' Eleanor told her. And she was tired, aching with it, wanting to lie down. 'Close the curtains if you please. I don't want all Paris to see me in my bathrobe.'

With the curtains closed, the lamps lit, coffee poured, croissants buttered, the television flickering into focus, the day began to feel more normal. I'll have my breakfast, Eleanor thought as she drank her coffee and then I'll have a nice relaxing bath and then...

'Seal Island on the south coast of England,' the newsreader said, 'has been struck by a tornado.'

The word stabbed into Eleanor's brain like an electric shock. It can't be, she thought. We don't have tornados in England. What is she talking about? But there it was on screen, the Sailor's Arms, eerily floodlit, groups of firemen pulling thatch from a wrecked building, a house torn open as if it had been hit by a bomb.

Panic surged through her. She put down her cup, wiped her fingers on the napkin, and took up the phone, dialling nine for an outside line. She could see her mother lying under the wreckage, squashed and bleeding, lying on the ground injured and alone, lying on a hospital trolley, white faced and dying. Her fingers shook as she dialled again. Hurry up! she urged. Get me a line. And at last the phone was ringing in Seal Island, the familiar tones increasing her panic. Come on! Come on! Answer somebody. And then her mother's voice. 'Hello.'

'Mum,' she said, limp with relief. Thank God! 'Are you all right? You're not hurt or anything are you? I've just seen it on the television.'

'Ellie!' Gwen said, sounding wonderfully normal. 'How nice to hear you! Where are you?'

'Paris,' Ellie said shortly. 'You're not hurt, are you? I mean, you'd tell me if you were.'

'I'm not hurt.'

There was a babble of voices in the background. 'What's all that racket?'

Her mother laughed. 'That's my refugees. I've turned the tower into a rest centre. We've got rather a lot of homeless here after last night.'

Typical, Eleanor thought, and was flooded with warmth and affection for her. Then a spasm of quite sharp pain made her draw in her breath and it took a little while before she could speak again or respond to what her mother was saying.

At the other end of the line Gwen was alerted by the odd gasping sound and the long silence. 'Hello?' she said. 'Ellie? Are you all right?'

'Little pain,' Ellie told her, trying to be casual. 'Nothing much. Something I ate. I've had indigestion all night. Not to worry.'

'What sort of pain?'

'Quite sharp actually. It's been coming and going all night. I shall have to get some health salts.'

Even at that distance Gwen knew what they were talking about. 'Have you seen a doctor?' she asked.

'No. Course not.'

'Perhaps you should. Just to be on the safe side.'

'No. I'm fine.'

'You're also very pregnant. They have doctors in hotels don't they?'

'Probably.'

'Then call one.'

'I'll see.'

'Call one,' Gwen insisted. 'Seriously. If you've had pains all night you need to know what they are.'

Eleanor gave way, partly to placate her mother and partly because the pains really were getting a bit much. 'OK,' she said. 'If it makes you happy. Look, there's someone at the door. I shall have to go. Look after yourself. I'll phone again later.'

The someone was Monica Furlong, who was now her second in command, and arrived dressed and perfumed and irritatingly ready for the day. She hesitated in the doorway, looking at

422

Eleanor curiously.

'Are you all right?' she asked.

Too much concern made Eleanor tetchy. 'You're as bad as my mother,' she said. 'I'm fine. A bit of indigestion that's all.'

'Only you've got a funny colour, sort of ... well as if you've got a temperature or something.'

'Well I haven't,' Eleanor told her sharply. 'Like I said, I'm perfectly all right.' But she glanced in the mirror just to check and was alarmed to see that she had a round patch of unnatural colour on both cheeks and that her eyes were oddly bright. 'Lack of sleep,' she said. 'That's all. But if it's any consolation to you I'm going to let the *médecin* check me over, just to be on the safe side.'

Monsieur le médecin was a small gentle man who spoke in French but brooked no argument. He paid no attention to Eleanor's diagnosis, but laid a professional hand on the top of her belly as the next pain gathered and faded and then announced that there was no need for alarm and that he would arrange for her to go into a clinic, *immédiateinent.*

'Out of the question,' she said. 'I've got work to do.'

'*Mais oui,*' the doctor agreed, smiling at her. 'The hardest work you will do in all your life. It is an excellent clinic, Madame. Organised according to the teaching of Frederick Leboyer.'

Eleanor didn't care whose teaching it was. 'I can't go,' she said, in English and firmly. 'I just need some indigestion tablets, that's all.'

The doctor smiled. 'No, No, Madame,' he said,

answering in her own language. 'It is the birth which arrives.'

And as if to prove him right, the next pain gripped her so strongly it made her groan.

'*Voila!*' he said. 'I arrange the clinic.'

She wanted to argue, to refuse, but her body was sending her treacherous signals. 'All right then,' she sighed. 'If I must I must.'

'Don't worry about the presentation,' Monica said eagerly. 'I can handle it.'

That was exactly what Eleanor was afraid of but the pain was holding her in a vice and she didn't have the energy to answer.

The doctor was on the phone, talking in a French so rapid and technical that neither of them could understand a word of it. Not that Eleanor cared. It was the wrong time and the wrong place but she was in labour and caught in a maelstrom of so many conflicting emotions that it was all she could do to contend with them; excitement and fear, annoyance at her bad timing, and an unexpected happiness because this child was finally coming.

The doctor was bending over her. 'They send an ambulance,' he said.

'I'll pack my things,' she told him. And was pleased by how calm she sounded.

In Seal Island a slow dawn was rising, rain-washed, sweet smelling and, after the traumas of the night, extraordinarily peaceful. Gwen and Lucy stood in the porch with the door open to the air, breathing the freshness of it. Behind them the scarlet room was sour with use, littered with dirty cups and discarded coats and anoraks, heaped with mounds of duvets, choked with the breath of too many sleepers.

'What a night!' Gwen said.

Lucy was looking round the garden. 'Your daffodils are up,' she said. And so they were, their green spears erupting from the dark earth wherever they looked.

'New life,' Gwen said, relishing them.' I wonder how Ellie is. I wish she'd ring.'

Lucy didn't want to talk about her sister. This night had been hers and her mother's, and rewarding for that reason above everything else. Ellie had no part in it. 'She'll be all right,' she said carelessly. 'Hello. Look who's coming. It's your number one fan.'

'Hello there!' Mrs Smith-Fernley called. She was wearing her best black coat above a stout pair of green wellies. 'How are you all making out? Everything all right? I've got breakfast organised. Nine to ten thirty in the school hall. Mill Lane should be clear by then. Mr Langley's seeing to it.' She'd reached the porch and stood before them beaming at them as if they were old friends. 'All pull together eh?' she said. 'That's the style.'

'Would you like to come in?' Gwen offered.

'No, no my dear,' the lady smiled. 'I only called to give you the information. But if you'll tell Teresa she can have her breakfast at Rose Cottage with me, I should be obliged.'

There was a flurry of stale air behind them and Mr Casterick blundered into the porch, rubbing the sleep from his eyes. He was bristlingly unshaven, grubbily bare-footed and coughing up the smoke of his first ciggie of the day. 'Morning Mrs Smith-Fernley,' he spluttered.

'Yes,' Mrs Smith-Fernley said, giving him her most disparaging look. 'Well I must be off. Things to do, you know. Things to do.' And went at once before she could breathe in any more of his germs. 'Your daffodils are coming out,' she called to Gwen as she went. 'You're going to have a fine display. Yes, indeed, a very fine display.'

To their credit, Gwen and Lucy didn't laugh until they'd tumbled into the tower but then they shrieked and giggled until the noise they were making woke their guests. Then the entire tower was thrown into such a turmoil that it was over an hour before they had a chance to speak to one another again and, in the middle of it all, Jeff arrived, freshly shaven and in clean clothes, to tell them that Mill Lane was being cleared and should be open to traffic in an hour or so, that Mr Rossi was on his way down to see the risk assessors and that the caravanners were to be back on site by mid-day.

'Milk yield's down,' he said, 'but that's only to be expected. The heifers are OK. What sort of night did you have?'

'We was on the telly,' the youngest Casterick told him. 'We seen it.'

Jeff grinned. 'Fame at last!' he teased, looking round the room. 'Good God! However many cups of tea did you make? It looks like a canteen.'

'That's just about what it was,' Gwen said. 'They're all off for their breakfast now, courtesy of Mrs Smith-Fernley. Once they've gone I can clear up. And I suppose I'd better phone the school.'

'I'll leave you to get on with it then,' he said. 'This is just a flying visit. If you'll take my advice – which you probably won't – you'll stay at home and let that school look after itself.'

That was Mr Carter's advice too. 'We saw it on the telly this morning,' he said when Gwen phoned. 'Stay where you are. We can manage. After all, it's only a day and then it's half term. If you can just come in for an hour or two next week to catch up with the mail.'

'I'd forgotten about half term,' Gwen said to Lucy as she put the phone down. 'Now then where shall we start?'

There was a lot to clear. The kitchen was cluttered with dirty cups and saucers, the bookcases hidden by piles of tousled bedding, both baths full of sodden towels and every tread on her new staircase encrusted with dried mud. And to make matters worse they'd run out of tea and there wasn't a mouthful of milk in the house.

'It makes me feel weak at the knees to look at it,' Lucy said, looking at it. 'Tell you what, let's go down the village and get some more milk and a loaf or rolls or something and then we can have a bit of breakfast before we start. If we clean first and eat afterwards we shall collapse.'

'I don't really want to leave the tower,' Gwen said. 'I mean, I ought to be here in case Ellie phones again. It's nearly three hours now and if she is in labour this'll be just the sort of time she'll ring and tell me.'

Ellie again, Lucy thought mutinously. It's

427

always Ellie. I can't even have twenty-four hours with you without her pushing in somehow or other. And she found a shopping bag and left before she could say something she might regret.

She had a relatively clear passage through Mill Lane, for enough of the fallen tree had been cleared to leave a pathway, and the High Street was absolutely normal, all shops open and trading, groups of villagers exchanging tornado stories, the postman doing his round, a delicious smell of new bread from the bakers. It didn't take long to stock up on milk, tea and biscuits and to treat herself to a nice new loaf and two fresh croissants and then she wandered up the High Street towards the place where the TV vans had been the previous evening to take a look round. She'd never seen the aftermath of a tornado before. It would be interesting if nothing else.

It was certainly dramatic. There was an enormous crane towering over the damaged buildings, the police had the road completely blocked off and had put one of their blue and white cordons all along the damaged side of the street, there were builders' vans all over the place – they got here quickly – and fire engines from one end of the road to the other with firemen busy everywhere she looked, up ladders, clambering over roofs, pulling down a chimney, shouting to one another, the white stripes on their yellow jackets bright against the dust and destruction all round them, and the two television vans had been joined by three more. It was quite exciting. So this is what happens when you're national news, she thought, and walked closer to the action.

There was a small boy standing by the barrier all on his own and looking doleful.

'What a mess!' she said, feeling she ought to try and comfort him. 'Is this where you live?'

'It's my dog,' he said, looking up at her. 'He's in the garage.'

Now she could hear an animal whimpering. 'Call him,' she suggested.

'I have,' the boy said. 'I don't reckon he can get out an' they won't let me go in an' get him. I did ask an' they said I couldn't.'

The dog was howling. Poor thing, Lucy thought. It wouldn't hurt them just to let it out. And the thought gave her an idea.

'Look after my shopping,' she said, handing her bag to the boy. 'Stay there and don't move and I'll get him for you.'

It was a moment of bravado and stupidity, driven by emotions that she recognised as reprehensible, even then – a desire to be part of this extraordinary event, the swaggering thought that she could be a dashing heroine like her mother, a niggling ambition to upstage her sister.

She lifted the cordon, ducked underneath it and walked briskly towards the garage, holding up her head as though the cameras were already following her. The garage door had been bent open by the wind and now lay at an angle, looking dangerously squiffy, but she could hear the dog whimpering inside and a little danger wasn't going to deter her. She put both hands under the twisted metal and gave it a tug. And at that, things happened so quickly that they were over before she could take them in. The garage wall seemed to be roaring and the door was falling out of her sight. She knew she had to run away and turned to start but something was hurtling towards her, striking her in the back, pushing her forward and off her feet, and she was falling, hands outstretched, calling 'Oh! Oh!' like a child. Then there was a sharp pain in her nose and another in her arm and she was lying on her side, spitting blood and groaning.

Feet moved into her limited vision but she couldn't keep her eyes open long enough to see whose they were. A voice was speaking, close and urgent. 'Lucy! Oh God! Lucy my dear, darling girl. Oh God! You mustn't be hurt. I couldn't bear it. I love you so much. So much. Open your eyes. Please!'

It was a struggle but she opened her eyes and did what she could to focus them.

'Oh thank God!' the voice said and she looked towards it and saw Neil's face gazing at her with such anguished affection that she began to cry.

Now there were other voices. 'Shall I call for an ambulance Neil?' 'Can we move her?' Neil answering, 'No. Don't touch her.' And leaning towards her, saying tenderly. 'You're OK. The ambulance is on its way.' Then there was a rustle of activity as though they were kicking up fallen leaves. Fallen, she thought, fallen, falling. Only I'm the one who's fallen.

She struggled to form a sentence, aware that blood was running from her nose and that she wanted to clean herself up. 'Can I have a tissue?' she begged. And after what seemed a very long

time, a wad of tissues was put in her left hand –
why not her right? – and she dabbed at her nose
and was upset to see what a lot of blood there
was on the tissues when she lowered them. 'I'm
hurt,' she said.

Neil was still beside her. 'Yes,' he said. 'You are.
Don't worry. The ambulance is coming. I'll look
after you. I won't leave you.'

Something rattled over the broken bricks and
two paramedics were looking down at her,
smiling reassurance. 'What have you been up to
then? Can you tell me where it hurts? Right. I
see. Right. I should say you've got a little fracture
there. Does it hurt anywhere else?'

She suddenly felt very tired and was glad to let
them take over. Whatever was going to happen
next was out of her hands.

'Where's Neil?' she asked. 'My policeman.'

'He's seeing to your shopping,' the paramedic
said. 'Don't worry. He's coming back.'

When her doorbell rang, Gwen was on her hands
and knees polishing the stairs. She'd washed the
cups and saucers, put the wet towels in the
washing machine, and hoovered up most of the
mud, but the treads were stained and needed a
good rub over.

She was very surprised to find one of Jet's
tormentors standing uncomfortably in the porch.
The smallest one. Nathan wasn't it?

'Yes,' she said coldly. 'What do you want?' Then
she saw her shopping bag and was afraid. 'Something's happened,' she said. 'Tell me quickly.'

'I got a note for you,' Nathan said, and handed

431

it over to her, looking very anxious. 'From that policeman.'

She read it, hands shaking, had to read it a second time before she could take it in. *Don't be alarmed*, it began, alarming her terribly, *but Lucy has had a little accident in Seadrift Lane. She is not too badly hurt.* What does he mean, not too badly? Oh God! This is all my fault. I should never have let her go off on her own in all this chaos. I should have gone with her. I would have done if it hadn't been for Ellie. Not for the first time in her life, she felt she'd been caught between her two daughters, crushed between their conflicting needs. She turned back to the letter, hoping it would tell her more at a second reading. *We thought she should go to hospital for a check-up. Some cuts need stitching. The ambulance has just arrived. I am going with her. Will phone you when I have more news. Neil.*

She was too concerned about Lucy to be more than marginally surprised at his reappearance in their lives. She took the bag from the boy's hand, vaguely and without paying any attention to it, thanked him, and then, still tremulous with guilty anxiety, she went to look for her car keys.

432

CHAPTER 29

The ambulance that came to collect Eleanor from her hotel was discreetly up-market, impressively equipped and obviously designed for comfort and privacy. It was just big enough for one mother and her uniformed attendant, who in Eleanor's case was a cool blonde who introduced herself as Amélie and spoke almost perfect English.

'We have mothers of every nationality, you see,' she explained, as their well-ordered vehicle purred them away. 'So naturally we have interpreters. Our aim is to do our very best for mother and baby.'

It was a good start and even Eleanor had to admit it. But now that she was on her way to the clinic, she had changed her mind about how she would handle this situation, and had decided that, as soon as they'd confirmed that she was in labour, she would take the Eurostar back to London and the caesarian section she had booked for herself. There was no way she was going to endure the pain of an actual birth and there'd be plenty of time to get back because everybody said that a first labour took hours and hours.

'You will wish to go to your own room I do not doubt,' Amélie said, when they arrived at the clinic. 'The doctor will see you there. It is en suite

433

as you see, with every convenience.'

And decorated in the palest lemon yellow and a great deal of pristine white, with a white crib waiting for the baby beside a wide white bed. 'Yes,' Eleanor said, exercising her French while she still had the energy for it. 'It is admirable. But it might not be possible to stay here. It might be necessary for me to return to England.'

'Do not disquiet yourself,' Amélie told her calmly. 'It is all arranged. Your company has insurance for this eventuality. You do not need to be concerned at all. You would like a bath, perhaps, before the doctor comes to examine you.'

Eleanor was disquieted that her hint about returning to London was being ignored, but she agreed that a bath would be acceptable. And so it was, for the water was wonderfully warm and the bath oil pleasantly scented, and afterwards there was a warm bathrobe to envelop her and towelling slippers for her wet feet and the white coverlet had been turned back ready for her occupation, as if she were in a hotel. So she lay under the coverlet while two more pains came and went and tried to think of the right French phrases to convince the doctor that she ought to go back to London.

The doctor was grey-haired and extremely gentle. She took her patient's blood pressure, checked her temperature and stood with one hand on her tightening belly while another pain came and went. Then she sat by the bed and asked the sort of gentle questions that Eleanor had come to expect – dates, allergies, health during pregnancy – all of which were translated by Amélie and easy enough to answer.

'You have another pain now, *n'est-ce pas?*' she said, as Eleanor winced her way through it. 'The previous one was ten minutes ago. You progress, Madame.'

'Ouf!' Eleanor said as the pain receded. 'That was nasty.'

'With the pains of *enfantement,*' the doctor said, 'it is a matter of who is in charge. Have you been taught the art of relaxation?'

When have I had time to be taught anything? Eleanor thought. 'I've been at work,' she said and her voice was tetchy.

'Ah yes,' the doctor said, her calm unruffled. 'I understand. Then allow me to explain. In childbirth, either the pain will control the mother or the mother will control the pain. Which is it that you wish?'

It seemed most peculiar to be asked such a thing. 'Do I have a choice?'

'But of course.'

'Then I would like to be in control.'

'Excellent,' the doctor said. 'In that case, Amélie will show you how it is done. It is late, but as you say in your language Better late than never. First we will give you something to drink.'

Painkillers, Eleanor thought. At last. They could have done that when I first came in. She waited impatiently for the drugs to arrive and drank the proffered cup, screwing her face against expected bitterness, but it was actually quite pleasant, a bit like warm fruit juice – with an aftertaste of raspberries.

'*Alors!*' Amélie said, as she set the empty cup on the bedside cabinet. 'We will begin.'

It was the first time in her life that Eleanor had embarked on any activity without knowing exactly what it would entail. The thought was quite exciting and made her feel daring. I expect it'll be some sort of drug, she thought, with a push button so that I can administer it myself.

But no drugs were offered. Instead she was asked to turn off her mobile phone – 'You will not want any interruption' – and then to settle herself on the bed – 'with the maximum of comfort'. Pillows were mounded and repositioned and mounded again until she was perfectly at ease. Socks were provided to keep her feet warm.

'And now,' Amélie said, 'I teach you how to push the pain away. Let us put it at a distance.'

It seemed ridiculous to be asked to relax your hands and arms to deal with a pain in your belly, but Eleanor humoured her. She was too comfortable to argue about it and when the next pain began it did seem a little less arduous.

'When your legs and hips are relaxed it will be better still,' Amélie promised.

And to Eleanor's surprise and relief, it was.

'Relaxed muscles reduce pain,' the midwife explained, 'and increase pleasure.'

'Not that there's any pleasure in this,' Eleanor said as the next pain took hold.

'Ah, but there will be,' the midwife said. 'Soon. I promise you. The pleasure is to come. But for the moment we must permit your body do its work. Let us see if you can relax your face.'

'I must look like an imbecile,' Eleanor

complained when she'd allowed her facial muscles to fall.

'You look *magnifique,*' Amélie told her. 'Like a mother.'

That made Eleanor want to laugh but she was oddly drowsy and could only manage a smile. It was as though all this deliberate relaxation was sending her into a trance. She felt as though she was drunk, head-swimmy and woozy and far too comfortable in her mound of pillows to want to move out of it or even alter her position. If this is what birth is like, she thought to herself, as another pain rose to its now oddly distant crescendo, I can handle it. She had quite forgotten that she intended to go back to London.

When Gwen finally arrived in Accident and Emergency at St Richard's Hospital in Chichester, she was out of breath and very worried. But she asked for news of her daughter as calmly as she could and was directed to cubicle twelve.

It was completely empty, although there were smears of blood and mud on the examination couch, and Lucy's bloodstained jacket was folded over the back of a chair. Oh God! She is hurt.

There was a nurse at her elbow. 'Are you looking for Lucy? We've just sent her down to X-ray. Go through that door there and follow the signs.'

Signs were followed, heart juddering, another reception desk was found, more instructions given, and then she was in a long corridor, where various people in plaster casts and metal casings were waiting their turn and talking quietly to their companions. And there was Neil Morrish sitting at the end of the row, biting his nails.

'Neil!' she said, walking up to him. 'How is she?'

A door was being held open and a porter was pushing a wheelchair out into the corridor.

'I'm fine,' Lucy's voice said. 'Bit battered. That's all.'

That's putting it mildly, Gwen thought, wincing at the sight of her daughter's stitched, scarred face, noticing that her right arm was in a sling and obviously painful because she was supporting it with very tenderly with her left hand. But she tried to speak lightly, as that was equally obviously what Lucy wanted of her. 'What have you done to yourself?'

The answer was almost matter-of-fact. 'I've got a broken nose and a broken collar bone and they say I shall have two black eyes by tomorrow morning. That'll be pretty. Oh and they've stitched me up and given me a tetanus injection. Everything's being taken care of. And now I've got to go to a place called Max Fax, so that they can look at my nose.'

'Oh Lucy! My dear girl!'

'Don't fuss,' Lucy said sternly. 'I'm fine. It could have been a lot worse, couldn't it Neil? You ask him.'

But she didn't like to. Not when she was dreading what she would hear, and not while Lucy and the porter were listening. Fortunately their next stop was just around the corner and this clinic was private. The porter had to key in a set of numbers to gain admission, and Gwen and Neil were left to wait outside.

'So tell me,' she said, as the door closed. 'What happened?'

He gave her a brief and careful version but even that upset her.

'All this for a dog!' she said. 'What a good job you were there.'

'More by luck than judgement,' he said. 'I only came down for the day. Just to see my mates. Tidy up. That sort of thing. I've got a job with the Met now I'm a sergeant. Starts in ten days. And then I come down here and walk straight into a tornado. How's that for timing?'

'I'm glad you did,' she said. 'My poor Lucy.'

'She's going to need a lot of looking after for the next few days,' he said. 'It's not easy with one arm out of action. I broke my collar bone once so I know.'

'She won't like being looked after,' Gwen said. 'She's hideously independent.'

'I could give you a hand if you'd like,' he offered casually. 'It might come better from a policeman.'

'I thought you were only down for the day.'

'I could stay on,' he said, still carefully casual. 'I expect Sergeant Jones would put me up if I asked him. He's a good bloke.'

He was smiling straight at her. She thought what attractive eyes he had and was surprised she hadn't noticed them before. 'So tell me about this new job,' she said.

It was just as well there was a lot to tell, for they had a long wait. It was nearly an hour before the door opened and the wheelchair reappeared. But Lucy seemed better pleased than she'd been when she went in.

'Just a broken nose,' she said. 'No need for an operation. It'll be better in a few weeks. Now all I've got to do is get this arm in a proper sling and I can go home.'

'Just as well I've got my car then,' Gwen said. 'I'll take you both back. You came in the ambulance, didn't you Neil?'

It was a certainly a happier return, although Lucy was still in a lot of pain and winced at every corner, and had to allow Neil to help her in and out of the car. But at last they were back in the tower, and Gwen could find her some paracetamol and then busy herself preparing something for them all to eat.

'Soup,' Lucy said. 'I shan't be able to bite anything. Or chew.'

She also found that even drinking tea was difficult. She couldn't lift the cup with her right hand, her left was inaccurate and even when the rim was in the right position, her face was so swollen it was hard to sip.

'You need a straw,' Neil said and went off at once to buy some.

'He's been so kind,' Lucy said when he'd gone. The painkillers were beginning to take effect so she felt a bit better. 'He came with me in the ambulance – did he tell you? – and stayed with me all the time and he didn't have to. He's not on duty.'

'I know,' Gwen said. 'He's on leave. He's got a job with the Met.'

The news was a disappointment. 'Oh!' Lucy said. 'I thought he'd come back. Still I suppose we all move on, don't we. When's he going?'

'Not yet,' Gwen told her. 'He'll be here for a couple of days, so he says. He's staying with his sergeant.'

Lucy closed her eyes as the pain ebbed away. 'What's the news from Ellie?'

'Nothing more since this morning,' Gwen said. What a long time ago that seemed. 'Unless she's left a message on the answerphone.' And she went to see. 'No. Nothing. We'll just have to wait. It takes a long time, especially with a first. Anyway, whatever she's doing, she'll be in good hands, if I know her. You're the one who needs looking after.'

It was a sweet moment for Lucy, even if she'd had to break her collarbone to reach it. 'Yes,' she agreed, closing her eyes again to enjoy it. 'I am.'

But her pleasure was short-lived. When Neil returned with the straws she discovered that she couldn't suck and breathe at the same time, and that sucking didn't quench her thirst. 'I need a throatful,' she complained, putting the cup on the table. 'If I could just blow my nose and clear all this gunge.' But that had been forbidden. She had to endure a new snuffling swollen self that was depressing to think about, leave alone look at.

Gwen tried to comfort. 'It'll soon get better, chick.' And was rounded on for her efforts.

'No it won't,' Lucy said. 'It'll be weeks and weeks. They told me so.' The bruises were beginning to colour the puffy skin round her eyes

441

and her shoulders sagged with misery. 'Weeks and weeks of not being able to do anything properly. Weeks of being a complete bloody nuisance. I can't even get out of this chair without someone to haul me up. You see?'

Neil was beside her, with one arm round her, easing her to her feet.

She didn't even have the grace to thank him. 'I'm going to bed,' she said. And headed for the stairs.

'Do you need a hand?' Gwen asked.

'No,' her daughter scowled. 'I need a new collar bone.'

'How will she manage?' Gwen said, speaking softly because although Lucy was probably out of earshot, she didn't want to risk being heard.

'She'll manage,' Neil assured her, speaking equally quietly. 'She wants to be independent.'

'I know,' Gwen said. 'That's half the trouble. She always did. She and Ellie both. They always had to do everything for themselves.'

'It's all going wrong,' Eleanor cried, struggling out of her nest of pillows. Her lovely peaceful relaxation had suddenly become intolerable. 'You must do something.'

'You are not comfortable?' her midwife asked in French.

'No, I'm fucking not,' Eleanor said in trenchant English.

'What is it you want?' the midwife said.

Eleanor didn't know what she wanted. She only knew what she didn't want. Not to lie down on that fucking bed, for a start. Not to walk about

442

either. She'd tried it and it didn't work. Not to stand still, for the next pain screwed her belly when she was standing and the pain of it was excruciating. Not to lean on her midwife. That just irritated her. 'No, No,' she cried, her face distraught. 'That's not it. Do something!'

'It is transition,' Amélie announced, appearing beside her. 'Stay calm. It will pass.'

Calm was out of the question. 'I should be having a caesarian,' she cried, panting with anger and distress. 'I should be in London. I don't want to be here. I don't want to be pregnant. It's all a mistake. I want this to stop.'

Finally they wheeled in a chair. Even in her shattered state she registered that it was most peculiar, as big as a throne with footrests and armrests and levers sticking out at every angle. She didn't like the look of it at all, but it had arrived in the nick of time, for the next pain was gathering to spring at her, and as the wretched thing was there, she sank into it, leaning on the padded arms, glad not to be standing. And it was perfect, holding her in just the right position, with supports for her feet and supports at her back.

'Why didn't you bring this in before?' she said. And then speech was impossible for there was only the pain and a new overpowering need. 'I want to push,' she gasped as it took hold. And pushed, lowering her chin to her chest, panting and grunting.

There were faces all around her, approving. *'Parfait! Superbe!'* But they meant little to her beyond the fact that they approved. The footrests were adjusted between pains, she was hot with striving, someone wiped the sweat from her eyes, Amélie was encouraging her. 'You are doing well. Your little one will soon be here.'

The room darkened as she laboured and after a while she was vaguely aware that they were all bathed in a curious blue-green light, as though they were all under the sea, where sounds were subdued and there were no sharp edges and hands flowed like fishes. She gasped at a new sensation and a voice murmured that the baby's head had crowned, which seemed exactly right to her, sitting in state in that great throne of a chair.

'Look down,' Amélie said in her ear as the next pain rose. And she looked and there was the baby's head between her legs, dark and damp and turning slowly, slowly, slowly until it was face upwards and she could see its features, all screwed up as though it had been making as much effort as she had, snub nose wrinkled, eyes tight shut, mouth stretched, steady pulse beating under the tender skin of its forehead. And as she watched, it opened its mouth and gave a sharp mewing cry, once, twice, three times.

'It is hard to be born, *n'est-ce pas,'* the midwife said in her gentle French. *'Mais alors,* you will soon be in your mother's arms.'

'Yes,' Eleanor said rapturously. 'Oh, yes.' And pushed again, watching as the rest of her lovely baby slithered out into the waiting hands of the midwife, and saw that she had a boy, and that he was perfect in every detail, with plump limbs and the prettiest face and the most delectable hands and feet she'd ever seen. He was protesting again,

444

his cries clear as a cat's, his eyes screwed up at the indignity of it all.

'Don't cry, little love,' she said and she put down her hand to stroke his head, very very gently, and was caught up in a happiness more extreme than anything she'd ever experienced in her life. 'Don't cry, my little darling!'

And at that the midwife lifted him up and lowered him into her arms, skin to soft skin and he stopped crying and opened his eyes and looked straight at her, as if he knew where he was and had known her for centuries. 'Oh how I love you,' she said, gazing back. 'I shall love you for ever.'

She held him for over an hour, breathing in the soft new smell of his skin, answering that intense look, kissing his cheeks and exploring his hands and feet with tremulous fingers, even feeling the little throbbing pulse in that tender fontanelle, rapt and enraptured. Her two attendants eased her through the third stage of the birth and presently Amélie came and stood beside her and told her that all was well. She was glad to hear it but it didn't concern her, for her world had shrunk to the few magical inches that lay between her baby's peaceful breathing and her own. She was totally and irrevocably in love.

CHAPTER 30

'There are times when I just don't credit you,' Jeff said to Gwen. His voice was sharp with exasperation. 'She rings you up, she tells you the baby's born, and you don't ask her!'

'I couldn't,' Gwen said easily. 'She was too happy.'

She could still hear Ellie's rapturous voice, 'I've got a son. Joshua Francis and he's absolutely gorgeous.'

'He'd only just been born. She was still high. It wasn't the right time. It's not a problem. She'll be here in a few days. She said she'd come down as soon as they sign her off. I shall ask her then.'

He snorted. 'The right time is when you make it the right time.'

'So you keep saying.'

'And I'm right.'

'Not always,' Gwen said but her voice was still easy. 'Only sometimes. I can remember when I first told you about the girls, you said I ought to stand back and let them make their own mistakes. You were right about that. Only I couldn't see it then. I still wanted to wrap them up in cotton wool and protect them. The way you did with Dotty when she was so ill.'

'That was different. She was dying.'

'OK. It was. But there are similarities. We were both overprotective. We both had to learn to

446

stand back.'

He snorted again. 'And this is what you're doing now, is it? Standing back? I'd call it chickening out.'

Gwen was arranging daffodils in her scarlet vase. Now she stood with the blaze of their golden bloom before her and looked at him shrewdly. 'You're such a bully,' she said.

He argued against that at once. 'I am not.'

'You are,' she said, but it was a statement of fact, not an accusation. 'It's being a farmer I think. It's in the nature of the beast. Sometimes it's quite attractive. I liked it when you bullied Mr Makepeace for me and sorted out the yobs. But sometimes it isn't. You're too used to getting your own way. That's the crux of it.'

'If I don't, the farm goes to pot.'

'Quite possibly,' she agreed. 'But it's different when it's us. If we're going on with our affair, you've got to let me live my life my own way. I don't tell you how to run the farm, now do I? OK then, you mustn't tell me how to handle my daughters.'

He was suddenly and totally serious. 'Are we going on with it?' he asked. She left the flowers and came and put her arms round his neck. 'Yes,' she said. 'I want to go on with it. That's why we're talking like this. But you've got to let me do things my own way. I've got to be independent. You must see that.'

The anxiety she'd provoked was calmed. 'Trouble is,' he said. 'I think I love you.'

She smiled up at him. 'That makes two of us. So you'll do what I ask? You'll stand back?'

447

He'd recovered enough to tease. 'On one condition.'

And so had she. 'I knew there'd be a condition.'

'You come out to dinner with me tonight.'

'Well it's a tough one, but I daresay I could manage it.'

'Pick you up at seven-thirty. Now I must go or the farm'll fall to pieces.'

She walked to the door with him, breathing in the first mild air of the year, lifted by the colour in her garden. In the chill days after the tornado the daffodils had suddenly come into bloom, as though they were defying the weather and the world. Now the beds were burgeoning with them, bouncing and fluttering in the strong sea breeze, and below their bold trumpets the violets were emerging too, in shy patches of tender blue. 'It's nearly spring,' she said.

'Where are the other two?' Jeff asked, as he climbed in to the Land Rover. 'Have you got rid of them?'

'Neil goes back to London tomorrow,' she told him.

'Well that's one blessing.'

'You're such an old grouch!' she teased.

'I don't see you much when you've got a house full,' he pointed out.

'No, that's true. But I won't have a word said against him. He's been a real help to me these last few days. If it hadn't been for him I'd never have got that garage door down, and he's helped me clean the place up and coped with the insurance man and looked after Lucy and everything. He even washed her hair.'

Jeff wasn't impressed. 'Bully for him,' he said. 'So where is he now, this paragon of all the virtues?'

'He's taken her to St Richard's to have her stitches out.'

Lucy had woken feeling much better that morning. Her stitches were still horribly obvious, like spiders straddling their black legs across her nose, but her scars were shrinking, the purple bruising round her eyes had faded to yellow and green and she'd actually managed to sleep through the night without being woken by the pain in her shoulder. Now as she strode out of the afternoon clinic she was beaming with relief.

'How do I look?' she asked her police escort.

He wanted to tell her she was beautiful but controlled himself in time. She might take it the wrong way and they'd been getting on so well over the last few days he didn't want to spoil things now. 'Much improved,' he said. 'They made a good job of that stitching. The scars are fading already.'

'It's great not to look like a gargoyle.'

As they walked arm in arm to his car he asked, 'Do you feel well enough for a stroll?'

'Depends where you want me to go.'

'How about the lagoon?'

It was bleak by that great stretch of water, even in the afternoon sunshine, and instead of leading her to the footpath, he headed off towards the graveyard, which was even bleaker. 'This way,' he said. 'I've got something to show you.'

'In a graveyard?'

'Yes,' he said. 'Look!'

They'd reached a small oblong building with roughcast walls, colour-washed pale yellow, and covered by a deeply sloping roof, its terracotta tiles patterned with grass-green lichen.

'What is it?'

'Come inside and see,' he said and led her through the door.

She knew what it was the minute she stepped over the threshold. There was such peace there. It washed around her like a warm tide, enfolding her and buoying her up, timeless and sustaining. She saw that there was a small table piled with hymn books beside the door, four rows of pews for about two dozen people facing a simple altar – a narrow marble slab holding two red candlesticks and a small red and gold cross – and on the wall to her left, a tombstone in bas-relief, commemorating a knight and his lady and dated 1537. They were in a church.

'This is what's left of the original parish church of Norton,' he told her. 'It's actually just the vestry. They pulled the rest down and re-erected it in Sutton when the population moved but they left the vestry here like a sort of chapel. I found it the first day I came. What do you think of it?'

'It's very old,' she said. 'Do they still hold services here?'

'Oh yes. I asked. You could – um – get married here if you wanted to. I thought of it the moment I saw it. I stood here and I thought, if I ever find my girl this is where I'd like to marry her.'

She was intrigued. 'Are you religious then?'

'Not particularly. I don't go to church if that's

what you mean. I had too much of that in the homes.'

'So why do you want to get married in church?'

'For the service,' he said seriously. 'I read it when I was little and I thought it was perfect. It says everything. For better for worse, for richer for poorer, in sickness and in health, to love and to cherish till death us do part. I knew if I ever said it I'd mean every word. And I will.'

She was so moved she was afraid she might cry. So she took refuge in a half-joking question. 'Are you proposing to me, Neil Morrish?'

He'd been so caught up in his dream that he came down to earth with a jolt. 'Well yes,' he said. 'I mean. No. Not if you don't want me to.'

She laughed at that. 'Make up your mind.'

'Well then yes if you think it's...'

'When I was lying on the ground half conscious,' she remembered, 'you said you loved me.'

'I did. I do.'

'But we're not lovers. I mean, you've never even kissed me.'

'It wasn't the right time. You were injured. I didn't want to upset you or hurt you or anything. You mean too much to me. I've loved you from the first moment I saw you, the night of the crash. I don't suppose you remember.'

She remembered very clearly. 'Extraordinary.'

She spoke so coolly he was worried. 'If I'm speaking out of turn...'

'No,' she said. 'You're not. It's just I've never been proposed to before. It takes a bit of getting used to. Most of the men I've known up to now

451

would have run a mile rather than propose to anybody. Commitment freaks the lot of them.'

'So you're not annoyed or cross or anything?'

She stood before him, gazing out over the pale blue waters of the lagoon. She felt she had to be honest with him, even if it was painful. He was too good for anything less than the truth. 'I don't love you,' she said. 'You know that don't you? I'm very very fond of you. You've been wonderful to me these last few days. I don't know how I'd have managed without you. But that's not love. At least, I don't think it is.'

'No,' he said humbly. 'But it might be the start. Unless there's someone else.'

'No,' she said, 'there's no one else.' And it was true. Her love for Pete seemed to have withered away. 'I just thought I ought to level with you.'

He was taut with distress. 'Well thanks for that anyway.' Then he didn't know what else to say. His declaration had cost him so much he was suddenly weary. 'Better get back. It's getting dark'

As they walked through the graveyard she took his arm again. 'I tell you what I think,' she said. 'I think you ought to come back to London with me and live in my house for a while. See how we get on. You might not like me when we're living together. Helen and Tina have moved out so I've got the place to myself and it's much too much for one.'

It made him feel weak to think of it. 'You mean live together?'

'If you could face it.'

His senses were roaring but he struggled to be

sensible. 'You'd have to let me pay half the mortgage.'

That was what she expected and only proper. 'Right.'

'And...'

'And?' she prompted.

'Could we get engaged?'

'You're so old-fashioned,' she said. 'Can't you live with me unless you've put a ring on my finger?'

'No,' he admitted. 'I can't. It wouldn't seem right. It would be like taking advantage of you. You know how I feel about it. I want to marry you and look after you for the rest of our lives, not just live together. I'm not saying no to that mind you. It's just I want you to know how I feel.'

He's so honourable, she thought, looking at him. He makes Pete look shabby. And he really does love me. He'd never do anything to hurt me. It might just work And it's certainly worth a try.

The affection on her face was too much for him. He pulled her into his arms, taking care not to touch her injured shoulder, and kissed her wind-damp hair, her wind-chilled forehead, her wind-white cheeks, aching to kiss her mouth, murmuring that he loved her. And standing warm against his ardent body she thought how easy commitment was after all and how natural. And was ridiculously happy.

Gwen was out in the garden, cutting another armful of daffodils before the light faded, when she heard a car approaching. They're back, she thought, and looked up expecting to see the

453

Mondeo. But the car turning out of Mill Lane was Ellie's Espace. It was such a lovely surprise she ran to greet her, daffodils and all.

'Oh Ellie, my dear,' she called. 'How are you?'

'I'm fine,' Ellie said happily. 'Signed off this morning.'

'And how's baby?'

'Villainous,' Ellie said, and bounded from the driver's seat in a swirl of grey silk to kiss her. She was glowing with health, full-bosomed and buxom, her fair hair longer than usual and very thick, her blue eyes shining. 'Aren't you my bad lad,' she said, looking back into the car, and there was so much affection in her voice that Gwen was quite touched by it. 'He's a little Pigling Bland.' She lifted the carrycot very carefully from its anchor on the back seat and held it out before her so that her mother could see the baby's sleeping head. 'You take the cot and I'll take his bag and the daffodils. I can come back for the rest later.'

'How long are you staying?' Gwen asked as she carried her precious burden into the porch. The baby was so well tucked up that all she could see was his profile.

'As long as you'll have me,' Ellie said. 'Put him on the sofa and I'll get him out so's you can have a good look at him.'

Gwen wanted to see him very much but she didn't like to have him disturbed. 'Leave him be,' she said. 'I can wait. Let him wake normally.'

Ellie looked at her watch. 'He'll be awake in ten minutes anyway,' she predicted. 'He's got a monstrous appetite. That's why I had to stay in the clinic so long. He sucked me raw.'

454

'Oh Ellie!'

'Yes,' Ellie said, making a face. 'Very painful. But they showed me what to do about it and it's better now. All part of the process. He's got to be fed.'

Gwen blinked in amazement. This new tough Ellie would take a bit of getting used to. 'Would you like some tea?' she said.

'Would I ever!' Ellie smiled. 'I've got a thirst you wouldn't believe.'

She was on her third cup when Joshua Francis woke and called for sustenance of his own, 'A-la! A-la!' his little red tongue like a clapper against the pale pink arch of his palate.

'Hark at him,' Ellie said lovingly, as she scooped him from the cot. 'You'd think he was starving. Oh you're a little Pigling Bland. What are you? Just watch him. He'll suck till it comes out of his nose.'

He was certainly a hearty feeder and oblivious to everything except the joy of the moment, patting his mother's breast and gazing up at her rapturously. When he'd fed until he was too full to take another mouthful, Ellie put him gently into her mother's arms. 'Now you can look at him all you like,' she said, 'while I get the rest of my luggage.'

He was soft and warm and amazingly light-weight. Gwen had forgotten how beguiling the newborn always are and how easy it is to be hooked by them. She sat with her satisfied grandchild in the crook of her arm, breathing in the scent of him, stroking his delicate skin with one much too rough finger, learning him feature by feature. I'll ask her now, she thought, as soon as she gets back with her bags.

But when Ellie came back, she was arm in arm with Lucy, and Neil was following behind them carrying all the bags. 'Look who I've just found,' she said. 'She says a wall fell on her. Come and see my baby and tell me all about it.'

So the baby was admired and the tale told and Gwen took a good look at Lucy's face now that the stitches were out and Neil carried the bags upstairs into Lucy's room. They were making such a noise they didn't hear the doorbell until it was rung rather more insistently for a second time.

Pete Halliday had driven down to Seal Island on a sudden impulse. He'd been prepared for an important business meeting that afternoon and his clients had called off at the last moment. At first he was very annoyed to have his careful arrangements ruined so carelessly. Then he saw that he'd been given an opportunity.

'Right,' he said to his secretary. 'If that's the way they want to play it, I'm off to the seaside to see Mrs M. I shan't get another window as wide as this for months. You've got my number if you want me.'

It was dark by the time he arrived and the windows of the tower were bright as a stage-set against a lavender dusk. Lots of cars, he noticed, so she's got company. As he drew up, he realised that one of them was Lucy's and was pleased to think that he'd be able to see her again too. Poor kid.

It was Lucy who opened the door to him, her right hand dangling from a sling. Noise and warmth seemed to be pulsing all around her, washing over him as he stood in the little ante-chamber of the porch. He realised that he was feeling rather too much like a thing apart and more than a little uncomfortable, and her opening words increased the feeling.

'Good God!' she said. 'What's brought you here?'

Boldness was called for. 'Luce!' he said, and he seized her free hand and pulled her towards him so that he could kiss her. He was a bit put out when she averted her head so that only the edge of her cheek was available, but he kissed that nevertheless. 'What have you been doing to yourself?'

It was too good an opportunity to be missed. 'Actually,' she said, standing back to let him into the house and speaking clearly so that he and Ellie were both bound to hear. 'I've just got engaged.'

He congratulated her as he walked into the room. Engagement parties and congratulations were things he could deal with. 'Who's the lucky man?'

'I am,' the policeman said.

But there wasn't time to say anything else, for the room erupted into squeals and shrieks. Gwen was on her feet rushing at her daughter, flinging her arms round her, hugging her. 'My dear chick! That's wonderful. Neil my dear! Congrat-ulations.'

And Ellie's voice rose from the depths of the

sofa. 'That's great Luce! Fantastic! I'm really happy for you. And you Neil. Absolutely. Come and kiss me.'

The shock of seeing her there stopped Pete in mid-stride. There was no way he could avoid her, even if he wanted to, and he wasn't at all sure he wanted to because she was looking absolutely delectable, wearing grey for once instead of black, which made her look softer, and with a longer hairstyle which was more feminine than her very short cut had been. He was smiling at her almost before he was aware of it. 'Hello Ellie.'

'Hello Pete,' she said, smiling back. 'Come and see your son.'

How could he refuse when they were all looking at him? It would mean losing face and that was unthinkable. He walked to the sofa as slowly as he could, smiling his handsome smile and trying to think of something light and witty to say. And looked down at the infant, lying sleepily across her lap.

'Jesus!' he said. 'He's just like me.' And he suddenly felt weak at the knees and had to sit down on the sofa beside her. 'Jesus on a bicycle!'

'Well of course he is,' Ellie said. 'What did you expect, you stupid man? You fathered him.'

Lucy and Gwen were beside them, laughing and talking at once, warm with baby worship. 'Isn't he a sweetie! Look at those dear little fingers.' He put out a hand to touch them, tentatively, and the baby curled its fist round his outstretched forefinger and held on. 'Oh my God!' he said. 'He's holding my hand. Look at that Ellie! He's holding my hand.'

458

Ellie smiled at him tolerantly. 'He does,' she said. 'He did it as soon as he was born. So. What do you think of him?'

'He's fantastic.'

'And you were the one who didn't like babies.'

'I don't,' he said, defending himself. 'As a species they're horrendous. But this one's rather different. I mean most of them are absolutely hideous but this one's handsome.' He was still looking down at the trusting face of his son. 'No one's going to run out on you,' he promised. 'We're going to give you the best of everything, best clothes, best food, best school.'

'Who's this *we* you're talking about?' Ellie said and her voice was sharp.

'Us,' he said seriously. 'You and me. His parents. Who else? We shall have to look into schools Ellie. You have to live in the catchment area for the best ones. We'll find out where they are and then we'll buy a family house in the area. Richmond maybe. Or Wimbledon. Somewhere leafy and near a common. A Victorian house with a big garden.'

'And where's all the money coming from?'

'You don't have to worry about money,' he told her. 'Shelton's gone multinational. Part of J.R. Grossman's. And I'm on the board. We can have what we like.'

'Now look,' Ellie said. 'It may have escaped your notice but this is my baby we're talking about. If anyone's going to make decisions about him it'll be me. Not you. You walked out on him.'

Oh God! Gwen thought. They're going to row. How can I stop them? And while she was struggling to find something soothing to say, there was the sound of a key in the lock and there was Jeff, stamping into the room, bringing the tang of the sea and the smell of the byre into her quarrelling circle.

'Ready for the off?' he said.

'Oh dear,' she said. 'It's never half past seven.'

'Seven twenty-five,' he said. 'But who's counting?'

'I've got my whole family down,' she told him, gesturing towards them and thinking how silly she was being when he could see that for himself.

He took it calmly. 'So I see. Hello Pete. Lucy. Eleanor. Nice baby.'

Ellie preened. 'Yes,' she said. 'Isn't he?'

He looked at her boldly. 'So who's going to look after him when you go back to work?' he said. 'Have you got that settled?'

The question fell into the group like a lead weight, pulling the line of his enquiry until it hung in the air between them, taut and unavoidable. Gwen caught her breath in shock. He comes crashing in, she thought, after all we said, crashing in, saying things, not giving me the chance. Why couldn't he wait to find out like everybody else? Pete looked at Ellie, anger suspended; Neil looked at Lucy, alert and curious; Lucy looked from her mother to her sister, wide-eyed with apprehension. Only Ellie was calm.

'Well I am,' she said coolly. 'Who else?'

The answer sent a frisson of surprise and relief through all her hearers.

'Aren't you going back to work then?' Pete asked.

'No I am not,' Ellie said forcefully. 'Not for ages anyway. I'm not handing my baby over to someone else to look after. No way. Some of these au pairs are absolutely dire. I've seen them. You wouldn't believe the way they go on. And the nannies aren't much better. They wouldn't have the faintest idea how to handle him. He's mine and I'm looking after him. I know his ways.'

'Quite right!' Jeff approved. 'Mother knows best.'

And at that the tension broke and they all began to laugh and talk at once.

'Ten minutes,' Jeff said to Gwen, 'and then I'm going without you.'

She hesitated. 'Well ... I ought to stay here and feed this lot.'

'Oh for heaven's sake,' Neil said. 'We can feed ourselves. Can't we Lucy? You don't have to stay here on our account.'

'Actually, I've got to go in a minute,' Pete said, glad of the chance to extricate himself. 'I was only checking how you were after the tornado. Flying visit sort of thing.' And he went while he could. 'I'll be in touch,' he said, as he kissed Gwen goodbye. 'Best of luck you two.'

Ellie didn't look at him. 'See you around,' she said.

'So you got the right answer,' Jeff said as he drove into Mill Lane.

Gwen was tempted to scold him but thought better of it.

The relief of knowing was so strong it made her annoyance look petty. The question had been

461

asked, even if it had been done precipitously, and the answer had been given. That was all that really mattered. I can stay in my tower, she thought, and go on being a school secretary, and see Jeff whenever I want to. He'll always be heavy handed and too outspoken but that's the way he is. It's all part and parcel with the rest of him and the rest is tenderness and intelligence and dependability and all the things that make me love him. And Ellie will look after the baby and make a good job of it because she loves him. What a difference a little love does make. The future spread before her, spangled with sunshine. When I've been here a twelvemonth, she thought, I shall throw a party and invite all my new friends and Jeff's sisters and my whole family, poor old Pete and all. 'Yes,' she agreed. 'I did.'

The publishers hope that this book has given you enjoyable reading. Large Print Books are especially designed to be as easy to see and hold as possible. If you wish a complete list of our books please ask at your local library or write directly to:

Magna Large Print Books
Magna House, Long Preston,
Skipton, North Yorkshire.
BD23 4ND

This Large Print Book for the partially sighted, who cannot read normal print, is published under the auspices of

THE ULVERSCROFT FOUNDATION